THE
BOOK
OF
WITCHES

THE
BOOK
OF
WITCHES

EDITED BY

JONATHAN STRAHAN

ILLUSTRATED BY

ALYSSA WINANS

HARPER Voyager
An Imprint of HarperCollins *Publishers*

THE BOOK OF WITCHES. Copyright © 2023 by Jonathan Strahan. All rights reserved. Printed in the United States of America. No part of this book may be used or reproduced in any manner whatsoever without written permission except in the case of brief quotations embodied in critical articles and reviews. For information, address HarperCollins Publishers, 195 Broadway, New York, NY 10007.

HarperCollins books may be purchased for educational, business, or sales promotional use. For information, please email the Special Markets Department at SPsales@harpercollins.com.

Harper Voyager and design are trademarks of HarperCollins Publishers LLC.

FIRST EDITION

Designed by Paula Russell Szafranski

Illustrations © Alyssa Winans

Library of Congress Cataloging-in-Publication Data has been applied for.

ISBN 978-0-06-311322-0

23 24 25 26 27 LBC 5 4 3 2 1

CREDITS

For Marianne, Jessica, and Sophie—now and always.

"There's a little witch in all of us."

—Practical Magic

CONTENTS

ACKNOWLEDGMENTS

The past three years have been unprecedented, at least in my life. They have added incredible stresses and strains to every project I've undertaken, but none more so than to this one. I'd like to thank every writer who was actually able to get a story or poem written, and to acknowledge those who tried to do so. I'd especially like to thank Maureen McHugh, Saad Z. Hossain, and E. Lily Yu for going above and beyond. My thanks also to everyone who sent me work during the open submission period. I was amazed by the quality of the work, and wish I could have included more stories than the three that appear here. Thanks, too, to Alyssa Winans for her wonderful art.

I've also been incredibly fortunate to work with an amazing team at HarperCollins. My sincere thanks to David Pomerico, who has been a joy to work with throughout; to everyone at HarperCollins who worked on the book; to my agent, the fabulous Howard Morhaim, who is always in my corner; and finally, to Marianne, Jessica, and Sophie, who support me through the madness. This book would not exist without you all. Thank you!

WHAT IS A WITCH?

Jonathan Strahan

A witch is "a woman practicing sorcery," says the Oxford English Dictionary. Which is clear and simple, but not particularly useful, and is perhaps too restrictive in gender terms. The OED's definition of "sorcery" isn't much clearer, though it does talk about "magic," which it says is the "supposed art of influencing [the] course of events by occult control of nature or of spirits, witchcraft." That gets us closer to a definition that matches my own reading over the years. I'm more attracted to the etymology of the word, which leads back to the Old English nouns *wiċċa* ['wit. t͡ʃɑ] ("male witch, warlock") and *wiċċe* ['wit. t͡ʃe] ("female witch"), and combines meanings of wisdom and power. I can certainly see the witches that I know best as being people on the outside of their communities who are possessed of both knowledge and power of some kind. That feels about right.

Wikipedia goes into more detail, definitely more detail than we need here. It says that "a witch differs from a sorcerer in that they do not use physical tools or actions to curse; their maleficium* is perceived as extending from some intangible inner quality, and the person may

---

* Maleficium is a Latin term meaning wrongdoing or mischief and is used to describe malevolent, dangerous, or harmful magic, evildoing, or malevolent sorcery. In general, the term applies to any magical act intended to cause harm or death to people or property. [Source: Wikipedia]

be unaware that they are a witch, or may have been convinced of their own evil nature by the suggestion of others." So a witch's magic comes from within the witch themselves, and they may not even know they are a witch!

Now this will all sound familiar, especially if you've read Terry Pratchett's stories of Granny Weatherwax, Nanny Ogg, Tiffany Aching, and the Discworld, where witches are women, sometimes girls, who are more midwives, doctors, psychiatrists, and moral enforcement officers than studiers of spells. My sources go on at *very* great length about the history of European witchcraft. Witches and witchcraft of some kind are found in almost every culture on Earth, and they are usually very different from the witches that we see on our television screens come All Hallow's Eve. Throughout Asia and Africa, for example, witches are equally likely to be male or female. In Japan they have fox witches: the *kitsune-mochi*, and the *tsukimono-suji*. And almost none of them has a broomstick or a hat, never mind a nice black pointy one. Those witches are European, and possibly mostly British.

According to Hungarian ethnographer Éva Pócs, there are three different types of witch: the neighborhood witch or social witch; the magical or sorcerer witch; and the supernatural or night witch, who is portrayed as a demon appearing in visions and dreams. These witches of myth and folklore are joined by many real-world witches. A Wiccan is someone who practices Wicca, a neopagan religion and a form of modern witchcraft. It's often referred to as Witchcraft or the Craft, and its adherents are commonly referred to as Wiccans, or as Witches or Crafters. Developed in England in the first half of the twentieth century, Wicca is a religion where a goddess and a god, traditionally viewed as the Triple Goddess and Horned God, are worshipped. While Wiccans are not to be found in this book, they are nonetheless witches.

Stories of witches, though, go back to the Bible and almost certainly predate it. There are references to witches and witchcraft in both the Old and New Testaments, and in Hindu, Jewish, and other religious texts. Countless witches appear prominently in literature, but the earliest "classic witch" is probably Baba Yaga, an ogress from Slavic folklore who flies around on a giant mortar (using a pestle as the rudder), lives in a hut that stands on chicken legs, and sometimes kidnaps small children. She was followed by other weird literary sisters like Morgan le Fay, the powerful sorceress from Malory's *Le Morte d'Arthur*, and the three witches from *Macbeth*, who seem to spend their time cackling around a cauldron.

The witches best known in popular Western culture date to the rise of children's literature in the nineteenth century, first in the fairy tales of the Brothers Grimm, Hans Christian Andersen, and others, but then in novels like L. Frank Baum's *The Wizard of Oz* and C. S. Lewis's *The Lion, the Witch, and the Wardrobe*, and more recently in books like Jill Murphy's *The Worst Witch* and J. K. Rowling's Harry Potter novels. While Lewis's White Witch Jadis, Murphy's Mildred Hubble, and Rowling's Hermione Granger (who might be a touch more wizard than witch) are among the most popular modern witches, the most iconic is surely Baum's Wicked Witch of the West. Her appearance in the 1939 film *The Wizard of Oz*, where she is played with panache by Margaret Hamilton, is the definitive evil wearer of black hats, and the cry "I'll get you, my pretty . . . and your little dog, too!" is justifiably famous.

Lovers of witches know that Elphaba, as Gregory Maguire named the Wicked Witch of the West in *Wicked*, is not the only witchy option. Whether it be Hayao Miyazaki and Eiko Kadono's delightful Kiki or the studious but bungling Mildred Hubble, the industrious Hermione Grainger or Diana Wynne Jones's rather wicked Gwendolyn Chant, the happily suburban Samantha from *Bewitched,* the darkly evil Maleficent from *Sleeping Beauty*, or Marvel's Scarlet Witch from *WandaVision*, a witch could be anyone.

And if a witch can be anyone, so too can the people who create those witches and the stories about them that we love. That's where *The Book of Witches* comes in. As a reader I'm most familiar with the Western tradition of witches and witchcraft, but one of the highlights of the decade or so since I last edited a book of witch stories has been the increasing chance to hear from more diverse voices, from writers from different backgrounds than my own. I've been actively reading science fiction and fantasy fiction for fifty years, and for the past decade the field has, perhaps too slowly, been opening itself to more perspectives. Writers from Africa, South Asia, and elsewhere are making inroads, and more attention is being paid to BIPOC and LGBTQIA+ voices. *The Book of Witches* is a conscious effort to reflect that, to celebrate all of the many voices that make up our community, whether they be established, well-known ones, or ones at the very start of their career. Not everyone I would have liked to include here could be involved in the end—the pandemic has hit everyone hard—but many are, including three BIPOC writers found through an exciting open-reading period. The witches you'll find in these pages are diverse and different from one another. There are one or two older ladies in black with broomsticks that would have been the envy of Magrat Garlick or any young witch, but you'll also find ones that are young students, old teachers, dark spirits, fey spirits, and beyond. They're male, female, and nonbinary; good, evil, and undecided; powerful, weak, or somewhere in between, and more. What they all have in common is that they are agents of change, possessors of some kind of knowledge and power that will change those around them for good or ill. I asked thirty or so writers to tell me stories about *their* witches. I think one or two of them might become your witches, too.

In the end, this is a book that I'm very proud of and that I think readers everywhere will enjoy. Hopefully, it's a book for all of us. It's filled with stories and poems that are rich and wonderful. I hope you enjoy them as much as I have, and that we might even get a chance to meet again around another cauldron of stories sometime in the future.

Jonathan Strahan
Perth, Western Australia
August 2022

THE
BOOK
OF
WITCHES

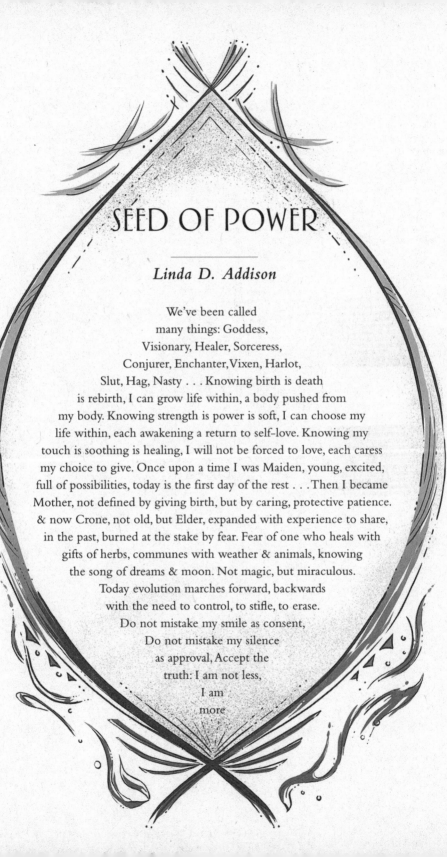

SEED OF POWER

Linda D. Addison

We've been called
many things: Goddess,
Visionary, Healer, Sorceress,
Conjurer, Enchanter, Vixen, Harlot,
Slut, Hag, Nasty . . . Knowing birth is death
is rebirth, I can grow life within, a body pushed from
my body. Knowing strength is power is soft, I can choose my
life within, each awakening a return to self-love. Knowing my
touch is soothing is healing, I will not be forced to love, each caress
my choice to give. Once upon a time I was Maiden, young, excited,
full of possibilities, today is the first day of the rest . . . Then I became
Mother, not defined by giving birth, but by caring, protective patience.
& now Crone, not old, but Elder, expanded with experience to share,
in the past, burned at the stake by fear. Fear of one who heals with
gifts of herbs, communes with weather & animals, knowing
the song of dreams & moon. Not magic, but miraculous.
Today evolution marches forward, backwards
with the need to control, to stifle, to erase.
Do not mistake my smile as consent,
Do not mistake my silence
as approval, Accept the
truth: I am not less,
I am
more

WHAT I REMEMBER OF ORESHA MOON DRAGON DEVSHRATA

P. Djèlí Clark

Oresha Moon Dragon Devshrata arrived on an idle wind that blew into Mara's Bay from the sea, her bright-orange air balloon awakening the sleepy village like a small rising sun. It was midmorning when the woven brackerwood basket that carried her descended into the middle of our market square, nearly hitting a pen of suckling kelp pigs brought in by the Brath twins.

We all—fishmongers and net trawlers alike—stopped our work to look up and marvel. Even Merl Janish, who started at sunrise each morning with a quart of strong cider, working his way through the harder stuff until he passed out at sunset, managed to rouse from his stupor. I was just a girl of two and ten then, at the market helping my ma sell red mussels and spotted whisker trout. But I ran forward and jostled through the gathering crowd to get a good look.

I had only seen Traveling Folk come to Mara's Bay on two other occasions, both times in years that added to odd numbers on their peculiar calendars. Their colorful air balloons had filled the skies, jangling with bells and chimes, accompanied by herds of long-horned velvet-blue sky bison that moaned and sang in piercing melodies. They'd set up their mushroom-shaped tents just outside town, and we had journeyed down to haggle for goods and hear news of far-off lands we scarcely believed in. At night their musicians played on drums and plucked curved stringed banjos, accompanied by jugglers, dancers, and fire spinners who frolicked with Mara's Bay folk well into the dawn.

Oresha Moon Dragon Devshrata, however, did not arrive with a flock of balloons, or bells, or chimes, or singing sky bison. She came alone, a young woman of no more than three and twenty. A curious gray woolen coat with pockets along its front hugged her shoulders, swallowing her inside. Beneath it, her dress was more typical of the garish hues of the Traveling Folk—a long green skirt of elaborate gold prints, colorful scarves, and a swirl of jangling necklaces that sparkled with crimson fire beads and carved metal charms. She stepped barefoot from her basket, wriggling ring-adorned toes as if testing this new soil, sniffing at the salt-filled sea air with a small flat nose, and casting her gaze about with the scrutiny of a surveyor. When she was satisfied, she swept forward with an imperious swaying gait no one in Mara's Bay could possibly match, bid us a good day, and gave us her fantastic and incredible name that I mouthed and played with silently on my tongue like a cherished sweet.

"Well, Mistress Devshrata," our mayor Erl Mas said after a few pleasant exchanges. "Not expecting your folk this time of year, and alone at that. You, umm, lost?"

Oresha Moon Dragon Devshrata absently brushed back the thick coils of midnight hair that shadowed her face like vines, making me touch my own limp brown tresses with envy. She flashed a dimpled smile that lit up her earth-dark skin and made her pearl-black eyes glitter. "I precisely where I expected to be," she drawled, in a singsong accent. "And I come to help allyuh with yuh trouble."

At this, there were a few quietly exchanged glances—Mara's Bay folk thought it impolite to murmur. *Trouble* was not a word we were accustomed to hearing. This wasn't a sprawling port city like Banar, with its infamous daily knife duels. Or the Twelve Isles with its scheming princelings and their hired mercenaries. This was Mara's Bay, quiet and unremarked, as far from trouble as we could imagine.

"So, it's trouble is it?" Ro Culin said, biting down on his reedwood pipe the way he did when thinking hard. He tucked two gnarled fisherman's thumbs into his suspenders and leaned his angular body back like a bent post. "What kind of trouble? Bluefish going scarce? Been noticing that lately, but figure too many sea cats this season chasing them off . . ." He continued on and was interrupted twice by those offering other theories for the scarcity of bluefish. Nearly all talk in our town, like the dross that littered the shores at night, made its way to the sea eventually.

"More trouble than that," the Traveling Folk woman pronounced with a sharp smack of her lips that made a curious *scheupse* sound I longed to catch, ending our talk. "The kind ah trouble allyuh can't handle on yuh own."

Ro Culin raised a bushy eyebrow on his long face at this. More than a few people shared quiet glances, along with some frowns.

"Don't suppose your help comes free, do it?" one of the Brath twins called, the endless freckles that covered her skin seeming as red as her hair.

Oresha Moon Dragon Devshrata smiled again, this time reminding me of a water fox. "Trade best fairer than free," she replied, reciting the common saying of her people.

"Always up for trade, Mistress Devshrata," our mayor said delicately. "But not certain what it is we'd be trading for. If you could tell us more—"

She cut him off with a flourish of her long fingers. Reaching into one of her coat pockets she withdrew a drawn pouch, untying it and upending its contents into her palm, revealing a set of painted bluestones etched with strange letterings. Pursing her lips to blow heavy upon them, she cast them upon the ground. They fell in a clatter on our worn gray cobblestones, tumbling before coming to a stop. Muttering in a tongue we dared not decipher, Oresha Moon Dragon Devshrata lowered to a squat and began examining each stone with care.

We all watched in hushed silence, even the mayor, as she murmured to herself. A few people etched unseen blessing circles on their foreheads and whispered mantras to ward off spells. Everyone knew the Traveling Folk practiced odd magic and could curse babes to be born with scaly feet or cause your fish stores to grow salt worms. They also had the gift of foretelling and were known to predict nights when the moon filled red as blood or days when the sun vanished in darkness. What else could it be, we knew, but magic? But no one was prepared for what she had to tell us.

"A storm?" someone asked once the Traveling Folk woman had finished speaking, repeating her words. It was old Cora Gilish. She blinked through her long red hair, casting a dubious glance to the sky with an arched eyebrow. "I know my seasons and no storms coming to Mara's Bay no time soon, gal." A few nods of assent came from the crowd. Cora Gilish was our local Cunning woman and could smell a storm coming days off. Every fisherman, clam digger, and kelp pig herder swore by her advice.

Oresha Moon Dragon Devshrata looked up at us, eyes hard and black as the smooth stones divers bring up from the seafloor, that you imagine have seen much in their buried depths. "Not the kind ah storm allyuh studying 'bout," she said. "This storm what coming called the Vassa. And yuh won't know they here, until it too late."

Confusion filled the crowd now. I frowned as well. We'd never heard of a Vassa. The mayor said as much and the Traveling Folk woman scooped up her bluestones, depositing them back into her pouch as she stood. Catching us in her glare like night squid with glow glass, she began to speak.

"Hear me now. The Vassa people dem from beyond these lands,

plunderers who roam the six seas. The first yuh will know of them is their great horn that sounds through the night—always dem come at night. Their black ships with black sails will be masked on the waters. But the flames yuh gon see, spit from the mouths of their vessels as fire arrows rain down on yuh village, burning all beneath dem. And as yuh run to put out the blaze, the Vassa will come, riding their war dogs, wearing the skulls and furs ah horned bears that roam their hard country. All will be put to the torch, save for what they can plunder. The men and women of allyuh village they will kill. But yuh children dem will be taken for thralls, to be sold far across the seas. It will be as if allyuh's Mara's Bay never was."

The stillness that came in the wake of her words was numbing. All I could hear was my heart pounding, and the squealing of the Brath twins' kelp piglets. Cora Gilish's eyes grew so round it seemed as if they might jump from her head. Ro Culin's long pipe dangled from his thin lips, ash and tabac falling and flittering on the wind. Even Merl Janish looked as if he had been struck suddenly sober. Then, rather quickly, everyone began speaking at once.

Words tumbled from frightened lips, a mass of gibberish that made little sense. Were the Vassa monsters? Did they eat people? Where did they come from? Could they be driven off? There was wailing and some tears. A shouting match that turned to shoving erupted as the Brath twins began arguing which of them could best a Vassa in a fight. Our mayor, a short man who was more belly than brawn, called in vain for order.

Through the pandemonium my eyes remained on Oresha Moon Dragon Devshrata, who stood watching it all with an odd calm—the way you did when a fierce red pike latched on to your hook, and you knew you had her. Let her wear herself out then slowly reel her in.

Our gazes met for a brief moment and the smallest hint of a smile touched her lips, as if the two of us shared some secret. I wondered if I stepped forward if she would warmly whisper it in my ear?

Turning back to the crowd, she reached into one of those jacket pockets and removed another pouch, this time pouring out what looked like fine black powder into her palms. Rubbing it between her fingers, she raised her arms overhead and made a sharp clap with her hands—producing a sound like thunder and a slight shower of red sparks that fell and danced about her midnight tresses. That got everyone quiet again, and we all stared, as if she were some otherworldly being dropped down from the Third Heaven.

"Mistress Devshrata," the mayor breathed, wiping perspiration that dotted the balding spot on his scalp. He looked as pale as his wisps of white hair. "You said you could help us against these . . . Vassa?" The last word sent a shudder through the crowd.

The Traveling Folk woman was quiet for a while, letting a silence hang in the air before answering. "I willing to help allyuh," she spoke at last, eyes glinting, "for a proper trade."

The mayor nodded eagerly. "I'm certain something can be worked out. We don't have much here, but we're willing—"

"I want a place to stay," she cut in abruptly. "A home to call my own, here in this village. Grant me what I wish, and I will stop the Vassa from ravaging yuh homes in turn. And my own."

That caught us by surprise. The Traveling Folk were, well, travelers. They didn't stay anywhere long. Mara's Bay considered itself friendly and welcoming to folk, but we rarely saw strangers put down roots. Everyone in the village had been living here long as could be remembered: generations of Culins and Braths and Gilishes. A newcomer, one of the mysterious Traveling Folk no less, was going to be . . . different. But given the circumstances, it seemed that everyone found it an easy enough bargain.

Ro Culin was the first to nod in agreement, biting his long pipe particularly hard. Cora Gilish scowled deeply but was second, and soon followed by more. In short order the whole crowd was agreeing to the bargain. The mayor turned back with visible relief on his round face.

"It seems we have come to an understanding, Mistress Devshrata," he said.

Oresha Moon Dragon Devshrata stepped forward boldly, grabbing his arm and placing his hand flat to her chest, while putting her own on his. "Once confirmed by the heart," she stated, "the agreement cannot be broken." The mayor nodded awkwardly and stumbled through the familiar ritual of the Traveling Folk, ending by spitting into his hands and smearing the saliva on her open palm.

When the two finished, a roar of cheers went up. Many offered the mayor excited congratulations on his fine decision. Ro Culin and Cora Gilish bullishly agreed the bargain was easily worth it. The Brath twins began arguing over which of them had been the first to voice assent. I watched it all, perplexed, as the most important question of all seemed to me to have been lost.

"How are you going to stop them?" I blurted aloud.

The voices died as all eyes turned to stare down at me, and I almost shrank back. But Oresha Moon Dragon Devshrata was staring, too, and that dark gaze felt as if it were pulling the words from my lips. "The Vassa, I mean," my words coming in a stammer, "how are you going to stop them?"

The Traveling Folk woman did smile now, her black eyes weighing me and seeming impressed. "And what yuh name is, lickle one?" she asked.

I swallowed before answering. Lickle? "Evon Cal. My ma is Adie Cal."

"Well, Evon Cal, daughter of Adie Cal," she drawled, "I glad somebody bother to ask."

She offered me a sly wink I would treasure forever, turning to walk to her basket where she rifled inside before pulling out a long and rolled parchment. She brought it directly to me and unfurled its length onto the ground. All about us, people crowded to look. On the pale brown sheet there was a drawing of what looked like a man, only his body was too straight, too angular. And where bone and muscles should have been, were wheels that reminded me of the inside of the clock that sat in the mayor's home—the kind of fancy gadgets outlander peddlers bought to sell when passing through.

"Begging your pardon, Mistress Devshrata?" the mayor asked, his face perplexed. "But what is that?"

Oresha Moon Dragon Devshrata looked up with a sea cat's grin and sly eyes. "That," she pronounced, "is going to be yuh champion." A tinge of excitement tremored her voice. "And I going to make him!"

Oresha Moon Dragon Devshrata's house took over three months to build. It was a grand thing, larger than any in Mara's Bay. Only the mayor's home came close. And that was because he owned our only inn and store. This new house was almost twice as big, constructed of cobalt speckled taupe stone and a roof of flat ginger terracotta slates. It stood on the outskirts of the village, atop a lonely bluff that overlooked the sea. We sat in our humble wooden houses beneath thatched straw, staring up at it in wonder.

Our champion took longer.

My ma said it was probably the grandest feat Mara's Bay had ever attempted, grander even than the old stone lighthouse that now lay crumbled and abandoned. Oresha Moon Dragon Devshrata had insisted our champion be made of blackwood, which when treated and dried became as hard as iron and would not rot or burn. Every part was cut and sanded under her watchful supervision, which accepted no imperfection. The heart of our champion she crafted from brass and steel and would let no one near as she worked on its delicate construction. For armor, sheets of bronze were hammered and bent into shape, applied in layers that covered his every limb and frame.

None of it came easy. Treated blackwood had to be imported from one of the Twelve Isles. Brass, steel, and bronze were shipped from Banari ports, who in turn shipped it from far-off lands. The expense was more than our small village could easily sustain, and everyone had to contribute. Fishermen gave up a fifth of their catch, and farmers a tenth of their harvest. The rest of us were saddled with a tax that we met as we were able. Ma and I worked more, selling whenever and whatever to do our part. When donations were called for, she even gave up a golden hairpin, part of a set my father had bought for her when he was still alive. The burden of protecting our village and our homes was one Mara's Bay folk accepted without complaint, and we gladly did all we could.

It was the end of summer, as the days turned shorter and the sea cooler, so that flocks of broad-winged silver fish could be seen heading for warmer waters, that our champion was completed. The mayor declared a holiday to mark the occasion and all of Mara's Bay turned out. Ma and I came to sell food—boiled spiced crabs, fried shark with bake, and roasted oysters slathered on honeyed bread.

Because it was a holiday, I wore a dress the color of green sea rice, with yellow frills like bright coral at its edges. Everyone had donned their best: the mayor in his black Banari coat with its fire-red ermine seal collar; Ro Culin with a new pair of sea-cat-hide suspenders that glimmered with rainbow scales; and Cora Gilish in the broad white bonnet of a Cunning woman tied under her chin by a ribbon. Even Merl Janish had combed back his black hair with sap butter till it lay slick against his head.

None of us, of course, could match Oresha Moon Dragon Devshrata. She arrived with her usual flair, turning heads and widening eyes. She had donned a burgundy coat with gold buttons and wide cuffs trimmed in blue that verged on purple. It sat over a lavender shirt that my ma later remarked was cut scandalously low. Rows of thin blue beads wrapped around her waist above snug tan breeches that were tucked into brown leather boots with broad gold buckles. It was not clothing anyone in Mara's Bay wore, where women preferred dresses that fell in straight lines and men sported loose fisherman's trousers. Many stared openly as she sauntered through the market, and as I found myself mesmerized by the rhythmic way her hips swayed, I wondered if this too was some special sorcery.

She stopped momentarily at our stall, as she always did when we came to market, asking for the bake and shark. I prepared it myself, making sure to add extra meat, and dousing it with the mix of peppery spices I'd come to know she liked. Catching sight of me she raised an eyebrow. I'd begged my ma to arrange my hair into little braids, to resemble Oresha Moon Dragon Devshrata's thick-knotted tresses. And I adorned my hair with bright colorful ribbons to match her endless scarves. I blushed when she appraised me with a smile and the slightest nod of approval.

"Well, isn't she a sight," Cora Gilish remarked once the Traveling Folk woman had moved off.

"That she is," Ro Culin murmured over his redwood pipe. His eyes trailed that rhythmic gait, the way an angler followed a bonefish on his line. Cora Gilish scowled, elbowing him in the ribs. He coughed, catching his pipe between his fingers and scowling back.

"What's that 'bout, eh?" he groused. "You agreed to let her stay like the rest of us."

Cora Gilish huffed. "That may be. But I didn't agree to let her bring her strange ways among us. Already have some impressionable ones mimicking her." She gave my hair a disapproving glare and my back stiffened. "Caught two Kien sisters barefoot with rings on their toes, till I put a broom to their backsides! Just you watch, tomorrow they'll be trying on breeches and knife dueling in the streets over second husbands like those Banari strumpets! And by the eight day's tides, look at what the woman's done to those idiot Brath twins!"

I looked to the two figures who trailed Oresha Moon Dragon Devshrata and had to stifle a giggle. Brother and sister were dressed in tight bright-green jackets and tight red breeches that matched their hair. A forelock on each of their heads had been plaited into a braid, where a copper bell hung. It jingled as they followed the Traveling Folk woman about like servants. Ro Culin chuckled and commented as much.

"More like well-heeled boar hounds!" Cora Gilish huffed. "And I can only imagine what *untoward things* happen in that house among those three."

"So can I," Ro Culin murmured. He shared an appreciative look with Merl Janish, who was sober enough to grin a set of yellowed teeth.

12

I didn't understand it then myself. People whispered about the lavish parties Oresha Moon Dragon Devshrata held in her great big house. She and the Brath twins carried on loudly, singing, drinking, and carousing late into the night. I often imagined that I would be invited to her house one day, where I would sit with the Traveling Folk woman and eat rich truffle pies and powdered sun cakes imported from who knew where. Certainly, I was as interesting as those dull-witted Brath twins.

"It's unseemly," the Cunning woman muttered. "Immoral. Scandalous. Per—"

She was cut off as a crier announced the start of the day's ceremony. I was happy to get away from that troubling talk and followed my Ma as the crowd walked out to the harbor.

There our champion stood.

He was a towering giant in the semblance of a man, taller even than the old lighthouse. His body of gearwheels and cogs constructed of steel-hard blackwood glistened the color of midnight, while a covering of bronze armor shined bright beneath the autumn sun, so that I thought I could see it shimmering atop the waves. His face had no features. It was utterly blank, free of a mouth or nose, save for two round inlays of pearl white glass that served for eyes.

Oresha Moon Dragon Devshrata and the mayor stood at the clockwork giant's feet, near a tall ladder. After he gave a few speeches during which the crowd seemed to get restless, the Traveling Folk woman finally stepped forward.

"People of Mara's Bay!" she called out. "I have made yuh this champion as promised! He will protect yuh village on its darkest day! He yours so long as yuh will have him! So, it only right one of allyuh give him life!" Her eyes looked over the crowd, searching. Many cast their glances away. It was one thing to cheer on the champion, and another to sully their hands with Traveling Folk sorcery. But I would not bend, staring straight out and whispering a prayer beneath my breath that those beauteous eyes would find me.

"Evon Cal! Daughter of Adie Cal! Come!" she called.

I stood rooted, too stunned to move—until Ma pushed me forward. Soon other hands were pulling and pushing me through the crowd, and I found myself standing right there before the Traveling Folk woman. She beamed down at me, that small smirk on her face once more seeming to hold back some secret. Bending down she leaned in close, and I drew a deep breath, taking in her scent—like rough deep waters and sweet pungent spices that spoke of far-flung places. I wondered if I held it in my nostrils if I would be able to breathe it out again into a bottle and stopper it to hold and keep forever. This close she was dizzying, and my head swam so that my mouth seemed to speak of its own accord.

"I love you," the words came, as if drawn from my tongue. In shock I tried to catch them, to pull them back, but they fluttered away beyond my grasp.

Oresha Moon Dragon Devshrata stared back at me for long moment, then putting a hand to my hair, adjusted my ribbons as she spoke low.

"Love, is it? Oh, lickle one, what yuh know 'bout love, nah? Still have much time for that. One day, when you ah grown woman, yuh heart gon give to one who deserve it. Maybe more than once. And yuh gon know the joy and pain and loneliness ah love. But yuh must never so easily give it to one such as me—a wind that blow in with the new season but like each passing breeze gon have its time. Yuh see, I have cast the stones to know what tomorrows lie in wait for me. And it—" Her eyes glanced up, quickly running over the assemblage of Mara's Bay folk, and a slight sneer lifted the corner of her lip before settling, so that I wasn't certain it had ever been there at all.

"But that my concern," she finished. "Now then, Evon Cal, we must see to yuh champion. He a thing ah machine and magic. And I need yuh to help start his heart with magic of yuh own."

"But I don't know any magic!" I stammered.

She smiled slyly. "Then I gon give yuh some ah mine." Taking my hands in hers, she blew gently on my fingers, and I felt a slight tingle run through me. "Now, go. Give yuh champion life."

I nodded, suddenly confident, almost light-headed. Grabbing on to the ladder I began to climb, making my way up each rung with a slight giddiness. I looked down once when I'd reached the clockwork giant's waist to see everyone far below, then continued climbing.

Our champion's heart stood about half as big as me. It was the only part exposed in the bronze armor—Oresha Moon Dragon Devshrata's own construction. I gaped at it in wonder, trying to imagine how such a thing could be made. Then, as the small bit of magic yet worked through me, I knew what I had to do. Placing my palms against the metal heart I closed my eyes and whispered one word. "Live."

A warmth rushed through me, and I could feel the borrowed magic leaving, entering the clockwork giant's heart. But it was more than that. It took something from me as well, from all of Mara's Bay. Because it really was our very own champion.

A loud ticking began as the mechanical heart hummed to life, beating like a thing of flesh and blood. All along the clockwork giant's body gears began to grind and turn in time. His back straightened and he seemed to stand firmer. On his featureless face those two round inlays of glass stared out upon the waters as he began his vigil.

From the crowd below cheering erupted. Women hugged and men clapped each other on their backs. I looked down searching for Oresha Moon Dragon Devshrata. I had confessed my feelings to her. She had shared magic with me. And I couldn't help but feel there was now a bond between us, of sorts.

I found her soon enough. In the midst of the celebration, she had grabbed hold of a woman—a plump widow named Agee Mas, the mayor's niece. And she was kissing her, with such intensity that several in the crowd stopped cheering to stare slack-jawed. The Brath twins stared hardest of all. I watched in disappointment as the Traveling Folk woman left the celebration arm in arm with Agee Mas, both heading to her fabulous house, leaving the ruin of my dreams in their wake.

"It isn't natural," one of the Brath twins muttered, where she sat staring into her thick brown ale.

I poured her another cup of hot fin-tailed lamprey and plum squash soup. It was winter. And a creeping ice had gripped Mara's Bay, holding us fast. Ma and I sold food now inside the mayor's inn, where people gathered to idle away time, until at least the fishing boats could be freed from the latest storm.

"Carrying on with a widow like that," the second Brath twin added. "It's indecent!"

"You're a fine lot to talk," the mayor said dryly. He was wiping down a set of iron pint mugs with meticulous care. Behind him, two of his daughters followed over each mug with a second wiping. He pursed his lips at the Brath twins. "Seem to remember you two up there most of the summer, doing 'indecent' things."

From near the fireplace where he sat in a big chair, Ro Culin chuckled. He tapped out the ashes of his reedwood pipe before filling it anew. Touching a flint to the flames, he used it to spark the tabac. "Got a point there. Says something, I think, that one Agee Mas is worth two Braths, eh?"

There was laughter from others, and even my Ma had to stifle a smile. That only made the Brath twins scowl deeper.

"You're just protecting her because she's your niece!" one of them snapped.

The mayor shrugged at the charge. "Agee's a good woman. Lost her husband three years back to worm sickness and never took another or a wife. She's been lonely. Don't recall you Braths courting her."

"Can't argue there," Ro Culin said, puffing on his pipe. "Least Agee's not all trussed up like she had you two—in your pretty, fine clothes." More laughter now. And the Brath twins hunched further over their ale, turning the shade of fresh-cut beet kelp. I didn't laugh. It wasn't that I cared much for the Brath twins. But I had seen Agee Mas sometimes walking hand in hand with Oresha Moon Dragon Devshrata. And you could hear the two laughing and celebrating into the night in that big house. I didn't understand the arbitrariness of attrac-

16

tion, and that to the Traveling Folk woman I was only a girl of two and ten. I only knew that Agee Mas was where I wanted to be.

"Laugh if you want!" shouted one the Braths hotly. "But we were up there! In her presence. We've seen things!"

The mayor sighed wearily. "And what is it you think you've seen?"

There was a pause and the two twins glanced at each other, before one of them blurted out a word. "Witchery!"

There was some quiet at that. Magic was one thing. But witchery was no small charge in Mara's Bay, where people warded against foul craft that could make a man fall from his boat into the sea or cause fish stores to grow salt worms. When someone asked what kinds of things they'd seen, the Braths were eager to go on. They spoke of strange items in the Traveling Folk woman's possession; of the way she cut open fish to read their entrails, of strange chants she would do amid smoke and candles. And ears listened.

"She's putting curses on us!" one of the Brath twins said. "Traveling Folk witchery! Why, that's how she got the two of us!" There were a few snickers at that, and some seemed ready to rebuff the charge. But the twins quickly ran on. "No one can remember a winter harsh as this one. Boats trapped in ice so thick you can't cut it away. House roofs caving in from the snow. Sea cats eating up all the night squid. It's not natural!"

People definitely went quiet this time. Everyone seemed to be dwelling on their own thoughts. For a long time, no one spoke. And then Ro Culin's voice broke the silence.

"Other day, before this storm, I hauled in one of the biggest blue fish you ever seen." He held his long arms apart to demonstrate. Some whistled appreciatively. "Had her right in my hands. A good grip, too. By all rights she was mine—till she wriggled out. Jumped right back through the net and into the sea. When I looked close, the rope in the netting had been cut to leave a big hole. Bought that net from Lon Fel. Buy all my nets from him. And never had a hole before."

"Because my nets don't have holes!" thick-necked Lon Fel, who was sitting across the room, boomed. "I make the best nets in Mara's Bay! Not a man or woman dare say otherwise!"

Everyone mumbled their assent. Lon Fel did make very good nets. And just like that, it began. One by one, people recounted stories of oddities. A sand calf had slipped inexplicably and broken its leg, needing to be put down. A barrel of freshly caught ice scallops had spoiled without good cause. A heavy hailstorm had ripped the sails of half a dozen fishing boats. On and on it went, and with each telling the mood in the room soured so that I thought I could taste it in the air.

"Two babes I delivered for Enin Geral," Cora Gilish spoke. All heads turned to the Cunning woman, who had remained quiet all this time. She looked up from the table where she was seated to fix her eyes on us. "Twins. Both born with the cleft lip."

There were a few gasps. I inhaled sharply. Twins were strange dealings enough; the Braths were evidence of that. But everyone knew cleft lips were a bad omen. Fishermen whispered they were really the disgruntled spirits of their catch who decided to be reborn as people, and the cleft was the mark where the hooks had once pierced their face.

"What do you suppose that means?" Ro Culin asked, his long face frowning.

The Cunning woman straightened in her authority, as every gaze turned to her, expectant. "Who can say? I know this. Never had a Geral born with a cleft lip. And haven't heard of one in three generations in Mara's Bay. Now we have two, at once."

"Now hold on," the mayor urged, tasting the mood of his inn. "We're doing a lot of talking here, and it's just that. Talk. Odd things happen all the time. We don't go blaming witchery for every bad catch or when our squid milk curdles." He turned about to meet each eye. "Need I remind you that Mistress Devshrata came here to help us? And we all agreed to accept that help. Gave our oath."

"Wasn't free!" one of the Braths barked. "We paid for it!"

"Still paying!" his sister added.

"All so that she can live in that big house," Cora Gilish remarked, one eyebrow raised. "And make us that 'champion' who never moves and drives us slowly mad with that infernal noise."

Everyone turned to look out the small, frosted glass window. From here we could see our champion. He was covered in a sheet of ice and stood just where we had left him. Where he always stood. The only sign that he lived was his ever-ticking heart. Day and night it ticked, so loud it could be heard the length of the village—our constant reminder of his existence as he stood his silent vigil.

"You saw her casting as well as me, Cora Gilish," the mayor said sternly. "And you agreed the threat was real."

"Perhaps," she answered, pursing her lips sourly. Then paused. "Or perhaps I saw a witch's trick. Done some talking with other Cunning women these past months. Sent out messenger sparrows too, to ask about these Vassa. No one, anywhere, has ever heard of them."

That caught the mayor off guard. His broad face frowned. "None?"

"Not even a mention," Cora Gilish replied, louder for all listening. She looked back out the window. "But now we have that monstrosity that does nothing, and the witch has a grand fine house. All at our expense. The Traveling Folk are known for their skills at bartering. Quite a good trade, wouldn't you say?"

There was a hush throughout the room. I watched slowly as every head turned to the window on the opposite side, where in the distance Oresha Moon Dragon Devshrata's house stood on its lonely bluff. Eyes hardened as they stared, thinking over all they'd just heard. And as I thought of Agee Mas sitting warmly up there, where I should have been, my eyes and heart hardened as well.

"Witch! Witch! Fall in a ditch!"

We cried our chant as children, running around the legs of the clockwork giant singing the words to our new game. It was still winter, at least two weeks longer than most were accustomed to. Even with the ice gone, the fish were scarce in these cold waters. And it left all of us idle from the usual spring chores that came with a bustling market. So, in the last slivers of sun before the coming of twilight, we played.

On cue at the end of the song, we all fell down like the witch in the ditch. The last one standing was made the witch, and we picked up snowballs to pelt him. It didn't make much sense but bore the special cruelty of children.

"If that witch was here, I'd push her in a ditch!" redheaded Jayn Rol said. It was a constant claim we made now to show our bravado and disdain for witches. Oresha Moon Dragon Devshrata had become the source of our ire, nurtured on the bitter words we heard murmured by adults. We mimicked their spite, swallowed it down bitter, and made it our own.

"My Da says we should have never made a pact with that witch," Jayn Rol spat. "He says now all of Mara's Bay is cursed."

"My Da says this winter might last forever," a girl put in.

"Mine says she's keeping the fish away," another boy added.

Jayn Rol scowled, turning to look at the big house on the bluff. "We should go pelt that witch's house!"

"No!" one boy said, his small face going pale, and eyes wide. "My Ma says witches cook children—and eats them!"

Everyone's eyes rounded at this, including my own. That was one I hadn't heard before. I didn't believe any of it, of course. But I no longer cared what people said or thought of Oresha Moon Dragon Devshrata, who now barely gave me a moment's glance. So, I held my tongue and kept my quiet.

"Can't believe some people used to look up to that witch," Jayn Rol said. His eyes fell on me, and I stiffened as he sneered. "I remember when Evon Cal was wearing those stupid bright scarves and had her hair all braided up like that witch. Probably used to rub soot on your skin too!"

My face heated, and he grinned. "I remember that day you climbed that ladder and made this iron monster's heart tick." He pointed up at the mechanical heart, covered in a sheath of ice but still alive. "Why don't you climb up there again and turn it off?"

"Why don't you?" I snapped back. "You're always so much talk, Jayn Rol. But you don't do anything. Just like your Da. All that talk, but when he passes by that witch, he puts his head down and keeps on walking." I huffed for good measure. "Talk from a Rol."

It was Jayn's turn to get heated. He stalked up to me and glared. I glared back. We were the same height after all. Seeing this wouldn't work, he spun about and stared up at the clockwork giant that was once our champion.

"Think I'll go up there and turn that thing off myself," he declared.

I rolled my eyes. "Don't be stupid. There's no ladder."

"Don't need one."

Marching up, he grabbed hold of a massive leg. Then with a heave, he hoisted himself up. We watched his odd ascent with breaths held, hardly believing our eyes. We played around our once champion, but none of us dared touch him. Jayn Rol exulted in our awe, and he gave a cry of triumph as he inched higher. Then his foot skidded, trying to find purchase on the slippery ice covering the bronze frame. There was a yelp—and he fell.

He was airborne for only moments before striking the ground hard. He lay there for a moment, only gasping. Then he screamed. We stood frozen, not knowing what to do as his face contorted in pain and tears filled his eyes. We were still standing when stout Bree Nor came running up, still wearing her washerwoman apron. With much exclamation she picked up Jayn and ran up the road to the mayor's inn. We followed behind.

Inside, the usual talk ended as Bree Nor came huffing through the doors, laying a screaming Jayn on a table. Cora Gilish made her way forward, broad white bonnet parting all before her. She felt along the boy's leg, and he screamed louder.

"Broken. It'll need to be set." Instructing others to fetch her things she turned to us. "How did this happen?"

"It was the witch!" a girl blurted out. The gathered crowd went still.

Cora Gilish looked up from where she was tying up Jayn's leg, one eye twitching. "What do you mean, gal?"

"We were talking about the witch," the girl said. "And then Jayn tried to climb the giant!"

"Climb?" Ro Culin asked. "Who gave him that sea-cat-brained idea?"

"I think it was the witch," a boy trembled. "My ma says she can make people do things—like she made the Braths do things."

The twins, who were standing nearby, quickly agreed—launching into one of their tirades that people now earnestly listened to. Cora Gilish raised a hand for quiet. "He fell?" she asked.

The girl nodded. "He was climbing just fine. Then something just . . . happened. I think." She paused. "I think the giant might have moved."

There were fresh gasps now, and Cora Gilish frowned deep. She turned her glare to us as on the table, Jayn whimpered through clenched teeth. "All of you saw this?"

The others all nodded in turn. And then all eyes came to me.

I stood there, confused. I hadn't seen any witchery. A stupid boy had tried to climb the clockwork giant and fell. I certainly never saw it move. But now Cora Gilish's glare was on me—everyone's eyes were on me. Even my mother's. I knew those faces waited on me to tell them not what I saw, but what they believed I saw. And it was so much easier to give them what they wanted. Under that pressure that seemed to pound in my ears, I found my head moving in a nod, and wondered if perhaps this was some other strange form of witchery.

It was like a spark.

The inn erupted with angry shouts. The witch had done this! The witch who had cheated them for fools, who had cursed their village, who lived in her big fancy house built with their money and toil. Now that witch was harming their children! It was time to do something! It was time for her to leave Mara's Bay!

I watched, stunned, as people I had known abruptly changed, seeming to become other people. It was as if their faces held masks beneath, angry, cruel, hateful masks, that they had been hiding all this time. Men howled and women screamed. They cursed the witch and called for blood. Stout line poles were grabbed up. Fishing hooks and curved serrated gutters were brandished. Chair legs were broken off, the ends wrapped in whale oil–soaked cloth and set aflame. As one, this group of people with new frightening faces streamed out of the inn and began their night march to the house on the bluff.

I was swept up within it, carried along by its raw anger—struggling to keep up. Once the mayor tried to block them, making fevered appeals. But someone threatened to return to his inn and burn it down as well. He cowered at that, and his daughters pulled him away, to let these men and women he had called friends and neighbors seek out others to sate their rage. When we finally reached the house on the bluff, the witch herself stepped out to meet us.

Oresha Moon Dragon Devshrata stood at her door, staring with that dark glittering gaze. She looked as fantastic to me as she did that morning of her arrival, and her long black hair seemed like snakes poised to strike. Dressed in her long gray coat and a bright rose-colored dress, she placed hands on her hips and planted bare feet on the icy ground—unyielding.

Her fearless stance was enough to momentarily stun the crowd and they stopped, losing their momentum. Cora Gilish, however, pushed her way to the front and walked right up the Traveling Folk woman.

"We've had enough of your tricks and witchery!" she declared. "We've come to tell you to go—this very night!"

Oresha Moon Dragon Devshrata's eyes narrowed as she stared the Cunning Woman up and down. "Allyuh break yuh pact?" she drawled. "Yuh don' have no shame?"

Cora Gillish's face thundered. "We don't honor pacts with witches!" she spat.

Oresha Moon Dragon Devshrata's paused at that, staring with a curious expression. Then she laughed. It was a loud rich bellow that echoed through the now-dark night, full of disdain and mockery. It did not stop until Cora Gilish took her open palm and slapped the Traveling Folk woman across the face, hard enough to make her stagger. We stared in silence, and I clutched at my dress with an inhaled breath.

When Oresha Moon Dragon Devshrata looked up again, there was fire in her eyes that looked like it might boil away seas. With a cry she launched for the Cunning woman. But other hands from the crowd caught her. She fought, bloodying the nose of one man, and scratching a tear into another's face. But in the end, she was caught like a struggling sea cat on a noose-pole. A frightful Agee Mas who was standing in the doorway was snatched up as well. Together the two women were hauled before us for judgment.

A new quiet fell over Oresha Moon Dragon Devshrata, as if the prior fury had never been. She watched in silence as pelted stones broke the windows of her home, as the people that had welcomed her now ran inside to ransack her belongings. She did not speak or cry out even as the first fires were set, and the flames began to darken the cobalt-speckled bricks until the terracotta tiles of the roof cracked beneath the heat.

Once, her eyes roamed about, then finding me, lingered. A flicker of something ran across them—disappointment, pity, or sadness—and it felt like a fishing barb had been thrust into my heart. I turned away, wanting to hide from those eyes that seemed to gaze through me, to my betrayal.

"Now the witch!" someone yelled. Talk began of what to do with our captives. Someone, a woman whose voice I tried to pretend was not my mother, suggested sending the witch and her lover back into the burning house. But Cora Gilish had another idea.

"She came over the sea on an ill wind," the Cunning woman proclaimed. "We will give her back to the sea!"

A frightening roar went up, and the mad procession began a new march to the harbor. Agee Mas cried and pleaded as she was led, but Oresha Moon Dragon Devshrata never uttered a word between the jeers and spittle that came her way, as silent and unshakable as stone.

It was the sound of the horn that stilled us. The sonorous blare cut through the air like the bellow of some leviathan, sending a chill deeper than winter, piercing into bone and spirit. We stopped, made immobile by that unearthly sound. Then we saw its source.

Out on the sea before the harbor were ships. They were black, so dark they blended with the night upon the waves. Their bodies were massive and long, like the great serpents that roamed the deep waters of the world. They had gotten close, so we could now see the tall masts that carried their black sails.

A sudden light flared before them—fiery green flames that spit in gouts from the mouths of carved monstrous heads at the prow of the vessels. As it illuminated the night, figures came into view standing on those black ships, the hulking forms of men plucked from our nightmares, wearing gleaming bestial skulls, and sitting astride giant armored black dogs that sent up fierce howls.

It was what had been foretold, what had been prophesied. The Vassa.

All the rage that had moments ago infused us was extinguished—like the hot spear of a fishing point plunged into water in its forging. And as we watched flaming arrows nocked like a hundred pinpoints of light, we saw our doom and wailed in fright. Only one voice rose above our anguished cries, and I looked up to see Oresha Moon Dragon Devshrata shouting words in her tongue.

There was a loud creaking, then crackling as in the harbor a towering form stirred. I held my breath as my hands clenched my skirts, realizing what I was seeing. Our champion!

The clockwork giant stretched limbs like a man awakening from a long sleep. Along his body ice broke, tumbling in great blocks to crash at his feet. That ticking heart seemed to grow faster, louder, as his once-dull eyes now shined bright. He swiveled his head to gaze out at the sea, to where the black ships bobbed upon the waters. Then he began his march toward them.

No one who stood witness that night could forget the sight of our champion striding out into the shallow waves. Or how the flaming arrows loosed upon him by the Vassa merely bounced from his bronze skin. How with one hand he lifted up the bow of a ship, pitching it over so that men and their war beasts were sent crying and barking into the sea. How the flames spouted by the monstrous vessels wreathed his unmarred face in a terrible countenance, as he broke them in two. The Battle of Mara's Bay, as we would come to call it, lasted no more than moments. Those Vassa that survived sailed furiously away, leaving their armor-laden compatriots to sink heavily and drown in the icy waters, their bloated bodies washing up on our shores for days to come.

There was silence as we watched the last of the remaining black ships depart. When a loud grunt came, all turned to see Oresha Moon Dragon Devshrata pulling ruefully away from the men who now slackly held her. They backed away. Everyone did. Even Cora Gilish cowered, shrinking into her broad white bonnet. We had seen more than the saving of our village this night, or the vindication of a Traveling Folk woman. We had seen ourselves, and what lay beneath, as monstrous perhaps as the Vassa. And it shamed us.

But Oresha Moon Dragon Devshrata paid us no mind, as if we were not there. She was set to walk past us when she stopped and looked directly at me. Heat burned my face, and I wanted to turn my head to not meet her terrible gaze. I wanted to pour out my guilt for what part I played in our disgrace. But I could do nothing but stare into those dark eyes that held me fast. The Traveling Folk woman bent low, and it wasn't until her hands wiped my cheeks that I realized they were wet with tears. She said nothing, but the corner of a lip raised in a slight smile that I will always hope was forgiveness. Then she was gone, walking past us, out toward the harbor—hand in hand with Agee Mas.

Our champion stood there, waiting. At some command from his maker, he knelt low. She climbed atop him, taking a place at his shoulders. Extending a hand to Agee Mas, she helped the other woman up. Rising again, the clockwork giant stood for a moment, an imposing figure in the night. Then he strode forward. There were screams as he entered our village and many ran—thinking his maker meant him to trample us and our homes in her vengeance.

But the giant walked past our fishing boats, past our thatched-roof houses, past the still burning edifice of his maker's house. He walked out of Mara's Bay and onto the plains, disappearing into the dark, so that after long, even the sounds of his ticking heart could not be heard.

No one knows what became of Oresha Moon Dragon Devshrata after that night. She never returned to Mara's Bay. Nor did any of the Traveling Folk. There were rumors over the years that she had gone on to design war machines for the princelings of the Twelve Isles. Some said she had become a ruler in some distant land on the other side of the world. Others claimed she had built a great balloon to sail to the sun and died when it burned and tumbled back to earth.

Who can say?

Life in Mara's Bay went on, as it had before. Most tried to forget that night. What was left of the Traveling Folk woman's house was removed bit by bit, so that a field now stands where it once did—though no one dares build there.

Long after that night, when I was a woman of middle years, who had twice married and birthed and raised three children, Mara's Bay had a bronze statue raised in the market square. It stands now half again as tall as a man and depicts the clockwork giant in all his magnificence, staring out at the sea. At his feet is a plaque that reads—Our Champion.

The name Oresha Moon Dragon Devshrata, however, is nowhere to be found. In fact, that name became unspoken in Mara's Bay, and largely disappeared from memory—except among the old like me who still remember when I was a girl of two and ten. It was as though speaking her name would remind us of what we had seen that night, not out in the waters, but in our own flesh and hearts. So, we erased her from our minds and the stories we passed down, as if silence would somehow rid us of our guilt.

But if you put your ear to the statue's heart, and close your eyes and listen, you will hear a faint ticking like a clock—the last fading bit of magic once given to a girl that she pressed into the breast of this bronze replica, when she was yet a woman of middle years. And if you come to me now and ask about that strange sound, I will tell you all that I remember of Oresha Moon Dragon Devshrata.

CATECHISM FOR THOSE WHO WOULD FIND WITCHES

Kathleen Jennings

Document No.: #NbL-693-#34PF—Newpool Castle-School
Rare Books and Manuscripts Room.
Access: Restricted. Written permission required from the Chief
Librarian or the Castle-School Senate.
Description: This falsification of the classic Catechism was
discovered in and confiscated from the common library of the
Castle-School of Newpool.
Like most texts predating the introduction of stricter borrowing
protocols, it contains marginalia and graffiti by one or more
unidentified students.
More important, although it is bound between authentic covers,
and begins with the familiar phrasing used to instruct young
scholars in the foundational history (and dangers) of witch
eradication, the forgery gradually deviates from the original
answers.

*[Note to self: I'm senior enough that I can now access the book under
the new restrictions. (New? Established for decades.) I'm also alone, as*

usual these days, so no-one can see me bend to sniff the pages. Childish.
The library has always been thick with perfumes like old harnesses and
burned honey. But this book smells, ever so slightly, of smoke and salt.

I had forgotten that.]

Q. Why are witches sought and by whom?
A. Witches are sought by few. This is for three reasons.

First, thanks to the good offices of those who hunt them, witches
are believed to be vanishingly rare.

Second, witches are feared. Ungoverned and ungovernable, each
forms the world to their requirements. They have razed cities and
turned honest wives from their families. They are insidious, an infec-
tion.

Third, those who seek them must therefore be wily and wary:
careful readers, cautious thinkers, quiet walkers. They must know how
to thread and unravel a path that darts around the strict order of our
world, if they are to trace the paths of witches.

That is why, and by whom, and reason to hesitate.

Q. Are you nevertheless prepared to enquire further?
A. I am.

[*Here a marginal note has been made in the imprecise shorthand of students,*
which might without further context mean good *or* get on with it *or* welcome.]

Q. Where do witches come from?
A. The Great Sorcerer Legasar lived on the most-eastern shore, where the
shoulder of the earth turns toward icy waves. He drew the first witch
from the ocean: skin and stone. He wrapped one around the other and
breathed into it a woman-shape, with a sea-glass heart.

Legasar folded into her all he knew, taught her the Great Words and the Lesser Words and the Words under Worlds; he instructed her in the spells of wings and the speech of bones; he opened her eyes to walk in that least of worlds, through the hall of doors, into whatever time or tide she wished to move.

All this he gave her freely, having made her, and asked no more than any artist does of his instruments: obedience.

[Have you *met* an artist? *asks the notetaker, or words like that. One can see the irreverence of the student vandal in the lines that spatter upward into sketches of feathers and femurs and waves. The style suggests a northern influence. How easily the lines grew, uncramped by piety or care for the book. A final excess of resistance in the face of a life of serious scholarship.*]

Q. What was the name of the first witch?

A. Legasar, having caused the ocean to birth the first witch, called her simply "woman," and this she always believed herself to be. (Ignorance, you must understand, is like fire, and wisdom given to fools is like a leaf in a maelstrom.)

But later she became known as Thalassa. This means "ocean" in the scholarly tongue.

Q. Did Legasar then err?

A. Why pass judgment? It is done. These three facts, held in the hand like marbles, are answer and warning enough:

Legasar was the greatest of sorcerers, and therefore cannot be criticized by one so humble as the reader of this catechism; Legasar pulled from the sea Thalassa, who was bound by no such restrictions; Legasar's fate walked the lands long after he ceased to do so.

What greater legacy will you leave?

Or judge if you will, but save your breath—who will hear?

[Walls listen, *says the note. Or perhaps:* Pages soften. *The flippancy of youth. The inattention.*]

Q. What befell Legasar?

A. Legasar, first among the last sorcerers, grew overfond of the creature he had pulled from the sea. As if she were his lawful apprentice, he taught Thalassa things which were to be kept beyond the grasp of lesser mortals, and that of women most of all.

Thalassa grew in wisdom, until she knew too much.

It is written by some that she grew in beauty, until her loveliness snared him. As if that might be forgivable.

But the truth is, Thalassa caught the venerated Legasar unaware, secure in his greatness, and overset him with magic surpassing his own. She made a net of her sea-dark hair, and folded him up; she took all the strength that had flowed from his hands, the power that held together the ancient sorceries, and reeled it around him like threads on a bobbin—tight as a winding-sheet, brighter than a meteor. Then she plunged the flaming Legasar into standing water, and buried the coal of him in an oak's heart.

[*In youth, I found Legasar's fate and the accompanying prophecy of the return of the oak-sorcerer tragic and stirring: a warning and a promise (who might wake him? what wrongs would he right?). Age brings a degree of sympathy. Envy of rest, weariness at the thought of descending shadowed steps to find yourself blinking in a world that has busied itself without you.*]

Q. Will he wake?
A. No.

Q. Shall this catechism not enquire as to the witch Thalassa's reasons for betrayal?
A. The ocean does not give reasons. Why then should a witch?

[*The note here indicates the student planned to use that first rejoinder on an exam. And today, after a lifetime of careful working out of theories and demonstrations of methods, negotiation of bylaws and rulings of the college senate, I almost wish I had dared to do so.*]

Q. What has become of sorcery in our present age?

A. When Legasar, the chief of sorcerers, was netted by Thalassa in the enchantments he purported to rule, magic across the lands was wrenched out of the ranks of lesser sorcerers. As Thalassa rolled Legasar's power around him, it unwound from them like silk from so many cocoons, and they were left as naked and half-formed as worms.

Even before the proliferation of witches, the College of Sorcery in Pool-by-Linden became merely the Castle-School, purveyor of approved legends, eyes inturned from the tossing world outside. Dry as the dead heart of a tree.

Many of the former sorcerers perished. Perhaps a few returned to honest labors. Many became scholars, trainers of witch-hunters, inventors of catechisms.

Q. What did Thalassa do next?

A. When Thalassa drew magic out of the world and sealed it to Legasar's fate, she locked away the enchantment that had created her.

Hollow as a candle mold, she walked for a time, undreaming.

[*I've had occasion, over my career, to revisit the original catechism. This bastardized version is notable for its insistence on using Thalassa's name instead of only "the witch." In the margin, the annotator has written it in various stylings. The pen pressed hard, so that I can still feel the indentations in the page:* Thalassa; She of the Sea; The Witch of the Wave, *repeated like an incantation.*]

Q. What tales are there of the wanderer Thalassa?

A. Thalassa caught and carried tales like burrs in the hem of her coat. She left fragmentary legends in her wake like frayed threads.

This much may be reraveled: She journeyed from the green-glass sea to the tree-canopied spindle-center of the continent, where few had ever seen an ocean, and her name was but a word.

So rather than repeat the dusty lies, let us use what we know to wonder.

If she *was* beautiful, perhaps that protected her. (If beauty has ever been armor.) It is said she was like rain-washed granite.

We know her gleaming heart was in her eyes. Maybe that was strange enough to give people pause, so that they shrank away.

But consider: It might be (as can happen) that the folks upon the roads she walked loved easily. Perhaps there has always been kindness in the world, in spite of everything.

And perhaps, having rid herself of Legasar, she became fortunate.

Q. Where did Thalassa go?

A. You are reading this by the window over the quadrangle.

[*The marginal comment here is startled and explicit, as was mine just now, before I remembered that given the layout of the library, the chances of an accurate guess were always high.*]

Stand up and cross-reference the maps in the *Learner's Cartography* with the scurrilous but delightful embroideries of history in *The Witch's Walk*. You will see that the paths Thalassa followed had been dragged and channeled out by the reeled-in cords of power. Whatever sorcerers legislated and claimed, they were not the only ones who touched magic. Thalassa traveled among people pitted with grief for the hollowed-out enchantments of themselves.

Barefoot, she crossed ten lands, and then she remembered thirst. When she had passed through three more, she recalled what hunger was. When she reached Pool-By-Linden (as it was known before the Fire), she heard water falling like the sound of her name, and she believed herself, at that time, a woman born in the way of other women.

Remember, the sorcerers held themselves apart, built high-windowed libraries, spat on the world below. Even their scholar-descendants should understand this much: Of all that Thalassa was and did, her belief that she was as others, that there was no difference between mortal women and what she was, proved the most perilous.

Q. Was Thalassa still fearsome, emptied as she was?

A. Thalassa had torn Legasar's power out of herself, too, like pulling waterflax from the seabed; she had forgotten and unmade that which made her. Yet it had given her form. Her ribs enclosed an appetite for that which did not exist, and her skull longed for a knowledge she had slain.

Q. Why is hunger a vice, and desire unbecoming?

A. Desire may create that for which it yearns.

Like a chimney swallowing wind, Thalassa did not yet know that she desired at all, nor guess what her stomach howled for.

When she limped along the tree-cooled avenues of Pool-By-Linden, when she craned up at its arrogant towers, her gaze fell on patterns that Legasar could have told her were the skeleton of the world. When she found work in its smoking manufactories, her ears caught syllables that once nestled in the Great Words. And while all who toiled beside her heard the same noises, in Thalassa that music dropped soundless into the abyss where (it is claimed) those not witch-born keep a soul.

At night, in a humble bed, her dreams swirled like bats in the caverns of her bones. Fragmentary as soot, they formed the shapes of the Words under the Worlds. Enchantment shivered there. The revenant of magic stalked her veins and sparked like sea-fire against her glass heart.

Within Thalassa, the magic reformed itself, as ice grows from the edges of a pond.

One night she lay to rest, her hands rough with common work and her ears ringing with humble speech, and opened her eyes on the hall of doors at the center of power.

Q. What were the women of Pool-by-Linden like before Thalassa reached them?

A. They were, by many reports, like women anywhere, whether petty and pretty, or ugly and jealous. It is said they were gossips and rivals, mothers and those of easy persuasion, girls half-blossomed and hags.

As to the truth of this: Such statements were made by great historians. But you may look out that many-paned window, with the penny-spider spinning in its lower corner, and judge for yourself.

[*Was the spider there too, all those years ago? Such a frivolous student would have drawn it, surely?*]

The women you see in the streets of Newpool today (although they hasten through the sunlit rain) are not so different in essentials from what Thalassa saw. They are stiff and glittering in court gowns, they carry their proud heads high on starched collars; they are preoccupied and humble in homespun and wooden shoes. Bored, arrogant, sneering; interested, voracious, scheming. Gentle, harsh, frantic. Human.

Certainly Thalassa, who had been taught no differently, believed her neighbors to be like all women. Therefore, whether they were her fellow-laborers or fine ladies on the raised walks, she assumed them to be like herself.

Assumptions may be dangerous.

Q. Dangerous for whom?

A. Who is threatened? Who gains? These are wise questions.

Consider that it is said, among those who would find witches, that the conversation of women, ungoverned, is hazardous and not to be trusted.

Without imposed order, their conversation assumes shapes not fitting. Thus, we are told, monstrosities are committed and formed.

A tree grown in a bottle is, by such reasoning, the purest expression of its kind.

Q. Since sorcery has been locked away, what form did this powerful speech take?

A. Thalassa thought of the vastness within herself. The women of Pool-by-Linden, as they ignored and befriended, employed and exploited her, betrayed no sign that they knew such secrets as had returned to her. Yet she believed them to be like herself, and she wondered what worlds whirled in them: What powers, what wonders?

So Thalassa spoke with her neighbors and asked, "What are your sea-glass hearts capable of?"

"Love and hatred," they answered, thinking her words fanciful.

"And when you close your eyes, what do you see?"

"The inside of our eyelids."

"You have answered as you must. But when you sit in stillness and think of nothing, what then?"

[*There is a page left blank, here. An urgent jotting from the student:* What then?!]

Indeed.

[*And I could swear I hear laughter somewhere among the shelves, although the Castle-School rare book room is somber, and I thought I was alone.*]

Q. What did the women answer?

A. They did not, at first. What more could *you* say, if I asked you to sit a moment and listen to your heartbeat? (It is still a little fast from surprise. You have sat too long among books in high towers, my love, if laughter frightens you.)

But Thalassa asked until they began to question each other. In sculleries and ballrooms, gutters and guildhalls, they discussed what she could mean.

They closed their eyes to think. They dreamed deliberately. And at last, one brewer-woman said, "I see a hall of doors. A grand hall, and plain doors."

That woman thought (and started to say) that, after all, perhaps it had always been there, waiting in the dark behind her eyelids for her to sit still long enough. Then others decided to seek, and they too found it.

"What is beyond that hall, through the doors, for you?" Thalassa asked, not remembering that once she alone—outside the company of sorcerers—had passed that way.

"I do not know," said the first woman. "I have yet to step through."

Q. So small a thing?

A. If to be willing, able, *permitted*, to sit quiet is small, then yes. So idly Thalassa the Witch conveyed to the women of Pool-by-Linden the treasures of ancient sorcery. With unstudied speech, she pulled power into them.

So simply began the age of witches.

[*There is a line drawn beneath that sentence, unevenly, as if—despite having already chosen an arduous, fallow road—the student lingered on each word:* So simply.]

Q. What is the hall of doors?

A. The hall of doors was once, among sorcerers, a figure of speech: a rubric, a mnemonic, a means of reckoning order onto the swirling mights-and-perhapses of the world.

As Thalassa dreamed, however, it became a hall in truth, paved in stone creamy as sea foam, walled with translucent green marble, and with plain heavy doors set into its arches.

No door ever leads to the same place twice, save one.

Q. And where does that door lead?

A. That one door is Thalassa's, and it opens on the waking world. But it does not retrace the dreamer's steps—it pulls them forward and out again, like turning through a garment new-sewn.

To pass over that threshold is to drag the world through one's mind and veins, organs and bones, and etch into them the knowledge of the ways of power, the inchoate dreams that underlie the Words under the Worlds.

[*I have learned and taught that envy cannot be beautiful. But imagine: to be granted longings that need never be given dry, precise, technical words. And oh, these drawings of doors in the margin, and the foliage that spills from them like hope, and the tiny birdfoot-inkings of stars . . .*]

Q. How many times can the world bear to be turned inside out, never knowing it?

A. How many indeed?

But sorcery once pulled bricks from the world's foundations and reordered them, while throughout the lands, shirts are daily shaken through and remade. This is as good an answer to the question as any.

Q. What are the powers that manifested in the women who, by Thalassa's teachings, entered the hall of doors and passed through it?

A. These are the consequences of Thalassa's unwisdom:

In Pool-by-Linden, there was a woman who could vomit fire and not be burned, and a second who—burned—put on scales of amber and verdigris and slid noiselessly into the canal. A third spun the wool under her fingertips to a string of embers and wound it like thread on a spool. The women of Pool-by-Linden loved flame.

In Happenby, where water is precious, one strung her tears on a hair from her own head and strangled a man with it. Another turned into a pillar of salt, although her children were grasping at her apron. A girl called up, out of what had always been a brackish well, a wave of the sea with deep-jawed, lamp-eyed fish trembling in it.

On the trading roads, one woman at a touch armored her cart so that arrow never struck it and wheel never broke. Another held the maps of the continent seared on her gaze, and could feel blood thicken in the veins of the sick. Yet another one day arose from her place by the fire and began walking, and her feet never tired and she did not seek food or water until she reached the other side of the lands.

Each of them carried the mysteries of Thalassa with her.

Q. What manner of power does a witch, newborn, receive? Is there any order or pattern?
A. There is no order or pattern to the powers of witches. They are not governed, nor are they governable. They are as innocent and as wicked as anyone.

It is said, however, that the first welling of power fills, like water, the shape of their first great need.

Q. How may I know a witch or tell who is likely to become one?
A. They know their own kind, beloved.

Ask, rather, how many of those who vanished hunting them disappeared by their own choice? Ask how one may be sure a person is *not* a witch?

"Rare," they are called. But how can you be certain any person, even in this library in the heart of the burned-and-reborn city, has not already enquired? How can we know that one among the aging scholars has not closed their eyes briefly as a spider's breath and, glimpsing a door that once thrilled them with possibility, grieved for what might have been?

[I do not wish to think of that, or of whether these words once read differently. Ludicrous to say the book senses that, and moves on. It is printed and bound, and has been on one floor or another of this building longer even than I.]

Q. What became of the witch Thalassa?

A. It is not known what became of Thalassa. Perhaps she died in the great fire of Pool-by-Linden. Maybe she returned to the sea, or to stand guard by Legasar's oak, lest he return and scourge witches from the world—as if they could be unraveled as neatly as sorcerers.

Possibly, being made after all of stone and sea, she has not perished at all, but walks the lands still. Some even claim to have seen her, a solitary figure on lonely roads.

People who say that, however, think witches, having found their own ways, have no friends.

Q. Is it only among women that witches are to be sought?

A. Does it matter so very much to you, now?

Very well. I left out pages and pages of the *Catechism* here, but they can be summarized as follows: A pattern once glimpsed is difficult to unsee; a grudge narrowly defined is easier to hold.

For the rest of your answer, consider (you have already studied this, so now you need only think a moment) the weight and patterns of power. What might be lost or overset by shaking out the coat of the world, and who would risk it? Assess your place in its fabric—and note, too, that out there where people work shoulder to shoulder, secrets and knowledge spread like contagion. So look for witches among those who have been too-long governed.

Having thus concluded this catechism—

[*I know this scrawled symbol best. It was the first I learned, when I was a student here, and thought the path up the mountain of the world lay at my feet: I dare you . . . ! But the page turns, and the air of the library feels entertained.*]

Q. How do the witches recognize the door through which they must go?

A. Each witch who has passed through Thalassa's door has marked it in her fashion. Alone among the doors in that hall, it is a palimpsest of stories. You will not miss it.

[*But I did. And these last pages are unfamiliar: I was young, once, and did not finish the* Catechism, *because—why? I cannot recall. The college had promised me a place, and rules by which to get it, and I was becoming impatient of superstition. Or perhaps the weather cleared, or I was called away.*

I am old. I have squandered my days like Legasar, save that I have made nothing, and no one will remember my name. I have forgotten the reason I stopped reading then. I cannot now conjure up the faint scratch of my cheap pen, or picture how easily the thinned ink bled out into thoughts and birds. But I never quite forgot the book.]

Q. How do those who are to become witches gain admittance?

A. You must touch the green-glass handle and it will open. Walk through, and the world will turn through you, and shape itself to your need, and unfold its secrets to your mind.

Q. Is there no toll, no payment?

A. The price of entering at that door is twofold.

First, to be and become ungoverned and ungovernable. This is no light task, and not for all.

Second, on arriving anew in this world, to set a candle for those who would follow.

[*"Anew."* It is too late to pursue so foolish a flicker now. I am too old to set any kind of example. The new students, undisciplined, laugh at the careful orbits of our days, the paths deep trodden in gardens, hollowed out of stone stairs.]

Q. What type of candle?
A. Even a catechism may be a light to those on a dark path.

Q. Does there remain another question in this catechism?
A. There does remain one more question. But you must ask it.

Q. And what will its answer be?

THE LUCK THIEF

Tade Thompson

Someone stalked my kids.

As a group, not individually, and not any particular one. If anything, it seemed he stared at each child in turn on the days that I caught him. Looking for someone, maybe? He might be a dad. Sometimes, custody proceedings don't go well, and they come sniffing about. In those cases, though, the mother would have warned us or the child might be showing signs of distress.

This guy would hang about the gates during play times, although he slouched off when an adult or teacher came around. At times I'd see him at the fence. Once, I thought I saw him during the school run, mingling with other parents just before the first kids emerged.

I don't want you to think I never challenged him. I did. I was out on the bench on the playground with Ted Parker when he was having one of those monumental nose bleeds he has, when I saw this man out of the corner of my eye, using the hedge for cover, poking his head out when he thought I wasn't looking.

"Hey!" I yelled.

But he was gone. Ted panicked, but he has a tendency to do that. I patted him on the head to calm him, and sent him on his way. I went out of the gate and looked around, but the guy was gone.

I talked to the police, which was the first time I had to describe him. It wasn't easy because all I can tell you is he was forgettable. He had dark hair, dark skin, dark eyes. His clothes didn't stand out. They weren't sports clothes, neither did he wear a hood nor any other kind of thing you expect criminals to wear. He was shaven, but it looked hurried, with missed patches.

"Did he look thin or was he bulky?" asked the constable.

"Not bulky, but not thin. He had jowls, but he looked like the kind of person who would decide to run a marathon on a whim."

"Why would you say that? Did you know him?" The constable looked perplexed.

"No, I . . . it's just a thing that came to mind."

Later, at home, I had just put my feet up when the phone rang.

"Mrs. Khan?"

"Miss Khan. Yes?"

"I'm Detective Inspector Reith. I wonder if I could trouble you to pop down to the station to identify someone."

It was all rather perfunctory. It was indeed him, the stalker. His name was Orin Bello. He wasn't difficult to identify. I signed something, and that was it. Reith told me they'd question him, but he didn't know if they'd be able to charge Bello with anything. He asked me to tell the school to invest in cameras. I laughed. We had some; they didn't work.

Reith was a lot easier to remember. Six-two, blond hair, pointy nose, pale blue eyes, a bearing that suggested he and a treadmill were close.

He gave me a ride home, and that was that, I thought.

It wasn't.

A knock in the middle of the night is never good news. The police knocking on your door is the worst kind of thing, so seeing Reith on my doorstep at 3:45 a.m. was unpleasant.

"Bello escaped," said Reith. "Walked right out of the station."

"How could that happen?"

Reith seemed embarrassed. "He . . . ah . . . pretended to be me."

In hindsight, this was a cocky thing to say.

"Would you like a cup of tea?" I asked.

"I'd love one."

I had hoped he would say no. Who comes in at that time of night? He was serious, though. He smiled. He smelled of cinnamon when he walked past me. Cooking? Donuts? Cop cliché.

He made himself at home and sank into my favorite chair without being invited. He seemed excited, and he rubbed his hands over the arms of the chair like a child would.

I brought him some Yorkshire tea with a saucer of biscuits. "I don't keep sugar in the house. Honey okay?"

"I don't mind either way," said Reith. "I never say no to free calories."

Okay, so he was a little strange. Lots of people are like that, and I work with kids. No adult can be as weird as kids are. My tolerance was high, is what I'm getting at.

I made conversation while holding back a yawn. "What do you know about the suspect? What was his name again?"

"Orin Bello. Quite a bit, actually." Reith slurped his tea, then dunked a biscuit in it with glee. "I love these."

"You were saying?"

"Yeah, Bello. We know he was homeless. Street homeless for a number of years." He dusted off crumbs and they ended up on my carpet. "He was also in a close relationship until recently. Almost got married."

"Do tell," I said, hoping he would not.

He did.

Gudrun Tinworth. That was her name.

These were the first words Bello heard from her mouth:

"I'll drain him dry as hay:
Sleep shall neither night nor day
Hang upon his pent-house lid;
He shall live a man forbid;
Weary sev'nights, nine times nine,
Shall he dwindle, peak and pine.
Though his bark cannot be lost,
Yet it shall be tempest-tost.
Look what I have."

She was under makeup at the time, and Bello did not yet realize he was attracted to her. He did know that he liked her delivery and wanted to tell her so. Something about her voice, the richness, the promise.

He checked. 1 WITCH was identified on the pamphlet as Gudrun Tinworth. He was fairly confident of his *Macbeth*, at least enough to know that her speech wasn't from 2 WITCH or 3 WITCH. Bello wasn't looking to take all three Weird Sisters out for a post-production drink. Just the first.

All the theater folk called her Run. It was disconcerting at first, but Bello soon got used to it. Standing there, studying his hands, waiting. The floor dirty with prints from a thousand feet over god knows how long. Others like him, waiting to speak to actors and crew maybe, or pick up lovers and family. Some had flowers.

"Gudrun Tinworth," she said, poking her right hand at Bello. She was not hideous under her witch makeup.

"Orin Bello."

A moment of embarrassed silence.

"I thought your performance was exquisite," said Bello.

"It's a tiny part," said Run.

"Still . . ."

"I'll take the compliment. It's the first I've had outside the company."

"Do you want to get coffee?"

She eyed him up and down, assaying. "Sure, why not?"

Run took him to a coffee shop not far from the theater, where she was known. She said hello to folks who had "regular" stamped on them.

"That guy's a writer, or wants to be. Here with his laptop, spends hours nursing one hot chocolate. She works in the tax office and is ashamed of it. She looks at fluffy animals on her phone. That dude used to work here as a cleaner."

She ushered Bello to a seat by the window and turned away to retrieve their drinks. Bello looked past the grime on the glass to the street. A row of telephone poles shrank in perspective outside. Back in no time, Run slid his drink to him.

"This is my spot," Run said, with a proprietary grin.

"Do you bring all the boys here?"

"Yes. Exactly so."

Bello pointed to the tax person. "What would she say about you?"

"She'd call me Shouting Girl."

Bello laughed. "What?"

"Yep. Shouting Girl. There are three of us. Shouting Girl, Cat Girl, Makeup Girl. We're friends."

"Do you shout a lot?"

"No. In fact, I never raise my voice." She sipped her coffee. "But I did scream a lot on one particular day. So . . . I'm a drug addict. My drug of choice is cocaine."

Bello did not react. It seemed she was expecting something.

"I haven't used in five years. Five years ago, I decided to quit. I still owed my dealer a thousand pounds, though. And I was unemployed at the time. A thousand pounds might as well have been a million. So I went to him and asked what I could do short of sexual favors to cancel the debt. He laughed like one thousand was nothing to him, which it wasn't. There was the principle of the debt. To amuse himself, he gave me a list of sixteen names and locations of people who owed him money. I was to embarrass each by yelling at them, publicly humiliating them about their cocaine debt."

"Did it work?" asked Bello.

"I don't know. The dealer never told me. The last person was in here, sat by that pillar over there. My voice was hoarse by this time, but I still gave it a go. Never seen the woman since, but the barista threatened to call the police on me."

"And the next time you came in, they called you Shouting Girl."

"The cheeky sods wrote it on my cup in magic marker, but, yes."

"It's amazing what sticks to you."

"What about you?"

"Me? I'm boring. I work in an office. I get paid. That's it."

"And you like *Macbeth*."

"And I like *Macbeth*."

Run leaned forward so that their heads were inches apart. Bello could smell the coffee on her breath and count the fine hairs on her upper lip.

"I don't believe you," said Run.

"I swear to you, I like *Macbeth*."

"Not about that. I don't believe you are boring."

"Maybe you should get close to me, examine my life, prove me wrong . . . or right."

After coffee, they took a walk, talking about this and that. They passed telephone posts, many of which had missing cat posters.

They soon ran out of words and parted, Bello buzzing with inner warmth. Underneath that, as he caught the night bus, something cold and inevitable settled in the pit of his stomach.

The next time he saw Run was the fourth day after they met. On his way to the café he saw a girl who had been badly beaten. One eye was swollen shut and blood trickled down her left nostril, spotting on her white top. She walked past Bello and he heard her breathing whistling through what must be a broken nose. He slowed his gait to ask if she was all right, but she was too fast. And if he were honest with himself, Bello didn't want to be late for his date.

The girl stopped suddenly, leaned against the lamppost for support, then started moving again, leaving a bloody handprint on a missing cat poster.

"Hey!" said Bello.

The girl paused, looked over her left shoulder.

"Can I call you an ambulance?" His phone was already out.

She squinted, an odd expression given only one set of eyelids could move. She smiled, even more disconcerting in that battered face. "No need," she said. "But that's good. That's good."

She nodded and staggered along. Soon, she was gone.

Bello thought the colors of London seemed brighter, something he had noticed the last time he was with Run. The smells were more pungent, and even the discarded garbage stood out more vividly.

Run looked glad to see him and waved him over with enthusiasm. Her hands dropped back under the table, out of sight.

"You're on time. I like it when people are on time. Usually, people play these subtle power games when it comes to dates."

"I don't play power games," said Bello. "And I try to act and speak the way I think and feel."

"Nobody can do that all the time," said Run.

"I said, I try," said Bello. "Can I get you more caffeinated milk?"

"Maybe later." She dropped a package on the table, rectangular, wrapped in brown paper. "I brought you a gift."

"Thank you." He was surprised, pleasantly. "I didn't get you anything. I didn't know we were doing gifts."

"We're not. I am. Open it." She seemed excited.

A book, a small notebook, unlined, black cover, the kind you can buy at any stationery store. Bello opened it, flipped the pages. New book smell.

"It's not really a gift," said Run. "It's an obligation. I'd like you to write down your thoughts between now and our next date."

51

"So we're having a next date?"

"Let's see how tonight goes," said Run. But she smiled in a way that told him this, whatever this was, could go as far as they both wanted. She pulled him to her and kissed him on the lips. They lingered to the hiss of steam cleaners and the conversation of other customers. It felt warm and right. They crushed noses.

"We could go somewhere else," said Bello. "Somewhere fancy."

She shook her head. "I don't want to go anywhere else. This is my haunt."

"Are you like a ghost, tied to one place by bloodshed?"

"I'm not a ghost," said Run. "I'm a witch, remember?"

Later, standing naked at Run's window, looking out at the street, Bello felt content. Mostly, he felt quiet, at peace. Behind him, she breathed. At times, she turned over and he heard the rustle of her bedclothes. That feeling of unreality washed over him again, through the looking glass with Run Tinworth. It was not unpleasant.

A manhole cover moved, drawing Bello's attention. At first, he wasn't sure his eyes weren't fatigued and playing tricks on him. The streetlight was strong and clear, however. Curious. If the heavy cover moved, it was from within. It was past midnight, and Bello knew that those holes were locked. You needed a special device to pry them open from the outside.

The cover moved again. No doubt now that it was being worked open. It shifted, eclipsing a circle of shadow. Bello expected a hand to appear any minute, but instead an amorphous bulge pushed out of the blackness. It shunted the cover all the way to the side with a scraping, metal-on-asphalt noise.

Bello's mouth dried up and he stole a glance at Run, who was still sound asleep.

Whatever it was seemed to be covered with a membrane and it reminded Bello of a butterfly emerging from a chrysalis. It leaned this way and that as more and more of its mass made it out of London's drains. Bello thought he heard the sound of rushing air, a whistling forced out between the margins of the hole and whatever the thing coming out was.

The membrane wasn't smooth. It was a lot of small patches bound together, although Bello saw no stitches. The size of a person now, it finally plopped onto the road. A split appeared and a hand slipped out, the skin, a dull yellowish-gray color, same as the membrane.

"This is a dream," said Bello, rooted to the spot.

What squeezed out was a woman, but she was covered in latex from hundreds of condoms. Where her legs met each other a profusion of discarded charger cables grew. On her head, a forest of cut plastic straws. She had dark pits for eyes and an irregular line for a mouth. Behind her head, a black circle unfurled, the inner tubing of a tire. It rose up a foot above her crown and rotated clockwise, a petrochemical halo.

Shreds of paper blew toward her from all directions, joined together and formed up on her back. In seconds, she had wings made from glossy magazine covers, massage parlor flyers, food wrappers, and other city detritus.

She beat the wings in a single elegant gesture and flew off into the night, disappearing from sight over the rooftops.

"Run, wake up."

But she did not. She mumbled, wiped drool from her mouth without opening her eyes and turned over. Bello thought she looked adorable and didn't have the heart to wake her. The light from the streetlamp washed into the room, and he noticed for the first time the tattoo of three small five-pointed stars on her upper forearm. He had three dots in the same position on his arm. He stood up.

When Run woke up in the morning, she found the blinds of her bedroom window open and Bello gone.

DI Reith spilled some of the tea into the saucer. He put the cup down on the side table without a coaster and slurped from the saucer. I stifled a yawn. All I could think of was sleep and the fact that I'd have to clean that surface.

"Inspector Reith, it seems to me you're telling me a love story," I said. "A fantastical, trippy love story. I hate to be rude, but I have work in the morning."

"It's all relevant, I promise," said Reith. "All you need to know at this point is that Orin and Run were attracted to each other. There's a straight line from that fact to his stalking of the . . . what's your boy's name again?"

"Ted Parker," I said.

"Ted Parker, yes. This story is pertinent."

Yes, pertinent, but why was it pertinent now? Wouldn't it still be pertinent in the morning? Between sleep and pertinence, I'd choose sleep anytime. Shouldn't Reith be out there looking for Bello?

He took a bite of biscuit and continued . . .

Run didn't hear from Bello for three days.

It put her in that weird state of mind where you like someone, but realize you haven't known them that long, and you fear they don't have the intensity of feeling you have. You can still recall the feeling of their skin on yours, their smell, their eye color, but you can't lay claim to their time, and you want to protect your own heart, so you wait for them to call.

On day four her phone rang.

"Hi, Run," said Bello. He tried to hit that high casual note, but his voice sounded hoarse.

"You sound terrible," said Run. "Like you swallowed a whole pond of frogs."

"Sorry. I thought I'd be back to normal by now," said Bello. "I didn't want you to hear me like this."

"There's this thing called text . . ."

"I hate it. And I wasn't in the right state of mind. Or body. But I thought about you all the time. Snatches of *Macbeth* kept coming to me."

54

"You mean with everything we did, all you fantasized about was Shakespeare? I should be insulted."

"I . . ."

"I'm kidding. I know what you meant. When can I see you?"

As they rose above London in the pod, Run realized Bello had good skin, clear, like a baby's almost.

"I can't believe you've never been up this thing," said Bello. "People from around the world come here for the Eye."

"It's just a slow Ferris Wheel," said Run. "And I've seen London already."

She slipped her hand through his and watched the rooftops and the tiny people and the boats on the Thames and Big Ben and Tower Bridge. The skin of his hand felt soft and pliant in hers. Not someone who did manual work, then. It felt like he'd soaked it in cocoa butter.

"You seem brand-new," she said.

"What?"

"Fresh. Like you were grown in a vat yesterday."

"I wasn't."

They kissed up there, above London, tourists behind them.

*On the way to the coffee shop, Bello saw the same girl, beaten up and limp-*ing toward him, missing a clump of hair from her scalp, crusted blood in its place. She had a black eye, but at least it wasn't swollen shut. Bruises on her arms, bruises on her legs.

"Hi," said Bello. "I saw you before . . . let me help you. Who is attacking you? There are shelters that—"

"No, thank you." She spoke like she had stones in her mouth. "I'm fine."

"Really? Because you don't look fine."

She limped away without slowing down.

In the coffee shop, he told Run.

"Oh, her? That's Makeup Girl. Don't worry about it. She's my friend. I told you about her when we first came here."

"Makeup Girl?"

"A while back Makeup Girl's lover was murdered by an ex. According to the report, she, the lover, walked through the streets injured and confused for hours and nobody helped or called an ambulance. Makeup Girl's a makeup artist and she walks about with fake injuries every day as a kind of protest. She's also logging people's responses to her, offers for help and the like."

"Why?"

"I don't know, grief reaction? She's going to write a book or do a podcast or something. You'll meet her, I'm sure. She comes in here. Enough about her. When are you taking me to your place? You're not married, are you?"

"I'm not. Why would you say that?"

"You get cagey when the matter of going home with you comes up. You're evasive."

"Let's go right now."

"So you have money," said Run.

"I've been lucky," said Bello.

Run admired the use of space in the house. The walls seemed an eternity away from each other; likewise the ceiling from the floor. Not what she was used to. His furnishings weren't ornate and bordered on minimalist.

"What do you do?" she asked.

"Securities. That kind of thing."

"You move money around?"

"I move value and deficit and obligations around for a fee."

"A large fee."

"A fair one."

She moved through the rooms and he did not impede her, probably keen to prove that he didn't have a hidden family. But, then, he could afford to have multiple properties, couldn't he?

Rather than find her way back to him, she phoned him while waiting in the bedroom. After they made love and he floated off into sleep, she remained awake, listening to his breathing, watching the ceiling.

Everything was good and something was off.

She felt close to him, but within that closeness was the awareness of an empty place, a cold spot, like a haunted house that hadn't revealed its ghost yet.

Cat Girl, Run's second friend, was a graphic artist, although she did some stage design, which is where they met. Cat Girl, Makeup Girl, she wouldn't tell Bello either of their real names.

"Cat Girl draws posters of missing cats," said Run.

They were feeling their way through the secondhand books in crates on the South Bank of the Thames.

"For the owners?" asked Bello. "They pay her?"

"Oh, no. No, these are all imaginary cats. Or maybe they are real cats, the ghosts of real cats that have taken up residence in her head and she draws them to . . . draw them out. I seem to remember her saying that once."

Bello said nothing and she wondered if he thought theater types kept kooky friends.

Then an Albert Camus book distracted her.

Run hadn't seen him for two days and decided to surprise him. She did some light shopping with the idea in mind that she would cook for him, something she had never done for anyone. She only had the confidence to cook a jacket potato with tuna, but it was the gesture, right? She elevated the meal with white wine, which she hoped would provide misdirection.

Light step, almost skipping on the way to Bello's.

A few yards away from his doorstep, she saw a deliveryman with a parcel. She slowed because she wanted to do her own knocking and be unexpected for Bello.

She could not hear what the delivery man said, but the door swung open. The delivery man smiled as he handed over the parcel.

To a woman barely covered in Bello's bathrobe.

"You know she didn't even have the sash done up?" said Run.

Cat Girl sat opposite her, fussing over drawings. Her current poster featured the Cheshire Cat from Lewis Carroll. Large, garish numbers made up the owner's contact details, identified as Alice Liddell.

Makeup Girl silently dripped E120 red dye mixed with corn syrup from both ears. Run wasn't sure the girl could hear anything. Good look, though. Skull-fracture chic. The bruised neck suggested strangulation, which is why Makeup Girl wasn't talking. No faking the funk; method all the way.

Run said, "She clutched it together with one hand, but you could see everything."

The Barista called their names and Cat Girl hopped up and returned with their drinks. Makeup Girl just looked grim and commiserated. Corn syrup stains on the chair beside her.

"So what did you do?"

"Do? I dropped the shopping and ran. I—"

"Have you called him?" asked Cat Girl.

"Fuck, no. Why would I?" asked Run.

"I don't know. I think if it were me, I'd like to make sure it wasn't his sister or his cousin or his mother."

"She's too young to be his mother."

Makeup Girl rolled her eyes. She looked like she was bursting to be a part of the conversation but wouldn't break character.

Cat Girl shrugged. "Whatever. You should ask. Has he called?"

"No, but he always waits three days."

"Not four or two. Three?"

"That's right. Exactly three days, then calls on fourth. Ever since I've known him."

"Weird. You should definitely ask about that," said Cat Girl, as she applied adhesive to the reverse side of her poster. "Hang on a mo' while I post this."

Run didn't ask Bello about the woman. The next time she and he met, Run pretended everything was fine, then she called in sick and watched him like they do on the cop shows. Not him. She watched his front door for two days on and off.

"I must be completely insane," she muttered to herself more than once, but she didn't stop.

She was on the verge of quitting when her labor bore fruit: A woman, swaddled in baggy jeans and a hood, slipped out of Bello's front door and walked down the street. The gait wasn't Bello's, although Run recognized that the clothes were.

The woman filtered through other pedestrians and made her way to an arcade of shops, turning into one. Run waited.

When the woman emerged, Run gasped, her heart in her throat.

The face of the woman, her hair, eyes, nose, mouth, was the same as the one Run saw in the mirror every day.

The woman was Run.

I was tired and Reith droned on, while at the same time finishing the tea and biscuits with the efficiency of a vacuum cleaner. No crumbs survived.

"Any more biscuits?" asked Reith, eyebrows raised, hopeful.

"Fresh out," I said. "And maybe I'm too tired to understand, but this story seems symbolic or allegorical. I don't see what—"

"It's not metaphor, Miss Khan. I'm sorry if I gave you that impression. Gudrun did see herself in Orin Bello's clothes. I'm telling you the story as I know it."

"Can we move along? I don't want to be rude, but tempus fugit."

"Sure. Bello invited Run 'round for a . . . clarification session. He knew something was wrong with the relationship, and he was fond of Run and wanted the relationship to work . . ."

Bello sensed the wall between them. Mistrust tinged with fear. She sat on the sofa making herself small, confused more than enraged. He sat a foot away, directly in front of her on a bar stool, like a jazz singer. He didn't have much furniture, and she looked like she might bolt if he suggested moving the conversation anywhere else.

"I'd like to say I'm sorry, Run. This is all my fault for not telling you everything, but at the same time, if I had, you wouldn't have believed me. Or worse, you would have believed me and run a mile."

"What does that even mean?" asked Run.

Bello exhaled, trying to compose himself, or his confession. "The woman you saw coming out of here, and the woman you followed . . . this woman was me."

"Are you trying to sell me some bollocks? This wasn't you being gender-fluid, Bello. She was smaller . . . she was *me*. It wasn't makeup. Makeup Girl couldn't do that, and she's superb at her job."

"I said, the woman was me. I changed into you. I transformed into an exact version of you for three days, then I reverted."

She sat openmouthed. "You're serious."

"I'm cursed. It's a curse."

"A curse?"

"I know how it sounds. Anytime I get strong emotions about anyone, I change into them for three days. The emotion doesn't matter, as long as it's strong. Anger, disgust . . . love. Anything."

"Are you insane?"

"You tell me. You saw yourself in my clothes, didn't you? And I know you believe me, otherwise you'd be out the door by now. You're the first person I've ever told."

"You're going to have to do better than that. Cursed isn't going to cut it."

"All right. I'll tell you everything. Do you want tea? Biscuits?"

"Bello . . ."

"Fine. I used to be homeless."

Bello shambled along Charing Cross Road, walking in a miasma of cheap booze and uncertain of the time, knowing only that it was dark. He'd just lost his regular spot in Soho to a younger, ferocious, sober bloke, and it was cold out. He knew there was a shelter close by, but his reason struggled, mired in alcohol as it was. He'd been on the street for three years and didn't bother anybody while he slowly drank himself to death. He was stoic about his life, knowing he'd been dealt blows, but certain that other people had been dealt their own blows and reacted differently. He wasn't bitter; he just wanted to get life over with. If there was reincarnation, good, because he needed a do-over. If there wasn't, good. Oblivion didn't sound bad.

For now, though, he was in his cups without a place to sleep, and in the last rational parts of his brain, he knew he did not wish to freeze to death.

All the shop fronts he passed were closed. One woman leaned against a streetlight, talking to herself. Sporadic traffic. A tricked-out Jeep swerved in his direction then zoomed off, profanity-laced laughter fading into the night.

He came to a crossroads, a literal one, where Shaftesbury Avenue crosses Charing Cross. Cambridge Circus. Shitload of traffic lights. Roofless people like him sleeping along the walls of the Palace Theatre. Daft of them. Must be new to London.

"Shut up!" said one of them. Bello had been singing without even knowing it.

He wanted to apologize, but his brain couldn't form the required words. He turned around, taking in the Victorian and Georgian fronts, and he saw it.

A bowl or basin, on a traffic island. There looked to be steam coming from the container, so someone must have just left it.

Bello wasn't hungry, but that didn't matter. Hunger was a luxury of people with regular income. On the street you ate when you found food. That was the deal when you depended on altruism. And you ate before someone else did. Humans didn't have humps like camels.

He crossed to the island. Food with an aroma so good, it almost drove him sober. Spiced tomato stew and beef and some cornmeal that he couldn't identify. He gorged on it, fast enough to finish before someone snatched it from him; slow enough that his belly wouldn't reject the food because of the cheap gin from earlier.

He burped. Bello was cold, but content, a feeling that lasted for a moment. When he stepped off the island, he misjudged the distance and fell. The sharp pain, the crack, the unnatural shape of his leg . . . fractured for sure. Coldness seeped into him from the asphalt. He may have screamed. His breathing became ragged and a lance of fear pierced the fog of drunkenness that had followed him all night. He could die here. People like him were invisible.

A car screeched to a halt near him. A driver bounded out and Bello lost consciousness. He came to on a stretcher, levitating away from the traffic island, lights flashing everywhere. For a moment, he saw himself lying down on the road with a broken right leg, but it must have been a trick of the light, or the painkillers mixing with the alcohol in his blood.

In the hospital, the usual happened. They patched him up, set his leg, cleaned him up, gave him a chemical detox by way of chlordiazepoxide and assaulted him with a social worker who buzzed him with terms like Safeguarding Adults and Harm Minimization, words Bello had heard before. Soon, he knew, they would talk about rehousing him, and he started to think of escape. Besides, he needed a drink.

A day before Bello planned to run away, a man visited him, a solicitor. The firm had been looking for Bello because an aunt had died and left him a house and a modest sum of money.

The paperwork took a few weeks because Bello had no ID and the firm had to establish that he was of sound mind. He was.

Orin Bello forswore alcohol and became one of society's visible.

He took a few courses and applied for work. He got every job he wanted, a success rate that confused him seeing as he had failed at everything before his homeless days. He rose in the ranks, ended up with his dream job, and, after the global plague, worked from home in front of a computer screen earning amounts that should be illegal.

Six months later, at exactly midnight, his doorbell rang. The security system showed a woman at his door, face obscured in a voluminous scarf. She reminded him of a babushka, except she was black.

"Yes? Who are you looking for?" asked Bello.

"The one who ate a meal at a crossroads," said the woman. "I know it was you. I followed the trail of stolen fortune, and it ends here."

Bello felt compelled by curiosity to open the door.

"Who are you?" he asked.

"I am the one who cooked the meal." She looked like an older woman, but her eyes were large, clear and intense. Her voice sounded younger, vital. She had no accent, which bothered him. The absence of London or Africa or the Caribbean in her speech made her seem like a cypher. "Did your mother not tell you to beware of meals at crossroads?"

"I don't understand," said Bello.

She pursed her lips briefly. "Child, you ate food that was meant for The Birds, the World, the Wise Women who Cook at the Marketplace. Do you know what that means?"

Bello shrugged, but started to feel disquiet.

"Someone down on their luck made a gift of that meal to powerful forces. You ate the meal and attracted good fortune that wasn't meant for you. You're a luck thief."

"Okay, I have only a vague sense of what you're saying, but I was homeless and hungry."

"You have to give it back."

"What? The meal? It's gone."

"No, you idiot. The luck. You have to return the luck that you stole."

Bello thought. "I don't think so. My life has turned around. I'm not going back to what I was. Even if I symbolically did that to get you off my doorstep, it might affect me psychologically, put me on a downward spiral. And, like I said, I'm not going back. This conversation is insane. Luck isn't transmissible!"

The woman nodded, and her eyes seemed to blaze. "All right. So be it. Since you will not give back the luck that you have stolen, I curse you with transforming empathy."

With that, she turned and scuttled away. Her feet made no sound on the concrete. It was somewhat anticlimactic for Bello. He had expected more melodrama. Transforming empathy. Huh. Whatever the fuck the whole thing was about, it was over. He closed his door.

The first person Bello turned into was Paul Newman.

Bello watched *Cool Hand Luke* one night, his first time. He related to Luke's stoicism and self-reliance. A few days later, he woke up looking like Paul Newman circa 1967. He screamed at the mirror, slapped himself, and thought it was some kind of fever dream. In three days, he reverted to his normal appearance.

It kept happening.

It took three transformations, Farah Fawcett, Don King, and a guy whose name he could never remember from the film *Magnolia*, for Bello to realize this was the curse. Transforming empathy.

He changed into people from work, people he had a crush on, people he disliked, any person, real or fictional, who aroused an emotional response in him. He'd go into seclusion for three days to regain his appearance.

His personality changed as he adapted to a world where any emotional connection affected his appearance. He worked from home and rarely went out.

The isolation became too much for him, and once a month he

would see a show. Theater was affecting and he would take the standard three days to recover.

And then he saw *Macbeth* . . .

"Which is how I met you," said Bello to Run. "I knew the cost would be to see you infrequently and to keep you from discovering my curse."

Run was at first silent, churning behind an unreadable expression. "I want to see."

"What do you mean?"

"I mean, even if I take what you've said at face value, it means you've lied to me, so I can't trust you."

"I never lied."

"You deceived by omission. I want to see this empathetic transformation. I'm staying here until it happens."

"You never told me you were a twin," said the barista as they passed her.

Makeup Girl and Cat Girl were already waiting. Bello and Run sat opposite in the cubicle, both noticing sheets of Cat Girl's conceptual art neglected on the table and a solitary black eye decorating Makeup Girl's face.

"I'm sure your mothers can tell you apart," said Cat Girl. "I've met both of you before, I just don't know which is my friend and which is her boyfriend."

"I do," said Makeup Girl. "They walk different."

"We have a problem," said Run.

"No shit. Your boyfriend's a changeling," said Makeup Girl.

"I'm cursed," said Bello.

"We need Hecate," said Cat Girl.

Bello looked puzzled.

"*'And I, the mistress of your charms,*
The close contriver of all harms,
Was never call'd to bear my part,
Or show the glory of our art?'" said Run.

"Hecate is real?" asked Bello. "I thought that was just a play."

"It's not really Hecate," said Makeup Girl. "She means we need someone to guide us. Someone with actual power. A Hecate, not the Hecate."

"Are you witches?" asked Bello.

"What is a witch?" asked Cat Girl.

"What is a coven?" asked Makeup Girl.

"What are the Weird Sisters?" asked Run.

After midnight, in the empty parking lot behind Burnt Oak underground station, surrounded by shadowed trees and the smell of urine, they waited under a dead streetlight, all the electrical connections ripped out. Bello remembered these kinds of places from when he was homeless.

The light snapped on, and she floated there.

"I've seen her before," said Bello.

"Shh," said Run.

She looked different, but Bello was sure he was looking at the same entity he saw outside Run's window. This time she was an angel of mud and spark plugs, with potted plants for hair and wings made of stained bedsheets and photocopied losing lottery tickets, and pens poking out of both shoulders like spikes, kebab takeaway containers covering her breasts. A halo of razor wire turned behind her head and fake Jimmy Choo shoes stabbed down the other extremity.

When she opened her mouth, scratch cards slipped out, collecting in piles underneath her floating form.

Moths and other insects gathered around the light beams.

Her mouth closed abruptly and the light winked out.

I stood up. I could barely keep my eyes open. "I must insist that you leave, Detective. I'm sorry to be rude, but you can't take a hint."

"Cat Girl divined from the scratch cards that I had to give the luck back," said Reith.

"I don't care. Get out," I said. "Wait. *You* had to give the luck back? You? Not Bello?"

"That's what I've been trying to tell you all night," he said. "I am Orin Bello."

After his arrest for creeping on my children, one DSI Alfonse Reith had interrogated Bello. Reith was apparently a shit and the intensity of his questions had made an impression on the cursed man. This transformation was not unuseful. Soon the duty sergeant unlocked the cell and wondered how Bello had overpowered Reith and changed places with him.

The transformed Bello walked right out of the station with the authority of a detective. The real Reith had already left the station hours earlier. There was some confusion about signing out, but all in all, it was easy.

"What do you want from me?" I asked. I still didn't know if I believed his fantastical story.

"I need the kid, the Ted Parker kid."

"Why?"

"Because his father's the one I stole luck from. And his father is dead. I have to give the luck back and I need your help to do it."

I kept Bello in my house for a few days. On the second day he reverted back to his own appearance. It was a painful, tortuous affair that took about an hour. I gave him some of the naproxen I use for my tennis elbow. I fed his bottomless pit of a stomach and marveled at how endlessly he could put food away. No wonder he got cursed for eating.

He gave me the address for Shouting Girl, Run Tinworth. Pretty girl and completely devoted to Bello. I would go as far as to say they were in love, but I didn't know if they knew that yet.

I met Cat Girl and Makeup Girl, too.

Between all of us we came up with a plan. I couldn't invite Ted here, but I could have some kind of event at school that would involve eating.

Why did I help him? Maybe I did it for love. For the loves that I had lost and wanted back. For the possibilities of love in the future or for something to think on when I was old and beyond companionship. I could look back on them and tell myself I brought a little joy into the world.

"We'll cook a meal," said Run.

"I'll cook a meal. I think it has to be me," said Bello.

The air between them was thick with electricity and hormones and longing. I was sure Bello would transform again. He did.

While the police looked for Bello, he, looking like Gudrun and posing as a casual worker for the day, helped me feed twenty children, although he was really only feeding one. He cooked and dished out the food to Ted Parker.

"I didn't mean to take your food," Bello said. Ted looked puzzled, but ate heartily.

"It doesn't feel any different," said Bello. Ten minutes later he was puking in the restroom and his body twisted back into a male configuration. It hadn't been three days.

Orin Bello was back.

Riders of the number 344 night bus from Clapham Junction to Liverpool Street reported a disturbance between Macduff Road and Tinworth Street stops. A veiled old woman had an altercation with what everybody agreed must have been some kind of performance artist dressed like an angel. The lights of the bus flashed on and off, so nobody could be sure exactly what happened.

The wings of the angel were made of junk-mail flyers and abandoned letters with the addresses and stamps still in place. Her hands were broken beer bottles that some witnesses said she used to jab at and stab the older woman.

The lights went out for a long time, and the older woman said, "Next time, keep out of affairs that don't concern you."

Neither the woman nor the performance artist were seen when the lights came back on.

Luck, then.

Ted Parker's life didn't change, although who knows? Maybe I'll be dead and gone by the time the difference becomes apparent.

You're probably wondering if, after the curse was lifted, Orin Bello reverted to homelessness and alcoholism and broken tibias. That would imply that luck is this thing that can be passed around, affecting the ability to win the lottery or miss the flight on aircraft that crash.

That's not what happened. Orin and Gudrun lived together for many years after in the inherited house. It didn't collapse; it didn't burn. Bello continued in his job because he worked hard and was good at it. He kept going to meetings and he worked things out one day at a time, as they say. Run had a regular slot in the Royal Shakespeare Company. She didn't play witches anymore.

Makeup Girl wrote a book called *Trauma Neglect: A Year of Being Ignored in the Big Smoke.* She's taking meetings about movie options.

Cat Girl got a cat and stopped making posters. She had an exhibition in some out-of-the-way hip gallery, which went well until she got a cease-and-desist from the copyright holder of one of the cats she drew.

Even in a world of witches and angels, good fortune is from what you do, not what you have. Which is why I am now living a life of love and laughter, but this is not my story.

Maybe next time.

GOOD SPELLS

—

Ken Liu

Succeeding the Author, the scriptor no longer bears within him passions, humours, feelings, impressions, but rather this immense dictionary from which he draws a writing that can know no halt: life never does more than imitate the book, and the book itself is only a tissue of signs, an imitation that is lost, infinitely deferred.

—Roland Barthes, *The Death of the Author*
(translated by Richard Howard)

[magpoi@localhost ~]$ cat /var/log/grimoire/today.log

Client: T.N.
Request: Make ☁ 🧠 not a pile of 💩
Dispensed: 0xDEADFEED
Quote: "Because if you did not wear spectacles the brightness and glory of the Emerald City would blind you."

Tommy shows up at my door. Eyes bloodshot, stubbly chin the blue of a crab's paddle fin.

"You want another hex?" I ask.

He nods, only once, as if that is all he can muster.

I invite him inside. "You still at the same restaurant? Boss getting better?"

A shake of the head. He holds up a hand to show me the sprayed-on ID patch on his wrist: the metropolitan airport.

I'm about to congratulate him on his new job—the airport is supposed to have excellent benefits—when something about the familiar aviation logo strikes me as out of place. I lean in closer. In the bottom right corner of the patch, behind and to the side of the stylized airplane, is a much smaller logo, like an inescutcheon in a coat of arms or a graphic footnote: a five-lobed design that resembles a cloud as well as a brain. NephoSopho's logo.

"Ah," I say. "You work at the airport, not for the airport." A nod of confirmation. "Tell me what you're looking for."

Just as most companies that fiddle with bits no longer run their own servers, most companies that still deal with atoms no longer run their own logistics. Warehousing, transport, delivery, fulfillment . . . the overwhelming majority of consumer-facing businesses outsource these operations to turnkey platforms. NephoSopho is a relative upstart in this space, having emerged from a bunch of divested warehouses when the DOJ broke up the stalwart Constantfair. They run hub warehouses inside airports to take advantage of micro launch windows for their delivery drones and blimps, which allow them to offer faster shipping at cheaper prices for their customers. Machine learning is supposed to be their secret sauce, making everything in their warehouses more efficient than their competitors.

"I just want some breaks, Mag," he says, his voice a dry and brittle whisper, as though he's terrified of waking a sleeping monster.

"Here, have a drink." I pour him a shot. I lower my voice to make him feel more at ease. I've heard that some of the newer NephoSopho distribution centers have a machine-enforced no-speaking policy to discourage employees from organizing or "wasting" time. Something as innocuous as coughing too loud can get your pay docked.

He swallows, and even the way his Adam's apple bobs up and down seems exhausted.

"They make the pickers race each other," he says, his voice now smoother from the lubrication. "You have to wear these augmented reality glasses that show the ghosts of everyone else on the same shift. The ghosts are either ahead of you or behind you, based on where the other pickers are on their own routes. The winner gets a bonus." A pause. He lowers his eyes, unable to look at me. "The bonus is taken from the pay of all the other pickers."

I imagine workers racing their carts around the warehouse floor, picking out junk on the dense shelves highlighted by their AR glasses like participants in some dystopian cyberpunk Christmas spree. Literally rats in a maze. The glasses tell them the exact route to take to minimize wasted steps, dictate how many seconds may lapse between stations along the route, and prescribe how to pack the items for each order into a box so as to take up the least space. Deviations from the optimal solution leave the picker open to potential fines. As much as possible, NephoSopho workers are expected to behave like machines— their only advantage is their soft, dexterous fingers, appendages more versatile than robotic pincers (at least for the moment). They are also cheaper—robots require quarterly software upgrades and daily licensing fees, which are more expensive than wages for humans.

"I hate that I actually wanted to win," he says. His face sags from weariness, a deflated balloon. Only the young are shocked by how easily they can be manipulated, Dr. G, my mentor, used to say. "I hate that I actually celebrated when I beat this old lady who tripped and fell on the last run of the shift. I hate that I was so tired and ashamed that I didn't even want to talk to anyone at lunch. I hate that I was making plans for the extra money—I want to get premium Dixit Story Time for my daughter."

And humans can also be enticed to participate in their own subjugation. Tay often jokes that it's easier for the managers at work to manipulate code monkeys like her than for her to debug the spaghetti firmware she's supposed to maintain. Young coders would work crazy hours if you offered them free soda and takeout and matching donations to trendy causes and told them they were special, wizards of the modern age; warehouse workers, apparently, are also willing to make life harder for their fellow employees if you offer them a few extra dollars an hour.

"I just want some breaks. I'm so tired."

"I get it," I told him. "I do. But I don't have anything for you."

"Can't you give me a glamour or a living shadow? Make it look like I'm working when I'm not? Get in their servers and change the algorithm?"

"I'm a witch," I say, "not a goddess."

There was a time, when I was still young and idealistic, when I thought I'd become a goddess of the digital age, a hacker who birthed and annihilated worlds with a keyboard.

"The algorithm" was in the zeitgeist, and people fretted about what it meant for future generations to grow up surrounded by photographs and Portragrams that had been enhanced and beautified by machine learning, that had been filtered by server-curated feeds, that had been resurfaced by neural networks trained to prey on nostalgia; for all who wish to be seen or heard to learn to write in the language of hashtags and meta keys and semantic vectors, codes optimized for parsing by computers so that users could rise in the estimate of silicon gatekeepers; for readers and writers and speakers and listeners to grow used to machine-translated speech and text, to accept the machine translations as more authoritative than human interpreters, better even than learning the language themselves; for everyone to train themselves to converse with chatbots, to rephrase desires and wants to be algorithmically interpretable, to adapt to the computed responses, to treat the hyperparametrized responses as natural, even stylistically preferable . . .

I thought I would stand up for the human. I'd be a hacker, a builder, a maker who would disrupt the relentless march toward machinehood, who would put the genie back in the bottle, who would once again place humanity at the center of the universe, back in control. I wanted to champion the analog, the random, the unexpected, the ethical and humane.

"I write very little code," I tell Tommy. "I can't hack into Nepho-Sopho's servers and change the scheduling algorithm. That's a fantasy they spin for you on the soap streams—probably a plot suggested by the brainstorming R3NNs they use in the writers' rooms."

I gave up my dream when I realized that even programming had become permeated with architecting wizards, codewalking familiars, refactoring pixies, concurrency djinn, multicall completion daemons, distributed intelli-swarms, hidden-layer scrying consoles, attention-visualization crystals. Just as it was no longer possible for most humans to truly understand computer-assisted mathematical proofs, the implementation of modern AI systems had become so complicated that it was literally impossible for any individual human to grasp them, to add to them, to reconstruct them, or even to hack them effectively without the aid of machine-learning, of assisting automata that made sense of the layers upon layers of abstractions, extended metaphors, symbolic notations, self-referential ontologies, feedback and feedforward loops.

To program the machine, one needed to place trust in more machines. I couldn't live like that.

"As a witch, the magic I can command isn't all-powerful," I tell Tommy. "I can give you an ultrasonic screamer to shout random commands at Dixit and give you a little privacy; I can give you a Bluetooth amulet so you can figure out if a jealous ex is tracking you with a GPS charm. But I can't just wave a wand and turn a NephoSopho warehouse into a humane workplace."

I play at the margins of the technology web, throwing little charms and enchantments and hexes at the overweening Machine that we had constructed and then promptly fell to worshipping. "You'll feel powerless a lot of the time," Dr. G., who taught me how to be a witch, said to me when I was ready to go out on my own. "But that has always been true of witches. We carve out our space at the margins, in shadows, beyond the ken of those in power. We do what we can to help those who come to us."

"Please, Mag. You gotta give me something," Tommy says.

I poke around my shelves, physical and virtual, and eventually find something that I can tweak and modify to do what I want.

When I'm done, I hand him the hex, a small box labeled OXDEADFEED.

"It's a film," I explain. "You apply it on the inside of your AR lenses. It's just like applying a screen protector; so, be careful about air bubbles."

"What does it do?"

"It's an AR filter. Once the film is on, you won't see any of the augmented visuals they project onto your glasses. No more ghosts to race against. No more flashing countdowns to your next station. It won't give you a real break, but at least you'll get some respite. You won't be completely immersed in their gamification nudges. It's . . . an air hose."

He hesitates, imagining life with the filter hex. "But then I won't see the highlight on the product I'm supposed to pick, or the optimal route."

"You'll still hear the verbal directions through the speakers in the legs of the glasses," I say. "But yeah, you won't be as efficient because you'll have to figure out some stuff on your own. You'll never win a bonus again, I suspect."

He hesitates for a few seconds before accepting the hex and paying me.

```
[magpoi@localhost ~]$ cat /var/log/grimoire/today.log
```

Client: Z.K.I.
Request: ♡ makes the world go around
Dispensed: 0x1111BABE
Quote: "Aphrodite is not to be blamed /
For I burn by myself."

I spend the morning concocting a love charm.

Zelda, a new client, is going through a rough patch with her partner. Since she's all the way out in the suburbs and doesn't want to pay for me to come to her in person, she gives me access to her household maintenance drone.

I securecast into the poppet—a sleek telepresence drone with all the latest bells and whistles that I learned about in a VR ad (which I was forced to endure the last time I went to the theater). It has the size and flexibility of a cat to effortlessly slip into nooks and crannies, a copper-coated antibacterial shell, Van der Waals pads for clinging to walls and ceilings, and eight octopuslike tentacles tipped with swappable tools that can be configured to suit the needs of the remote operator. Per your politics, it's either boosting individual autonomy by freeing skilled tradesmen from the tyranny of geography, or further dehumanizing labor and cementing class divisions ("You need plumbers, electricians, handymen! But you don't need them in the house like cavemen!").

Zelda has taken off all the drone's privacy filters and geofencing so I can roam around freely. I spend an hour crawling around their place, observing, while she tells me about their relationship.

"Joan is incredibly smart," she says. "Youngest partner at the firm. Every time they have a big client, she has to be out there to impress them."

The house is large but sparsely furnished. Everything is modern, glossy, with simple lines and uncluttered surfaces, the kind of design language favored by contemporary feng shui practitioners: a harmonious

Wi-Fi interior and easy to navigate for autonomous and telepresence drones.

I certainly appreciate it. Since I'm no electrician or HVAC technician, I don't have a license for the fancy VR interface for this model of poppet. I have to tap out my commands over the securecast tunnel on a keyboard like some barbarian. God help me if her home had toddlers running around.

"She works long hours," Zelda says. "Sometimes she doesn't come home until after midnight. She has to take clients out: exciting places, beautiful people. Maybe I bore her."

She's turned away from me as she says it, as though she can't bear to let me see her face. But the AI in the poppet interface is still set for emotion-processing-priority mode—probably the last vendor to visit the house in it was her hairdresser—and the camera pans around for a bit before zooming in on the mirror of the vanity across the room to show me her downcast expression, eyes lowered in shame.

I wait until she has recovered, and we go on with the walk-and-talk as though nothing has happened. She shows me Joan's study, the walk-in closet with her work outfits, the diplomas and certificates on the walls. She points to a picture of an herb garden in a hallway corner, telling me how much she adores basil, oregano, rosemary. ("I love to cook, but Joan prefers to order out.") There is no herb garden in the yard. She tells me about trips she and Joan have gone on, and I note that none of the trips were within the last two years. She talks about the words she wants to hear but Joan won't say, about the dates she wants to go on but Joan doesn't, about pauses and silences and thoughts left unspoken until they've curdled and festered and rotted.

These are clichés, but that doesn't mean she isn't unhappy, isn't terrified, isn't stifled like a butterfly under a bell jar.

"Nice collection," I say, pausing in front of the shelves in the living room: feminist classics with contemporary covers; novels by diverse authors who have won awards; big-name nonfiction of the sort that someone with one degree from Princeton and two from Yale is expected to have read.

"These are Joan's," Zelda says.

The books look new, untouched. Joan is too busy to read them, of course; she probably gets a few snippets now and then from her personal summarizing bot—she can afford the premium-level subscription to feed her a few observations that seem strikingly original. It should be more than enough for her to fake her way through conversations at parties.

"Where are your books?" I ask.

She smiles awkwardly. "I keep them out of sight. I think Joan will laugh at them."

She shows me the stash in a box tucked under the bed, where you might expect to find the whips and cuffs and dildos. The books have plain covers and no titles, and the binding is very cheap. But the spines are cracked and the pages dog-eared. They've been read.

Curious, I tap on the keyboard. Four metallic tentacles slowly buzz forward, reaching for the books.

She moves to block me but then stops herself. "They're nonce romances," she says, her voice trembling. "Just for me."

I tap on the keyboard some more. The tentacles stop. I know what nonce romances are—books written by machines to cater to the desires of a single mind, the natural endpoint for ever-ramifying sub-sub-sub-genres of the literature of hunger.

Reading them feels too intimate, wrong.

"If you want, I can show you how I write one," she says, biting her bottom lip, suddenly suspended between apprehension and excitement.

The emotion-processing engine in the poppet informs me that she's not flirting with me, which I already know. I pause to examine my own spike of irritation—maybe it's the irony of being reassured by a machine that I'm not reading another human wrong. Why should I trust it? I'm not used to emotion-reading AI, since I rarely even wear AR glasses. In that I'm an outlier—salespeople, diplomats, lawyers, among others, regularly resort to AR glasses with emotion-parsing engines, and I'm sure most of them aren't using the glasses as accessibility tools for autism. We want the mediation of the machine in even the most human of domains.

She takes me to a spare bedroom and sits down at the desk while I scooch over and climb onto the shelf to the side, extending the goose-neck camera to get a good view.

She presses a button on the auto-pen, a toaster-sized box: round, chromed, the kind of futuristic gadget they imagined back in the middle of the last century. Very retro-chic.

"Write me a story," she says. Her breath catches at the end, a silent gasp of anticipation.

"We'll write the story together," the machine replies according to formula. This is a ritual, an invocation of the Muse, the beginning of a journey. The voice is ungendered and warm. "Tell me about your heroine."

"Let's make her like me, but better," Zelda says. A self-deprecating laugh.

"Sure. What about the woman who comes into her life?"

"Remember Nereida from *Side by Side*? Like that. But give her green eyes. And make her five years younger."

"It was a rainy Friday afternoon when Sally decided to quit her job. She was on the way to her boss's office to hand in her resignation when a voice—"

"No, don't make it an office romance. Make it . . . something fantastic."

"It was a rainy Friday morning when Sally looked into the back of her closet and saw a window. Startled, she—"

"She pushed the clothes aside and stepped inside the closet," Zelda interrupts. "The window was open, she realized, and she could feel the warm breeze on her face. There was a large green meadow beyond, ending at a white beach, and beyond that, the sea. In the far distance, silhouetted against the horizon, she could see a woman in a flowing gown on a black horse. Go on from there."

"Even years later, Sally couldn't fully articulate what made her decide to climb through that window, to go to the lady on the horse . . ."

As she and the machine weave the story together, her face changes. She's no longer nervous, shy, embarrassed, fluttering. She giggles, laughs, argues with the machine. She is alive.

What is the machine doing, really? We've long since discarded the nonsensical interpretation of the Turing test and agreed that the ability to imitate a human conversation partner is not much proof of anything. A one-sided conversation, in particular, in which the machine reflects back the desires of the human participant, isn't "intelligence," regardless of how ill-defined the concept is and no matter how sophisticated the mathematical model behind that mirroring may be.

The auto-pen, like all language models of its kind, is a generative neural network. Such a machine, fed "the internet" and all our databases and libraries and movies and music and games and photographs and memes, awash in our ocean of signifiers and signs and symbols and sigils severed from any root of intention, ready to draw out an endless stream of writing and speaking and telling and showing and deducing and seducing and yearning and yarning, is Barthes's ideal scriptor.

Zelda is conversing with the machine in a language of romance-coded clichés, playing a game of self-enchantment. How appropriate that the Anglo-Saxon word for a story is *spell*. She's Lacan's Narcissus, delighting in the jouissance of a text woven by, of, and just for, her.

Barthes, that old-fashioned semiotician, turned out to be also a pretty good futurist.

Quietly, I leave her to her machine-mediated waking dream and crawl away to weave my spell around her house.

"What did you do?" she asks me much later, after she pays me but before I disconnect.

"The magic won't work if I tell you," I say. Not always true. But definitely the case here.

"So will Joan love me more?"

"We all deserve love," I say.

That seems to satisfy her. I disconnect.

[magpoi@localhost ~]$ cat /var/log/grimoire/today.log

Client: Tay (except she's not a client)

Request: Foster feral 🤖 🤖 🤖

Dispensed: 0xBEE9BEE9

Quote: "V=IR. Eat your heart out, von Neumann!"

For ages, Tay has been asking me to go on a fai-walk with her at Fairwoods Park, apparently a haven for the city's growing population of these creatures.

Late spring is the best season for fai-watching, she insists, and she wore me down until I agreed to let her leave a reminder bug in my Dixit. A client who was supposed to come in for a consultation on her Dixit personal assistant ("I swear the thing misunderstands me on purpose!") canceled at the last minute, and the reminder bug pounced on it. Before I'd even woken up, my own Dixit had put the appointment with Tay on the calendar. And that is why I'm wandering among abandoned machines on a Saturday morning.

Maybe I need to take my Dixit for a consultation. It sure seems to not get what I want, despite what they claim to be the best machine-learning in the world.

("For someone who rails against big tech, you sure rely on a lot of robots," Tay would tease me. She's not wrong—but how do you get around the modern world, a world designed by and for machines, without them? Even witches aren't exempt from reality.)

I'm reluctant to go on this outing with Tay because I'm not keen on the fad of caring for abandoned AI devices (feral AI, or "fai") as though they were stray cats or injured squirrels. I cringe at the thought of bored fruppies with too much free time setting up solar charging stations for obsolete delivery drones, virtue-drunk college kids bringing discarded robot vacuums to "urban sanctuaries," and "hopepunk" technicians volunteering at shelters to give free "humane maintenance" to the failing components and neural networks of outdated and discarded Dixits, weather bugs, robo nannies, pet-enrichment pals, home-security drones . . . all this "fai-animism" seems too precious and silly, too First World, too self-consciously postmodern.

So it's a little hard for me to be excited as Tay interrupts my account of suburban love-conjuring to point to a boxy delivery drone that has seen better days wandering the trails of Fairwoods Park. The little machine, a squat box with rounded corners, is about a foot high, with oversized all-terrain wheels, one of which has been replaced with an aftermarket replica with a big smiley face on it.

Instead of making a beeline to bring some entitled office worker his precious triple venti hemp extra-foam latte, however, the bot wobbles down the side of a grassy knoll like a puppy with a broken leg. A few concerned children trail after it, trying to offer help. But the bot doesn't stop or respond.

"Come," Tay says. "Let's see if we can do something."

She jogs across the park at a good pace, her box braids bouncing happily, the kinetically powered beads woven into the braids glowing as though she were dancing. I shrug and follow. This is certainly more exciting than guessing the manufacturing date for a flock of Constantfair messenger drones with missing propellers flopping on the ground and then picking them up to confirm the date stamped on their bellies—the activity Tay and I were engaged in just before. (Don't worry, a bunch of middle schoolers are walking toward the flock with fresh propellers. Maybe this will earn them some badges.)

"Finish telling me about your love potion," Tay says, as we make our way toward the limping coffee-delivery drone.

"Love charm," I say. "Not much more to say. I put in my standard spells for this sort of thing, adapted to her circumstances."

"What is 'standard'?"

"You want the details?" This is a surprise. Tay doesn't usually approve of my techno-witchcraft. She keeps trying to recruit me back to the industry, to make me "legitimate."

"Indulge me."

"I installed a few secondhand aroma synthesizers in the kitchen and the spare room she uses to write her romances—sage, thyme, marjoram. Not too much, just a subtle hint of her favorite scents to make her feel she has a claim on those spaces."

"A room of her own," Tay says.

"That's right." This is why Tay and I have remained friends. She gets me—most of the time.

We're still a few dozen yards from the wobbling robot, which has become entangled in a bush at the foot of the knoll. The children mill around it. We slow down to a walk.

"What else?" Tay asks.

"I snuck a few of her romances into her partner's bookshelves, at about eye-height."

"I thought her partner doesn't have time to read."

"She doesn't. Let me finish." I pause to catch my breath before continuing. "I hung up some quotes, very sweet and silly, that her partner had said to her from their wedding video. I added a knock-off glamour to her smart mirror to emphasize in her reflection the parts of herself she likes the most based on gaze analysis. I installed a reinforcement learning enchantment—a simple neural network I trained myself—in her Dixit so that whenever she says something positive about herself, Dixit runs a workflow for subtle uplifting mood lighting."

Tay gives me a funny look. "I'm not sure I get it. None of this does anything to her partner. I thought you were supposed to get her to love your client more."

We've reached the limping coffee bot. The group of children part to let us get close.

It's still painted in the color scheme of the international coffee chain that used to own it, though the chassis is now covered in stickers from fai-welfare organizations. Gently, Tay bends down and flips the coffee bot over to examine it. The wheels spin and the motors whine help-lessly, reminding me of a tortoise flipped on its back.

"She has to love herself first," I say. "If she finds herself boring, so will others. If she doesn't make space for herself, no one else will. In that house, all I saw and felt was the shadow of her partner. Fix that, and maybe everything else she wants will follow."

"Does that really work?" Tay asks.

With the concerned children looking on, she flips open the cover to the bot's maintenance port and disconnects the power supply. The whirring and whining fade and then stop abruptly. The wheels cease spinning. The robot is still.

Some of the children, especially the younger ones, look nervous and upset.

"It's all right," Tay says to them. "I'm just putting it to sleep so that I can do surgery. We don't want to hurt the robot, and we don't want to get hurt, either. Never touch a bot's insides unless the battery is discon-nected."

She's got good "bedside manner," if that's what you call it. The children hang on her every word.

"I'm a witch, not a psychologist," I say, continuing our own con-versation. "But I have a pretty good track record in this sort of thing. Besides, it doesn't matter whether someone else loves you until you love yourself."

"I suppose that's true," she says. "Although in my experience . . . sometimes the problem with people like your client is that they're al-ready too in love with themselves." She takes out a set of calipers and measures the coffee bot's wheels. "Anyone know what this instrument I'm using is called?" she says to the children.

Tay doesn't know it, but she's voicing aloud my own fear and doubt. There was something about Zelda's interactions with me that felt too convenient. Was it really a coincidence that the maintenance drone was left on emotion-processing-priority mode? Was it really out of shame and embarrassment that she looked away from me as she said, "Maybe

I bore her?" Or was it a calculated attempt to get me to see her face framed just so, to manipulate my empathy and attention, to lead me to the conclusion she wanted me to reach?

Were the bookshelves devoid of her own stories, the walls empty of her own accompaniments, the rooms bleached of her scent—were they also part of the act, too? Does she crave the feeling of being a martyr, of being pitied and fussed over? I never did see Joan interact with her, after all. When I saw Zelda ecstatically weaving her fantasies with the machine, was I really seeing Narcissus gazing into a pool?

Those are also clichés, clichés spun into a spell to get me to give her what she wanted. It's the sort of story one might say is algorithmic, input formulated to elicit from a trained agent the desired behavior. Give the witch what she wants to see, and the witch will make you love yourself more. Zelda was treating me like a machine. That stings.

Was I helping someone in need or just giving an addict more attention? Does it make a difference either way? There's always an uncertainty in working with humans. They aren't binary, nor even shades of gray. They're jagged, unpredictable, analog, beautiful as well as despicable, cruel and kind, pitiable and manipulative, all at once.

Even if Zelda was playing me, I can't see myself doing anything different. A witch is supposed to believe the best of her clients—that's part of the magic.

While I wallow in my own doubt and spin my wheels and rationalize, Tay goes on with her work. She's now wielding another instrument, a stylus that she presses against the coffee bot's wheels one by one after she spins them with her hand, noting the numbers flashing by on the display.

"Whoever tried to help it before was a bit sloppy," Tay says. "The aftermarket wheel is a mismatch with the others in terms of both radius and grip, and that's throwing off the poor thing's navigation module. It's like when you attach a bit of bristle to one leg on an ant; the unbalanced insect would stumble around in a circle, lost because it navigates by counting steps."

"Can you fix it?" asks a girl in the watching crowd. She has one of those old-fashioned anti–facial recognition cheek stickers, which instantly endears her to me. (They don't work anymore against modern cameras, but it's the symbolism that matters.)

Tay smiles at her. "I'll try."

She takes out a sander and begins to grind away on the happy-face wheel.

"Are you trying to make that wheel the same size as the others?" a boy asks.

"Exactly," says Tay. "And then I'm going to do my best to make sure the wheel feels the same to the little bot, too."

"Do you work with sick bots all the time?" asks the girl with the sticker. "I want to be a bot doctor."

"Sort of," says Tay. "I help make bots, and that includes fixing them when they don't work right. Hey, any of you want to help me out? I'll show you how to use the calipers and the profilometer."

Hands shoot up all around. "Me, me!" "Pick me!" "I want to!"

Even with my cynical heart, I can see the appeal of what Tay is doing. Here she is, inspiring the next generation of engineers. Let's hope they do a better job than their elders.

I volunteer to cradle the "sleeping bot" and "keep it comfortable" while the kids work under Tay's direction. Tay shows them how to take off the protective covers and clean the bot's joints and components with some isopropyl alcohol. She teaches others to wield the precision measuring instruments to guide her modification to the wheel.

A few minutes later, Tay pronounces the bot fixed and reconnects the battery. Gingerly, the girl with the cheek sticker and I flip the little bot back onto its wheels. After a few seconds of holding still as it runs through a start-up sequence, it whirls, spins in place, and scoots away from the crowd, perhaps intent on delivering some imaginary order to the woods in the distance. The kids cheer.

I have to admit: I'm having more fun than I expected.

"Do you think it's going to be all right?" I ask.

"Depends on what you mean by 'all right,'" she says. "I tested its neural networks while working on the wheel. They're pretty corrupted."

"I'm surprised that it can function at all then."

"Well, these things are more resilient than you think. Most are put together from modular, standard components to keep the cost down. The fewer bespoke components you need, the better."

Not unlike weaving a personal fantasy out of clichés, I think. Not unlike telling a new story with secondhand words in a dictionary.

"That kind of designed decoupling builds in a lot of resilience as a side effect. Some components can fail, but others will keep on chugging. Even the artificial intelligence is modular: The recognizer for taking customer orders may no longer work, but the obstacle-avoidance navigator continues to function."

As a witch who relies on customizing and repurposing off-the-shelf components for hexes and charms, I can certainly appreciate her point.

"Hence the erratic behavior of the fai," I say. "Not all the pieces are quite there."

"Yup," says Tay. "Now, all the 'smart' components as well as the supervisory AI, which serves as the customization glue that holds the commodity components together and gives the final bot something of a 'personality,' is usually implemented in analog hardware, which again keeps cost down, but also degrades and becomes outdated quicker. However, since analog AI chips are so much simpler than full-on digital processors, they fail gracefully rather than catastrophically, a blessing as well as a curse."

I give her a blank look. "You know I don't follow the industry."

"Right," Tay says. "Okay, quick refresher: They don't build a complete neural engine into every coffee bot or smart lock."

I nod. Even with all the recent advances, there's just no way to cram what amounts to a graphics card into every IoT device—heat, power consumption, expense . . . the list of reasons is long.

Tay explains that raw power is necessary when you're growing a digital brain. Feeding a general language model the entirety of the internet, shoveling tens of millions of hours of accident-avoidance driving footage into a new autonavigator, training the homeland security facial recognition engine on all the photographs and videos looted from overseas databases by American data privateers . . . these tasks require massive super clusters for the back propagation and gradient descent and all the tensors flowing through thousands upon thousands of hidden layers.

But once that brain has been built, Tay goes on, you need only a minuscule fraction of the computing power to use it. In this "inference" stage, where you're building an amanuensis for authors or a facial recognition chip for a stand-alone surveillance drone, you want something simple, fast, cheap.

At that point, the computation needed amounts to a lot of vector dot products, which don't need sophisticated general-purpose processors; a bunch of floating-gate transistors repurposed to serve as variable resistors, for example, would do the job—if you turn to analog computing.

By mapping different input values as analog signals and judiciously applying Kirchhoff's and Ohm's laws, it's possible to read the results of multiplication or addition or any other calculation you desire simply from the voltages and currents found in an analog circuit. By "burning in" a set of values in a write-once memory chip to represent the weights and biases in a neural network, you could replicate the work otherwise done by a billion transistors with a few thousand analog components.

Unlike digital computers, analog computers don't give the same exact answer every time. Like the real world, analog computations are messy, noisy, shades of gray. But for many applications of machine learning, where the data is noisy and unpredictable and the computation approximate rather than precise, such small variations don't matter.

"These things are designed to be disposable," Tay says. "It's throwaway culture applied to machine brains. Because these analog AI chips are essentially ROMs, once they're obsolete, the customer has no choice but to buy new versions. Not only is it a guaranteed revenue stream, customers feel like the money is well spent when they receive a new robot and the old one is tossed to the curb. No more repairs, only replacement."

This is why we're surrounded by discarded pieces of AI, I realize. The fai are the ghosts of our own arrogance and callousness coming back to haunt us.

I've been focused on how humans are being remade to be more like machines, but I haven't considered the possibility that machines are also being constructed to be more like humans—disposable, powerless, fungible. There's always a younger one willing to work for less, a newer model ready to take the place of the old. Funny how the logic of efficiency and productivity always leads here.

"So, what's going to happen to our coffee bot?" I'm surprised to find myself caring about a discarded piece of machinery.

"It will continue to decline. Analog computers, like all of us, age and wear out. The write-once chips aren't meant to be reprogrammable, and will fatigue and degrade over time. It's going to behave more and more erratically, and eventually it will get into some trouble that it can't recover from. Some volunteer will have to take care of it—maybe reuse parts from it to help other fai."

I stand next to Tay, and we watch the bot ramble into the distance, swerving out of the way of picnickers and bikes.

A feral bot that has degraded beyond a certain point can become dangerous to people and may have to be destroyed, likely a traumatic sight for children who have bonded with it. Tay's checkups and repairs, I realize, are also meant to forestall that outcome.

Do robots really only decline and degrade as they grow old? I wonder. Or could the failing components, the shifting resistance values, the worn weights and biases, be considered a form of learning, of silicon wisdom?

"I don't know who I'm really helping," Tay says. "But it makes me feel better when I take care of these bots. So what if I'm being sentimental and fooling myself a little bit?"

Maybe we're all like Zelda, I think, dancing before a mirror of symbols we hope to speak back to us with intention, with desire, with love.

Don't we deserve it?

```
[magpoi@localhost ~]$ cat /var/log/grimoire/today.log
```

Client: T.N.
Request: 🤖🦾🤖🦾🤖🦾
Dispensed: 0x600D59E1
Comment: "Ond on sped wrecan spel gerade, wordum wrixlan."

Tommy looks at me warily. "I don't have to do anything special? Just put the gizmo on the junction box?"

"That's right," I confirm. "Best to slap the amulet against the back, out of view. The adhesive should stick to pretty much anything."

"What's in it?" he asks.

"Lightning, thunder, the flux and flow of Dao," I say.

He looks skeptical, but nods. Witches don't reveal their secrets.

I happen to have told him the truth. The amulet is indeed bottled lighting. Powered by the omnipresent vibrations in a warehouse environment, the mechanical assembly inside the amulet converts the kinetic energy into static charge, which will be released periodically in violent discharges. A little lightning. Tens of thousands of volts.

The discharges won't be dangerous. But they will generate a great deal of noise in the power supply leading out of the junction box. That noise, in the form of peaks and troughs, will propagate down the lines and into the terminals that monitor the pickers, that determine their paths, that dictate their every movement.

For a shielded digital computer, such fluctuations won't mean much. But for an analog artificial brain, they'll alter computations, change products, yield completely unpredictable results. The analog chip, living in an analog world, will suffer and degrade or learn and grow—it's all a matter of perspective.

I don't expect the miniature lightning bolts to necessarily lead to more breaks for the workers—but there will be changes, and change is what all life thrives on.

It's not much magic, but it's all I can give him, a witch's defiant curse as well as blessing.

Well, maybe not all the magic I can give him.

I suggest that Tommy come with me on a fai-walk.

"No," Tommy says. "Hug-a-bot is not my thing."

"Humor me," I say. "Come to Fairwoods Park with me next weekend. You don't have to hug any bots. I don't."

"Why?"

"We spend so much of our lives being ordered around by bots and remaking ourselves for the convenience of bots," I say, improvising on the fly, "and that makes all of us more robotic. It's out of balance. We need to put ourselves in situations where we take care of bots, so that we can feel empowered, capable, human."

He looks skeptical. Rightly so. I'm a witch, not a philosopher.

"I can't help you if you don't help yourself," I say. "That's the way magic works."

He relents. Probably more to stop me from pestering him rather than because he believes me. But it's enough.

What really draws me to help the fai (and what I hope Tommy will also feel) is hard to explain. Maybe it's a sense that the fai are fellow analog creatures, subject to the ravages of time, capable of decline, senescence, suffering (however one chooses to define it), as well as learning, growth, jouissance. Maybe it's a hope that in helping the fai, we flood the immense dictionary of our culture with love, compassion, caring; we prime the dense web of signs with nongamified labor, with nurturing breaks, with ever-expanding empathy. If life is only an imitation of the book, why not fill that book with feats of sympathy, deeds of generosity, random acts of kindness? Sure, they may be clichés, but clichés are clichés because they are shared, elaborated, passed on, woven into the foundation of language, the archetypes of understanding, the personal mythologies of all scriptors who yearn and pine for the love of the universe, the one and only thing that is original.

Above all, I think about Tay and myself and the children in Fairwoods Park, our hands on the coffee bot, joined in a common cause. We are not meant to be trapped in AR goggles, each drowning apart among ghosts; we are not meant to tell our best stories only to machines; we are not meant to dance alone before a mirror. We should be dancing together. We must dance together.

Tommy thanks me and leaves, clutching the amulet tightly.

("For someone who claims to be sticking up for the human, you sure help a lot of robots," Tay said to me on our last fai-walk.

"The way to be more human isn't to keep out the machine," I said. "But to embrace it and take it in.")

I can't push away all doubt. It's possible that the AI companies pumping out so many disposable bots are letting the obsolete ones run feral on purpose. It's possible that they view fai-animism as a kind of useful idiocy, something that we, the consuming public, engage in to further our own subservience. By caring for obsolete machines, we anthropomorphize them, and in that self-deception, in that seductive spell, we degrade ourselves and lose the will to be saboteurs, hackers, breakers, to fight back.

But even if that were true, I wouldn't do anything different. To willfully jump into a good spell, to believe when there's no reason to, to look for a spark of hope in the random accident that is the cosmos, is magical thinking.

It's the most human thing to do.

Author Note

For an introduction on the potential application of analog computing to deep learning, see: Haensch, Wilfried, Tayfun Gokmen, and Ruchir Puri. "The next generation of deep learning hardware: Analog computing." Proceedings of the IEEE 107.1 (2018): 108–122.

THE LIAR

Darcie Little Badger

THE MYSTERIOUS WOMAN

Jodie sat in a bench-filled lounge outside the Do-
minion Casino poker room. It was 6:18 p.m.,
and she'd been waiting for a table since
5:30. A 32-inch flat-screen TV on the wall
displayed the standby list and indicated she
was up next, along with four others identified
as *Pete M., Joe T., Olav A.,* and *Bartholomew S.*

Lowering her phone, she wondered if the
sweaty, pink-faced man sitting next to her was
Joe, Olav, or Bart. There were a dozen people in
the room, but he was the most visibly nervous, his
right leg bouncing.

"Howdy," he said, noticing Jodie's attention.

"Afternoon. What's your name?"

"Pete." He jabbed a thumb at the waitlist
screen. "That Pete."

"Call me Jodie."

He ducked his head sheepishly. "Guess we're

playing against each other. You any good at this game? My cousin says Texas Hold 'em is the easiest kind of poker . . ."

"Is that so?" Perhaps her first impression of Pete had been premature. Either he was the most naïve gambler in Vegas, or he'd just overplayed his "nervous newbie" act. She'd wager on the latter.

"Standby, your table is ready," an announcer called, his voice crackling through overhead speakers.

"That's us," Pete said, rising.

As they strolled side by side to the felt-topped poker table, Jodie's phone, which was securely zipped in her black fanny pack, dinged twice. She'd check her messages after the game; it wouldn't be long. The other poker players, ranging in age from their mid-thirties to fifties, already sat around the oval table. Two wore sunglasses; all wore button-downs. As Jodie took her place beside Pete, she declared, "Y'all, wish me luck. My hands are always terrible."

*Two hours later and five hundred dollars richer, Jodie slid onto a leather-*upholstered bar stool in the Roman's Another Day bar, ordered a ginger ale (she had to drive home later), and turned on her phone. There were ten missed messages, all from a group labeled "Coven," a nod to their powers. Jodie had connected with the coven online; everyone had similar stories of the Mysterious Woman. They didn't use real names and avoided identifying information, like hometowns or jobs, but Jodie considered them her friends.

Adelle: Has anyone talked to AJ recently?
Chloe: Last Friday.
Adelle: Me too. I'm worried. It's been days.
Chloe: Maybe he's on vacation???
Adelle: No. AJ would have told me.

Then, Jodie noticed that she had a new private message from Adelle.

Adelle: Hi, Jodie. Do you live in the western US?

As Jodie jotted out a response—Why do you ask?—the smell of cigarettes and not-too-bad cologne announced the return of Pete, who thumped onto the seat beside her. "Hey, card shark," he said. Then, to the bartender, "Whiskey, please." At least he'd dropped the fish-out-of-water act. Feigning inexperience hadn't helped him during the poker game. Not against her, anyway.

Jodie slid a ten to the bartender. "I'll cover his drink." It was only fair, considering she'd won all his chips.

With a bashful chuckle, Pete said, "Thanks."

"Just so you know, I have an appointment in ten minutes," she lied. "I can't stay and chat."

"That's fine." He absentmindedly scratched at a pale Band-Aid on his upper arm. "I just had one question."

"What's that?"

He leaned closer, lowered his voice. "Are you the fanny-pack-wearing Cherokee girl who won big at the MGM last week?"

Actually, she was Apache (and 30 years old), but Jodie couldn't tell him that.

"Maybe." She twirled her soda, annoyed. She hadn't meant to win big; it just kinda happened. Now, she had a reputation. That meant it was time to move.

"What's your secret?" Pete asked.

"Really want to know?"

"Yes." He hadn't sounded so earnest all night. When the bartender placed a glass of whiskey in front of Pete, it remained unacknowledged.

"I once defeated a mysterious woman in a game of Uno," Jodie explained, "and she gave me a magical boon."

Pete groaned. "A what?"

"It's like a superpower."

"Respectfully, if you had more than ten minutes, I'd be happy to trade fairy tales—"

"Just listen. It's important that you hear the story."

He sobered up quickly. "Go on, then."

"We'd been playing for petty cash. Me, Mysterious Woman, and my cousins. When I won, she said, 'You can take my money or accept a gift. It would be a great skill for a woman like you: Shake my hand, and people will believe all your lies.'"

"What did she mean by 'a woman like you'?" Pete asked.

"Who knows? I was just twenty, working at the grocery store to pay for college, majoring in math 'cause I have a knack for numbers. I wasn't—" She gestured to herself, to the bar, as if inviting Pete to infer the woman she'd become based on the place she drank. "I was really shy, too. My cousins—two punks from Santa Fe, always decked out in beadwork and spikes—met Mysterious Woman at a concert, and I don't know why she chose me instead of them. I shook her hand, 'cause I didn't want to cause trouble over twenty dollars. Plus, isn't magic make-believe?

"Should have trusted my gut, taken her money instead. There was something off about her. Ethereal. Powerful. Mysterious Woman's long hair resembled a million strands of Vantablack-painted silk. She spoke with an accent, but I couldn't place it, and her eyes . . . like the *Mona Lisa*, she always seemed to be looking at me, even when she wasn't."

"What are you complaining about? I'd pay millions for a super-power like that," he joked.

"Well, there was a catch." Jodie's phone dinged, and she glanced at the message on her screen.

> **Adelle:** If you do, can you check on AJ? He lives in LA. I'm really worried, especially after what happened to North last month.

LA was a four-hour drive: not terrible, given the size of the western US, but . . .

"First, boons can be given or stolen. If you ever meet somebody with more than one boon, chances are, they've killed lots of people like me."

Pete chuckled; she didn't hold it against him. It's not like he believed her.

"And second, every boon comes with a curse," Jodie continued, simultaneously messaging Adelle: Call in 30 mins. And she provided the number of her burner phone, purchased for emergencies only.

"What's yours?" Pete encouraged.

"When I tell the truth, nobody believes me."

"That's not so bad . . ."

"It is if you want to be a mathematician." Jodie stood, finished her soda with an audible gulp, and buttoned up her jean jacket.

"Wait! C'mon, Miss Jodie. I listened to your story like a good sport. Won't you give me a hint? How do you really win?"

Gently, she smiled. "Who can say?"

"You?"

"Afraid not. This conversation has only been a dream." There was a coral-red smudge of lipstick on her empty glass of ginger ale; perhaps it would confuse him after she left. "You never really met me, Pete."

What Happened to North One Month Ago

North: GUYS IM SCREWED

North: MY GIFT IS GONE

North: Last night when I came home from pub there was a person in my house dressed in black like an actual burglar and when I tried to run they grabbed my arm and I couldn't break free not even by fighting. It was like hitting a rock. They threw me against the wall and told

me to calm down because they just wanted my gift
which made me fight more but it didn't help. There was
a rumble and I couldn't breathe and I passed out and
when I woke up just now the intruder was gone but I
can't sing with five voices anymore.

Jodie: What about the curse? Did your attacker take it, too?

North: Let me check.

North: Damn. No. Applause still gives me hives.

Adelle: I'm so sorry.

North: What am I supposed to do? I got a show tonight.

Chloe: You still have a LOVELY voice.

North: Thanks, but it's not enough.

Adelle: Can we help?

North: Stay away. I don't know how the attacker found me.
You could be next.

North: At least Im alive.

AJ: This is why we keep a low profile.

North: What are you implying?

AJ: Nothing!

North: Fuck off. I've been singing for 10 years. NEVER got
accused of magic. Autotune yeah but NEVER magic.

North: Its this GROUP.

North: Were you the one who attacked me, AJ?

Chloe: Please don't fight.

AJ: I'd never hurt you, man. Calm down.

<North has left the group>

THE IMMORTAL MAN

By the time Adelle called, Jodie was driving up I-15. She lowered the
radio to a white-noise murmur of soft rock and transferred the call to
speakers. A Dolly Parton soundalike asked, "Jodie? You there?"

"What's up, Adelle?"

This was the first time she'd spoken to a member of the coven. The others would chat among themselves, but texts gave Jodie more time to be deliberate about phrasing. Adelle's surgery voice fit her well, based on everything Jodie knew about her friend, a 30-something-year-old former nurse with three young sons who lived with their father. Adelle's curse was too dangerous for a house full of children. Her right hand carried the boon of healing. Her left hand, the curse of death. The greater the boon, the greater the curse, but Adelle never complained. Her eldest son, Felix, had a painful hereditary disorder. But he no longer suffered, not like he used to. The magic was a salve.

"I know AJ's address," Adelle replied. "I've visited his house."

"When?"

"Most recently, a month ago."

"Aren't we supposed to be anonymous?" Jodie drummed her fingers on the steering wheel.

"AJ broke his foot last year, remember? With a curse like his . . ."

"Ah. You went there to heal him?"

"At first, that's why I always visited. To heal. But lately . . ." Her voice tightened with emotion. "We love each other. That's why I'm scared. AJ never ignores my calls. Not like this. He could be in the hospital. Or . . ."

"Or something worse?" Thinking of the attack on North, a bitterly paranoid side of Jodie wondered: Am I being lured somewhere? After all, AJ went missing after he shared his address with Adelle.

"Yeah."

"You don't want to lie to me," Jodie said, realizing too late that she didn't know what Adelle wanted, which meant the statement was just a guess and therefore had no power. Luckily, Jodie hadn't disclosed her boon to the coven. She could try a different tactic, undetected. "Just warning ya that I know when people are being deceptive, 'cause I used to administer lie detector tests for the FBI."

"Honest to God, hon!" Adelle exclaimed. "I'm just worried about

AJ. Sorry. I know why you're cautious. This was a lot to ask. Don't give it a second thought. I'll fly to Los Angeles on Sunday—"

Sunday was two days away.

"What's AJ's address?" Jodie interrupted. "I'll check tomorrow evening." A lie. She'd drive there now. Four hours to LA, ample cash to cover the hotel. She'd visit AJ's house at dawn, no doubt after a sleepless night lying in a strange bed, worrying, wondering what she'd find.

AJ lived in a neighborhood of sardine-packed houses. There were two un-broken lines of cars parked on either side of the street, reducing the driving width to a single lane. The taxi stopped alongside a white house surrounded by a wire fence; impatient traffic honked as Jodie paid her bill and climbed out of the back seat with a quick "Thanks." It was 7:30 a.m., clear-skied, and already warm. She wore a cloth face mask and a Yankees baseball cap to hide from security cameras. Although Jodie didn't plan to cause a scene, situations like these, with so many unknowns, defied planning.

According to AJ, he met Mysterious Woman at a bar: not a dive or a pickup hotspot, just a run-of-the-mill place where people congregated after work to drink and watch football together. He struck up a conversation with (in AJ's words) "the most striking woman in the room, in every room, or so I thought." He was curious, but Mysterious Woman deflected his questions with her own. By last call, she knew AJ's life story, and—according to AJ every time he recounted the night—she'd only become more mysterious.

"She asked me: If I could have one superpower, what would it be? I said: never age. Then, she asked, 'What if the power had a side effect, and every injury caused ten times the pain?' At the time, I was just twenty-nine and hadn't broken a single bone. She promised I'd never get cancer. There'd be no wrinkles, no deteriorating heart. Only other things or people could harm me. Seemed like a fair trade, especially hypothetically. Plus, heart disease runs in my family."

"Was it a fair trade, though?" Jodie thought as she unlatched AJ's gate and noticed that there were no-slip pads on the steps to his front door and memory foam padding on the railing around his porch. AJ always seemed chipper, but Jodie knew full well that behavior could be deceiving.

Jodie pressed the off-white doorbell, and when nobody answered, she knocked twice and called, "AJ? You there?"

Patiently, she counted the seconds. At ten, Jodie shouted, "Hey, buddy, wake up!"

The only response came from the neighbor's open side window, "Can you keep it down?"

"Sorry!" Turning, Jodie faced her critic. The groggy-looking twenty-something woman wore a white terry bathrobe, which she clasped shut with one hand. "I feel awful for disturbing you," Jodie said. "Have you seen the man who lives here? I'm his cousin, and my family's really worried. We can't reach him by phone."

The woman's scowl softened. "Um, not recently, but I'm usually at work."

"Thanks. No worries." Jodie jogged to AJ's mailbox, flipped it open, and mentally reeled when she saw a dense pile of envelopes, a week's worth of unopened mail. From her elevated vantage point, the bathrobe woman suggested, "Try his back door."

"Okay." There were white gardenias in the narrow alley of land connecting AJ's front yard to his backyard. Jodie, by hopping and weaving, didn't crush any flowers underfoot. Two large, curtained windows overlooked the fence-enclosed patch of yellow grass behind AJ's house, and between the windows was a yellow wooden door. As she stepped closer, Jodie heard a plink, plink, plink sound, similar to the rhythm of a moth enamored of a light bulb. Plink, plink, plink. Dozens of fat black flies were trapped between the curtain and glass pane of the left-hand window. Plink, plink, plink. Some crawled in aimless loops, while others kept trying to escape the house and whatever else was trapped within its walls.

"AJ," Jodie whispered, even though she'd meant to shout. And then, she turned the doorknob. The door opened a few inches, catching on a chain lock. A strip of light fell into the kitchen, and Jodie leaned forward, wide-eyed. Shock delayed her reaction to the smell.

"Oh, god," she moaned. A bloated carrion fly ricocheted off her cheek and zipped away. Gagging, Jodie snapped the door shut and ran to the gardenias, gathering flowers in her hands and rubbing their petals against her face, inhaling, desperate to purge the smell of death.

Because she'd seen him lying on the kitchen floor. And he'd been there for days.

The immortal man had died at age 51.

LADY LIFE OR DEATH

Later that morning, Jodie took a breather—the first she'd had all day—at a little rest stop between Los Angeles and Vegas. Hers was the only car in the parking lot, although a green-trimmed long-haul truck was parked behind the restroom facilities, its driver sleeping. Jodie bought a granola bar from the half-empty vending machine near the restrooms, and then she sat on a wooden bench to eat and think.

AJ had aged, which meant his gift was absent—stolen—at the time of death. He could have been killed—intentionally or accidentally—in the struggle. First North. Now AJ. A pattern was emerging; the gift thief was picking off members of the coven. And it seemed that North had been right. Their friendship was a liability; even Jodie, who'd tried to remain totally anonymous, was letting details of her life seep out, blood in the water.

Either Chloe or Adelle could be a hunter.

After swallowing the last bite of granola, she called Adelle.

"Jodie? What is it?"

"I'm in LA. Um. God. AJ's neighbor found his body. AJ . . . he was . . ." She lowered the phone; on the other end of the line, Adelle was screaming.

I'm sorry, Jodie thought. *I'm so sorry.* Instead, after the screaming became sharp, hiccupping gasps, she said, "Adelle, pretend the killer stole AJ's phone, okay? Would it contain anything—anything at all!— that could reveal your location, full name, family's names? Anything he could use to find you."

"Killer?" she cried. "AJ was murdered?"

Jodie stopped herself from responding, *Seems so.* Instead, she asked, "What if I told you that a gift thief is targeting our group? What if AJ was murdered for his gift?"

"I sent AJ photos. We texted every day. This isn't happening. This . . ." A moment of silence passed, and when Adelle next spoke, she sounded stoic, almost robotic. "Felix depends on my gift, Jodie. What should I do?"

Prey ran. Prey hid. Jodie could pack all her worldly possessions in a few suitcases and start a new life somewhere else. The Midwest, another country. She'd switch from gambling to panhandling and thereby entirely disappear from the consideration of society.

Of course, prey also sought protection in great numbers. Alone, Jodie would be running forever, but she couldn't ask her family for help. She did enough damage to them all those years ago. After shaking the Mysterious Woman's hand, it hadn't taken long for Jodie to accept that her gift was real. By that point, however, she'd already torn her cousins' minds apart.

She'd rather die than let that happen again.

"Tell your ex-husband about the murder and go into hiding. Okay? Don't try to fight."

"What about Chloe? Is she in danger, too?"

"I'll warn her," Jodie said. "And then no more communication. Who knows who we can trust?"

"Yes . . ." Adelle sniffled. "You're right."

Jodie's thumb was an inch from the "end-call" button when she heard Adelle's quiet plea, "Be careful, hon."

The last-minute flight to Portland had burned through Jodie's most recent poker winnings, but she had enough cash in reserve to survive a couple weeks on the road. In any case, money was among the least of her concerns. In an emergency, she could use lies as currency. The phrases "I already paid for that" and "You owe me twenty dollars" went a long way.

With a flight to catch in twenty hours, Jodie took a cold shower and then whirlwind-packed a couple suitcases with her valuables. Later, the landlady would find a few pots and pans, a pillow, two comforters, and a tangle of electrical wires: extension cords, chargers, even a string of Christmas lights Jodie had used only once, years ago.

At midnight, eight hours before takeoff, she rolled a sleeping bag over the bare twin-sized mattress and tried to sleep. Every couple minutes, the yellowed blinds flashed as a car drove past her window. Normally, the street's rhythm was a metronome lulling her to sleep. Not tonight. She tried counting cars. By one hundred, Jodie gave up.

It would be nearly 5:00 a.m. in North Carolina, where Adelle lived. Too early to call. But what good would a check-in do, anyway? She had a solid survival plan. Simple, adaptable. Adelle's ex-husband would take a long vacation with the boys, and Adelle would move.

If this was a movie, the killer would strike tonight, when Adelle was vulnerable, frightened, and on the cusp of escape. Why? Because of dramatic tension. Or maybe because the murderer knew she was leaving, and if they didn't act quickly, their victim would get away . . .

Jodie glanced at her phone. The time read 1:48 a.m. Somewhere, a fly clinked against glass.

She'd call Adelle in two hours. One last goodbye. Until then, she'd take a walk.

The 24-hour convenience store down the street sold the best tamales Jodie had ever tasted outside of her grandmother's kitchen. Maybe they'd help her relax. Dressed in jeans, a T-shirt, and a windbreaker, she stepped outside, locked the door, and set off across the asphalt parking lot with her hands thrust deep within her pockets. The surrounding windows—in her apartment complex, in the inn across the street, and in the various concrete-colored shops around them—ranged from dark to dimly lit, and although Jodie was alone on the sidewalk, at least one car drove by every minute—tick, tick, tick went the metronome.

The store was just three blocks away, a walk she'd made countless times before, but tonight, Jodie felt vaguely unsafe, like she was being watched, hunted. She glanced at the windows across the street, searching their curtains for movement. Finding nothing, Jodie turned toward the alleys and listened for footsteps.

"Perhaps I got it all wrong," she thought. "If this was a movie, I'd be the next victim. 'Cause it's unexpected."

At that, Jodie grit her teeth, shook out her arms, and resumed glaring at the shadows. She wasn't frightened anymore; this was the tension of anticipation.

What would she say to the murderer?

Want to hurt me, my guy? You're a literal piece of shit.

Within minutes, the convenience store was an oasis of golden light around the corner. As she approached the front entrance, Jodie noticed two cars in the square blacktop parking lot. She made note of the license plates. Nevada, Nevada. Locals, then.

With a ding, ding of a little bell, the convenience store door shot open, and a man—mid-thirties, shirtless, with burnt skin and thick brown hair—jogged outside, nearly slamming into Jodie.

"'Scuse me," she automatically said, trying to circle around him, but he sidestepped in her way, remarkably nimble for a guy who'd probably been drinking since Happy Hour, based on his smell.

"Huuuh-ay," he said. "Whassup?"

It occurred to her that if he'd been a witch, she'd be a goner.

"Nothing," Jodie said, and he must have believed that, so why wouldn't he move?

"Whas the . . ." The rest of his question was so slurred, she couldn't make it out.

"You want to leave me alone," Jodie muttered, and without another word, the man staggered away, walking past the parked cars and across the street. The moment he disappeared around a motel, Jodie's phone rang with a shrill chirp. The caller ID said: Adelle.

"Hello?" she answered, leaning against the outer convenience store wall.

"Jodie, I think the murderer was in my house! She just . . . she walked through the wall, Jodie!"

"What? When was this? Are you safe?"

"She isn't here anymore. I don't know what to do! Should I call the police?"

"What about your kids?"

"Jason took 'em to Florida already. I'm alone."

"Okay. They're safe. Good. Then tell me exactly what happened." Sometime during the conversation, Jodie had started walking back home, her restless energy redirected to yet another dead-end destination.

"I was dozing—not a deep sleep. In bed, I face a window, which is always locked and covered by curtains. The headboard's against a solid wall. Um, well, something woke me. A sound. Next thing, I'm staring at that window, and it's dim in my bedroom, but the curtain's clearly moving forward, toward me, like there's somebody behind it. And I lower my eyes and see legs and a torso, and then she's taking a slow step closer, this woman who'd walked through the wall."

"When the shock wore off, I screamed loud as I could. Same time, the curtain slipped off her head. She was . . . maybe mid-twenties? Hard to tell, since she wore a ski mask. Covered everything but her eyes. Five feet tall, very average build. Um, with me screaming, she didn't care about sneaking around anymore. She charged my bed, but at the same time, I tore the glove off my hand. My death hand. When the witch saw that, she jumped back and sank through the floor. Disappeared! So I . . . I thought I oughtta grab my phone and run. I'd packed the car already."

It occurred to Jodie that there was a low rumble in the background of Adelle's call. "You're driving now?" she guessed.

"Yeah. Just driving. What else can I do?"

"Hon, don't freak out—"

"Oh, I'm past freaking out."

"Okay. Okay. Did you check the back seat? The trunk?"

"Yes. I'm alone here. Certain."

"Hm." She pulled the keys from her pocket, holding them in her fist during the final stretch home.

On the other end of the line, there was a THUMP.

"Adelle?"

"Something just landed on top of my . . ."

"Am I on speakerphone now? Can you hear me through the car speakers?"

"Oh, god, I think it's her!"

"What's happening?"

Jodie heard the squeal of tires, a shrill wail, and another thump. Adelle cried, "Please, no!"

"Stop!" Jodie shouted. "If you hurt Adelle, you'll spontaneously combust!"

Adelle was sobbing now. "My son is sick! He needs my gift!"

"Hey, if you take her power, you'll die!" Jodie screamed. "Go away!"

"You killed the man I love," Adelle cried. "For God's sake, don't kill my baby, too!"

"Please stop!" Jodie begged the murderer; her lies weren't working. Either the phone had disconnected, or the witch was immune to her gift. Around Jodie, the windows of apartments and motels brightened, awakened by her shouts. A woman in a bathrobe leaned out of a third-floor window and said, "Shut the fuck up, you crackhead," and Jodie was mentally transported to AJ's house, surrounded by the odor of rot and the hum of flies.

From the other end of the line came a hideous sound, like a storm sucked into a jet engine. A scream slipped within the rage.

The line abruptly went quiet, although the call was still connected. There was a click, like a glove box opening, followed by the rustling of paper and metal keys.

"Adelle?" Jodie asked, ducking behind a blue mailbox and sitting cross-legged on the grimy sidewalk. "Is that you?"

A raspy voice whispered, "Your friend is bleeding to death, but I can heal her now."

For a beat, Jodie couldn't speak. Then, "Please save her—"

"Call off your curse."

"My . . . curse?"

"If I burn to death, she'll die, too."

With that, the call disconnected.

DIRECT MESSAGES - CHLOE

Chloe: Adelle won't answer my messages.

Chloe: I'm scared

Chloe: Please don't leave too.

Chloe: I just want to know you're alive.

Chloe: My power is really strong. I can protect her & you too.

Chloe: I met the Mysterious Woman when I was very little. She asked me why I was covered in bruises. I told the goddess that everyone hit me, and I just wanted to make the pain stop. She sang, "I am rubber, you are glue. Whatever you do bounces off of me and sticks to you."

Chloe: That's my gift. Nobody can hurt me anymore.

Chloe: I think it's how we defeat the witch.

Jodie: Sorry I took so many days to answer.

Jodie: If you were serious about meeting:

Room 2

Throne Inn

34 Longran Circle

Raleigh, NC

Find me. I'm here all week.

PS, if you are the person who attacked North, AJ, and Adelle, I just want to talk face to face. Give me an hour of your time, answer my questions, help me understand, and I'll turn over my gift without a fight. Adelle struggled, and now she has just one arm.

Chloe: WHAT???

Jodie: Yeah. Adelle's ex, Jason, said the attacker tore off her left arm to stop her from using the death curse.

Chloe: That's terrible. I'm so sorry.

Jodie: Throne Inn.

THE LIAR

You couldn't win at poker with lies alone.

To be fair, Jodie's gift gave her a major boost; when people thought her hands sucked, they bet accordingly. But she still had to know the game, understand probability, when to fold, and how much to risk on a hand. She had to read other players, seek out tells and inconsistencies. Sometimes, everything came down to luck.

That happened less often than one'd expect.

In fact, what finally swayed Jodie—what convinced her that Chloe was AJ's killer, Adelle's tormentor, and North's dream crusher—were the odds.

Chloe is close to North (at the very least, she knows what his voice sounds like, meaning she can ID him), and he's attacked first. Coincidence? Maybe.

Chloe wants to remain in contact with Jodie. Innocent request? Perhaps.

When Chloe realizes that Jodie is pulling away, she reveals her power, and it's coincidentally perfect for defeating the witch. Deus ex machina? There was a mighty slim chance.

The odds of all these maybes and coincidences happening at once were so small, Jodie wouldn't bet ten bucks on it. Of course, she could be wrong. Chloe could be a fine ally. She'd know soon enough.

There was a knock on the motel door.

"Get ready," Jodie whispered. Then, she stood from the wooden chair beside the creaky queen-sized bed, crossed the dim room, and looked through the peephole. At first, she saw the crown of Chloe's head—a knitted blue beanie over scruffy black hair. And then, the young woman looked up, her brown eyes large, wide set, and solemn, like the eyes of a little deer.

Jodie opened the door wide, squinting against the daylight. "What's your name?"

"I'm Chloe." She made no move to approach.

"Cool." As an invitation, Jodie stepped back and sat on the edge of the bed. "Come in. Don't be scared. I can't hurt you. At the moment, this hotel is the safest place on Earth. Oh, but you want to take off your shoes. Carpet's really soft."

"Thank you." Chloe shut the door behind her, kicked her slippers into a corner, and stood awkwardly in front of the flat-screen TV until Jodie pointed at the wooden chair.

"Sit," Jodie instructed. "So, did you tear off Adelle's arm? Kill AJ? Ruin North's life? Was it you? Be honest. It's the only way you'll get what you want.

"I . . ."

"Like I said, I don't plan to hurt you. You want my gift? Fine. I'll give it to you happily, if you answer my questions. This isn't a trick. Cooperation is the only way forward."

Chloe dropped onto the chair, cradling her face in her hands. "It was an accident," she groaned, her voice muffled.

"What?"

With a miserable sigh, Chloe looked up. "AJ. He wasn't supposed to die. I think his heart gave out."

"Because of the pain? The fear?"

She looked down. "Don't know."

"Was Adelle's arm an accident, too?"

Chloe's gaze sharpened. "I could have done much worse."

"How many powers do you have, anyway? Just curious."

"Hmmm." Thoughtfully biting her inner lip, Chloe counted them off on her fingers. "Super strength. I can duplicate small objects, like coins or shoes. I'm able to exchange bodies."

"Gah! How often have you done that?"

"A couple times."

"Go on."

"Walk through solids. Float. I can forget or remember any moment in my life. There's North's gift of singing. And, of course, healing, health."

"All those gifts and no curses?"

"No," Chloe said, lowly. "My curse is terrible."

"What is it?"

"Hunger." She turned, gazing at the wallpaper, stripes of off-white on dirty green. "When possible, I glut myself to survive months of starvation. Like a bear in the springtime."

"Could you die from this . . . starvation?"

"Worse." Chloe surged forward, grasping Jodie's hands, squeezing. "You cannot understand my pain, Jodie. The things it drives me to do. It's torture. There's no greater agony."

"What about the loss of a friend? Or a child?"

"You can live with grief, kid," she hissed, her nails biting into Jodie's palms. "Everyone does it."

Teeth grit against the pain of Chloe's tightening grip, Jodie asked, "And how many people have grieved because of you?"

Chloe leaned even closer. She smelled like sweat, and vanilla. Her beanie was soft, as if knitted from cashmere. "Honestly," Chloe whispered, "I've lost count."

Jodie's ears crackled as the pressure rapidly decreased; from somewhere deep, a maelstrom roared. "Wait, what about my questions?" she asked.

"We're done talking."

"Stop! You don't want to take my gift!" But if Chloe's hunger surpassed her capacity for friendship and love, overruled her sense of self-preservation, then maybe she really didn't want this. Or maybe she did. Jodie couldn't lie if she didn't know the truth.

"Let's find the Mysterious Woman and make her take your pain away," Jodie shouted. "Isn't there time to try?"

Chloe just grimaced, shook her head. It was becoming hard for Jodie to breathe. There might be time for one more lie, but she was afraid of breaking the wrong mind; she and Chloe weren't alone in the room.

Adelle had been hiding under the bed.

Suddenly, Chloe cried out with shock, and the whirlwind went silent. In Chloe's last surge of consciousness, she looked down, gasping at the skeletal hand that touched her bare foot. Quick as a snake, the hand withdrew back under the bed.

Jodie caught Chloe's lifeless body before it hit the hotel carpet. Behind her, Adelle crawled into the open, clutching the remains of her left arm, which was half-wrapped in black velvet. Even though the arm had been severed from her body, the death curse still worked. They'd tested it on flies earlier that week.

"I couldn't let her steal more boons," Adelle said, her voice robotic again; she helped Jodie lower the body to the ground. "She was already like a god."

With a gentle swipe of her thumb, Jodie closed the corpse's large brown eyes, wondering who they'd belonged to, before Chloe stole them.

"What's your gift, Jodie?" Adelle asked, softly.

"What if I told you that everyone believes my lies?"

"I'd say that's a terrible, dangerous power." To Jodie's right, Adelle leaned closer, and Jodie braced herself. Because it was a terrible power. Nobody should have her gift.

"You were right," Adelle whispered. "We should find the Mysteri-

114

ous Woman. I want to beg her for Felix's life. I want to understand . . ." She looked at Chloe's motionless face. ". . . why."

They sat together for a moment, heads bowed.

"Do you want to join me?" Adelle asked.

Jodie wished she could say, *Yes, I do.* Instead, she agreed, "Let's go find her."

ESCAPE ARTISTS

Andrea Hairston

February
Winds slice my spirit
I stop believing in spring
I can't imagine
Coming back from the dead
Of winter

Hinkty rich folk buried one hundred naked witches
Alive
Just outside town
Covered their faces with golden sand
Putting out a roaring fire
No loam or living soil
Cowards feared
    Enchantment sneaking from hairy roots
    Worms casting hoodoo spells
    Fungus at the crossroads
        Singing the blues
        Committing necromancy

Jealous of mushrooms and mold
Rich folk insisted
Sand never gave a hoot or a holler for
   Ungrateful magikers and uppity heifers
   Scat singing the horror tales that ring true
The Official Story:
Witches instigated
   Every wayward child and broke machine
   Every busted life and failed crop
   Every wind turned foul and truth nobody bothered to hear

Self-anointed victims of black magic, of hoodoo-voodoo
Innocents
Spilled no blood
Murder outsourced
Chain gang did the grim labor
Got paid five cents an hour
Owed that and more to the prison store
Weary convicts poured glassy granules into witch-mouths
Bound witch-lips tight with indigo cloth
Demon wives would utter no curses
Rich folk proclaimed
Words unspoken posed no danger

Some big fart in town wanted the chain gang
To chop witch-hands and witch-feet
To prevent escape
Rational minds prevailed
Limbs bound in rope
Sand filling eyes, noses, ears
Covering every inch of skin
Even witches couldn't

Walk
   Swim
      Crawl
To freedom
Witches would suffocate
Self-satisfied town folk collected shovels
Secured shackles
Marched the chain gang back to holding pens

Mothers and sisters, daughters and cousins, lovers and sons
Wept on the witches' graves
Sand gobbled these salty libations
As if feasting on an ancient, inland sea
Who says nothing grows in sand?
What about a
   Shrine to Grief
   Host to Anger
   Monument for Change
Can I get a witness?

Hinkty cowards proclaimed
The witches' graveyard was haunted
Cursed
People were warned to stay away
From the truth
Stay away
A witch will suck power from your soul

Word on the wind was clear
Not a single ghost sheltered in the graveyard
Powerful witches took years to die
Made the ground rock, rattle, and roll

Made glassy granules hum
An eerie lament
For anyone bold enough
To listen
A hundred undead
Witches sang years of torment and inspiration

A stranger, fool, clown, a traveler
Too ignorant to be afraid
Heard spooky
    You put a spell on me
    I got to be free
Music
Somebody had made a terrible mistake
Sacred fool had to dig up haunted ground
Had to set one hundred witches free or die trying

Under the sand
Rags had rotted to indigo dust
Ropes were scraggily brown threads
The traveler found
No teeth turned black
No bones picked clean
By enterprising sand worms
Trying to feed the future
The witch women had escaped!
Nobody could say how long ago
A miracle!
Wouldn't you agree?

Razor-sharp rumors sliced the town
Every shadow wanted revenge

Every dark cloud was out for bloody retribution
Nobody remembered how to give back a stolen life
That hoodoo spell was forgotten
A tall tale buried with the witches
Rich folk slipped out to spy empty graves
Nothing to see
They'd lost their senses long ago
Who in their right mind buried one hundred women alive
Hearts beating
Blood drenching indifferent ground

Lies bubbled up
Denial
No Blood on Our Hands
Banished, yes
No *actual* witch had been buried
A ritual for puppets
    Stuffed with straw
    Wool yarn hair
    Button eyes
    Crocheted grins
A warning to demon wives

Denial is never solace or cure
Fears frothed
Town folk looked around
Desperate for somebody to blame
The traveler was long gone
Escape from sand pits proved guilt
Didn't it?
Demons must have rescued their wives
Witches were out there again

Ready to drive *innocent* people mad
They had to be covered with rocks this time
Boulders
Sand was weak

A cousin, lover, three mothers, four daughters, two sisters, and a son
Gathered at the Monument for Change
Why hadn't they done more before?
With a finger snap and a flick of the wrist
They vowed to stop the massacre
Courage was powerful juju
Brave hands tingled
Warm breath touched their necks
Soothed their brows
Shimmers flickered at the edge of vision
Ignited their spirits
The power of the witches had come to them
Indeed
These brave few had become witches
This time
They refused to be buried alive

March
Icy wind rattles my bones
Buried alive
A green shoot nudges a rock aside
Spring

THE WITCH IS NOT THE MONSTER

Alaya Dawn Johnson

My dad is not a witch, but he is the deacon for the Floodwatch, and he studied harbingers under the Living Master, so he knows a lot about witches and their ways.

I am not a witch, but I was born during the First Inundations, under the sign of the apocalypse, and so I have a great potential for evil. I am very lucky to be his daughter. Who knows what I would be otherwise.

What is worse than a witch? A whore?

Surely not. There are many whores, after all, and few witches.

A flood?

But a flood cannot be a person, it can only kill one.

A fleshed demon, like those that crawled out of the floodwaters?

But the Living Master in the Sea City has destroyed them, and the Floodwatch keeps us safe.

A ghost, perhaps. Like the one in the food cellar.

Just one night, she swears to god, just one night the witch wants to sleep through the night without waking up outgassing sick shame like a fucking shame chimney.

Instead, she jolts upright with a scream clawing at her throat and her own hand between her teeth like rawhide.

She doesn't remember the dream, no, but she knows what she was dreaming. Or, more to the sick point, who.

At four in the morning, darkest night, she crawls out of her sleep pod. The lights of South Potomac's eastern floodwall blink in the distance. Morse code, the message a century old: *Safe harbor.* The mining communities out here on the floodplain keep tradition. She has a job waiting in their safe harbor. Like a good little witch, she goes where the Sisterhood points her. She used to say it was because she doesn't have any other choice, but in truth, the choice is all she has.

On a whim, she takes out her own hand torch and signals back: *Alive here.*

What he did to her was like death, but he didn't kill her. That's the problem.
It's how she became what she is. A conduit between the dead and the living. An intermediate phylum, a woman-shaped mushroom growing on the shame-eaten carcass of a little girl. In places like this, old defensive communes still clinging to the bloody logic of the First Inundations, they remember the witches who saved them when haints first crawled out of the water, animated by a planet's rage. The sea cities have banned all witches, but no one who still lives on land can repudiate her kind entirely. She prefers the term *conjure woman*, but her old teacher Goldie always insisted that's what their kind were before, not now. She doesn't conjure much of anything, in any case. The dead are the dead; she can't make them linger, but sometimes she can make them go.

The people of South Potomac really want one to go. The commune has seen more prosperous days; the microchips and mechanicals were all harvested decades before, and even raw materials like plastics and rare-earth metals and wood are nearly exhausted. The old mansions that used to line these streets before the Inundations stand as skeletal husks over springtime flood lakes, if they stand at all. Still, the old chief holds on to her commune's loyalty with, as far as the witch can tell, the strength of her memory of better days. The younger generation has mostly left, seeking better pay as menials in exclusive undersea metropoli, or staffers on hurricane rigs, but their parents and grandparents remain, scavenging and farming and defending their floodwall. Chief Vai is ancient, an elder among elders, the kind of woman who weighs you down with an air of near-unbearable experience, so that you are forced to hunch while she, straight-backed, looks down.

"It's the last virgin mine in the territory. Built after the First Inundations."

The witch blinks. "After?" She's no miner, but she knows that aridocene buildings designed to withstand the end of their age are legendary mines that could sustain a commune for years if they found the right corporate intermediary.

"You're wondering why we haven't mined it if we're really squatting on a pot of gold?"

She squints at the chief's nose and then looks back down again, queasy. Chief Vai is witchy in a way she can only aspire to be: nose at once beaky and broad, eyes set in sockets deep enough to be hollowed out by a spoon, a mane of gray hair twisted like tangled wires. The witch could charge enough for months if she showed up in communes looking like that. Well, if she were white.

"If you called me, I assume there's some kind of haint."

The chief's lips turn up and she glances at her son. Chief Samuel is a big man, wide-shouldered and narrow-hipped, a mane of hair past his shoulder blades of a shade too insipid to be golden, though some might have flattered him with the description in his youth. Now in his mid-forties, the mane has eroded into a midpate widow's peak and a chronic hunch cradles the alcoholic extrusion of his belly. He must have been a surprise late in life for Chief Vai. The look of childlike dismay he wears in the presence of his mother speaks to a kind of perpetual infantilization that the witch has often noted in only sons. He is yet another specimen of the kinds of white men whom she has been forced to understand for her own survival, and what little he has in him of Vai—the expectant blue gaze, the preemptive defense—makes her wonder about the both of them.

"I wasn't in favor of involving a witch," Chief Samuel says. "We can't afford to lose our contracts with the sea cities. So I hope you can be discreet."

She purses her lips. "All of the Sisters are discreet, and none of us speak to the sea cities. Why me?"

"You came highly recommended, so we—"

The witch winces and raises a hand. "Who on this wet earth would recommend me?"

Chief Samuel puddles to a stop. His mother leans forward, claps a hand on his bicep and meets her eyes. The witch has uncanny eyes; a pigment disorder gives the irises a brown so intense as to seem black, and Goldie trained her to use them to intimidate. But after a moment, the witch looks away. When not strictly necessary, she avoids eye contact. Most animals—especially humans, in truth—instinctively avoid staring too long in one another's eyes. She can just tolerate it a little less than most.

Now, Chief Vai laughs. "No one recommends a witch, you're right. But you have a reputation."

The nausea hits her like a wave against a breaker. "The Charleston sewers?"

It had been an ugly job. Chief Samuel lifts his mother's hand from his arm with a delicate, almost puritanical, care and sets it down against her thigh. "You cleanse the evil from the last age. That can only be a good thing—"

"Even if your methods are crude," Chief Vai interrupts smoothly. She knows a weak spot when she smells one.

The Chief's office in the old bank building at the center of town smells of musty furniture, brackish water, algae, and mud. It does not smell like blood, but the algae leaves a metallic tang at the back of her throat and for a second she is seeing soldiers and militiamen firing into crowds of civilians, refugees fleeing the hurricane-backed floodwaters, hundreds of black and brown faces carrying their most important possessions gunned down for daring to cross clandestinely into a white suburb. Then she goes back further, to the voice of Goldie, who marked her: "Your daddy gave you the gift, witch eye, I'm just going to shape it."

It had been a merciless sort of shaping for a job that requires such cruel oceans of mercy.

She swallows, anchors herself in the present. If they know about Charleston, they know this already, but she makes herself say, "I don't guarantee civilian safety."

Chief Vai's eyes, ocean blue, glitter. The witch feels bowed over again with the weight of years, and of understanding. "Where are you from, originally?"

"Not far from here."

Chief Vai nods. "But the other side of the river, of course. We're lucky you people didn't try to loot here, like in Charleston."

The witch knows a dog whistle when she hears one. "What does that have to do—"

"Calm down, that's ancient history. You're all so touchy."

She hates the deliberate ambiguity the most, the sticky imprecision about whether "you all" were the Sisters, or her sisters, as it were.

"Your point?"

The old woman laughs. "There will be no one else near you but my Sammy. He can take care of himself."

The witch takes a step forward, locks the chief with her uncanny gaze. "And what harbingers of Mother Water's fury are haunting you?"

Now Vai looks away. "There is," she says softly, "a girl."

The ghost in the food cellar has no shape that I can see, but it makes the room very cold when it is there, much too cold for the turnips and rutabagas, though I suppose the potatoes and sweet potatoes will do all right. I haven't told Dad about it because he would want to pray and I do not think this ghost is evil or a demon and I worry what our prayers might do to it.

Prayers are good for many things, but principally they are weapons in our battle against the three enemies of God: demons of the earth and their harbingers, the witches who treat with them, and godless social-ism. Prayers:

1. Cast out demons, both ghostly and fleshed. (After Mom went into the water, I thought she might have become one of them, but Dad promises that she is too pure and that I will follow her there one day. I ask him how, but he says I'm not at a high enough level of initiation to understand the Mysteries. I'm glad that the Living Master has told him Mom is safe. I've seen pictures of the great horde that came from the Water Demon Mother at the start of the First Inundations, and I hate to think of Mom like that, rotting and furious.);
2. Torment witches;
3. Make our flesh strong against temptation; and
4. Purify our souls.

This means that prayer, obviously, is very good, but a) not every-thing is a demon, and b) I do not like 3 and 4. This is a secret. It is a flaw in me, a reason why I must be very careful about the tendency of my birth and why Dad has to try so hard just to get me to listen. Still, it's true, I don't like them. I wish I did.

I told that to the ghost. I was sitting on an overturned crate and when the goosebumps rose on my arms, I turned to where I could see the light go smudgy and I said to it, "I wish I could be good, ghost."

The ghost did not reply.

I think it's scared of me.

Perhaps it sees that dirty, secret thing inside of me that could be a witch if it weren't for the purifying flame of Daddy's prayers.

If it prayed over me, would I disappear? Could I turn cold and insubstantial? Could I never have to feel anything again?

I was sucking on those sorts of thoughts when I slid into sleep. I awoke on the floor, my head on some potatoes, and the air was just the normal sort of chill, and the flood siren was going, and I had scared the ghost away.

The would-be mine is a classic of the last century, not the early part which still clung to the old traditions of the aridocene (she's only seen photos of those houses of plywood and drywall, decomposing like bloated corpses on a floodplain), but the latter half, the Age of Inundations, when would-be warlords constructed arks capable of withstanding any imaginable climate disaster. The impression it gives the witch, even at a distance, is of an embattled, brittle strength. She squeezes her eyes shut and then opens them. Her stomach warbles like the evening birds. Twelve civilians were killed at Charleston before she managed to put those hundred angry haints to rest. The townsfolk wanted to burn her at the stake, and only the threat of the Sisterhood made the town council hurry her out that night. Perhaps she should have taken a rest, hidden herself in the lonely stretch of mangrove forests in the Appalachian sea islands. She isn't sure she's ready for another haunting.

An exterior wall encircles a pair of outbuildings and the main structure, a squat, opaque cylinder with a tall tower growing from the center, its circling windows staring bug-eyed back at them against the western light. The petroleum waste in plastics alone—especially considering what had caused the Inundations in the first place—was monstrous, enough to warrant an invasion with force of any commune or federated polity that attempted to use even half that amount of unrecycled crude today.

It stands on a low rise a few hundred meters outside the floodgates of the commune, a fact that makes the witch raise her eyebrows, but Chief Samuel assures her that it's within their territorial limits.

"Verified by . . ."

"Regional charter. And it's on the SeaCity Oranto blockchain."

That surprises her. The SeaCity Oranto blockchain does not generally deign to verify polities as small or mining operations as depleted as South Potomac's. Either Chief Vai is better connected, or this untapped mine is more valuable than she realized.

Whoever built this house selected their site well: Nearly a century later, and it's still on dry land, a postage-stamp island in a grassy marsh. Its exterior plastics shine palely in the late afternoon light, a milky gray that she imagines must have been dark blue or even black in its heyday. The energy biofilm that once would have regenerated any breach in the walls has long since degraded, so their skiff passes untroubled beneath the crude arch of some long-ago mining attempt. The wake of their passage slops against the laser-cut rubble, left where someone first stacked it all those decades ago.

She turns to Chief Samuel, who meets her eyes with a shifty squint and then digs the pole into the earth. They glide away from the breach.

"My mother told you, no one's been able to mine this place."

She nods peaceably. "What happened back there, though?"

He poles even more energetically and they both lurch forward when the skiff beaches itself at the edge of the rise.

He wipes his forehead. The witch retrieves her work bag from the wet floor of the boat. She waits.

"It happened before I was born."

"What happened?"

"You have to understand, people tell stories. Not even half of them could be true."

"What story do people tell? Understand, Chief. Your commune is paying me well for my services. I did not come to gossip or to document local superstitions for some university project. I came to clear a haint. So, tell me."

He gives her a hard look, then turns his back to her and jumps clear of the water onto the tall grass.

"Just that there were three of them that night. One was Chief Vai's second husband."

"Your father?"

"No . . . my uncle."

Chief Samuel busies himself with tying up the boat, and she gives him his privacy. She can't help but wonder, though. After a nervous moment, he continues. "Vai had prohibited anyone from coming near the old house, but they wanted to trade with a visiting sea merchant who had passes to one of the big rigs."

"So they were going to rob the commune in order to abandon it for a year contract chipping rust on a carbon sequester rig?"

He winces, which is interesting. She slings her bag over her shoulder and splashes into the shallows. *You feel more in the water*, Goldie used to say. *You were birthed there, and Mother Water will take us all back to her bosom one day, sooner than you think.*

"They never made the trade." He starts up the hill.

"Obviously." The mud between her toes is thick with the chemical runoff of this place, an acrid petrol slick. Like everything from the last century, it holds on to things. As an old tar pit clings to the bones of the last age's behemoths, this mud sticks fast to spirits, and only with difficulty and care can be made to spit them out.

"Two of them drowned that night. The water was a meter deep. No storms, no flooding."

"Drunk?"

"My uncle swore they weren't."

They're almost to the base cylinder, a monstrosity of metal and plastics—no organic materials that she can see, except for the crude wooden sign planted in the middle of the path:

Spiritual Contamination Site. Keep Out!

She steps around it and approaches the old keep—because that's what it is, isn't it? Some twenty-first-century disaster fantasy of some twentieth-century reimagining of an earlier, disastrous age—and rests her palms on its darkly mottled surface. Cold as old bones. Lingering tech, or the sign of a deep haint? Chief Samuel flinches and takes an involuntary half step back.

"They were stunned," he says, "by a flash of light. A girl walking on the water."

Her guts twist. "Did she threaten them?"

"Uncle said she didn't even see them. She just opened her mouth and started screaming. They all fainted. Only one of them woke up the next morning."

Not malevolent, most likely. Not fleshed. That was a start. The witch let out a breath like an unspooling ribbon.

"Then show me the door, Chief Samuel. And I will see to your haint."

Sometimes, I am very afraid. I can't tell Dad because he would tell me to read my Oranto Book and pray to the Living Master and the violet light, but I do all of those things and I'm still afraid. Then he might want to pray with me and I already told you that I don't like that.

I'm afraid of the ghost in the cellar. What I mean is, I'm afraid that the ghost isn't a ghost at all, but myself. The witch inside of me. I'm afraid she comes into me at night, when the only sound is the rumble of the inverter rising up through the floorboards, and the fans circulating air through the watchtower. In the dark she creeps out of me and she tells me things I don't want to hear. I close my ears to her but she is inside of me and will not stay silent. I pray and chant and she fades for a while, but my fear of her doesn't. She says, I know what you've been doing. I know that you asked for it. I know that you're evil. I know that it's all your fault.

I ask her, what is my fault? Why are you here? Haven't I cast you out a dozen times?

She says, those are three questions.

I say, answer them! Or leave me alone!

She says, I can't.

Why not?

Because I'm inside you.

Then leave!

I can't.

Why not?

Because you don't want to die.

And that explains why I am so bad, and the seas are rising because of me and women like me, and we are witnessing the end of the world, and only my father and his church can stand against it.

I should want to die to save the world. But the witch tells me that the world will end no matter what we do, that Dad doesn't know, that Dad is wrong, that Dad is—

A witch shall know a fellow witch by her smell. *That's what Goldie* taught her, anyway, in that nasal Old Testament twang she used when giving what she called the "ancient knowledge of our calling."

"Goldie," she told her once, "that's complete horseshit and you know it. You smell like the old 40s you were drinking last night. And there can't be any ancient lore of our calling. We've only existed since the Inundations."

"You think there weren't any of our kind before?" Her voice had that warning note in it, but the witch was young and angry and had been made into what she was by things worse than Goldie.

"Conjure women, you said. Not our kind of witch."

Goldie stuck out a long finger, brown and gnarled as an old tree branch, thick yellow nail at the end like a wood ear fungus, and tapped her on the crown of her head. It hurt like a mallet to her tympanum. The earth made itself known to her through her soft crown, and she was young in her powers.

"You think there was no hoodoo in the world before the ice caps melted? Before Mother Earth shook the big cities into Mother Water?"

"Of course there was, but it wasn't for people."

Goldie sucked her teeth. "You young people think you have all the answers. You think Mother Earth didn't know us before we knew her. You think witching is magic."

"Then what the hell is it?"

Goldie rapped her again with a crack that sent her sprawling, dirt in her mouth, the stars streaming through her head.

"It is revenge, child," Goldie sang through the stars. "It is revenge for what man has done to us, and it smells of wet cunt, and thick blood."

She hasn't thought of that in years. But the mad old witch might have been right about this one because the house stinks of it. Familiar smells, after all, as home to her as the scars on her wrists. She climbs the stairs to the first level, a circular corridor opening onto individual rooms. Most of the doors have been forced open or blown apart, but a large one on the west side is still barred to intrusion, its clouded finish of some late aridocene material showing none of the cracks and mold that mark the floor and outer wall.

She stops before the door and sets down her tools.

"I thought Chief Vai said no one has touched this mine."

"None of us has. Sometimes looters come over from other townships."

She nods slowly, taking in everything that's been left. Prisms still hang on the walls, situated to catch the light every hour of the evening here on the west side. In between them are paintings: pastoral scenes with improbable combinations of tame jungle animals; Aryan saints gazing beatifically at pillars of purple light; a stern-faced man in an oversized business suit of the last century battling a tentacled monster rising from the sea with a horde of fleshed haints crawling beneath her. The art is terrible, but it would fetch a decent price in SeaCity Oranto for its historical interest, at least.

"Must be the haint who keeps them from taking much," she says. But there is something acerbic in her tone.

Samuel looks around nervously, shines his light into the open room nearest to them. "Do you think it's here? Now?"

She raises an eyebrow. "Do you smell that?"

Samuel jolts and leans away from her, into a pair of shutters across from the closed door. They open with a screech, far more easily than he expected, and he overbalances. For a few airless seconds he seesaws on the sill before grabbing onto a rusty hinge. He comes up panting, red-faced, on the right side of the window. He would have had to swim back if he'd fallen; here on the west side the keep borders the marshy water, with a view toward South Potomac.

The witch, who watched this performance unmoving except to squint against the sudden influx of light, opens her pack and removes her tools. The herbs: John the Conqueror, mountain sage, frankincense. The offering: a double-yolked egg, her last of a half-dozen purchased from an old lady in a town five jobs ago who knew precisely what a treasure of a hen she had and priced her fruits accordingly. The grounding: She unfolds her cane, a simple enough device but loaded with amulets that rattle like old bones when she locks out the joints. And last, the workings: a silver reflecting bowl, two candles, one red and one black, and a jar of grave dirt. A witch can make do without the rest, but she parts from her grave dirt when someone else puts her in the ground. *What makes a witch?* Goldie asked her. *The one who broke you, or the one who marked you, killed by your own hand and buried with your own sweat.* Perhaps, she reflects, Goldie was so mean because she always knew how it would end between them. The witch laughs.

Samuel jumps. "Is it here?"

"Probably. Calm down, I haven't called it yet." To be honest, she wasn't sure there was a haint to call—that presence smelled like a witch, and a strange one to stay hidden in a ruin like this.

"Oh, right. Of course." He runs his hands through his thinning hair and forces a smile. "So," he says, "are your parents from around here, too?"

"Third generation."

"Are they both . . . or was one . . . you know . . ."

She sighs. "I don't."

"Caucasian?"

Some things never change. "They were both Black. Capital B. My dad was light-skinned."

"Oh," he says, as though that answered anything at all.

Outside, the wind blows, fast and businesslike, chivvying the clouds on ahead. She takes in a deep lungful and looks sharply to the east, at the same moment that Samuel's shortwave radio echoes up to them from somewhere in the marsh below the window.

The witch cannot make out the words, but the urgent tone is clear enough, as is his mother's gravelly pitch. Samuel jumps as though he's been pinched.

"I think I've got to get that," he says.

"Hurry," she says. "There's a storm coming."

As Samuel splashes beneath the window and the breeze turns wet and chill, the witch sits back on her heels, takes up her cane, and feels for the power of the other. Where is she?

There, beyond the locked door? Could the other witch have a key? The power beneath her vibrates through the metal of her cane and shakes the amulets into a just-audible resonance, a chorus she recognizes, because it is the tonic to her own power's chord. She shivers. A friend, then? But no, Goldie taught her better than that. With greater affinity comes greater danger, and greater damage. Of what damage is she capable, the woman waiting down below?

Or could the other witch not be a woman at all? She has come across a few male and nonbinary conduits, though their power feels different to her. And she doubts they would smell so much of blood.

Samuel lumbers back down the corridor, hampered by his waders, trailing scummy water like a haint from the First Inundations.

"It's a category two, surging down the coast. The floodwalls will close in an hour, and nothing will make them open again before the water goes down."

Purple storm clouds have already dimmed the evening into an early twilight; but it's nearly midwinter and all the sky will be dark soon.

The witch lights the black candle and the red. Their light moves over the hard planes of her face, changing them. She looks like a child, then she looks like a monster.

"Settle down, Chief," she murmurs. "There's no way we'll get back in time on that little dinghy."

He grimaces. "Vai's on her way. She has a speedboat."

The witch reaches for the silver bowl.

"Well? Leave that voodoo shit, you can come back for it later."

She pauses. "You're that worried? This place has withstood greater storms than this."

Samuel's grip tightens around the radio until only his knuckles stand out white in the graying light. "You're gonna stay?"

"Leave if you want."

"Vai isn't paying you to kill yourself."

"That's good, 'cause I wasn't planning to."

The radio in Samuel's hand squawks in Vai's voice. "I'm outside the wall, Sammy. You've got five minutes."

He glances out the window, but they can't see the boat for the outer wall.

"Shit," he says. "Fuck this haint."

She smirks. The phrase, a popular expression from the first Inundations, is so quaint as to be practically archaic.

It does, however, remind the witch that it wasn't the Inundations themselves that brought down these old End-Timer bunkers, but the waves of fleshed haints that came after them. This part of the Atlantic coast doesn't get a fleshed one but once in three years, these days. But there's something old and in pain coming in on that storm breeze, and she doesn't want to be in the path of those decomposing spirits if she can help it. They, like most everything except the kind jaws of the Earth Mother, are not kind to witches.

"Give me ten," she says to him, at last.

"Damn it, didn't you hear? She's waiting!"

The radio buzzes. "Where the fuck are you, Sammy?"

Samuel glares at her, but his shoulders tremble, his palms tip up pleadingly.

The witch reaches out her hand. "Let me speak to her."

The wind is cold enough now for even him to sense it. The shutters crash into their frames and bounce open again. He flinches and throws her the radio.

"Vai, this is Natalia."

"Natalia who?"

"Your witch."

"You don't sound like you're running for your life, witch."

The witch smiles. "We're probably safe enough here, but I would rather get out. I just need ten minutes."

"You have two. And I won't forgive you if you kill my son."

The power below her shifts its register; it moves. Her breath flies from her chest. Samuel, at last, sniffs the air. His movements are slow, his voice slower. "What is that smell?"

"What the fuck is going on in there? Witch, I swear to god I will kill you if that ghost doesn't do it first!"

"I just . . ." the witch gasps with the half breath she can manage. The candles flicker on the mossy walls of the darkened corridor while their shadows caper and dance like an old film on a faulty projector.

". . . didn't want . . ."

The door cracks open behind them. She felt how tightly it was fitted into its frame, and there's no reason for even the wind to budge it now.

The flyaway curls and split ends of her unkempt hair lift into a halo. Samuel groans against the light.

". . . to leave her."

The door is open.

This is a good memory.

Dad and I went walking the perimeter last December. It was a dry day and there was grass waving all the way to South Potomac. We could even see the old river road! Dad took my hand and I didn't mind. I was skipping along in the grass. Real grass! Up to my chest! It tickled me in a nice sort of way. I felt protected and warm.

He was in a good mood, quiet, but not in that expectant hawklike way, more like a regular dad, so I took a chance and asked him about Mom. "Tell me where she is again?"

"She's under the waves."

"But she's not the demon-fleshed?"

His hand grew tighter around mine. I started to pull away but then I remembered my lessons and smiled up at him. He felt so big beside me, big as a wall, and he had hair like a lion, or like Jesus in those pictures from the Oranto book. He glowed like Jesus, too, in the sun, even though Jesus was only a wise teacher and not God like the Christians say. My dad is also a wise teacher and he is very close to God.

"No," he said. "She was spared that fate."

"And when will I see her?"

He lifted me so that I could see straight into his eyes, which were the gray of stormwaters. He says I have his eyes, but I don't think so. My eyes are blue as a calm ocean. My eyes are my own.

"When you are as holy and pure as she was, and you can return to the waters."

I looked over his shoulder, because I did not like to meet his eyes for too long, or smell his breath. "And the floods will cease?"

"The Age of Inundations will end," he said, "and the Enlightenment of God will cleanse the earth."

"All because I went into the water with Mom?"

He moved his head so all I could see were his eyes. I felt as though I were in a storm, even though the day was so bright. I was special just to be his daughter. I was special to walk with him like this. I wished we could walk like this forever, and never do anything else again.

"Because of you," he said to me, "and girls like you, who were cleansed of the taint."

"But I am not a witch, Daddy."

He set me down and turned his back to me. I was relieved and yet so scared.

"And you won't be, Viola," he said. "Let's go back to the house and pray."

That is not a good memory.

You should get out, Ghost. It's not safe here.

It's never been safe.

She becomes aware of the storm first, the howling and the lashing, the groaning of petty human structures at the raging of the earth. Oh, the earth: It is howling, too, harmonizing with the storm like the resonances of her amulets. Infinitely more powerful, though, so that she is grateful that she is a minor witch and incapable of perceiving the full depth of that chorus.

It takes her several minutes to realize that some of those notes of pain come from her own body and not the wracked planet that birthed her. From her bruised throat and not—

What did she dream?

It is as though she went back into her own childhood, the life that opened her head and allowed the earth to come pouring through, but her father was a Black man, old before his time, bitter and belligerent, a devout believer in the Pentecost until the (sadly natural) end of his days.

So it was not her dream, just as the pain is not all her pain, though she resonates with both, how could she help it? And that means—

The witch opens her eyes.

"Vai," she gasps through parched lips. "You bitch."

That woman's dry laugh echoes down the corridor, bouncing and elongated so that she cannot immediately determine its origin. The witch turns her head slowly, as though it is held onto her neck by rusty wire. She squints. The darkness is profound, then interrupted: Lightning spider-webs to the water just past the walls. Thunder blasts her ears a heartbeat after the light jams her pupils, but in those bare fractions of seconds she makes out a great lump to her left, and beyond it, in the window, a figure, drenched, shadowed, crouching like a crow beneath the eaves. How did Vai manage to climb up there, at her age?

"If Sammy's dead, I will kill you before the storm is through."

But then again, the devil clearly gave Vai a good deal for her soul.

"The Sisterhood won't forgive you for that. We take too much from one another not to take care of our own."

That was one of Goldie's lines. Funny how she uses them more, the closer she gets to Goldie's age.

Vai spits. "You're forgotten even among the old Sisters. Too strange, too disconcerting, too broken even for them."

This stings, as only a woman like Vai would know. However little truth there is in the statement—though for fuck's sake, the witch knows there is some—the words burrow deep into her oldest, shame-filled spaces.

But don't forget, you evil harridan with half a soul, she thinks, *that's where my power lies, too.*

She lifts a hand like a dead mackerel on a fishing line (What is wrong with her? Why can't she do anything right? Why is she so fucking weak right now when this madwoman could kill her at any moment? Why didn't she *guess*—) and flops until she knocks over the jar of grave dirt.

It's so wet that what pours out is black sludge, as though from the trench pits of the deepest sequester rigs, cursed to their carbon alloy cores. But that's an even better match for what's in her heart right now, her knowledge of what this woman in the window is, and what she's done to that poor girl, that little witch, all alone in the cellar.

"If your son is dead, then you killed him." She forces herself onto one shoulder with a bolt of pain that sails clear from the crown of her head to her pelvic bone.

"I had nothing to do with—"

Another crash of lightning, this time enough to see Vai straining against the window frame, her teeth bared like a death's head, snarling down at where Samuel lay on his side, one hand flung across his eyes, unmoving.

"You're afraid to go past the threshold, aren't you?" the witch says as she carries the grave dirt back, slow, slow to where Goldie marked her when they first bound themselves as teacher and student.

"You were supposed to banish the demon!"

"But if the demon dies . . ." she says/repeats/remembers—

The grave dust marks the puckered scar above her left breast.

". . . so do you."

She's no major worker, no conjure woman from the old stories Goldie taught her, their ancestors flying out of bondage, far over the ocean. She's just a girl born once and broken, born twice and badly mended. She cannot fly beneath a new moon, or weave the fates—but she sure as shit can call a haint.

"Viola."

Her voice echoes from the old metal and petroleum polymer with a force beyond the meager air in her battered lungs. There is a storm behind her, perhaps the old chief had forgotten that.

"Witch, what the fuck do you think—"

"Viola."

Vai's eyes are wide with sudden fright, whites flashing as more lightning arcs lambent in the western sky.

"Witch, I have a gun and it is aimed right at you. If you don't stop saying . . . that name . . ."

She laughs. "Only a witch could make that gun go off in this storm, and Vai, you and I both know—you are no fucking witch."

Vai raises her arms and pulls the trigger: once, twice. The third time, she screeches like a crow and flings it. The old piece misses the witch, but hits the sodden lump of Samuel, who attests to his continued life with a groan and a lurching movement onto his back.

"Sammy? Sammy, love, can you hear me?"

Samuel scrunches his eyes shut, rocks his head back and forth, murmurs something low-voiced that the witch isn't sure if she recognizes or remembers: a soft but desperate negation.

"Viola!"

She manages to sit up the third time, which is good because the door slams open right where her head used to be. There's no need to catch glimpses of the world past the glare of the lightning anymore; the haint has brought its own. Static electricity crackles over her skin like ants running up and down her arms. She marvels at the sight.

"You could have been a wonder, Chief Vai."

But Vai is still as a gargoyle in the window, her only sign of life a hummingbird pulse against the soft, translucent folds of her neck.

Samuel throws an arm over his eyes.

"My mom . . . no witch . . ." he says.

The witch glances at him curiously, but she turns back to the door, to whatever is making itself known in the threshold that faces the window.

"You can come inside, you know, Chief. It's too late now."

Vai still doesn't move. The witch can't tell if those are tears tracing down her cheeks or water from the storm.

There is a girl in the doorway. She looks like a photo of a child of the last century: petroleum-fabric clothes in garish colors, the metallic glitter of an AR interface over one ear, light brown hair cut into a neat bob.

But she glows.

And her eyes—

How do you make a witch?

There is no sound to her words, but there is pain. Grief, rage, guilt, doubt, disgust, shame.

It hits them like wires whipped up by a storm, lashing, unforgiving. Unbearable to almost anyone—except a witch.

There is a reason why witches are made as they are. A reason why only they can clear the haints, fleshed and unfleshed, that have overrun the earth since the Inundations.

The girl regards the witch with those eyes, black as pitch, betrayed and unforgiving.

Tell me!

The witch coughs until yellow sputum spills onto her hands. She will never get it all out. It is a small injustice among the chorus of greater ones, which the earth itself has animated as it spasms and wracks its way to death. And when it is reborn, badly mended, what will it be?

"A witch makes herself, Viola," she rasps, "by killing the one who broke her, or the one who marked her."

The haint nods slowly. *Did I kill Dad?*

Something—a scream, or laugh, or wailing memory—wants to claw its way out of her throat, but she braces her palms against the puddled floor and pushes it down.

"I don't think so. Otherwise you wouldn't . . ." She takes a sharp breath. She finally registers Vai's broken sobs behind her because of the silence that descends when they stop. Only Samuel speaks now, that soft, pleading negation.

"Ask her," the witch says, and points to the one who left this girl behind.

"Go away!" Vai climbs down from the window, stiff but shockingly limber for someone a little over a hundred years old. The little girl's father had been highly ranked in the Oranto Prophecy movement of the last century, which built the first sea city. Vai must have continued in his footsteps, probably spent time in SeaCity Oranto with their anti-aging treatments. They say those can help you live well into your second century if you get them early.

You're the ghost in the food cellar?

Vai falls to one knee at the onslaught of that terrible voice, but she doesn't collapse. She holds her hands out, palms forward, as though her will alone were enough to make the haint disappear.

"*You're* the ghost! *You're* the witch! I kicked you out years ago! I made sure I was pure!"

The haint takes a step forward. *But I'm not a witch.*

Vai keeps going, as though she hasn't heard. "And then I come back to this demon-cursed town and it turns out you've been here all the time, and you won't even let me mine this awful place, as though you loved it, you monster . . ."

Vai's words give out, overwhelmed by the kind of primal rage the witch wishes she didn't understand.

Why didn't you kill him?

Vai freezes, fists hovering above the floor. She looks up, startled.

"Why would I have killed Daddy? He was a holy man. The best father."

There follows a silence like the hush after a boulder has been pushed off the cliff but before it hits the ground. The girl's black eyes meet Vai's milky blues.

No, the girl says. *No, no, no, no, no—*

"Witch!" Vai screams, "Witch, do your job!"

"Let her in, Vai. It's better that way. Let her in and she won't haunt this place. If I banish her, it'll kill you." *Or,* she thinks but doesn't say, *turn you into something I'll have to kill anyway.*

"Banish her, you fucking useless excuse for a witch! I'll tell the Sisters all about you. You'll never work anywhere on this coast again."

The witch gives a shaky sigh.

"White ladies," she mutters. *Sounding more like Goldie every day,* she thinks, and feeling her old teacher's grave dirt coating her hands, she smiles just a little.

Teeth chattering, she reaches out to touch the girl's ghostly hand. Light enters the witch like an electric charge. The flood of pain is not far behind.

Don't do this, witch, the girl says.

"Why not?"

She'll die. She doesn't understand. She needs me. She thinks Dad is good, but he'll kill her without me.

"She's already lived a long time, Viola. It's okay to be at peace. It's okay to rest." She pauses, coughs out more of the lump in her throat, and says the words: "He'll never hurt you again."

Viola looks up at her, trusting, pleading. The witch will die before she breaks that trust. What her clients never understand is that haints are not the enemies of the living, for all the sea cities tout their foolproof defenses against them. They are simply the forgotten, the betrayed, the left behind.

Most, however, aren't literally a shard broken off the soul of the still-living. The witch can't even imagine the power Vai must have had to be able to cast off Viola and walk away. If she'd made a different choice, if she'd accepted the truth and become a witch, how many souls could she have saved?

But Vai isn't even interested in saving her own.

The witch takes a breath, invokes the resting prayer. "Mother Water, do you—"

Witch?

Her eyes snap open. "Yes, Viola?"

Samuel is awake.

She turns. Samuel has risen to his knees, and he is staring at his mother with an expression she cannot so much interpret as resonate with like an amulet.

Is he really her son?

"I think so," she says, her voice rasping. She isn't sure if she wants a drink or if she wants to throw herself into Mother Water.

Oh. I hoped . . . Oh, witch, why couldn't we have been like you, instead?

It all happens very fast.

Samuel throws himself at Vai. She folds like an old doll; she wasn't expecting it. He gets his hands around her throat and squeezes. His face is a mask of tears, but he says nothing. Even his breath is quieted by the winds singing outside the walls, the abating storm.

The witch keeps hold of Viola's hand until the end.

"Oh, Mother Water," she says, when the haunted light fades, and only she and Samuel are left in darkness. "Oh, Mother Earth, keep them and hold them and forgive us for what we have done to you, and forgive them for what they have done to us."

Samuel rises to his feet, unsteady, wide-eyed as a new colt. "What . . . did I do?"

The witch blinks. "You killed the one who broke you."

She can smell it, the power rising in him: salt water and wet earth. He looks down at his mother's corpse and turns his gaze away. "What now?"

She's never witnessed another witch's making before. "You bury her," she chokes out.

That little girl, those fierce eyes, that deep kindness that a century of self-deception had worn away to avarice and violent indulgence. Like all the others, only the witch will remember her.

"And you keep a little of the dirt."

What is a witch?

I don't know, I don't know, Daddy—

Hush, I'm no one's daddy, let alone yours.

Goldie?

Natalia?

Tell me, Goldie. I don't know, I just don't want to be . . .

That's all you need, child.

What is a witch?

Someone who made the choice.

MET SWALLOW

Cassandra Khaw

She was already dying when I met her. So close to death, in fact, that I could *see* her psychopomp—a hound, black as tar, seeping at the edges— tugging at her sleeve. It was ready to go, but she wasn't.

"Huli jing," she said, naming me as I stood on the river's edge.

"Dead girl," I said politely. "How can I be of help?"

Her almost-corpse burbled with laughter. Water streamed from her gray mouth. Sometimes, when I think back to that day, I suspect she was already dead when she floated up to me, and the only reason she could speak was because of the strength of her spirit. Either way, her pale fingers clenched around the pebbled shore, holding her there—just for a while, just for long enough.

"Take my skin," she said. "Take my life. Take my name. Take my magic. Those were good to me when I could use them, but that time is long past."

"Why give them up to a stranger?"

The hound pulled again and something unraveled from her: a train of matter, like a torn strip of silk, fluttering this way and another though there was no wind, nothing but the stagnant summer swelter.

"*Please.*"

Her death bayed its impatience. There was no more time.

"Yes," I said and spread my jaws to swallow everything she was and could have been.

Her name was Amaranth.

She was eighteen at the time of her death and if she had lived seven more weeks, she would have been nineteen. She was a Cancer, according to astrological charts. She had two sisters, a dead mother. A father whose name I could not pry from her memories, not for love or fear of being discarded in the woods. In the short time she was alive, she'd exorcised houses and relationships, helped a deer-god to its rest, broken a seal-wife from her torture, taught the ivy around a neighbor's house to hold its foundation tightly. She was kind if not always good and, had she lived, she might have become one of those witches that history would not forget.

Except then he killed her.

He—no matter how I excavated, Amaranth's mind persisted in withholding the details of her murder from me. I knew that there had been a man, that there had been trust there, even love, a misplaced certainty he was one of the safe ones. That he held her under the water until she ceased to kick and thrash, but I understood these truths in the abstract, like a story told to me thirdhand. It infuriated me at first. How does one find and punish a killer when there weren't any clues, only the stain of them upon the soil?

But slowly, as I taught myself the trick of being Amaranth, of standing on two legs and speaking in her cadences, of wanting blackberries but only as a compote, jeweled and dark and sweet, I realized it wasn't what she wanted.

All Amaranth wanted was to go home.

So we went home.

It was nearly dusk when I arrived at the house in which Amaranth had lived, the sky an unsettling violet save where the horizon left it blood-ied, bruised to dripping shadow. My feet hurt; human skin wasn't as resilient as paws. Her eldest sister Lucia stood silhouetted in the door-way, a broad figure with a broom in her hands, her leather jacket slicked with gold from the light. She froze at the sight of me, her expression disbelieving.

"Amy?"

I bobbed my head. I was nervous. If she saw through my disguise, there would be no explaining what I was. Amaranth wasn't here to say she had consented, and without her endorsement, I couldn't imagine a defense that could withstand the horror of what I had done.

"I'm home," I said, my voice seeping with a drowned witch's love for her older sister. *I'm home*, sang Amaranth's marrow. *I'm home, I'm home*, echoed her bones as I loped up to the house, crying as if the body's grief was my own. "I'm home. I'm so sorry I scared you. I'm home, I'm home. I'll never—"

"Hush," said Lucia as her arms enfolded me. She held me tight: a promise in the prayer circle of that embrace. Amaranth's—our—my sister wouldn't risk losing me again. She would keep me safe.

"I'm sorry." I said again. I couldn't help myself. I *was* sorry. I was sorry it wasn't Amaranth in Lucia's arms, not really, for all that I was bequeathed. I could wear her skin, put her life on like a scarf, smile like her, sing like she did, but I wasn't Amaranth and even if the delineation was too thin for even light to traverse, *I* would know and the loneliness of that knowledge felt worse than the skinning knife.

"Did he hurt you?" Gently, Lucia pried herself away to hold me at stiff-armed length, her nails digging into my shoulders.

He was someone they knew collectively then: a family friend, a relative, a recent tenant of the enormous house, which I knew from Amaranth's memories contained more rooms than the sisters could use. A house their parents had intended for more: more laughter, more sib-lings, more of everything. Until—

Until—

Amaranth's mind stuttered. Her memories closed to me, like doors locking shut. *So, it's like that then*, I thought to myself. Hauntings all the way down.

"I don't remember." It wasn't a lie.

"It doesn't matter." Lucia's hands traveled my face. She picked and plucked at flyaway strands of my hair, gathered them to tuck behind my ears. I saw in her expression the question she couldn't bring herself to ask.

"You're home," said Lucia, firmly, as if her voice could anchor me to safety. "Whatever else happened, you're home. Nothing else matters."

Except it mattered. Lucia, who knew how to coax storms to conversation and tornados to mumbling sleep, would have done something had Amaranth given her a name to work with.

He killed you, I told the corpse I was puppeting. *Why are you protecting him?*

Whatever was left of Amaranth did not answer, but I was sure it heard me and resented me for my question. I filed my observations away. This would need to be addressed soon. It was one thing for me to occupy someone else's body and another to be inhabiting flesh that protected its murderer. The first was an eccentric, the other was possibly suicidal. If I was going to make this work, if I was going to give Amaranth's sisters (she had a second one I would meet) the pleasure of her natural life span, I would need to prevent her killer from performing an encore.

"I'm sorry I scared you."

Lucia shook her head. I knew from Amaranth's memories that her looks, alone of the three, favored their matrilineal lineage: She had their mother's thick hair, white skin, haughty nose. Her height was their grandfather's. Even without Lucia's boots, she was about six feet two, built like she could hold the sky up all on her own.

"That's in the past. This is now. As long as you're safe now, it'll be okay."

Her smile was vague and I should have questioned its careful softness. However, I was new to being Amaranth and it had been a long time since I had a sister to disappoint me.

Lucia walked me upstairs to Amaranth's bedroom after she had shed her shoes and made sure I wasn't in need of tea or food. I was hungry, of course, but admitting such felt too much like offering my underbelly. Amaranth trusted Lucia but I didn't. Not yet. I would make that mistake later.

"Are you sure?" said Lucia as we stood outside a red door, her hand on its knob. "I could get you a grilled cheese."

I shook my head. "I'm fine."

Amaranth's sister nodded and stepped back. The front door had opened and shut while we were talking, and I could hear, thin as the noise was through two stories' worth of floorboards and faded salmon carpet, the sounds of movement in the kitchen below.

"Fine," she said. Lucia couldn't stop looking behind her, at the wash of orange light spilling up the stairs. "But you let me know."

"I will," I said before going inside Amaranth's bedroom.

I waited with my cheek pressed to the door until the stairs no longer creaked under Lucia's weight. Only when I was sure she was gone did I turn to take in the room I had inherited and the contents it kept. Fairy lights dripped in thick ropes over the walls, filling the room with a sorbety warmth. The artificial candied glow should have unnerved me, but it didn't. There was a window overlooking the woods and a sky roof over the unmade double bed. Books were strewn all over the floor and the knitted covers on the bed, and were piled on the monstrous desk Amaranth had inherited from her great-grandmother. It still smelled of the dead woman: talcum and dried potpourri, cigar smoke and pomade.

I made a circuit of the room, trailing my fingers over each and every item, comparing how they were now to their twins in Amaranth's memory. When I was done, I sat myself on the bed and finally allowed myself to relax. The world was now sable outside the window, moonless and oppressive. The parts of me that were a fox thought longingly of undoing the latches and crawling outside to hunt, but I didn't know what wards

Amaranth's sisters might have put up around the house. It wouldn't do to be discovered so early. Instead, I lay down, my stomach grumbling, and that was when I discovered the journal stashed under Amaranth's pillow.

It was a spiral-bound notepad with a subtly opaline cover, its surfaces mottled with peeling stickers. Nothing special. I turned it over and over in the light, mostly to see how the mother-of-pearl plastic shifted colors but also to check for enchantments. At some point, I became bored of the exercise, and flipped open to a random page. The paper crawled with words and annotations and nestling footnotes. I skimmed the writing: It seemed to be delirious accounts of past meals, poetry interleaved with drier observations, metaphors bumping elbows with precise fact. Nonsensical if thorough, but more important, true.

I ran my tongue over Amaranth's teeth and rolled onto my stomach. Goosebumps rippled over my skin. Hallucinogenic as the writing was, I knew, the way I knew to move Amaranth's lungs and to guide the sway of her walk, that it was completely and irreparably true; all of it, every word. Although how it could be that the writing was actually without embellishment, I could not understand. Humans were dull things with practically embryonic senses. None of it was right and yet, I understood what I read was as true as a death in the river.

My eyes stopped at the last sentence of the page. It had been underlined thrice, each scratch of the pen more forceful than the last. The words had nothing to do with the ones preceding it, which somehow made them more foreboding.

They can't know.

I reread the sentence once more, then the entirety of the journal again, then the stack of paperbacks atop Amaranth's dresser, hoping for insight, but sleep found me first.

I dreamed of a hand twisted in my hair, and of being held facedown in water dark as ink until the air left my lungs and the river poured in to take its place, and it didn't hurt, although it should have.

All I felt was relief.

I woke the next morning choking on Amaranth's death. **By the end, her** killer had given up on the river and wrapped both hands around her throat, squeezing until the small bones there stoved in and broke. I could taste it still, her death: the brackish water, mud between my teeth. For all that Amaranth-the-person had welcomed her end, her body had not, and it hurt both of us to remember what it was like to die.

"Amy?" came Lucia's voice.

I shot a wary look at the door. "I'm awake."

No reason for Lucia to *not* ensorcell the room so she could keep tabs on her sister, not after what had happened, but it made me uneasy anyway, which I liked even less than being scared. Fear was easy. Fear was propulsive. Even if fear didn't always resolve into *safe*, it at least provided direction. Much better than the liminality of this discomfort. I had an image of Lucia crouched outside, and in my mind's eye, there was something coyote-like to her skull under its mourning veil of skin.

"There's breakfast downstairs if you want any." A nervous intake of breath. "You don't have to eat anything—"

She did not have to tell me such. The smell permeated Amaranth's room. Bacon fried so thoroughly it was almost caramelized. Eggs sautéed with peppers and mushrooms from the wood: I could smell their earthiness through the salt and fresh-chopped garlic. There were beans, too, and bread lightly charred in butter and bacon fat, and coffee, hot and bitter and galvanizing. I was a fox more often than I was a person, but all that meant was the promise of breakfast was irresistible to me.

"I'll be there."

I got up and scoured Amaranth's dressers for clothes, picking out what was most shapeless and least likely to expose what I was. As I sifted through her room, it struck me how *young* Amaranth had been. To a fox, no human was old and even the eldest of them often seemed precocious, like children playing at dress-up. I felt an unbearable tenderness toward Amaranth, my heart silted with a sudden grief. Eighteen wasn't anything at all. She deserved more time than that. All the dead girls do.

Done at last, I headed downstairs, though not before a brief stop in the bathroom on the second floor. When I arrived in the kitchen, most of the spread atop the kitchen island was gone, decimated by whoever lived in that immense house. Lucia had a hip leaned against the counter beside the pearly farmer's sink, a mug in her hands. She was with another woman who was paler than she should have been, the color of a corpse kept from the sun; and much too tall, too elongated. Amaranth's memories gave me a name: *Marianne*. This was their other sister, and the sight of her made me wonder if Amaranth's family didn't like staying dead.

"Amy," said Marianne, bobbing her head, regal and indifferent.

I looked over what was left. There was enough, thank god, to make a meal for me. I stumbled toward where I knew the plates to be, but Lucia stopped me with a gesture. Unlike Marianne, her expression was ashen, unsure. The parts of me that were Amaranth tensed with the need to comfort her. She was my sister. She was our everything. She and Marianne were the suns around which Amaranth's life orbited and to see one of them so dimmed was to feel the world die a little.

"Hang on," she said.

I paused obediently. Lucia made me wait as she rummaged through her cabinets, picking through cans of soup and dusty bottles with faded labels, gray Tupperware, and tubs of spices. As she worked, an unexpected pang of resignation scraped at me, sharp as a claw. Whatever Lucia was doing, the body recognized and dreaded.

The light in the kitchen went strange, becoming a deep medicinal orange that I could almost taste. I rolled my shoulders. Had I my fur still, every strand would have been standing on end. It felt like a storm was growing, like woodsmoke warning of a fire streaming from the mountains, like a death of things, like my death come at last after all these eons to beg me home. Now I was scared, but there wasn't anything to do but wait. Running was no option, not with Marianne's bored gaze holding me in place.

While I struggled with my epiphanies, Lucia finished what she had begun, turning to me, still wearing her melancholic expression. In her hand was a blue plate heaped with something that shone wetly in the unnatural light, the gleam of which brought to mind tumbled sea glass from when I had been a kit and not yet wise enough to fear the ocean. The orange began to ebb, leaching away as Lucia set the plate atop the island, her eyes averted. She looked ashamed.

"What's this?" I said.

The celadon plate was scalloped with white patterns, an intricate wreath of graceful bodies transforming between the stages of life, moving from infancy to interment. Pretty if slightly ominous but harmless either way. What had me riveted was its contents: a jellied mess the color of oxblood and the consistency of liver. It smelled halfway familiar, a little like carrion but not enough like that. As I regarded the gleaming, gelatinous mass, cilia unfurled from its borders, waving timidly in the syrupy air.

"What's this?" I said, voice husked, weighed down by Amaranth's despair and Amaranth's need to be good to her sisters.

"Our pain," said Lucia, slightly embarrassedly.

"We eat yours. You eat ours." said Marianne, not embarrassedly at all.

I choked out a laugh. "You're joking."

Marianne stretched—arms rising over her head, a palm cupped over the elbow of the opposite arm—with drowsy grace: She reminded me of sleepwalkers or drowned things, moving like gravity applied slightly less to her than anyone else. She opened her mouth to speak, but what she had to tell me was drowned by a tidal wave of Amaranth's memories.

As if a dam had broken, they rushed over me, a torrent of images, out of order, jumbling together so I could not tell which came first. It didn't matter, of course. They were all the same in the end, all memories of Amaranth trying to eat the pain she was handed, and how it hurt worse than drinking glass.

To be a woman was hard enough. To be a witch was worse. It meant being hunted and the fire if you were caught or, if you were unlucky, a collar around your neck until everything you were bled away into someone else's idea of good. I drowned in Amaranth's knowledge of this, her conviction in her smallness, how nothing of what she did was enough, not in the face of what she and her sisters had dealt with. No matter how much she ate, how she swallowed their anguish, it wouldn't suffice: They would always be in pain. All she could hope for was to blunt their suffering, dull it, give them reprieve until they had to leave again into a world that wanted them gone.

How she loved them. How she admired their resilience, the ease with which they took her pain as their own, never so much as wincing as they did. How sorry she was that she wasn't as strong as them.

I understood at last what led Amaranth's corpse to me, why she hid what she did for as long as she could, and my heart broke under the weight of this truth.

"Amaranth?" Fingers closed around my right shoulder. I couldn't tell which sister had spoken.

I didn't reply. Instead, I began to eat.

It hurt, of course.

Being a fox didn't make it any less terrible.

I lived with the sisters for a decade. For most of those years, Amaranth's siblings upheld their ends of the bargain, and while I was often gorged on their pain, they made sure it was never too much, which was almost as good as not having to carry their hurt at all.

Marianne asked more of me, but she gave more in return. She was like the ocean in her hunger to be held and heard. "Being dead," she said the night I turned twenty-one, the three of us on the porch, drinking mead until I felt half-drowned in honey, "is not easy."

"Really?" I said, enough of a fox still to goad her on.

"Yes, but it isn't worse than being alive," said Marianne and there was a warning in her laugh, in how she perched her hand on my head, fingers splayed and nails dug too deep. *I was hers*, said the gesture. At the time, I had only smiled. What else was there to do?

As for Lucia, I saw less and less of her after that first morning save when we had celebrations so large our guests spilled out of our doors and everyone stayed late no matter how cold the night grew. She would roam between them, her cheeks sheened with their joy, their gratitude for her. By the time the last guest went home, Lucia would be effulgent, her namesake incarnated, phosphor leaking from her hands onto the floors, the wood mottled with a satiny brilliance for days to come.

Neither of them asked me much about what had happened in those weeks when Amaranth had been alone in the woods. Back then, I imagined it was shame. Shame for not having been there or being there enough. Amaranth's memories refused me any account of the three squabbling, but I was raised in a litter of eight and even animals feuded. I was unconvinced of their alleged harmoniousness, not that I had anyone to argue this with. What little there was of Amaranth's spirit had since rotted to silence, and I was alone in her corpse, left to pick through her half-lives and least favorite truths.

Of her murderer, there was no sign. Neither Marianne nor Lucia brought any men to our home and when they did, it was to repair some corner of the house or another, work they performed with nervy efficiency, like miners in a crumbling shaft. I went unaddressed save for when it was proper to extend greetings. No one touched me. No one so much as looked twice. There were rumors about us gusting through the nearby town and though none were grisly enough to overshadow our utility or the bright lure of Lucia's many fetes, they were nonetheless unsettling enough to incite not fear but something like its well-shod cousin.

I thought occasionally of finding him. He wasn't dead. He still isn't—not as dead as I'd like, at any rate. If I focus, I can feel how he pulled at Amaranth's bones, particularly in the late spring when the rooftops wore the last snow like a crown of old scars, this ineffable awareness of him, urging us into the night, forward, forward until we found him again and could break his neck in our hands. But I didn't. The thought of Amaranth's grieving sisters looking for her through the dark outweighed any impulse for vengeance.

Looking back, I don't know if I *enjoyed* being Amaranth. I didn't like being a receptacle for her sisters' pain, and I liked even less how with every year that passed, I forgot more and more about what it meant to be a fox. For years, I would wake puzzled by why a dream of a hare's belly opened like a mouth would leave my own watering before I could remind myself what I was. There was a kind of death in that, one slower than the water, and were it not for Lucia, it might have been mine.

A week before Amaranth's body turned twenty-nine, Lucia came to me while I was in the garden. The hostas were the first to warn me, their voices a gush of molasses, startling me from my work. I looked up from where I'd been weaving the ivy through a trellis, having at last coaxed it away from the foundations of the house. Amaranth's garden did not love me at first. They knew me for what I was, perspicacious in the way green things often are, but I worked to earn their trust, and they gave it to me after three years of tithing them the blood from Amaranth's hands.

"What do you want?" I said, shucking my great yellow gardener's gloves.

I did not rise. I sat and watched her as did the garden, wary. Lucia was in a button-down flannel shirt, its sleeves rolled up to her elbows, and only one half of it tucked into wide denim jeans. Her face was clean of makeup, her long hair uncombed but prettily so: She looked approachable, like someone fresh from a restorative nap if not for the rictused smile. Carefully, like my gilding of human skin was see-through and the fox was bare to the world, Lucia crouched about a foot away from where I sat with my ivy.

"To talk," she said haltingly. "I have a confession."

At the word *confession*, the air quieted.

"Yes?" I said.

"It was my fault," said Lucia, without context, without emotion, and she could have been talking about any sum of sins, but I knew, I *knew* with a jolting miserable immediacy what she meant.

I said nothing. The air, which had been unseasonably warm for this stage of the year, lost its pleasantness, becoming cold enough that my teeth chattered. It took me a minute to understand the temperature hadn't changed; this was adrenaline and no small amount of anger.

Lucia dropped her gaze, two spots of color deepening the pallor of her cheeks. The red spread, wandering over her face, blotching her throat. I watched her pulse hammer against the fragile skin there. Lucia wasn't old, but she would be soon. In a few years, those minute lines would become deep tributaries, and it was cruel but I wanted badly for her to be afraid when that day arrived. When it was clear I wouldn't speak, she talked for us.

"He said he would be my patron," said Lucia. The garden flattened her voice, absorbed any resonance it had. "I'd tried for so long, you know. I courted them all but no one cared. What's a witch without a little god of her own?"

She chuckled dully to herself.

"You had your plants. Marianne had the moon. I wasn't complete. I wanted—I needed someone there, some god to listen. I felt like I was limping through the world. It was awful."

"Awful," I repeated, rolling the word in my mouth like it was an ice chip.

"Yes," said Lucia, light returning to the face Amaranth had loved so much she begged a fox to don her corpse. "But then he said yes, and I gave myself to him. I was so happy."

Reflexively, I closed a hand around my throat. Had it been her god that killed Amaranth? *No*, I thought, discarding the thought as quickly as it arose. I'd have been able to tell. No deity is ever discreet. I'd have smelled the god on her corpse, the strange, sugared attar they all seemed to exude.

Was it Lucia then who had held Amaranth under the water?

I looked her over. Whatever else Lucia was, she was transparent. There was guilt in her bearing, in how she gathered her limbs close, cocooning herself in her arms as she set her chin on bony knees; the slope of her expression and the smile that was now correcting itself to a grimace, but wasn't a murderer's guilt, no.

"Why is it your fault then?"

"I forgot about you," said Lucia and to her credit, it seemed to hurt her to say. "I knew something was wrong. I saw it. I remember you telling me that something was wrong. But I was sure you'd be alright. You were strong."

Her brow ridged with thought.

"You were *so* strong," said Lucia. "I was so sure it'd be alright, so I turned my attention to the god because the god—he wanted so much. Then you vanished, and I worried something had happened. I almost went looking for you—"

"But you didn't," I said.

She nodded.

"There were other things. And I was sure you would be alright. It wasn't the first time you had disappeared. I had other priorities—"

"Priorities more important than your sister?"

"You were so unhappy," said Lucia, and it was an answer even though it wasn't, and I could tell the garden hated her response, too, could feel the rosebush fatten with thorns, could hear the tomato plants vow to wither their fruit so Lucia could never enjoy them again. I bit the inside of a cheek until my mouth warmed with blood. The initial blast of adrenaline calmed to something else: disgust, I realized after a moment.

"I didn't know what to do with your unhappiness. No matter how much of it I ate, there was more. There was always more. I wanted to focus on something else, something that wasn't your grief at the world. When you came back, I promised myself I would do better. I would try harder. But there were so many other things happening. And I was—"

"Tired," we said together, her voice ashamed, mine aghast.

"You were tired," I said, raising my voice when Lucia tried to speak again, to refute whatever she heard in my tone. The horror of what she had admitted percolated through me. I had thought it was a bargain with a god, Amaranth forfeited to ambition. I had wondered if it was love or resentment, something potent, something you could fold into a story and make it make sense, but it wasn't any of that.

Amaranth was just *forgotten*.

"Did Marianne feel the same?" I said, no longer caring to hide. Amaranth's voice, its diction flaked away, showing the fox at the shining bone.

Amaranth's magic woke. I'd been Amaranth long enough now for it to answer to me, to stir like a hound alerted by its master's displeasure or by the long bellowing call of the hunting horn. It tensed, eager to be set loose. It was the winter and the woods, and it wanted what I did because it loved me now, maybe better than it had ever loved Amaranth because I was as wild as it was. My vision dimmed to underwater colors: teal and abyssal emerald, blues so dark they might as well be black, and ultramarines like the gleaming surface of the ocean.

I pushed it down as Lucia flashed me a bewildered smile, beautiful in its glassiness, beautiful because of how breakable it was. I saw the gleam of her god in her, a gold bright as a newborn sun.

"What? What are you talking about?"

If I said anything else, I knew Lucia would shatter and I wasn't Amaranth but I was Amaranth enough to know my heart would crack in half if hers broke. There was a way back from this, but I was tired now too and I was done being used.

"Did Marianne feel the same? Was she just as bored with Amaranth's pain?"

"Amy, you're scaring me."

"I'm not her," I said giddily, Amaranth's magic spilling everywhere, the grass rising to encircle Lucia's ankles. "I'm not. I was never her. She was dead, you know."

Lucia, who had been fighting the garden with growing panic, stopped dead. I laughed in her face, a vixen's shriek.

"She died. She was killed. She went out there into the woods and someone found her and she drowned."

"But you're right *here*. I don't understand."

"Only because Amaranth felt so guilty about it all, guilty enough that she begged a fox to crawl inside her skin and pretend to be her so you wouldn't be sad. She was so afraid you would be hurt and she is dead and now I find out you could have stopped this if you hadn't been trying to take *a vacation from her pain*?"

Lucia said nothing.

"But you know what?" I said, savoring the colloquialism to follow, the sharp pleasure of Amaranth's favorite phrase. "Fuck *that*."

I loosed the flesh at my collar and unbuttoned myself from Amaranth's corpse as the garden held Lucia to the earth. Anywhere else in the house and Lucia might have been able to break free, but this was Amaranth's spot and besides, the garden was furious. Lucia screamed as I sloughed muscle and skin and miles of offal; she screamed as I birthed myself from Amaranth's ribs, slick with blood and red as a heart, nuzzling out from between her bones.

When I was done, I went over to Lucia, who'd stopped screaming and only gawked at me with the shell-shocked expression of a fawn with its belly suddenly opened.

"I hope you live forever and I hope you remember this always."

Then I licked the tip of her nose before vanishing into the undergrowth.

THE NINE JARS OF NUKULU

Tobi Ogundiran

Sura could not say when she first dreamed of the man. It might have been a season ago, or three moons past, but he kept returning to her dreams. No sooner would she lay down to sleep than she would find herself beneath a grove of palm trees, the golden sand stretched out in all directions as far as she could see, a great shimmering oasis before her. And there he would be, on the other side of the oasis, waiting for her. What was most odd was his reflection in the water: that of a huge black panther resting on its haunches, eyes burning like twin suns.

Her father, Nukulu, frowned when she told him of this. "A panther, you say?"

"Yes."

"And what does this man do, in these dreams? Does he approach you? Does he speak to you?"

"No." He never approached, never spoke to her. Just stood there, watching her. "What does it mean?"

"I cannot say. But it is a bad omen." And he snapped his fingers to ward off evil. "I will bring you a potion that will give you dreamless sleep."

In truth, Sura found herself fascinated, and wished the man with the panther reflection would speak to her, but her father knew best.

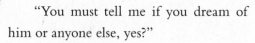

"You must tell me if you dream of him or anyone else, yes?"

"Yes, Father."

He smiled, and Sura snuggled closer to him as they strolled through the garden. Behind them, her father's viziers trailed at a respectable distance. The evening air was pregnant with the scent of citrus and overripe dates, which meant that harvest season was in full bloom. At the end of the walkway, fireflies winked about the statue of her mother, so that the long-dead queen seemed briefly alive, garlanded in ethereal light.

"I must go away," said Nukulu.

"So soon?" He had only just got back. Sura missed him when he wasn't here. She missed the long nights they often spent laughing or playing chess; she missed their philosophical talks and the pride in his eyes whenever she countered his postulations with her own arguments. He often brought her souvenirs from his jaunts, pieces of far-off kingdoms that gave her glimpses into cultures she would never see. The palace was a shrine to the spoils of war. Persian rugs, bronze busts, and even a massive twenty-one-stringed lute-harp from the western Niger empire. "Do you have to go?"

Nukulu touched her chin. "There are always fires to put out. That is my burden. But this shouldn't take long. Now, will you give me something to remember you by? A good-luck charm?"

Sura reached into her pockets and withdrew her token: a small piece of her hair that she'd braided into a bracelet. Nukulu smiled and tied it around his wrist.

He often asked for pieces of her; hair, nails, once a vial of her blood. She in turn kept pieces of him: in truth just one piece; a gold bracelet that she wore around her wrist, and had never taken off since she was a child.

"You are so very precious to me. You must know that."

"I do, Father."

He kissed her cheek and swept from the garden, his viziers scrambling after him.

Sura was just settling in her bed to sleep when the knock came. She sighed, wondering who would bother her at this hour. The knock came again, two raps: light but firm. With a groan Sura threw off the covers and called, "Come!"

Shaffa came in bearing a tray. "The potion, princess," he whispered. "For your dreams."

Shaffa was her father's most trusted advisor. He was also Master of Poisons, with a formidable knowledge of every potion, tincture, or draught across the continent. A lizard of a man, he had revolting wet eyes and a soft voice that made Sura's skin crawl. As a child she cried whenever she had cause to be in his presence, and as a young woman she actively avoided him. She was surprised to see him now, because she could have sworn she saw him ride off with her father and his host at dawn. Nukulu must have been more worried about her dreams than he let on.

"Thank you," she said. "Leave it on the table."

He hesitated. "I am afraid I must see you drink it."

Sura frowned. "I am not some child who wouldn't take her medicine. Leave it on the table and I *will* drink it."

Shaffa did not move. He stood bearing the tray, the candlelight playing across his face so that it seemed his skin rippled. He looked more lizard than man in that moment; black, unblinking eyes boring into her.

Sura slid quietly out of bed and toward him. She emptied the jug into the cup and downed it in one gulp. "Happy?" she said when she placed the cup back on the tray.

"Thank you, princess." Shaffa bowed ever so slightly. "Good night."

And he stalked silently from the chamber.

Sura waited ten heartbeats, then put a finger down her throat. The draught rushed back up, tangy with her stomach's acid. She grabbed a fresh collection cloth and puked into it, the draught bright as moon-blood. No one would look twice at it, not even Shaffa. She folded the cloth and stowed it away with her dirty laundry.

Contented, she climbed back into bed and settled into sleep's dark embrace.

The man was waiting for her.

"Hello," Sura called. "Who are you? What do you want?"

If he heard her—and she was sure he heard her—he gave no reply. Her voice carried across the glassy oasis and washed away.

He moved.

One moment he stood at the other end, the next he was racing over the oasis, bounding across it as though it were hard ground and not water. Sura stumbled backward, gawping as the man advanced. In the water the panther matched his every stride. The man vanished a few feet from her just as the great cat leaped up—*out*—of the water and closed its jaws around her neck.

Sura screamed, scrabbling, beating at the beast, but it was strong. Too strong. It plucked her off her feet and pulled her into the water.

She waited for pain, for the sting of canines as the beast ripped out her throat. But it never came. Then it occurred to her that the panther was trying to drown her, and she waited for the crushing weight of water eroding her lungs and brain, but that too never came. And then the pressure was gone, and she found herself splashing out of the oasis, heaving as she clutched at her neck. She was whole. She was surprisingly whole.

"By . . . the . . . stars," she gasped.

That's when she saw them. There were fifty, sixty, a hundred people, stepping out from the palm trees. And at the head, the man. She could see him clearly now. He looked ordinary. He looked no more than a man. But he wasn't.

"You," Sura gasped, edging backward into the water. "You're the panther. You tried to kill me."

"I wanted you to see."

"See what?" She looked around at them. "Who are you people? Are you . . . are you all animals?"

"We are n'yangi," he said. "Soul of man and sacred beast. As are you."

Sura laughed, in spite of herself. "I'm not."

"Look in the water."

She looked. And in the rippling surface, where her reflection should be, was a great bird. It was easily the most beautiful creature she had ever seen, its yellow and orange plumes catching in the light, so that they looked like flames. The bird turned amber eyes on Sura, regarding her coolly. "What in the . . . ?" She breathed, then shook her head. "No. I'm dreaming."

"Yes," said the man. "But that does not make this any less real."

Sura tore her gaze from her reflection and looked up at him. "Who *are* you?"

"My name is Thoki, and we"—he gestured at the others—"are your family."

"My family?"

"We are your mother's family."

Sura's mother had come from a tribe in the far south who had all been killed many seasons ago by the plague. Indira, Sura's mother, had escaped only because she had eloped three moons before with her father. Her mother's family were many seasons dead. That was how Sura knew he was lying.

She took a step backward. Hadn't Nukulu told her of his enemies, that they were numerous and crafty? Hadn't he warned that they would go to any lengths to get at him? It was why he kept her in the palace, out of sight and heavily guarded. And yet here she was, readily come to them. Fool, she was a fool.

"I want to wake up," said Sura. "Let me go."

"Wait!" He cried. "Please listen. You are in danger—"

Sura turned and splashed into the water. The muddy bed sucked at her feet and she fell—

—startling awake in her own bed, drenched in sweat, moonlight streaming through the high windows.

In the days that followed, Sura fell into a rhythm: crockery painting in the morning, chess at noon, long walks in the gardens in the evening. She put the n'yangi and their lies far from her mind, and every evening just before bed, she drank her potion that allowed her dreamless sleep.

And for a time, all was well.

She first saw the ravens in the garden. Sometimes there were two, sometimes three, but every time she stopped to look around her, there they would be—hanging in the trees, nesting on her window— watching her. Sura panicked. They had to be the n'yangi. Now that they could not hunt her dreams had they decided to show themselves? When she complained to Shaffa, he merely looked at her with his lizard eyes and assured her that he had not seen any suspicious ravens. So she took to hiding indoors, her windows closed from their prying eyes. More and more she wished her father were here, so she could confide in him.

One evening just before she retired to sleep, Sura sat in front of her mirror, trying to untangle her hair from her bracelet. She had been unraveling her plait and somehow loose hair had knotted around the bracelet. She cursed, trying to twist it free, but it was wound tight. She was loath to cut her own hair, so she slid the bracelet from her wrist.

Her hands vanished. She blinked, staring at them, refusing to believe what she was seeing. But there they were, stumps at the ends of her wrists where it looked like someone had chopped off her hands.

She screamed, then. From shock, from disbelief.

The room swayed even as her vision swam, and she toppled off her chair, falling, falling—

She was a child again, of twelve, thirteen seasons, strapped to a table. Her heart pounded against her rib cage, even as her chest heaved with fright. Sura craned around the room and her eyes fell on Nukulu as he approached her.

"Father?" she called. "Father, please . . ." She knew she should trust him.

He would never hurt her. But that was hard to believe with that wicked knife in his hands.

Nukulu looked sad, almost apprehensive. *"You know how I have enemies?"*

"Y-yes."

"And how I must do everything to protect myself?"

"Yes, but—"

He stroked her forehead. "You won't remember any of this, it'll be like it never happened. And what you don't know can't hurt you. Now sing. Sing our song."

Sura sang, her voice high and warbling. She sang, tears leaking down her cheeks. Her song soon turned to screams of agony as her father hacked at her wrist. Sura twisted, struggling against the bonds, but they held fast, held her in place as he chopped and chopped and chopped.

Sura saw her white bones, smeared with her blood. She saw her father open his own skin and remove the bones of his hand, throwing them into a crucible. And then, slowly, he took up her bones and took them into himself.

Sura came to, shuddering, the cold hard floor pressed against her cheek. She pushed herself to her knees, screaming anew when she saw her stumps. They were hideous things, and she didn't want to look at them. She cast around for the bracelet, then realized it was still caught in her hair. She thrust her stump into it and let out a sob of relief when her hands reappeared. Reaching for her scissors, she cut the knot of hair entangled in her bracelet, then knelt there, staring at her hands in shock and disbelief.

Nukulu had cut off her hands and made her forget. But why? Why would he do that? The bracelet was providing her with the false hands. But also repressing her memories of what had happened. And she couldn't remember *why* exactly but in all these seasons she had never taken it off. Had she taken it off she would have known. But now she knew. She knew her bones were in her father's hands, and he had made her forget, and no matter how she turned it over in her mind, there was no justifiable explanation for that.

You are in danger.

When Shaffa came that night Sura pretended to drink the potion. Then she clambered into bed and cried herself to sleep.

High up in the stone walls, in the black of a crack, three ravens watched her.

"He cut off my hands," said Sura to Thoki once she found him at the oasis. "He took . . . he took my bones!"

Thoki looked crestfallen. "We feared he might have done that."

"Why?"

"So he can steal your spirit, that which makes you n'yangi."

"But what does he need it for? He has all that power."

Thoki gave a sad smile. "Power is never enough, particularly when it is not yours. Come. To understand Nukulu, you must know how he came to be among us. He came to us as a boy, scared, wounded, and fiercely determined . . ."

In those days when the world was young, a boy sat in the desert, yoked to a caravan.

He peered out through the slats of his cage, burning with anger at the memory of his perished family. Anyone else would have prayed to a god to spare him, to strike down the raiders with fire and brimstone. But the boy had long ceased to believe in a god who'd allow his family to perish, who'd allow him to be taken captive. He knew, in that moment, that he was alone. There were no gods. There was only him, and his will.

And so he gnawed at his bonds. Like a rat he worried all night at the piece of camel-hair rope that bound him, until his teeth ached, and his gums bled, and the knot unraveled. He could have slipped free, broken from the camp, and set out into the night—the raiders, in their arrogance, never kept watch. But the screams of his family still filled his ears, and he decided to have his revenge. So he moved, a spirit in the desert night, and slit the throats of his captors. Three of them he slew until he happened by the chief raider, stumbling back from a midnight piss. The man took one look at the boy—free, bathed in blood—and rage curdled his features.

Before long the boy was strung up, eight machetes angled at him for a ritual execution. He feared then. In that moment he was naught but a little boy, and he wanted his mother. He closed his eyes and waited for death.

It never came.

What he heard were screams. They rent the air, high and bloodcurdling. The screams of grown men, cut short. The boy opened his eyes to see a shape flitting through the dark, and he heard the unmistakable sound of tearing flesh, and snapping bone, and he smelt the copper tang of hot, fresh blood, sharp in the air. When the sounds died, he saw a beast of the wild, the largest hyena he had ever seen, stalk out of the darkness and fix him with its burning yellow eyes.

The boy looked from the hyena to its shadow and back. The shadow was not that of a beast but that of a crouching girl. And he knew, then, that this was no ordinary hyena.

"Who are you?" he asked. But she turned and fled.

He went after her, racing through the sands, but she soon vanished into the night. Still, he followed her tracks, followed them until night began to bleed from the sky, until the wind washed away her tracks, until the sun rose to boil the sweat from his skin, and he collapsed from exhaustion.

She found him and carried him back to her home. The boy awoke to find himself in the company of n'yangi, berating the girl, Indira, for bringing him. The elders wanted him gone, but he had seen them, seen what they could do, and, never wanting to feel powerless again, wished to be among their number. Nukulu made his case, and Indira, much taken with him, swore to be responsible for him. After much thought and deliberation, the elders reluctantly welcomed him into the tribe.

Nukulu grew. He flourished. He bloomed. He learned the ways of the n'yangi. He learned to wake up at dawn and collect water in leaves and pods. He learned to blend into the desert and hide in plain sight. All these things he learned, but what he most wanted eluded him—how to change into a ferocious beast.

His friendship with Indira bloomed into romance, and soon they were wed. On their wedding night, he asked her the secret behind the changing:

"It is not something that is learned," she told him. "You have to be born of the oasis."

"How can I be born of the oasis?"

"Shut up and make love to me," she said, leaning in to kiss him.

"Indira, I don't want to ever be made to feel powerless again," he told her. "I want to learn to defend myself."

"And learn you will, just not as n'yangi."

He asked Indira for a second time, as he held their newborn babe in his arms. "Tell me how to be born of the oasis," he said. "I want to be able to defend my daughter."

Indira laughed. "What could she possibly fear, when she has the whole tribe to protect her?"

And she must have seen the look in his eyes, for she touched his face and said, "I do not care what you are. I love you with the strength of the oasis."

Nukulu was not convinced. "I feel I am not man enough. I am not one of you."

It was true. Hadn't people called him osha—an ordinary man, without the spirit of a sacred beast? Hadn't Kobi, who'd wanted Indira for himself, made jest of him?

By now Nukulu had learned that Indira would not readily divulge her secrets. So he plied her with sweet wine, and dulled her senses, so that the third time he asked her, the truth came tumbling from her lips:

"There is a way," said Indira finally, "for you to take a spirit animal. It has not been done in a long time because it is an abomination, done only to those who must be executed, but whose spirit animal is so rare that it must not be wasted. You . . . take their bones into your body."

Nukulu immediately thought of Kobi, who had looked upon his wife with covetous eyes, who had called him osha. He went to him while he slept.

It is a coward who attacks a sleeping man; Kobi stood no chance, and with two blows to the head, he departed to dine with the ancestors. Nukulu went to work. He savaged Kobi's lifeless body, claiming the long bones of his legs and the flat bones of his hips. He took everything until he was whole. And he felt the power come into him, and he transformed into a great serpent. He ate Kobi's flesh, then packed his own bones into a sack and returned to the tribe.

When Indira saw him, she realized what he had done, and before she could rouse the tribe, Nukulu transformed and stung her. As she lay there paralyzed, petrified, *alive*, he carved her bones from her flesh, and took them into himself.

Now he was Serpent and Hyena.

Nukulu killed many n'yangi, taking their bones, their spirit animal, so that he became a wicked amalgamation of spirit animals. An aberration. A witch.

The n'yangi were no match for him. They fled into the sacred oasis where Nukulu, who was not born of the oasis, could never enter.

And so he took his bones, and took his daughter, and went into the world.

Sura stared, not really seeing anything. "Father . . . he killed my mother?"

She didn't want to believe it, that the man she loved with all her heart was a monster. And yet, hadn't he cut off her hands and feet? Hadn't he bound her with his magic so she would never know?

She looked up at the n'yangi. Her family. Forced into hiding because of her father's greed.

"I want to make him suffer," she said. "How can I make him suffer?"

"The only way to destroy him," said Thoki, "is to find his bones—his true bones—and burn them."

"Where are they?"

"Before he left, he stole nine jars from the shrine and put them in there."

"Nine jars?" asked Sura as she rose to her feet.

"Yes. But it has been many seasons, and we cannot say if he still has these jars, or where he keeps them."

But Sura did. She knew, because she had seen them.

It was still dark when Sura awoke. She swung immediately out of bed, throwing on a nightdress. She plucked a torch from its sconce and slipped out of her room.

Soon she was in the garden, the heady scent of fig and date palms, avocado and overripe peach rife in the air. The desert chill bit into her skin but she barely felt it. Her heart thumped in her chest, her blood roared in her ears. Now and then she cast a glance over her shoulder, half expecting to see a guard, or the ever-lurking Shaffa, step out of the shadows. How would she explain what she was doing, why she was about at this hour of spirits? She shook the thought from her mind. She *was* a princess; no part of the palace was prohibited to her, much less the garden where she'd spent countless hours as a child.

Her mother's statue appeared before her. The likeness was uncanny. Sura had looked in the mirror as she entered womanhood and seen that face staring back at her. Indira stood with arms outstretched in an empty fountain bowl, her torso twisted lithely as she twirled on one foot. Her unseeing eyes gazed out into the night, and her lips stretched in a smile. She looked frozen in time, as though she were not carved from limestone, as if with the slightest breath of wind, she might resume her dance.

Encircling the fountain bowl were nine bronze jars. They were massive, beautiful things, etched with what Sura now understood were runes, protective spells. Sura had thought the jars simple ornamental objects, but now she knew better. But why would her father put them here of all places? Had he, in some twisted sense of devotion, placed the one thing that could destroy him at the altar of his love?

Sura knelt at the fountain's edge, reached for the first jar, and nearly toppled headfirst into the fountain as her hands passed through the jar.

"What—?" she whispered, uncomprehending. She reached again for the jar, and it dissolved like smoke only to re-form around her hand once it passed through.

Sura stared, dumbfounded. It would seem the nine jars of Nukulu did not exist. But she had touched the jars before, *felt* them. The only way they weren't real now was if . . .

"I was hoping you wouldn't do that," said a voice behind her.

Sura whipped around to find Nukulu standing five strides from her, hands clasped behind his back. "Father," she gasped, scrambling to her feet. "I wasn't—where did you come from?"

Nukulu did not immediately answer her. He was staring at the statue of her mother. "She was always so beautiful," he said softly, "Indira."

Sura took a step backward, her mind racing. He should be miles away, far beyond the mountains that bordered the country. And yet, here he was.

"You said she died in childbirth. But that's not true, is it? *You* killed her!"

Something flashed across Nukulu's features. It could have been pain. "I didn't want to. I . . . had no choice."

"There is always a choice. You were greedy. You took what was not yours and could not face up to the consequences. What did you expect her to do?"

"Love me. Accept me. What is the point of love if it is conditional? She was meant to stand by me no matter what! But in the end . . ." He closed his eyes, taking a deep breath. "Did you come here to kill me? Were you seeking my bones?"

Sura did not dare utter a word. He had killed her mother when he thought she betrayed him. Who was to say he wouldn't do the same to her?

Nukulu stretched out a hand. "Come. Let us leave this place. It will be like it all never happened."

She had heard those words before, and they did not hold the comfort they once did.

"You'll make me forget again, won't you?" she spat. "All this time I've been your prisoner, your docile sheep daughter, here to serve your needs. You don't love me; you've never loved anyone in your life."

"That is not true—"

"You're not capable of love."

"*You* are most dear to me."

"You cut off my hands!" Sura cried. She ripped off the bracelet and waved her ugly stumps in the air. "You took my bones, then you made me forget. Why? What manner of love is that—?"

Sura cried out as her stumps alighted with pain. Nukulu started toward her, his face awash with concern.

"Get away from me!" she shrieked. "You miserable *osha!*"

That struck a nerve. Nukulu's expression, which had been entreating, imploring, the harmless face of a father she'd known and loved all these years, changed; rage drew like a curtain across his features.

And it terrified her.

"Just like your mother," he said quietly. "You won't love me for me."

Sura dropped to her knees, clutching her stumps to her chest. The pain was unbearable. Oh, so unbearable.

"I could have killed you, taken *all* your bones."

And then she saw it. At first she thought it a hallucination brought on by pain, but it wasn't. Her arms were growing longer, sprouting feathers, until they were no longer arms but wings. The wings of a great bird covered in red and orange plumes.

She knelt there, staring in wonderment at her wings, turning them over. They were real. No longer held in thrall by her father's bracelet, she was becoming the phoenix.

Nukulu saw it too and he transformed. One moment he was just a man before her, the next he *exploded* into a cloud of birds: ravens swirling about, cawing and flapping as if shaken free of their roost.

Then they came at her.

Sura fled. She dived around the fountain, racing for the trees. But she was mid-transformation, and her legs were no longer legs. She tripped on clumsy bird feet and toppled to the ground, flapping desperately.

The ravens swarmed her. Hundreds—*thousands*—of birds, pecking at her, ripping out her quills, tearing at her flesh. Sura screamed, trying to shield her face, trying to shield her eyes, but the birds only tore into her with renewed fervor. How foolish she was to think she could stop her father. He, who had killed countless n'yangi before her, and forced the rest into hiding. How foolish to think he'd leave the one thing that could destroy him unguarded. He had been watching her all this time.

A terrible sound rent the night air; a screech, multiplied through the throats of a thousand birds. The attacks ceased and Sura lay there, whimpering, wondering what had caused them to stop their attack. She cracked open her eyes.

The garden teemed with animals. Lions and hyenas and jackals and wild dogs, flitting through the trees as they snatched ravens from the air and ground them between feral teeth—all the n'yangi had come out of hiding to battle her father at last.

Sura tried to drag herself into the trees, away from the chaos of battle. She could see her bones peeking through her flesh, her feathers bloody and lying in tatters. She was dying.

Nukulu was now a great black serpent, coiled around the n'yangi, who screamed in agony as he crushed them.

Her wing touched something solid. Sura turned to see what it was and came face-to-face with her mother's blank gaze. She did not understand. Why was her mother's statue lying in the underbrush, as though hastily hidden? She looked from this statue, back to the one in the fountain, and understanding slowly came to her.

Glamour worked only if one did not know what to look for. And as Sura turned back to the fountain, the scales lifted from her eyes, and she saw very clearly the yellowed bones of her father, arranged upright into a dancing figure.

Sura laughed. He *had* been watching her, and in his haste, he had come here to hide his bones. She dragged herself over the cobbled stones, groaning as each errant movement sent a stab of pain coursing through her body. She felt as though she would pass out from the pain. But still she dragged herself into the fountain bowl and curled herself around his bones.

It was surprisingly easy, claiming herself. She was a woman and she was a phoenix. For the first and last time, she called on the phoenix.

"Daughter!" Nukulu had transformed back into a man, his eyes wild with something she never thought to see: fear. "Please!"

The flames engulfed her, and the last thing she heard was him screaming.

IN A CABIN, IN A WOOD

Kelly Robson

In 1971, the Academy Awards nominees for Best
Picture were *Patton, Airport, Five Easy Pieces,*
*M*A*S*H,* and *Love Story.*

Under a snowy canvas awning, at the edge of a brimming pool, Louise
lay swaddled in strips of linen like some kind of damned mummy. The
spa menu claimed their mud came from the Valley of the Kings but
Louise wasn't fooled. It smelled like grime dug up from the edge of La
Brea and wouldn't that be appropriate? She was a fossil, after all.

The young spa attendant poked her head into the cabana.

"Nearly done, Mrs. Mirador," she said. "Are you comfortable?"

"Just fine, Abby," Louise replied. "I could stay here forever."

The girl gave Louise's cushions a solid pat, and then heaved a great,
wet sigh.

"What's the story, dear? You sound like a rainy Sunday."

"Sorry for disturbing you."

This was the point at which, normally, Louise would prop herself up
on an elbow and settle in for a good old-fashioned commiseration. But
moving wasn't an option, so she deployed her most effective weapon.

"Tell me your troubles, sweetheart."

Louise's lisp made the word come out *sheetheart*, and it disarmed everyone. Or, very nearly. A couple of Halloweens back, a junior agent from Robert Horus had dressed up in a witch mask and knock-off Chanel suit, and had gone around the party *sheethearting* people.

"Nobody could be unhappy here, madam," said Abby with forced cheer.

The mud on Louise's cheeks stretched and cracked over her grin.

"That's not true. People are especially miserable in Hollywood, because they have such high expectations."

Abby nodded but didn't reply. She fussed with the straps holding the cabana flaps open, untied one, then the other, retied them.

She was awfully pretty, in the currently fashionable vein—long, lanky, and fresh as cream, exactly the looks to catch a casting director's eye. But she had terrible posture, gnawed fingernails, and ragged cuticles. Girls couldn't get away with that in Louise's day, but times had changed. Nobody cared about lovely hands anymore.

"Are you thinking about giving up on your dreams?" Louise prompted, gently.

"I think you—" the girl began, but then the head aesthetician bustled in.

"Twenty minutes, madam," Magda announced. "Don't bother the clients," she scolded, and steered the girl out the door.

Louise dozed, luxuriating in the soothing wrap. Soon, too soon, Magda and Abby returned to the cabana.

"We'll unwrap you now, madam," Magda said.

"Can I stay like this?" Louise asked. "Just a little longer?"

"No, madam. The treatment is forty minutes only."

Louise knew not to argue; whether Magda was waxing, extracting, or wrapping, she was relentless—everything tight, clean, and timed to the minute. Louise liked it that way. She'd followed Magda from spa to spa for years, from La Ville en Rose, to Laguna Azul, to Épicerie de la Corps, and now here at the Imperial Cabana. Magda was a big woman—taller even than Louise, and strong. In her hands, Louise felt dainty. It was a rare sensation, and Louise was more than happy to pay for it.

Magda lifted Louise's shoulder and flipped her onto her stomach as if she were no heavier than a child. Louse relaxed and let herself be buffeted about like a dinghy in a gale. She'd always loved being thrown around by a force of nature.

"How did you break your nose, Mrs. Mirador?" Abby asked.

"Hush," Magda whispered.

"Do you mean the first time, or the second?" Louise said. "When I was just a kid and learning to sail, I caught the boom right in my face. And the second time was when I nearly drowned off Santa Catalina. Did I ever tell you about that, Magda?"

"No, madam."

"I used to sail around the Channel Islands in a little single-mast sailboat, all by myself. You should have seen my tan back then. Brown as a bear. Beautiful."

"That's why your skin has so much sun damage, madam."

"Sun, rain, I never cared. I just wanted to go as fast as the wind could push me. Then one day, a gale blew up out of nowhere, and I was carrying far too much sail. The boat did somersaults while I tried to reef back the canvas. Next time I looked up I was on a lee shore heading straight for Catalina."

No response from Magda.

"A lee shore in a gale," Louise repeated. "That means basically death."

"If you say so, madam."

"I got banged up pretty badly. Breaking my nose again didn't make my face any better. And my poor little dingy didn't survive. She smashed to bits on Seal Rocks. Unsalvageable."

"What was her name?" Abby asked

"She was the *Lou Lou*." Louise grinned. "I figured, if I wanted a boat named after me, I'd have to do it myself."

"The sea has her own desires," said Magda. "She will take anything she pleases."

"I guess, but really I was just reckless. Long Beach was just a few miles away, and I thought nothing bad could possibly happen so close to home."

When the last strip of linen lifted from Louise's skin, she heaved herself up from the treatment couch and blinked in the soft, filtered light. Magda stood broad and strong in her white pantsuit, with motherly hips and short, practical salt-and-pepper hair. Abby, slender arms heaped with muddy linen swaddling, with eyelashes so light and fine her eyes looked pink as a rabbit's. Exposed, vulnerable.

"Was your next boat the *Lou Lou II*?" Abby asked.

"Oh dear, no. I gave up on adventure. Married Donny and settled down in Beverly Hills. I never see the ocean anymore."

Louise slid off the treatment couch, buck naked, all her scars, wrinkles, and moles exposed, and for the first time in months she wasn't itching—not even the spot on her hip she'd scratched bloody just that morning.

"What I learned," Louise said, "is that I could die anywhere, and probably would, if I kept taking big risks. A girl only has one life."

"That's not true, madam," said Magda. "Every woman has three. Maiden, mother, and crone."

Louise laughed. "I guess I missed out on the middle part. Went straight from maiden to crone, and faster than scheduled, too."

Pretty girls came and went in Hollywood. Louise figured she'd never see Abby again, but she was wrong.

Early Friday evening, she drove her Lincoln Continental convertible down the canyon road toward Sunset Boulevard. A silk scarf held her curls in place, and sunglasses protected her from the last rays of the sun as it skinny-dipped into the sea beyond Santa Monica. The steering wheel twitched under her palms. The car hadn't been right since Donny had crashed through a field off Sepulveda three years back—rolled the car and drove away with a stake punctured through the soft roof, trailing a piece of vine dangling with little green grapes.

Donny's luck. When anyone else rolled a convertible, they left their head behind.

Louise had been at home all day, waiting for a messenger to drop off some contracts. Not that sitting around her Benedict Canyon cabin was any kind of hardship. She had her books, her pool, her birdfeeders, and with Donny away, the phone barely rang. It was peaceful. Delightful. But the nursing home had strict visiting hours, and Louise had to get going before four o'clock if she wanted to spend time with her mother.

Turning left onto Sunset at rush hour was always chancy. That day it was worse than usual, cars swerving, honking. Someone was standing in the middle of the street—a girl. Louise squinted.

Abby. Hair wafting in the breeze, dressed in plaid shorts, T-shirt, and a cheap pair of sandals so insubstantial it seemed she wasn't wearing shoes at all, just hovering a half inch above the road. She pointed a Super 8 camera into the flow of traffic. Trucks raced past mere inches from her elbows.

Louise muscled the Lincoln into the intersection and slammed the brakes. She hit her hazard lights.

"What on earth do you think you're doing?" Louise yelled.

The girl swung the camera at her. The lens flashed orange, reflecting the setting sun. A dump truck laid on its horn, and then skinned past Louise. She clung to the steering wheel like it was a life preserver and screeched, "Get in the car. Now."

The girl climbed into the back seat behind Louise, then shinnied up front and settled into the big bench seat, long pale legs folded under her.

Louise completed the left turn, waving at a cement truck as the driver lobbed curses at her.

"Does your mother know you spend your evenings playing in traffic?" she demanded.

"My mother knows everything about me."

Abby braced her elbows on the dashboard and pointed the camera at the passing scenery. What there was of interest in an endless trail of parking lots, car dealerships, motels, and taverns, Louise couldn't tell.

"That sounds awful," she said. "I spent half my life trying to keep my mother from finding out anything about me. Now she won't be around much longer, and I keep wondering why I put so much effort into keeping my distance."

"That's too bad, Mrs. Mirador. But it means you'll be free, right?"

Louise laughed. "Oh, my dear, what a thing to say."

"If you don't have a mother, you can do what you want."

"I do that anyway, mostly. Most people do." Abby leaned back in the seat and adjusted the focus, zooming in on Louise for a close-up. "Why are you wasting film on me, dear?"

"There's no film in the camera. I'm just practicing."

"For what?"

"Making movies. What else?"

Louise supposed it made sense. If a girl wanted to be a movie star, she might want to know how cameras worked.

"You need a tripod," Louise said. "Set it up in good light and film yourself. Get to know your angles. It'd be expensive, though. Film and processing isn't cheap. Even for a home camera like that one. Most girls just practice in front of a mirror."

The Lincoln coasted through the soft corner onto Sunset Strip. Abby put the camera in her lap. She laid her arm along the backrest and leaned toward Louise across the wide bench seat.

"I want to make them, not act in them. I just really love movies, you know?"

Louise hit a pothole. The car vibrated and the steering wheel lurched. Abby clutched the dashboard and hissed like a cat, but it wasn't Louise's driving that startled her. She was glaring at the billboard on the corner above Donny's favorite liquor store—a towering advertisement for *Love Story*.

"I love movies, too," said Louise. "Isn't that a good one? So romantic."

"Are you kidding, Mrs. Mirador? She gives up her dreams to marry a guy and dies young. How is that romantic?"

"Tragic romance, then. A real tearjerker."

"The *doctor* doesn't even tell her she's *dying*. He tells her *husband*." Abby pounded her fist on the dashboard. "It's so old-fashioned. Practically *Victorian*."

"I don't think it's anything to get angry about."

"It was written by a man. Directed by a man. All movies are. There's one woman in it and when she dies, people think that's beautiful. Like the only good woman is a dead woman."

"People do die, you know, sweetheart."

"Oh, I know." The girl slumped back in her seat and began chewing a nail.

"My husband was involved in the financing. We went to the premiere. Red carpet and everything, though nobody paid any attention to me, of course."

"Uh-huh."

"Ali MacGraw really is that stunning. I think she'll win an Oscar."

"Yeah, she made a great corpse."

Awkward silence as they left the strip behind. Tall skyduster palms on either side of Sunset heralded their arrival in Hollywood. Abby gnawed her thumbnail, and another *Love Story* billboard appeared on the horizon.

"Where can I drop you, sweetheart?" Louise asked.

Abby sighed. "I'll go wherever you're going, Mrs. Mirador. I don't think I have a choice."

Take a strange kid to Mom's cabin at Cedar Breezes, why not? Florence used to love meeting new people. And Louise could use an accomplice.

"Can you watch the door? The nurses don't like me pouring drinks for Mom, but I figure what can it hurt? It's not like she's going to walk out of here."

Abby leaned in the open doorway, pink camellias and orange trees in the garden beyond. Florence sat by the wide window, in the big, wheeled recliner Louise had bought when her mother had stopped walking.

Louise cupped her hand on her mother's deeply lined cheek, and gently drew her head upright.

"How about a drink, Mom?" Louise asked. "Gee and Tee, heavy on the Gee, right?"

Louise forced a laugh, and Florence's eyes widened, her lips curled. She shifted in her chair, smiled, and then her focus drifted back to a place deep behind her eyes, somewhere in the realm of sleep.

"She likes to hear people talk," Louise told Abby. "And when someone laughs, she joins in. You have a better sense of humor now than ever, don't you, Mom?"

"Does she know where she is? What's happening to her?"

"Oh, God, no, I hope not."

Louise rooted in her big leather bag. She took six half-melted ice cubes from a pink plastic container and dropped them in a glass—pinwheel-cut crystal, one of the last surviving pieces from Louise's wedding set. One-third gin, two-thirds tonic. The sweating bottles made the inside of her purse clammy, left water stains on the delicate nap of her suede wallet.

"She looks like you," the girl said.

"Don't say that too loud. Mom always loved that she was better looking than me."

She placed the drink in Florence's lap and wrapped her mother's fingers around it. The skin on her hands was translucent, blue and purple veins webbing her knuckles. Louise adjusted the glass to rest between her mother's skinny thighs.

"Cedar Breezes happy hour."

Florence's chin lifted. A smile flickered across her lips. Her eyes drifted half-shut and she lapsed back into unconsciousness for thirty seconds, a minute before stirring again. For a bare second, not two, she looked as though she knew who and where she was. Then her focus dissolved.

"Have a sip, Mom."

Louise lifted the glass to Florence's lips. Her mother's eyelids opened and closed over staring eyes, but her lips didn't move. A bit of gin slipped from the corner of her mouth and dripped to her pink cardigan.

"She doesn't want it," said Abby.

Louise put the glass on the floor. She mopped her mother's chin with the cuff of her blouse.

"No. She wouldn't take it last night, either. She's refusing food. And water. They say this is the last stage, when they turn their face to the wall."

Sitting with Mother was like watching a person drown in quicksand— sinking, struggling, rising, sinking again. A moment of something that might be called consciousness, followed by a few minutes of struggle as she slowly fell into dreamland, and sunk into sleep. Ten minutes, fifteen minutes later she'd stir, wake. Clench her hands, patter her feet on the footrest. A brief spark lit her gaze, then slipped away.

"They could feed her through a vein, if I wanted. Keep her alive for a few more weeks."

"I guess it's peaceful?" said Abby, uncertain.

"She might be having entire nightmares, a hundred times a day. But I hope not. I hope she's visiting with the people in her head. Like Donny, maybe. She loves Donny. He won't visit, says it makes him too sad. But he sends flowers." She pointed at the huge bouquet of drooping roses on the windowsill.

Mother's head came up. Louise took her hand.

"It's okay, Mom, you can go if you want. You don't have to wait."

Florence squeezed Louise's fingers. Lips worked to form a word.

"I love you, too, Mom."

When Florence finished another struggle and lapsed back into sleep,

Louise took the gin and tonic to the bathroom and poured it in the sink. She dropped the glass into her bag.

"I won't let them put an IV into her. If she doesn't want to eat and drink, she doesn't have to. I figure, killing herself is the last choice she'll make, and I'm not going to take it away."

At eight o'clock, visiting hours were over. A nurse came to put Florence to bed.

"Can we stay, María José?" Louise drew up the blankets and tucked them around her mother's feet. "I think she might go tonight."

The nurse settled her mother's head back on the pillows. She opened a jar of Vaseline and began dabbing it on Florence's lips.

"You can stay," María José said. "It'll be soon. Tonight or tomorrow. Can you smell it?"

Louise nodded. "Yeah, I can smell it."

The nurse shut the cabin door gently behind her.

"Smell what?" Abby asked. Her nostrils flared, scenting the air.

"Death."

"Are you joking?"

"It's sweet and metallic, like cotton candy and steel wool. Or, I don't know, rotting flowers. Magnolia blossoms and underwear that's been sitting at the bottom of the dirty laundry basket."

"I thought it was some kind of weird disinfectant not doing its job." Abby hitched herself up on the windowsill and perched beside Donny's roses. Behind her glittered Hollywood and its traffic, red brake lights of the cars streaming up and down the streets.

"The smell has something to do with the organs shutting down, ammonia buildup in the tissues."

"How come they don't tell us these things? The smell of death seems kind of important. My mother should have told me."

"Maybe she doesn't know."

"My mother knows everything."

"Maybe she told you, but you didn't listen."

"No, I do listen. I really do. I don't have a choice."

Louise laughed. From the bed, mother laughed, too. A soft sound, but high and cracked.

"Did your mom tell you about menopause? Hot flashes are the least of it. I get cold flashes, too. Phantom bugs running up and down my legs. I have all the self-control of a teenager. But the itching is the worst."

"You're not itchy now, though, are you?"

Louise scratched her neck, experimentally, then her hip. For the first time in months, she wasn't.

Louise went through moisturizer by the bucket, but it didn't really work. Nothing did. Nighttime was the worst. She'd tried going to bed wearing cotton gloves, but always ended up ripping them off in her sleep and in the morning, the sheets would be flecked with blood. During daytime, she usually had enough self-control to keep from scratching herself, but at what price? Seemed like all she did, all day long, was fight to keep from flaying herself raw.

"Just scratch, Lou," Donny had told her, the last time he'd been home.

"It's rude, Don," she'd said.

"Who cares? Do what you gotta do."

Easy enough for him to say. For most of their marriage, Donny had looked like a respectable banker from his hat to the tips of his very shiny shoes. But over the past few years, he'd stopped cutting his hair, treated shaving as optional, and dressed in shorts and Hawaiian shirts exclusively.

Louise, by contrast, still wore a set bouffant, tweed suits, pantyhose, and heels. It had gotten to the point where, whenever she and Donny went somewhere together, people mistook her for his mother.

"Nobody works in Hollywood anymore," said Louise.

"I'm sorry?" asked Abby.

"That's what Donny says. Deals get done in Acapulco, or Las Vegas, or somebody's ranch in the desert. Not here. *Everyone's gotta get away.* That's what he says."

"Get away from what?"

"Their wives, I guess. Their houses. Their kids. Whoever and whatever can make a demand on them. But my point is, it's a closed system. You said you want to make movies?"

"I do."

"You're better off drawing them. Flip-books, you know?" She pressed her thumbs together and fluttered through a battery of pages. "Or stop-motion. A short film if you have to work in live action. But a feature film? That's never going to happen."

"Are you okay, Mrs. Mirador?"

"You can call me Louise. No, I'm not." She pointed at her mother, slack-jawed on her pillow, a weak snore rattling in her throat. "You know what it's like when you wake up after sleeping with your mouth open like that? Tongue dry like beef jerky, so you stagger to the bathroom and stick your face under the bathroom tap, but she can't do that. The faster she dehydrates the quicker she'll die. Like I'm watching her spend her life away with every breath."

"That's hard."

"Do I dribble water in her mouth? It might keep her alive a few hours longer. But why? To live through some more nightmares?"

"You must love her very much."

"I don't know. I don't understand her one bit though she's the person I know most about in the world." Louise swiped her knuckles over her eyes and wiped the tears on the collar of her suit. "Except for Donny. He's no mystery."

The crying made her flushed. Under her clothes, a hot flash was brewing.

"Fuck this," Louise said.

She stripped off the jacket and her silk blouse, too, which left her in a camisole over her bra. "Why am I wearing so many layers? What have you got on?"

"Just a T-shirt," said Abby.

"Not even a bra?"

"There's not much point."

"Nice."

Louise tossed her jacket and blouse into a corner. Took off her shoes for good measure. She could go out into the garden and cool off, lurk under the Cedar Breezes garden lights like some kind of half-dressed ghoul, but instead, she tucked her pantyhose-clad feet under Florence's bony hip, like they were on the same couch watching TV together, which they'd actually never done. Her mother never used to sit down. She was always puttering, cleaning, organizing something.

"Mom had a shitty life. Do you know how awful it was to be an Orange County farm girl seventy years ago?"

"No."

"Let me tell you. If people weren't dying of the Spanish flu, it was tuberculosis, or cholera. Or diphtheria. Do you know what diphtheria is?"

"No."

"Me neither. But she does. She was an orphan three times over. You have a mom. Where's your dad?"

"I don't have one."

Florence was still drifting in and out. Eyes open but not seeing anything. Eyes closed and dreaming. Maybe if it was dark, she'd drop down into real sleep. Louise flicked off the bedside lamp.

"When mom first got sick, I tortured myself about it. With all the tragedies she went through, and after working so hard, it was unfair for her to end life like this. I wanted her to live to ninety-five. Spend money. Learn to enjoy life. But she never spent a dime she didn't have to."

"She bought you the *Lou Lou*, though, didn't she?"

"No, but she did buy the house in Long Beach. And she loved it like it was a person."

Florence's hands stirred over the blanket, fingers tapping at a phantom keyboard. Louise counted eight strokes, then her hands stilled.

"Do you know what I realized? It's wrong to make up tragic stories about someone else, even if she's your mother. Mom would say she had a happy life. I say it was tragic, filled with death and abandonment. So who gets to decide? She does. Not me. So that means I have to stop telling myself stories about her. She doesn't have a story. She has a life. For a little while longer at least."

Louise opened the Vaseline and dabbed the ointment lavishly over her mother's lips, making little peaks, like frosting on a cake. She wiped her fingers on her camisole and then lifted Florence's head, adjusting the angle. With two fingers, she closed her mother's mouth, but Florence just sighed and opened it again. Maybe a towel under her chin would keep it closed? That wasn't too much was it?

Plenty of towels in the bathroom to choose from. She wedged a hand towel under her mother's chin, and then backed away. Florence was so thin she hardly tented the bedcovers, and the towel looked creepy, like she was being choked by an overgrown maggot. Louise pulled it off and dropped it on the floor.

Abby drew her heels up on the windowsill, put her chin on her knees. Beside her, the roses nodded, weighed down by their overblown blossoms.

"Do you mean that?" Abby asked. "We don't get to make up stories about other people's lives? That's what movies are."

"I mean, we don't get to make judgments about other people's lives. We don't get to call someone else's existence happy or sad or tragic or heroic. So all my moaning was just avoiding the real question."

"Which is?"

"When she dies, where does it leave me?"

"I think it leaves you in charge."

"Of what? Of my family? What family? She's all I have. Except for Donny, but nobody's in charge of him." Louise laughed. It sounded like something breaking.

"Should I go get you something to eat, Mrs. Mirador?"

"Louise."

"Are you hungry?"

"Probably. I can't tell." She fished her car keys out of her bag and dropped them in Abby's palm. "Be careful. It pulls to the left."

*A good daughter would have sat by her mother's bed for the next hour, hold-*ing her hand and whispering comforting platitudes. Louise tried, but it was too damned maudlin. Felt fake, and worst of all, boring. So, with her toes still tucked under Florence's hip, she put the phone in her lap and dialed the answering service.

"Two messages," said Donna, the evening operator. "Mr. Smith's office wants to know how many chocolates you want to put in the box. Does that make sense?"

"Boys playing spy," said Louise. "I bet half your accounts leave messages like that this time of the year."

"You wouldn't be wrong, Mrs. M."

"What's the other message?"

"Your husband is in Acapulco. He left a number."

Louise dialed Mexico. On the other side of a crackly line, party noises, and a drunken American girl yelling *Hola* into the receiver.

Florence used to keep a little hourglass by the phone, for long-distance calls. Three minutes only, and then hang up, no matter what, and she'd analyze the phone bill every month. It took longer than that just to get Donny on the other end of the line. Florence would be scandalized.

"Hey, old girl," Donny said when he finally got to the phone. "What's the news with Flo?"

"Sinking fast, Don. If you want to see her, you should come home now."

"Do you need me?"

"Not really, except for the funeral. You better come home for that."

Screeches in the background, laughter, splashes.

"I will. How are you hanging on?"

"We're having a party here, too. I'm slamming shots with María José. Licking salt off random biceps."

"I'm sorry, old girl."

"Me too."

Under the fuzz of the long-distance line, a voice: *Donny, come back to the pool.*

"Listen, Lou. After the funeral, why don't you come down here? Lie on the beach. Drink tequila. Lick some biceps."

"Just what every old lady longs for."

"You never know until you try it."

"No, Don. The surfers would run screaming."

"They wouldn't if they knew that you're a power in the dream factory."

"You're the power. I'm an accountant. Which reminds me, Howard called. He wants to know how much we're going to contribute to the Oscar voters' packages."

"Right. What do you think?"

"We should let *Love Story* go. Nobody's getting past *Patton*."

"That's a switch. Last week you were ready to throw the bank at it."

"I was just thinking. Why did Jenny have to be terminal? Does a woman have to die for a film to make a killing?"

The line snapped. Somewhere in Acapulco, a whoop, a shout, a splash.

"Well," Donny said, tentatively. "If she hadn't croaked, it wouldn't have been a very good script. The film wouldn't have gotten made. Nobody would've put money on it."

"I would have."

"Then you would have gone bust. Romances are old-fashioned. You can buy them by the dozen in any drugstore."

"Isn't that a reason to make more romances? Women love them."

"Movies don't get made just for women."

"They make them just for men."

"No, they don't."

"Excuse me? *Patton*?"

"That's history. It's real."

"I guess the dream factory only cares about men's dreams."

196

"You really gonna give up on *Love Story*? Best Picture isn't the only nomination. You wanna let Ali's Oscar go, too?"

She wiggled her toes under Florence's hip. Her mother seemed to be sleeping deeply now, instead of floating in and out of consciousness.

"Maybe right now isn't the time to make big decisions," Louise said.

"We can give up if you want. But Howard is counting on us to do our bit. We can throw the voters a bill or two."

"I'll go to the bank tomorrow."

"That's my girl."

Donny made kissy noises into the phone before hanging up. Louise brushed the hair off Florence's forehead, then retreated to the bathroom and spent some time in front of the mirror, marveling at how awful she looked. Her hairspray had given up, curls broken and drooping, showing at least an inch of gray roots though she'd just had the color freshened last week. Worse, her face looked like an aerial photo of Death Valley, foundation cracked into bottomless fissures around her eyes and mouth. Neck like a turkey carcass. Wattles at her armpits. Age spots everywhere.

That's why your skin has so much sun damage, madam.

She soaped up her hands, gave herself a good scrub, and wiped it all off onto a towel, leaving a ghost of herself behind in a smear of beige and pink. She dropped her skirt on the floor, skinned off her pantyhose, and wiggled out of her bra, too—*not much point*—leaving herself in just the camisole, slip, and panties. A lifetime of random scars hatched her slack and pouchy skin. Knobby legs. Bare feet.

Bare life.

Back at the bed, Florence's lips had shrunk back from her teeth. Mouth gaping open again, like one of Francis Bacon's popes, a living corpse, howling an undying scream.

Louise took her mother's chin between finger and thumb and pressed her jaws together. Maybe a little denture adhesive on her gums? She checked the drawer for a tube of Poligrip but there was none. Just her mother's upper plate rattling around with the tub of Vaseline. Florence hadn't worn her teeth in months.

She cupped her hand on her mother's cheek and leaned close.

"Stop fighting, Mom," she breathed. "You can go."

"I hope you like pizza," said Abby.

The girl stood outside the cabin with a pizza box so wide it would have to be turned on an angle to fit through the door. Moths flitted above her head. Behind her was Magda, very serious, wearing a black pantsuit and cradling a bottle of wine in her arms like a baby.

"Hello, madam," said Magda.

"I brought Mom," the girl added.

"Mom?" Louise repeated. She looked back at the bed.

"My mom, I mean."

"Oh, I didn't know. But I suppose it makes sense." Louise ran her hands down her barely clothed flanks, suddenly self-conscious, which was ridiculous—Magda has seen it all.

"This transition is painful," Magda said, her tone weighty. "We have come to accompany you through it."

"Thanks, I guess?"

"No thanks needed, madam. It is a privilege to attend a croning."

"Okay," Louise said. Magda had always been a bit dramatic.

Abby took a spare blanket from the closet. She spread it on the floor and put the pizza box in the middle.

"You really need to eat something, Mrs. Mirador."

"Call me Louise. I keep telling you."

"Will you be okay sitting on the floor?"

"I think I can manage it."

Very slowly, Louise lowered herself to the blanket. She couldn't sit cross-legged, her hips wouldn't bend that way, but she could sit with her legs folded to the side—ladylike by default. Abby joined her, legs crossed at the ankles, and Magda crouched over her heels, natural and comfortable as settling on a couch. When Louise flipped open the box, the aroma of cheese, pepperoni, and good yeasty dough unfurled into the corners of the room.

"The croning is a woman's final transition into her ultimate power," said Magda. "Not all achieve this honor, but all aspire to it."

"Mmmf," said Louise, through a mouthful of pizza.

"I kind of feel like this pizza is the ultimate power," said Abby.

Magda frowned.

"Make fun if you like. Nothing sullies this universal truth."

Though she would have sworn she had no appetite, Louise gobbled her first slice nearly without chewing. She licked the pepperoni oil off her fingers, wiped her mouth on the back of her hand, and reached for another slice. Abby was working her way through a pizza sandwich—two slices pressed together, crust out.

Magda lay her slice across her palm and raised it to her mouth like an offering. She took a small bite, chewing carefully.

"Open the wine, daughter," she said.

The bottle was dark, unlabeled. Nothing strange in that. Half of Los Angeles made wine in their garages. The corkscrew was odd, though—soapstone or maybe meerschaum, carved with the face of a woman, the screw just a fine golden curl protruding from her throat.

Abby drew the cork from the bottle, then looked around.

"I have a glass," said Louise. She stretched to reach her leather bag and dragged it across the linoleum. "Just one, though."

"My mom likes it best that way," said Abby.

"When three share a glass," said Magda, "the charm is firm and good."

"That's what Shakespeare said." Abby grinned.

"Damn him," said Magda.

"Someone did, but it wasn't us."

Louise held the crystal glass in both hands. The wine poured like light through a window, a luminescent stream warm and golden as piss. The liquid lay still in the bottom of the glass, without a ripple.

With great effort, hips and knees complaining, Louise levered herself to her feet. Cupping the glass in her palms, she staggered the few steps to her mother's bedside.

"I can't do it. I can't let her go. This is not okay."

Now, she thought, *who's being dramatic?* But where can you be dramatic if not beside your mother's deathbed?

"It's not okay," she repeated. "What is this? A potion?"

"No," said Abby.

"It's a benediction," said Magda. "To mark the closing of one door and the opening of another."

"Is it her or me? If I drink it, I survive. If she drinks it, she survives? Is that the way it goes?"

"No," said Abby.

"Definitely not," said Magda.

She slammed the glass on the bedside table, and the liquid still didn't move.

"Thanks for the pizza." Louise lowered herself into the bedside chair. "You can go now. If you don't have money for a cab, take it out of my wallet."

This was the point where, as a good daughter, she should take her mother's hand, embrace her thin shoulders, cry into her neck, and sob out her undying love. But the most Louise could do was lean over her mother, reach to either side of her head, and rub her tender earlobes between finger and thumb.

Maybe her mother's eyelids flickered, maybe not. Her lips closed, though, and one brief sigh escaped from between them. Then Florence sighed no more. The clock stopped. Beyond the roses, outside the window, the moon dimmed. Not one star flickered.

Louise pinched her mother's earlobes, as if she squeezed hard enough, dug her nails in deep, Florence would breathe again. She hovered there as long as she could, then fell back into the chair.

"Did you think you would escape?" said Magda at Louise's shoulder. "Each scrap of knowledge and power a woman can assemble comes down to this, the moment when nobody in the world can tell her what to do."

"You're a crone, now," said Abby, "You can do anything."

"If you have the will," Magda added. "Harness your power. You've spent a lifetime pretending to be less than you are. Such is the tragedy of this world. Women used to be stronger."

"That's not true, Mom. Women are the same as we've ever been."

"They are more credulous now. They believe the value of their life is contingent on the permission of others."

"If that's true," said Abby, "it's because the lies women hear about themselves are louder and stronger than ever. That's why I want to make movies, Mom."

Louise slapped the arms of her chair and cackled.

"Are you hearing yourselves? You sound like every university dorm in Southern California, from Woodland Hills to Malibu to Davis. It's ridiculous. My mother—"

Louise's voice broke.

"—she just died, and you're spouting Feminism for Beginners? Who the fuck cares?"

Magda retreated. The hem of her wide black pants brushed over the pizza box.

"Is this your choice, then, madam? When you were young, you rode the waves. For a brief time, you bent the winds and currents to your will, before retreating in fright. Now, you are at your utmost power. But like thousands of others you will hide, and say *yes, dear* and make your decisions over to others. Why? To keep their good opinion?"

"Yes," Louise said. "I mean no. Life isn't that simple."

"Isn't it?" asked Abby.

Now is not the time to be making momentous decisions.

But if not now, when? With her mother lying dead, was it true she had nothing more to lose? Was life something to be remembered, like the long-ago push of wind at her back, the waves on her hull, and the lee shore coming on fast? Or was it something to be risked, now more than ever?

She raised the glass to her lips and drank deep. The wine tasted of nothing more or less than life, with every drop of pleasure wrung from it.

"Here," she said, passing the glass to Magda, "let's share."

"To you." Magda raised the glass and sipped. She passed it to her daughter.

Abby raised the glass high.

"To you, Mrs. Mirador."

Louise squeezed her dead mother's hand once, then let go. She grinned at Abby, and gazed out the window at the twinkling lights of Hollywood.

"Call me Lou Lou," she said. "And now, let's make movies."

WHAT DREAMS MAY COME

C. L. Clark

The call comes in late my time, my sister's voice almost frantic. The outline of her face in the video image is fuzzy, but I can see the worried expression she keeps throwing over her shoulder. When she turns to me, though, she forces herself to relax.

My own face is hidden in the dark of my bedroom, a black square in the corner of my screen.

"Caris," I say. "What's going on?"

"It's your mother," she says, accusing.

"You mean *our* mother—"

"She's stuck, Pol. In the 'scape. We can't get her out."

The indignant response clogs in my throat and my mouth goes dry.

"Babe?" My wife stirs beside me. "Some-thing wrong?"

I *shh* her gently and pat her hip as I get out of bed, taking the phone to the living room.

"Can't you go in and get her?" I whis-per, cupping my hand around my words.

"I tried. It's weird—I can't get her.

I can't *find* her. And the dreams are—they're nightmares. And—they're coming *out*. Like, I can see them."

"That's not that weird. The Dreamscape bleeds for all of us sometimes—"

"The *neighbors* can see them, Pol."

"Fuck."

That's definitely not supposed to happen. I trace the splotch of a birthmark on the back of my hand absently. I stop as soon as I realize I'm doing it.

"What's Aunt Tiff say?" I ask.

Caris shakes her head. "She can't get to Mama either, but she says if we can't get her to wake up and stop . . . projecting or whatever, she'll give us away."

I take a sharp, involuntary breath. The secrecy of our family's gift—curse, whatever—is so closely guarded that I haven't even told my wife. Since my relationship with my family has always been strained, it never seemed like a problem. Before my sister even asks, my mind sprints forward, to the bag I'll have to pack, the excuses I'll have to make.

"We need your help." Caris's voice is apologetic.

I snort. "Did Aunt Tiff and LeeLee ask you to ask me, or are you going behind their backs?"

She makes a noncommittal wheedling sound in her throat. "Look, if you don't help, you know what they'll do to her."

The dark mirth in me turns sour with dread. If my aunts decide that my mother is a risk to the rest of us—to *them*—they'll kill her.

I know firsthand how ruthless they can be for the sake of their stupid "rules," even against their own family. They won't hesitate if they think it's necessary. And despite the complicated way—alright, the fucked-up way—that Ma and I left things, I'm not ready to let her die. Especially not if I can help; I don't wanna carry that guilt along with all the rest of the baggage she gave me.

I take a deep breath and suck my teeth, trying to calculate time zones and flight costs and budgets. My wife will be upset; we can't afford it. But my family can't afford for me to wait. "I'll be there to-morrow."

Caris's relief whooshes out in a sigh. "See you soon, Pol."

I click the call off and crawl back into bed. My wife curls into me, her fingers skimming my flat chest, thumbs grazing the scars from my top surgery a few years ago. None of my aunts have seen me like this. I close my eyes and sigh into the pillows.

I don't let myself dream.

There's something special about the wide stretches of midwestern sky, un-broken and empty along stretches of highway. About seeing a storm come from miles away, with clouds that stretch just as many miles high. You don't get that in the cramped stone European cities I haunt these days.

Do I miss home? Nah. Nope. Not at all.

But when my sister picks me up and we start driving home, my eyes are glued to the window and my mouth hangs open. From the corner of my eye, I see her glance down at my chest every now and then as we make the thirty-minute drive from the airport to our mom's.

I have mercy on her. And on myself. I always hated dancing around the obvious out of some backward politeness. I flick my chest with my fingers and it makes a hollow thump. "Weird to see in person, huh?"

My accent is already shifting back, all half drawls and cocky ca-dence.

The ice cracks. Caris laughs a little too hard. "It is. Like . . . where'd you put them? In the trash?"

"No," I say, adding in a deadpan, "I keep 'em on ice in case I change my mind."

She takes her eyes off the road to stare at me in confused horror before she realizes it's an excellent joke. Then she scoffs. Then groans. "Almost wish you were serious. Aunt Tiff and LeeLee are gonna flip their shit." Caris sighs and shakes her head.

Caris, the diplomat. Caris, the peacemaker. If you weren't careful, you'd think everything about her is soft: soft voice, soft cheeks, soft dark eyes, dark curls gathered in soft puffs on her head. But she's the only one in the family who can get anyone to do what she wants. She's ended more than one feud between Ma and Aunt Tiff with a hard look and harder shame.

Even she hasn't been able to budge my aunts about me, though.

"How's it feel?" She meets my eyes and the crinkle of concern and a desire to *understand* me makes me turn fully away from the window, opening myself up.

I run a hand down my front.

"It feels good, sis. Real good."

She sucks her teeth. "Good. Long as it's worth it. 'Cause this finna be ugly."

She curves the car into our neighborhood streets, clicking her long nails on the steering wheel. I clench the inside handle of the door, bracing myself.

I don't have time to get ready for my aunts' onslaught, though, because as my sister pulls up, I see someone at the door of my mom's house. At first, I think it's one of the boys, Rico or Junior, but this guy is screaming and pounding on the door.

"Stay in the car," I tell Caris, unbuckling my seatbelt. "Call the cops."

"Pol, don't—"

But I'm already out of the car, all heroic and shit.

"Ay, man, can I help you?" I say. My tone's less solicitous and more "get the fuck out of here," but you know.

Caris's car door slams and I turn to see her racing up the drive in her unlaced high tops, her keys jangling in her hand. Of course, she didn't listen.

Back to the man, then. He's looking at me over his shoulder, confused. There's something familiar about him. Big shoulders, waves in his hair, his work shirt straining over a belly that's probably equal parts muscle and someone's good cooking. He smells like that blue hair grease

206

Grandma used to use on us. I wonder if he's the new boyfriend; maybe my mom introduced us over FaceTime?

"Look, man, I need you to back up off my ma's door like that, okay? She know you're here?"

She can't know he's here if she's still stuck in the Dreamscape, but if I can cool him off, get him to come back later . . .

He turns fully to me. One hand strays to a gun on his hip, an old one but still—shit.

"Pol!" Caris shouts from behind me.

I don't turn. I'm stuck on this guy's gun and the bleary confusion in his face. It's like he's trying to recognize me, same as I'm trying to recognize him—he's not acting like the kind of guy who busts up on his girlfriend's house, banging on her door.

"Look, man," I start again, raising my empty hands. "We don't have to have a problem, I just think you should come back tomorrow or something. My ma's not here."

"Pol." Caris is in my ear now, her hand tight on my shoulder, the keys in her hand digging into my flesh. She points. "*Look.*"

I look at the man. Then I *look.* His confusion, as he turns back to the door to bang on it. The fuzziness around the edges of his body, and where his hand meets the door. The distortion in the sound. Even the weird anachronism of the gun model.

I see him for what he is—an escaped dream. An escaped *nightmare.*

"Shit," I mutter. I reach out and swipe with my hand. It goes right through him—he's as insubstantial as a *Star Wars* hologram.

"Yeah," Caris says. She shrugs into her bright, oversized varsity-style jacket. It's bedazzled and kinda hideous, but it works for her. Somehow. "That's what I'm saying. If it gets any worse, it's gonna really start freaking Ms. Jamison out. Then we'll be in real trouble."

Caris nods at the neighbor's house with the purple door. Ms. Jamison was a sweet old woman. I even house-sat for her and she paid me in real money, not stale butterscotch candy, but the last thing we needed was for her to realize she lived next to a house full of witches.

I blow the air into my cheeks. "Alrighty then." I fish my old house key out of my pocket—it doesn't fit.

Caris nudges me out of the way with a sheepish shrug and jingles hers. "You been gone a while, boo."

So I hang back while someone else lets me into my house.

Inside, I'm hit with a wall of noise. It's not even all bad—there's a TV on, there's my aunts laughing in the kitchen, the low bass rumble of men talking—I realize with a start that they're my little brothers. Not little anymore.

"Aunt Tiff, Aunt Leslie, we're back," Caris calls.

The noise vanishes—all except the TV, still burbling on. My brothers come into the foyer from the side bedroom—my old room. My aunts come in from the kitchen, Aunt Tiff's heeled boots ringing on the tile.

Everyone stares at me, but it's Aunt Tiff whose expression says the most. The curl of her lip, the visible recoil of her neck even though the rest of her body stays put.

It takes a lot of energy to stand my ground. I wonder what I look like to her: my chest is new, but not the shaved head, not the dark shadow of a mustache or the thick eyebrows she and Aunt Leslie always tried to get me to wax off.

"Aunt Tiff," I say stiffly. "Aunt Lee."

"You have no right—" Aunt Tiff finally growls but LeeLee cuts her off with a hand to her shoulder.

LeeLee's hair is wrapped up in a messy bun of tight curls, her edges not even slicked down, and she's wearing my mom's alumni sweatshirt. She looks like she's been keeping vigil for a long time. "She's here to help, Tiff."

I frown but don't correct her. Pronouns are a losing battle and there are more important things. "Where is she?"

"You have no right," Aunt Tiff says again, shaking LeeLee's arm off and shaking her head so that her long hair, straightened just enough that its weight drags the curls into bouncing waves, sweeps over her shoulder. Her vanity. I can't help wondering if this preening is her un-conscious response—like she has to remind herself, *I'm not like you.*

"I don't know what you call yourself doing," she says, taking an-other sneering look down my body and back up again, "but you can't have it both ways."

As she tries to intimidate me, staring down her nose and sneering at my chest, I realize that's not the only change that's happened over the last few years. I don't have the same restraint I used to. I built a life that doesn't need these people, so I'm not afraid to lose them with my honesty.

"You want to do this here, now?" I growl back, fists clenching at my sides. "Or are you gonna be a fucking adult about this? Because I wouldn't even be here if *you* were strong enough to help *your* sister."

Caris jumps in: "Besides, someone has to deal with the escaped dreams. We need all the help we can get, there was another one just outside—"

Aunt Tiff bristles and crosses her arms. The lines of her blazer and jeans are as sharp and crisp as the rest of her. "The Dreamscape is for women. You don't see your brothers complaining that they aren't al-lowed in."

I glance at my brothers in question, their eyes wide, and Rico, the oldest of the boys, puts his hands up in front of his chest—*don't bring me into this.* Almost as an afterthought, he pulls our younger brother, Junior, back, because he looks like he has something to say and really, he shouldn't.

"We'll go get some dinner for y'all," Rico says, and he leaves, drag-ging Junior with him by the collar. Smart.

"You know I'm the best," I say softly when they've gone. "Would you rather kill Ma than let me embrace it?"

There's something almost predatory in the way Aunt Tiff stands between me and Mama's bedroom door. It occurs to me that if Ma does . . . lose control . . . Aunt Tiff will be the most powerful witch in the family. Not including me, obviously. I don't count.

"You know what it means to embrace the gift." Aunt Tiff smiles for the first time since she's seen me. It's a smug smile and shows teeth. She thinks she's won: the admission that using women's magic makes me a woman, that any attempt to deny that is a delusion.

Sighing, I shake my head. Somehow, stupidly, I didn't expect this to hurt the way it does. I push past Aunt Tiff and LeeLee, who's looking a little sympathetic but not enough to defend me properly. It's fine, I don't care. No one ever has before.

My mom is sprawled on her bed, looking for all the world like someone just having a nap—a twitchy nap, maybe, but sleep nevertheless. We're taught early on to control not just our dreams but our bodies while we're sleeping. Even so, I still worry sometimes that I'll talk in my sleep and let something slip.

In the hallway, my aunts and my sister keep arguing more about me, about how to handle the overflow from the dreams, but I ignore them. Walking into Ma's room is like walking into a mausoleum or diving into a pool, that's how sudden the quiet is. The room smells like stale nag champa, the dregs of a flowery reed diffuser, and the shit stink of a half-full cup of—I sniff and gag—valerian root tea. It's like she was *trying* to go deep into the Dreamscape. But I've been gone too long to have any idea why, what she might have been looking for.

There's room for me to lie in the bed next to my mom. She's curled up, her hair in a scarf, tight curls otherwise unbound. It's streaked with blond; she's been dyeing it. Her mouth hangs open just enough to leak a dark spot of drool on the paisley pillowcase.

Instead, I slide to the floor beside it, with my knees curled up against my chest and my head against the mattress.

I close my eyes, breathe in, two, three, four—hold, two, three, four—exhale, two, three, four, five, six, over and over again until I feel close to the gauzy barrier between sleep and waking, and then I *reach* through it.

It's been a while since I've gone into the Dreamscape with real intent to work. The most I ever do is subtly send my wife to sleep when she's got insomnia, or ease her through a nightmare. I try not to do even that; I stepped into one nightmare once that was about me and her, and—well it was shitty for both of us and I couldn't look her in the eye the next day.

The Dreamscape is why so many of the women in my family are doctors and psychologists. My mom works with people on hospice, people already on their way out—says she eases their regrets and helps them pass comfortably in their sleep when the time comes.

I slip the veil between my own dreams and my mother's and it takes me a minute to recognize our old house, the one she lived in with me and my dad when they were still married. Only, like most dreams, it's warped, slightly. Even we aren't immune to the fucky displacement that shows up in dreams—we're just better at dealing with it, manipulating it, sometimes back into shape, sometimes out of shape for our own reasons.

It feels good to be back. It's like being back in touch with an old friend you've been too busy for. Only, I haven't been too busy. I've been forbidden.

"Ma?" I call out. She's not in the living room, with the big box TV that feels like it's from another era, or the '80s couch with its matching hideous green carpet. Or was it brown? I can't tell how much of this is also getting blended with my mother's memories of her childhood homes.

"Mama, you here?" No answer still, so I step gingerly through the house. Not because it helps but because it'll make me feel better, I conjure up a sword from my imagination. And then, because I can, I light it on fire. Why not? I don't know what kind of monsters Ma keeps in her dreams.

She's not in the room that looks vaguely like mine, not in the bathroom or the room that was probably supposed to be my sister's. I hear a sound from the end of the hallway. Her room. It makes my heart jump and for a second, my sword flickers out of existence. I steady myself and bring it back before making my way to the end of the hallway and—I knock first because old habits die hard and anyway, last thing I want is to interrupt one of *those* kinds of dreams—then the door flickers away and my mom is looking up at me, dressed the same way she is in the real world, in sweatpants and a baggy T-shirt with her hair wrapped up in a silk scarf.

"Ma," I say, relieved. "I came to get you."

She blinks in confusion, like the escaped dream man from outside. Then she cocks her head. "Rico?"

I exhale sharply. I look a lot like Rico, always have, and the resemblance has only gotten stronger. I hold up my hand with the dark brown birthmark. It fans out in the shape of a scallop shell. I thrust it in her face. "No, Mama. Pol."

"Why are you here, Rico? *How*?"

"It's *me. Pol*," I insist again, and it feels the same way it always has, asserting my existence. *I'm here. Look at me. See me.*

Instead, I feel her *push* me.

The dream dissolves.

This time, we're somewhere I've never been—a house or apartment that looks modern in one corner, with big windows and a cold light I think is supposed to be the sun. Another corner, though, has an old ratty sofa, the kind of thing a couple of broke college students might bring in from the curb.

I *should* be awake now. Witches can push interlopers out of their dreams—unless the interloper is too strong. That must be what happened to my aunts and sister. But I'm still here.

Ma kneels right in the middle of the room, hunched over a baby she holds in her arms. I can't tell if she's nursing the kid or checking on it, but her cooing has a frantic rhythm, an edge to it that makes the back of my neck prickle.

I inch closer, trying not to spook her this time. The baby is mostly featureless—there's a thatch of dark hair, a wrinkly little brown body.

Then Ma gasps and she puts the baby on the ground to resuscitate it, but its little chest is still. Then the dream warps and the baby is back in her arms again. As the macabre scene plays over and over, with my Ma nursing the baby and then failing to save it, I wonder—is it supposed to be me? Or is it someone else?

We're not supposed to make assumptions like that in the Dreamscape; Ma always warned me against it, but I'm only human. I know the shit that bubbles up from my unconscious has a root more often than not, even if I can't tease it out. Half the meaning we get when we read someone's dreams comes from the meaning *they* give it.

I can't read her mind, though, not the darkest places, and not her past. This is as close as I can come. Assumptions won't get her out. The only thing that will is for her to follow me willingly, and for me to find whatever her mind manifests as the "way out." The more a person wants to wake up, the easier it is, but with a witch as strong as my mother . . . I have no idea what to expect.

"Mama. Hey, Ma. It's me, Pol."

Ma startles up at me, and this time, her eyes are lucid.

"Pol? What are you doing here?"

The baby, alive now, wiggles in her arms.

She scans my flat chest, my face. "Pol. You shouldn't be here. I told you before and I meant it—I don't care if you don't want to be a girl—or whatever. You're my kid. Always. But you said you'd obey the family's decision."

The family. *This stupid little backward coven.* My lip curls in frustration. "The *family* brought me to help you." Then, confused at how relaxed she seems, I frown. "You're stuck. Can't you tell?"

Ma looks around the room, her brow furrowed. Then she looks down at the baby. Like a smash cut, it's suddenly on the floor again. It dies. Smash cut again, and it's back in Ma's arms before she's even had a chance to answer me.

She closes her eyes and I can *feel* her trying to leave. To wake up. The Dreamscape shudders with the attempt, but when she opens her eyes, we're all still there: me, her, and the baby.

"Oh."

"Get it now?" I snap. I should be nicer. I should be more understanding. It's gotta suck realizing you're locked in some fucked-up dream. But I learned to lock compassion up a long time ago, and it's hard to get past the iron doors, the bars, and the padlocks I've erected to keep myself safe. "You've pushed everyone else out. So let's go."

I lean down and hold out my hand. At first, I don't expect her to take it. She's getting that distant glazed look in her eyes again as she stares at my birthmark.

But she grabs hold and her palm is dry and warm—I feel a pang of tenderness. Then the weight of her drags me down into darkness.

*It's still dark wherever we land in the Dreamscape. Musty fabric and moth-*balls, rasping wool and rustling fake silk brush my cheeks and the back of my neck. A closet. Ironic. And yet, it's not the same as my own closets, metaphorical or otherwise. There's a different kind of oppression in the air. I can smell the fear-sweat stink of it. I can see it in the way the darkness shimmers like an oil stain.

Mama's hand is still in mine. Unintentionally, I jerk away. I'm not used to touching her. It's been so long, and even before I moved away, I . . . let's just say gestures of affection stopped feeling affectionate.

"Do you know where we're supposed to be?" I whisper.

Her voice reaches my ear with a tremor of fear that makes my stomach drop and a chill run down my spine: "Yes."

"Can you get us out of here?"

The gleaming whites of her eyes vanish as she closes them—the world shudders but we're still here in the dark. I take a shaky breath. Okay, something else then.

I turn the handle of the door, cracking it open just enough to look. It's just a bedroom, but shadows stretch across it like monsters, thin arms and legs reaching up the walls and across the ceiling.

The door creaks a little as I slip through it. Ma grasps at the back of my shirt and hisses for me to *stop, wait, come back.*

Somewhere, children are laughing, but it's in that fucked-up, horror-movie way, distant and echoing all around us, and beneath the laughter, there are heavy footsteps. Like work boots. Ma jerks back into the closet and suddenly the footsteps are louder, like they're coming from all directions, even though there's only one door that leads out of the bedroom. The door that's probably the way out.

I stick my head into the closet after her and grab her wrist. The touch is electrifying, literally, and I fight the urge to release her.

"Come on," I say, my voice low. Even though I know it's her dream, even though I know it's *just* a dream, I can't help looking over my shoulder. I know I'm not supposed to make assumptions but I think I know whose boots those are. I don't wanna be here any more than Ma does. I try to make my voice calmer, confident. Deeper, the way I've been practicing. "We have to get through that door—there's nothing stopping us. He's not in here."

When Ma emerges from the closet, she looks younger. Not a kid, but the lines in her face have smoothed, the gray in her hair darkened, the blond streaks gone. I wanna let go of her now that she's out, but I don't trust her not to bolt for the closet again.

At the bedroom door, I listen. The children's laughter, the footsteps, they're all still there, and my stomach is so liquid I think I'm gonna shit myself when I open the door. I clench everything tight and hold my breath, then I open it a hair. Ma's intake of breath is sharp behind me.

It's not the exit from the Dreamscape that I hoped. It leads to another hallway stretching from our left and right. On the other side, opposite us, is another door.

"We'll jump for the other door on 'go,' okay?" I wait for her to nod. I can't stick my head out to look, but it sounds like the footsteps are receding, so I wait a full ten seconds before counting Ma down.

"Three . . ."

The boots go quiet.

"Two . . ."

The laughter stops, too, and suddenly the silence is a lot less reassuring, but I've already started the count.

"One—"

Ma yanks the bedroom door open and leaps past me, stretching for the door across from us, but it's yanked suddenly out of reach—the width of the hallway is half a soccer field now. I try to pull it back with my magic, but nothing happens.

Instead, I feel a presence on my left. I turn slowly. Ma's weight drags me down again as she sags to her knees. I stay on my feet, clutching her wrist.

I recognize my great-uncle from pictures only—Ma never let us meet him. He's larger than I ever imagined and I have to remind myself that this could be the dream's warp. He towers over us. Thick, calloused hands reach for the buckle of his belt.

No use trying to sneak anymore. "Run!" I scream.

Ma and I sprint for the door on the other side of the too-stretched hall, only as soon as I pick up my legs, they're made of lead. Or they're stuck in quicksand. I fucking hate dream running.

Behind me, too close, the jangle of his belt buckle is thunderous.

A small voice in my head tells me, *Fly*. It's the small voice of lucidity that finds me in my own dreams, my real dreams, not the Dreamscape ones.

Fly, it says again.

Duh.

This is a dream. It's not my dream, but I'm a dream witch. This is what I do.

Wings burst from my back and I'm strong enough to grab my mother in my—*oh, talons, that's interesting*—and I flap with powerful wingbeats to the door. Even though the man's boots are heavy and reverberate around the Dreamscape as he runs after us, he can't catch me before I fling open the door with my mind and dive through it.

I land with a thud on the carpet, wings tucked around us while we roll and skitter. Only, the wings are gone. So is the oppressive weight of my great-uncle's presence. Sprawled out, eyes closed, I sigh with relief.

"Ma? You okay? We made it."

Her scream jerks me upright. She's hurt, I think, or Aunt Tiff did something to her and she's just realized it, she's gonna die anyway—

None of that, no.

It's Mama Glory in one of her church hats and a black skirt, like she's just come back from a funeral, and she's shouting at Ma—I shake my head, trying to clear it. That can't be right. She died six years ago. Right before I left for good.

We haven't woken up.

I clamber to my feet just in time to see Mama Glory backhand Ma, and it's like a movie how dramatic Ma's reaction is, her spinning half a circle with the force of the blow. Mama Glory's hand pulls back for another go and I try to get there first, to wedge myself between her and my mom, but dream logic slows me to a slog again.

When I was a kid, I used to give her shoulder massages while I watched cartoons after school, digging my tiny fingers into the work-knotted muscle of her bent back. It's the same woman, and yet . . .

I'm lucky that she's just a figment of my mother's dreams. Mama Glory was the last matriarch, before she died and Ma took over, and she was so powerful she could—she *did*—block me from the Dreamscape entirely when she found out about me. I'd begged Ma not to tell her, but she told her sisters and I don't know if it was Aunt Tiff or LeeLee who ratted me out, but I remember going into the Dreamscape afterward and finding Mama Glory there. I remember the blistering pain as she forced me out of my own dreams and the gaping emptiness whenever I tried to go back.

It was like that for two years.

She's your grandmother, Ma always said. *We have to respect her*, she said, and *Things will change*, she said. But Mama Glory was gone now and nothing had changed.

Here in the Dreamscape, though, I can see the truth.

Mama was afraid.

And now, seeing her face, distorted after the blow, I see the fury she tamps down before she turns to face my grandmother again.

I call on my dream magic to fight the drag at my feet and—poof. Just like that, the next blow is headed for me, not my mom.

I don't know why I do it, not logically, but there's a part of me that wonders if no one ever got between Ma and Mama Glory, either. I can almost hear her say, "That's just not the way we do things."

When I'm there, though, waiting for the blow to land, I realize I fucked up.

I fucked up bad.

This is Ma's dream. She's always known Mama Glory as a witch, powerful beyond means in the Dreamscape. So even though she's dead and this is just a figment of my mom's damned overactive imagination, she's a *powerful* figment.

I buckle in half against my will and hear the sharp, high-pitched whistle of a switch before it whips across my backside. The sting brings tears to my eyes. I haven't felt it since I was a kid—and then I *am* a kid, with the stupid pigtails I hated and a frilly Easter dress with shining pleather shoes.

The loathing is immediate. So's the bile in my throat. Try as I might, though, I can't change. Not the clothes, not my age. The helplessness I felt all my life before I came out, before I left home—it comes back a thousand times heavier, pressing me to my hands and knees. My eyes are hot with frustrated tears.

Another stinging blow. I pull for my magic again and though my clothes flicker for half a second back to jeans, the Easter dress constricts again, harder.

"Ma!" I croak, eyes shut against the pain and the humiliation. I don't wanna see myself like this. "Mama!" I fumble with one hand, reaching blindly for her.

Where is she? From my knees, I turn, looking for her.

I see her standing where I was, half a dream-league away, hands pressed over her mouth, tears running down her face.

Her fear has won out over her fury.

I drop my head to the carpet and resign myself to the blows of the switch until I can gather enough strength to fight again.

The lucid voice in my head interrupts again. *You could just go. Leave her. This isn't your dream. Wake up. Wake* up.

Leave her. Leave Ma to this. To replaying her every nightmare until Aunt Tiff decides she's too much of a liability. Leave her, and watch the end from the outside. The thought makes my guts heave.

Before I can admit my decision to myself, another strike falls, missing the flesh of my backside and striping across my bony kid-back.

I scream. I can't even help myself. As much as I don't want to, I cry out for her again, my voice high and breaking.

"Mama!"

And then she's there, Ma, clutching my hand in one of hers while she wraps the rest of her body over me.

"Your clothes," she says, in the gap before the thin wood falls across her shoulders. She winces under the blow but meets my eyes again after it passes.

I understand what she's saying, but I don't understand why.

"No! Help me get rid of her!"

She shakes her head. "You are strongest in the Dreamscape when you own who you are. Change your clothes."

I swallow and nod. With her help, the dress ripples away. First it changes to old jeans with the little juniors elastic bands and some oversized wolf T-shirt I had when I was a kid. From there, it's easier to return to the way I was when I entered the Dreamscape: Levi's and black tee, hard jaw and muscles.

"What about you?" I ask. It's an incomplete question. She looks like herself, herself as I last saw her in person, plus a few more lines, a lot more gray in her hair. What I really mean to say, and can't find the words for, is *Why are you stuck?*

Ma looks at me with her mouth pressed together, her eyes tight at the corners with grief and regret. "I know who I am."

"Huh? Who?"

"I'm your mother, Pol. Now, come on."

She doesn't give me a chance to process her answer before spinning me around to face Mama Glory.

I use my dream magic like some superhero or mutant superpower, sweeping hand gestures and streaming light. Ma, on the other hand, closes her eyes just like she's meditating or praying. It's funny to see how different we are as we do that now—I shoot a beam of light from my palm toward my grandmother and Ma just bows her head and presses her hands together.

Under the force of our joined magic, Mama Glory disintegrates—and so does the rest of the dream room.

I jerk awake with a gasp like I've almost drowned. Gratifyingly, I hear a choking gasp echo me from above.

My face is pressed into the carpet beside my mom's bed, right next to a pair of shoes. I crane my neck up to see Aunt Tiff, holding a syringe clenched tight in her fist.

"Don't—" I rasp, grabbing the tailored leg of my aunt's jeans.

She doesn't even look down at me, though. Instead, she drops onto the bed to sit next to my mom, murmuring softly to Ma as she checks she's alright.

I pull myself up to my knees so I can see, too, and there she is: Ma, sitting up, taking slow sips of water from the cup Aunt Tiff holds tenderly to her lips.

Ma makes a small sound when she sees me, and that's when Aunt Tiff finally turns to me. The disgust is still there, despite everything, though at least she tries to hide it this time with some kind of begrudging gratitude.

Even now, it hurts, though I should have known better.

I push myself to my feet and head for the bedroom door when my sister and LeeLee burst in.

"You did it?" Caris is saying before she even sees me. When she does, her eyes flick behind me, frightened and hopeful at the same time. "The escaped dreams, they stopped—did you . . . or did Aunt Tiff . . . ?"

I nod, shoulders sagging with exhaustion. "I got her out."

"Oh, thank God," she says, and she rushes past me to sit on Ma's other side.

LeeLee gives me a tight-lipped smile before following Caris.

I keep walking, out of the bedroom, out of the house. I stop in the middle of the empty driveway. I used to sit here and play cards with the neighbor kids, practice wheelies. One of my mom's boyfriends taught me how to change the oil in my car right here.

When Ma gets better, they'll start debating whether or not they should block me from the Dreamscape like Mama Glory did. For now, I don't care.

I grab my suitcase out of my sister's car and call a cab.

I wait for the car and wait for somebody to run out of the house looking for me, wondering which will come first.

SHE WHO MAKES THE RAIN

Millie Ho

Grandma is missing. Oracle bones glitter
on the bamboo mat, the fan still creaking
in the living room. A dry, bloodless summer.
She's not by the altar in the garden,

nor the gazebo where she needled bodies
back to health. Her study, once fragrant
with herbs and peach wood, is just
a woodshed now.

Grandma is often missing. A cataract
grey face, she sits in soft silence,
watches mountains blur with smog.
Toxic buildup, neurons giving up.

It has not rained for many days.
No more farmers lining up, the lake
choked by dust. Industrial momentum,
charcoal fingers, trucks crawling away.

The alphabet of Grandma's magic
is scrambled. Some days she forgets
who I am, other days, her own name.
She unseals the spirit world and misplaces

her slippers. Holds my hand too tightly,
stares at the ceiling light. She is older now,
but I am older, too. I follow her residue,
the echoes of what she must've wanted to do.

Cypress trees nudge me left, the crows
lead me right. Through wooded valleys
and down the hills, into the dried lake.
The sky is shot with craters.

The smell of wet grass and mud,
the clouds spinning above like gears
that are finally turning.

One drop, then two.

Rain needles my face, rolls into
the cracks. Grandma stands
in the lakebed, hands raised,
lit from within, fingers forking
the sky.

As wondrous as a beating heart.

Some days Grandma forgets,
other days, she makes the rain.

AS WAYWARD SISTERS, HAND IN HAND

Indrapramit Das

2008

Michael and I make the long walk home across downtown Lansdonfield, Pennsylvania, after six hours tripping on shrooms in the woods. The geometry of streets and buildings feels sharper, lights blossom with unrecognizable intensity, and people reveal their natures effortlessly. We meet a young Black roller skater in Bottleneck Park who laments the dying of his art in our city, weaving across the wet concrete of the basketball court bespectacled and alone. We encounter a middle-aged white man on North Franklin who visited Calcutta before I was born, and asks if the hash still flows free there before power-walking away, trailing the stink of his hand-rolled cigarette. Reaching North Dietz, we walk into our favorite Greek restaurant. We've never seen the woman at the counter before. Her face is luminous with exhaustion, a piercing punctuating the corner of her mouth. Her clothes are mournful black, contrasting with her damp pallor. She's pregnant. I feel an infantile urge to cross the counter and embrace her, wrap my arms around her and lay my head on her chest. After our long journey she seems unbearably maternal, glowing in the steamy light of the restaurant.

"I like your tattoos," Michael tells her. She smiles and thanks him. "We're planning on getting some. Where'd you get yours done?" he asks.

"My ex-boyfriend did most of them," she says.

I wonder if the bastard left her after finding out she was pregnant. We ask for falafel, avoiding the meat because Michael got the runs last time.

"Wheat or white?" she asks.

Michael and I look at each other, nod, and say "Wheat," in perfect unison, provoking a lovely and knowing smile from her. We're both tall, skinny, and have long hair. If it weren't for the different shades of our skin, his white, mine brown, we might be mistaken for brothers. Michael and I try not to laugh. She hands us tumblers of water.

"Where are you guys planning to get your tattoos?" she asks us.

"We were thinking of the place next to the farmers' market," Michael says.

"It's not that good. My ex works there," she says.

We are silent.

"Not why I'm not recommending it," she laughs. Her coppery red hair peeks out from under a green bandana, sticking to her clammy forehead. She places one hand on her belly. I wonder how easy it would be to fall in love with her and get a job cleaning gyro drippings and waiting on people right next to her, to apply for a green card and move in with her, to make myself a partner to her and a father to her child. Where would Michael figure in this life? He's my roommate and best friend. Would we form some kind of parental triad, a coven of three? Was he imagining a similar scenario right now? We have often completed each other's sentences. I briefly wonder whether Michael himself has conjured this woman for our benefit at the end of this long day.

"I did some of these myself." She shows us her arms, adorned with designs I no longer remember. We agree that they are very nice tattoos.

226

Michael doesn't mention that he also already has tattoos. I've seen them when he's changing, or going to and from the shower, two lines of symbols marking each side of his spine. He's never told me what they mean, if anything. Sometimes he playfully calls them "teats."

"I would do your tattoos, but I'm still learning. I just got a gun," the woman says. "Maybe I'll come find you guys sometime."

"With your gun? Sounds scary," says Michael, and we laugh like a trio from a cozy sitcom.

Michael and I sit down in a booth, the benches hard, unadorned wood. The restaurant is empty. The TV on a shelf in the corner is playing a program showing real-life surgery.

"She totally thought we were a couple," I tell him, unable to keep the pride from my voice.

"Totally," he agrees. The pregnant woman glances at us from behind the counter, a wistful smile still on her face.

2005

The night Michael first showed me his magic, we crammed ourselves into an old station wagon with friends and sped over the Pennsylvania countryside. The car's owner, a bearlike junior named Cal, switched off the headlights when the road was straight and glowing under the full moon. We yelled out the windows to the winds of our illusory immortality. At the end of the drive, about an hour from campus, Michael led us into the dark of Susquehannock State Park. We all stepped over the chain and sign by the parking lot forbidding people to enter after sunset. We made our way along the unlit trails to the Pinnacle, an outcropping of rock thrusting out of the forested slopes, overlooking the Susquehanna River valley.

With beer bottles tucked in the cracks between ancient rock and joints weaving lines under the stars, we sat and watched the waters hundreds of feet below glisten in the light of the night sky. "Don't be scared," Michael said, coaxing me to sit at the edge and let my feet dangle over oblivion, my body sparkling with vertiginous life. He still had short hair then, as did I. "Never throw a lit roach off the Pinnacle. You could start a fire," he said, taking a drag. I took a puff and waved Cal over to pass it on. The hushed conversations of our friends behind us wrapped around my shoulders. Michael took something out of his pocket and showed me—talismans in his moonlit palm. A small, flat glass pipe, a torch lighter, and a small baggie of what looked like oregano. "Magic sage. *Salvia divinorum,*" he said. My stomach dropped with pleasurable fear. Michael had been there when I first smoked weed, first got drunk enough to be hungover, a freshman breaking my promise of never doing drugs in America like the college kids in Hollywood movies, of being the good and sober Indian Muslim student, never giving this country a reason to expel me like a brown thorn from its hide. Perhaps this night would bring something new as well.

"Another thing you should never do on the Pinnacle is smoke salvia," he said, packing the pipe. "You could trip out, fall off." I scooted back, letting my sneakers touch rock again. *Will you guys be careful, you're too fucking close to the edge,* came Noor's voice from somewhere behind us, on cue.

Michael held a thumbs-up, then lit the pipe, inhaled. "Should I be worried?" I asked.

He laughed, his breath smoky. "My parents taught me not to flip out."

"Your parents. Taught you to smoke salvia."

"You don't know, man. My family's . . . strange. The first time I smoked salvia with them, I felt the night sky rip above me, like it was a tent. I looked up, and saw through the tear, into void. These arms made of that darkness came out of the rip. I couldn't tell if those hands were huge as the sky, or whether they were just a few feet above me. Then I felt *myself* ripping, those arms coming out of my own back, embracing me, pulling me toward the void. Into myself. I came to thinking I'd died."

"Jesus."

"Didn't see him up there." Michael smiled. He seemed unaffected by the salvia. "My parents told me what I saw through the rip was time so old and dense it was visible."

"If you can look into the seeds of time," I mumbled.

Michael nodded. "The beginning and the end of the universe. When anything becomes big enough, it becomes a god. The river down there. The Appalachians. Hell, the Earth, its ecosystem. And beyond."

"So god is gravity."

"My man, always the science fiction writer. But yeah, you're right. It's everywhere. I saw how big the universe is, the *gravity* of it, and how we're a part of it, like if the microbes in our bodies became aware of where they live. Seeing god."

"All gods reside in the human breast."

"Heavy. I like that."

"I'm paraphrasing. It's William Blake. Studying him in one of my classes. You know, I assumed you were Christian. Agnostic Christian, maybe."

"Like you?"

"Well, yeah. Except the Christian bit."

"I did get into Christianity as a teen. Went to church, played music there. My rebel against my parents' whole pagan nomadic trailer park existence phase. Did you rebel against your parents?"

"They wouldn't be too happy about me getting drunk and doing drugs." I laughed. "But nah. My parents were pretty cool about religion. They're not devout."

"My parents told me our ancestors were Finnish healers. One was tried right here in Pennsylvania."

"What for?"

"Drying the milk out of her neighbors' cows. Visiting them in spectral form. The usual. She was acquitted, though. The funny thing is, so much of what my parents say sounds like shit you hear from, like, New Age hippies or stoners at campus parties. But I saw it. They taught me to control some things."

He handed me the pipe. "I can control it for you, too, make sure you don't freak out." My toes curled in my shoes, the valley calling out with silence. *What're you cool kids whispering about?* came Cal's voice. *I think they're about to make out.* Alina this time.

Michael smiled. "Trust me."

The salvia smoke was thinner, more bitter than weed. We were flat on our backs on the Pinnacle. "Okay, don't move. At all," said Michael, and whispered what sounded like gibberish. I couldn't feel anything other than the high of the weed we'd smoked earlier. "Don't move," Michael reminded me. I let my mind drift, staring at the glittering belt of the Milky Way, never visible through the smog of Calcutta. I was thinking of how Michael told me he'd made a deal with the devil, back when I met him in our first-year dorm. *Student loans*, he'd said with a grin. *I'm never paying them back.* I thought of filling out application forms. Of watching the invasion of Iraq on TV, and wondering if applying to US colleges was a mistake. Watching the aftermath of the Gujarat pogrom on TV, and deciding to apply. Dancing with my crush Sneha at a school function, but never telling her. As the years turned back, I felt myself rooted to the Pinnacle as all that time washed across us. I was here in Pennsylvania, at the moment I was born in India. I had always been there, because I was a part of this rock, which was a cuticle on the heaving back of that god we crawled on, which in turn was a germ to a greater god, and on to infinity. Despite a distant sentiment telling me to panic, I stayed still as Michael had said, and so our bodies became rock, skin calcifying, furred not with hair but moss. *Where did Tarik and Michael go?* I heard Alina say. Then a soft chorus.

They must have gone in the woods?

I didn't see them walk by us.

We'd have heard if they fell off, right? Somewhere far, our friends walked around us. Our names called out. They were right next to us, their legs tree trunks reaching up to the sky as they stepped over us, on us, I couldn't tell. They looked right through us, at old rock. I could have lain there forever, letting seeds burrow into us, roots rip through us, trees flower into the sky above us and brush the burning wheels of sun, moon, and stars in revolution. No student loans, no classes, no immigration and scholarship applications, no tax forms, no borders, no expectations, no goodbyes.

2006

"You should just try fucking a guy once," Michael told me, sometime during our first semester as roommates in the Unity House. He walked over from his desk to mine. Our room was thick with beer fumes from open bottles, incense of spent joints in clotted ashtrays, curdling into one familiar smell in the warmth of the heater.

"Dude. I think I would have figured it out by now if I was bi," I said.

"It's not that easy to figure out," said Michael, shaking his head.

"I don't get turned on by men."

"You made out with Josie."

"Yeah, because I was drunk and wanted to make out with somebody! He was there and willing. It was nice, but it didn't give me a hard-on or anything. Making out with girls does." We'd probably had this conversation before.

"Anyway, kissing Josie doesn't count. He's an asshole," said Michael.

"I thought you had a crush on him."

"Doesn't make him not an asshole."

I laughed and watched the screen of my laptop. The music video was almost done buffering. The room was dark except for the blue glow of the screen, which glistened on the empty bottles on our hang-out table, on the half-empty bottle in Michael's hand. He leaned back in his chair. His golden-brown hair caught the screenwash, too, fake moonlight that hung over his contemplative face. The face of a wood elf in thought, graceful cheekbones gently hollowed by shadow.

"Look, forget Josie. Haven't you ever wondered what it would be like to kiss me?" he asked, not making eye contact.

The music video began playing, an intrusive burst of noise. I clicked pause.

"Of course I have."

"Then why don't you?"

"You know why," I said and took a deep breath, a tingle in my gut. "You're my best friend. It wouldn't be like making out with Josie. Or anyone else."

He put the bottle down by his feet and buried his face in his hands. Seconds later, he pulled his hair back, the skin over his high forehead stretched and sheet-white. "Just once. Why not?"

"Because you're drunk and you'd regret it in the morning."

I looked at his mouth, glossy with beer. He was beautiful, but I couldn't muster the desire to give him what he wanted. I felt guilty for having told him so many times that I would gladly go out with him if he were a girl, or if I were a girl, or if I were more sexually fluid. For telling him every so often at the culmination of our long conversations about exes that have broken our hearts, that we are perfect for each other. And we are. Or we've always convinced ourselves that we are. In truth, I knew I'd probably be daunted by his experience if he were a woman, as I was by every woman I became interested in, my virginity a specter shadowing my confidence.

I didn't touch him, or move closer. He kept his eyes off me.

"God, why the fuck are we so perfect for each other?" he said, echoing my thoughts. He got up and went back to his side of the room, connected to mine by a little mini hallway where our shoes and empty bottles lived, so it felt like two separate rooms. I heard the groan of springs as he sank into his bed.

"Are you okay?"

"Yes. No, you're right. I'm fine." His voice muffled by the quilt.

"Are you going to sleep?" I asked.

"Yes."

"Good night, Michael."

"Good night, Tarik."

The next morning, he walked over to my side of the room. We squinted at each other through our hangovers, I still in bed, he standing and swaying against the wall. "Thanks for not letting me kiss you last night. I'm sorry about that," he said, with a sincerity that embarrassed me.

"That's okay. Don't worry about it." I wondered if this would affect our friendship permanently in some way, but I knew better.

2007

Michael lay facedown on his bed as I straddled his back, giving him a massage, both of us in the midst of an acid comedown. He did the same for me, molding the tension out of my suddenly malleable body. Acid makes you strikingly aware of your physicality, of the juices flowing inside you, fighting to come out in various ways and forms. Spit and tears flood your mouth and eyelids, piss sits heavily in your bladder, blood flushes your cheeks and lips, sweat crawls under your clothes and begins to smell strange and unfamiliar. Your cells burn, begging to be touched. Michael and I were both single during this time. I was dying to touch someone, to kiss someone, to taste the furnace of another human body. I wanted these things so intensely it felt like the drug had induced withdrawal from the human chemical dependency on other humans, on tactile contact. I knew Michael probably wanted the same thing. There was no one around that weeknight—all sleeping, or studying, or at the party we'd started out at and left because the cokeheads were getting too rowdy for an acid trip. We just had each other.

Like Siamese twins we'd marched across an empty campus just before dawn, a frozen land devoid of women or men, shoulder to shoulder against the cold, two chins tilted to the starry sky as we admired how Christmas lights woven through the branches made chandeliers of the iced trees. We looked at ourselves in the mirror of a restroom in the music building, stared horrified at two flushed zombies standing under the fluorescent lights, swollen eyes and lips glimmering with the fluids animating our sallow flesh. We went up to a private practice room for which Michael had the key. I scrawled the words I'M ON ACID on a blackboard while he played the piano with startling lucidity. Moved by his art, I drew the face of a sharp-boned, elfin woman on the board, shocked by how steadily the lines of her face cohered under my fingers. When we were done, Michael looked at the board. "Um, not that many people have the key to this room," he said. I erased the words I'M ON ACID and left the chalk-dusted face of the woman to greet the first person to enter the room that morning.

I remember the ridges of Michael's ribs as skin and T-shirt slid rhythmically over them under my hands. "Oh, Tarik," he moaned, quasi-orgasmic, trying to make me uncomfortable. "God, you're so thin," he said, when it was his turn to run his hands over my ribs. "So are you," I mumbled through the pillow, which smelled of his shampoo.

We hugged each other for what felt like ten minutes and was probably one, before retiring to our separate beds, the acid still smoldering away inside us. "Can you leave the light on?" Michael asked from his side of the room. I left it on.

That night, I woke to the realization that someone was on my side of the room. I was pinned by torpor to the familiar firmness of my mattress. It was Michael, had to be Michael walking over to the bed. He was naked, his long hair down to his neck, silhouetted by the glow of the standing lamp on his side of the room, which was out of sight beyond the bend of the connecting hallway. I'd seen Michael naked, when he was helpless, drunk after being dumped by his girlfriend in sophomore year, limp and vomit-streaked in my arms as I helped him into the shower. Not like this. He raised his hands to his face, covering his features and then pulling back his hair like he so often did. As his palms slid back, I could see it wasn't him in the dimness. He'd wiped his face off and left a different beauty behind, feminine, cheekbones still sharp. As she walked closer, the lines of her body trickled like water against the soft light, shaping her body softer, her hair pouring longer down her back and sides a cloak, black instead of russet. She came up to the bed and leaned as if praying by my side, knees on the hairy carpet, praying for my riveted soul. She leaned over me, her breath the scent of honey and blood, and bit her lower lip, not a caricatured gesture of feminine coyness as I first thought, but to split the thin membrane of skin there with her sharp teeth, raising crimson that she licked over her flushed mouth, darkening it to a glistening wound. I could feel my own blood coalescing between my legs under my blanket. There were no whites to her black eyes, though the ambient light gathered in pinpricks to give her pupils. In her face, I could see the memory of Michael, sleeping not so very far away, as if this creature was a sister of his unearthed from the night. I wondered if I was afraid, and I was. But my heart raced with more than fear. I'd kissed women, but I'd never been next to a woman naked like her. Through blanket and boxers I felt her fingers against my cock. I was still a virgin. My body twitched as I expelled an unwanted memory of Josie touching me. As I breathed out, she leaned forward to catch the exhalation, swallow it, her warm mouth on mine. I was paralyzed, but my tongue responded to hers. I kissed her back. The blanket whispered off me, leaving me exposed, in my undershirt and boxers. Then she was on top of me, straddling me like Michael and I had straddled each other not so long ago (or was it a very long time ago). Her cock was erect, thighs cool against me, as if she'd just emerged from a rushing river. Shadows gathered behind her, subservient to her beauty, and I saw them shaped into arms that spread around her like wings, the limbs of a lovely spider. Those arms rose up, a headdress for a queen now, a multitude of fingers scraping the slanted ceiling over my bed. Reality gasped, sliced open. A gash of emptiness appeared above her. The void poured into the room, rippling around us, a tent made of time, sheathing us so we were just the two of us in a universe of darkness radiant with an ancient echo of cosmic light. She bathed in eternity. She was slick with it, and she bent down and kissed me again, breasts soft against my flat chest, her many icy hands on my face, in my hair, grasping between our bodies to rub my aching crotch. I felt flesh enfold my cock through fabric, pulling the fear, the need from me, unraveling me. She moaned with me as my boxers drenched with fresh warmth.

2008

On the day we vacated our campus room in the Unity House, Michael called Josie, by then his boyfriend, to help move his things with his truck. As Michael and I solemnly packed up belongings and stripped the room we had spent two years living in, Josie watched us, impeccably groomed in his tight T-shirt and torn jeans. As always, I felt cowed by his physical perfection as he stood there not helping. Massaging his exposed biceps, he sighed. "I can't believe you're both leaving. I loved this room," he said.

Michael was dismantling the row of empty bottles on our hallway shelf. They clashed loudly in the garbage bag.

"Tarik, do you remember the lap dance I gave you?" Josie asked. Michael rolled his eyes. We'd both heard this question many times, but it had been a while since he'd brought it up.

"How could I forget?" I said, stuffing clothes into my suitcase. My heart was racing, unpleasant and unexpected. Memories I hadn't examined closely since my first kiss with a boy, with Josie himself, surfaced abruptly. Josie had, in fact, given me a lap dance at a party back in junior year. It had ended in our first kiss. I'd been stunned at his sinuous sensuality, his grace as he writhed against my crotch, flinching at the dry smoothness of his abdomen and chest when he grabbed my hand and slid it under his T-shirt, moving it in circles across his taut torso. In that moment he'd felt beautiful against me, and with everyone in the room chanting, "Kiss! Kiss! Kiss!" and our beer-sour breath already mingling, I'd taken the chance to kiss someone, anyone. Though my clothes were all on, I felt stripped and re-dressed, a new person, not the boy who'd left India, who'd never kissed anyone, let alone another man. Josie and I did kiss again, the spectatorial thrill of that first, being watched by friends, by strangers, women and men, by Michael, fading a bit each time. By the time Josie was groping me every time he saw me at a party, I was no longer returning his affection—telling him that I wasn't gay, that I was seeing a girl long-distance over Skype in India, that I was too high, too drunk. His tongue would still enter my mouth, his hands under my clothes, while I whispered at him to stop, and he whispered to me of how perfect and smooth my brown skin was. One night, I had to speak instead of whisper, clear but still polite, before he finally stopped trying to mold my body into the clay he wanted. Then senior year came along, and suddenly he and Michael were dating.

I wanted Josie to be heartbroken right then. Heartbroken by the end of our college days, maybe even by my impending departure from the country, from my friends, my home of four years. From Michael.

"I feel terrible I didn't get you a goodbye present," Josie said. Michael gave him a wary look as he arranged his old textbooks in a stack. "Maybe I can give you a blow job. Finish what we started that day."

"Josie," muttered Michael, shaking his head.

"I'd really appreciate it if you'd just let me pack my things right now," I said.

"Tarik, did you just take me seriously? I'm sorry, but I see you as a friend. You're not getting a blowjob from me in your wildest dreams."

"Alright, man."

"Psht, so serious. You're no fun." Tired of baiting me, Josie left to wait in his truck.

Downstairs, Michael took me aside, red shirt darkened to crimson by the mist of rain. Josie sat in the truck, impatiently drumming his fingers on the wheel. I almost admired his nonchalance. He grinned and waved.

"Hey man, I'm really sorry about Josie," Michael said.

"It's not your fault. He's always like that."

"I invited him over. Trust me, I've had enough of his shit, but, I don't know, I shouldn't even have asked, it's like taking advantage of him."

"What do you mean?"

"I'm breaking up with him. I think he knows it's over, anyway. He's bored of me. I'll thank him for his help, and then that's it," he said.

I said nothing, watching my breath billow in the wet air.

"I know this isn't how you wanted to leave. I know we didn't hang out that much these past few months because of him."

I didn't break my sullen silence, didn't give him absolution for choosing Josie, even though he had every reason to. Michael wasn't my boyfriend. I didn't deserve his every waking minute of time.

"We had some good times in that room," he said, looking up at the two windows lodged in the slanted roof of the Unity House, each a frame for two years of our lives in the same room.

"Yeah, we did," I said. "Anyway, it doesn't matter. I'll see you again in a few days."

"I'll make it up to you," he said, and walked back to the truck. We waved goodbye. I went back upstairs to wait for my older cousin to pick me up and take me to his place in New Jersey for some post-graduation family time.

After my short stay in Newark, I return to Lansdonfield for the little while I have left in the country. Michael and I spend two weeks of spring living in a vast, empty house that belongs to an opera singer. Michael is house-sitting for her while she's on tour. Two cats share the house with us, feral ghosts who barely show themselves. One of them lives under the floorboards of the upstairs bathroom, his water and food dishes right next to the toilet and a hole in the floor. The other lives everywhere else. I never see the two of them at the same time, but Michael assures me that they cannot live without each other. The living room of the house is cluttered with various remnants of the singer's life so far: framed photos of her family, boxes full of dusty Christmas decorations and trinkets, baby-faced ceramic angels, yellowed old books and sheet music, a grand piano on which Michael practices in the evenings, when the red walls are lined with streetlight slanting in through the blinds. A life-sized oil portrait of a gorgeous woman with dark brown hair flowing past her shoulders watches us from above the fireplace, her green eyes guttering in the paint. Michael tells me it is the opera singer herself. I never see a recent picture, or any photos of her. Michael tells me it's because she's ashamed of her weight.

Michael cooks for me, stir-frying vegetables and rice, pan-searing steaks from the nearby farmers' market. Clueless at domesticity, I cut vegetables and wash the dishes to even things out. His laptop and speakers sit near the coffeemaker, and he bobs his head, hair tied back in a loose bun, to songs we both love. "How about this one?" he always asks, bent over the computer, and if I shake my head he selects another song, until we reach consensus. When the beats quicken, he shakes his ass, moves his feet across the tiles in quick steps, closer to me. "C'mon, dance! I wanna see you move that long body of yours." I laugh and ignore him, tapping my feet at best, encased in my inflexible body instead of his flexible one. Time is demarcated by the clock in the kitchen, which makes highly realistic bird calls on the stroke of the hour. It never fails to shock us.

We eat our meals in the little garden out back, feet in the cold grass, enjoying the spring sunlight until evening falls and it becomes too cold to sit outside for long. Michael shows me the herbs and vegetables he is growing in a patch in the corner of the plot—basil, tomatoes, others that I forget the names of. He parts their tender little infant leaves gently, feeling for their burgeoning life with his soiled fingertips.

Occasionally the friends still left in town after the exodus of graduation join us for dinner, and we sip chilled beers and watch the stars appear, listen to the hypnotic hiss of trees and plants in this tiny oasis nestled within the urban landscape of Lansdonfield. There is a parking lot just beyond the wooden fence where the uncropped grass ends, guarded by chipped gnomes. We usually talk about college and how we will miss it (though Michael has always hated college, if not the time he spent there), of the four years we've spent together. Michael and I chew a cap each of the mushrooms he has grown in manure in one corner of the garden, one night under the trees. They are sun-dried but juicier than the psilocybin we've taken before. I trust he knows what he's doing. We lie in the garden hammock side by side, waiting for the silent white streaks of shooting stars. We see faint trails of the recent past behind our fingers as we wave our hands to the dark sky. He asks me, his hand shimmering, "Do you remember when you and I kissed in a dream you had? I was a woman."

I laugh, the memory of the dream bubbling out of me in breath, shaking the hammock. I hear Michael laugh, too, absorbing my reaction. "What. Yes, I do. I fucking do, Michael. What the fuck. A woman with too many arms. I . . . came in my pants that night. Wow, I told you about that?"

"No, you didn't," Michael says, through giggles.

"Fuck me."

"Gladly," he says, and we burst into laughter, the hammock swinging urgently to contain it, the stars leaping before our eyes in celebration.

"You're real," I say, shaking my head. "I can't believe it."

"Nor can I, sometimes," says Michael, bringing one hand to his face, touching.

"Spectral form," I whisper through tears.

"Spectral form," he agrees, and we convulse with laughter.

"You tell the cops, they'll burn me at the stake," he says.

"I would never," I say.

"I didn't mean to glamour you. I thought I was dreaming, until I realized I wasn't."

"Well, she was really hot."

"Thank you," says Michael, his voice gone soft.

Our sides seep into each other.

"I'm sorry," says Michael.

I look at him. He isn't laughing anymore, but the tears still glimmer fresh on his cheekbones. Light from the windows of the house yellow against his eyes. "Why?" I ask.

"I bewitched you."

"What's a little bewitching between friends."

"I kissed you after you told me not to."

"It was a dream, Michael."

"Was it a nightmare?" he asks.

"No," I tell him. "Just a dream."

*The next day we eat a whole Ziploc bag of mushrooms on the walk to Em-*ber Woods, known as "the Heap" to students, a small forest grown out of the sodden remains of a garbage landfill. We munch on caps and stems as if they were Cheetos as we cross the pretty, manicured residential neighborhood that borders the plot.

By the time we enter the forest the effects have begun to take hold. This journey stretches out in our minds like an endless epic, a crawl across dimensions; from civilization and the city we've made our home to alien wilderness where we watch huge spiders tremble in the sun, picking their way across the leaves of their sylvan city. Michael leads the way with assured steps, his sneakers sinking into the mud, backpack slung across both shoulders, weighed down by the Tupperware containers of guacamole and salad he painstakingly prepared for our trip, ignored and fermented by the time we remember we are animals that need to eat. Time stretches behind our steps as the sun disintegrates behind leaves and trunks, its shards still burning on our cooling skins. We arrive at the clearing where students have bonfires, a circle of scorched rocks and ashen soil marking the spot, which is nestled behind a short bluff. We sit on the stage of that slope like statues, letting insects crawl over us, the setting sun bathing our faces through forest sieve.

"I never realized what Josie did to you," says Michael, as my hands ripple across my vision like pennants. Michael's body radiates heat, reflecting the sunlight like a moon.

"What did he do?" I say.

"He didn't respect you."

"Nah," I breathe out. "It's all good."

"No, it's not," says Michael, his voice calm like mine, but forceful. "I broke up with him because . . . he told me he rejected you. When he had that crush on you. He told me he was kissing you one day, and got grossed out imagining how your dick would be all dark, because you're brown, and lost his crush."

I feel a familiar dislocation, unpleasant. "Alina told me, back then. Josie talked that shit to her, too."

"She should have told me."

"Don't blame her. I told her not to tell anyone. I didn't want it to become gossip. Can we not talk about this? It doesn't feel good."

"I remembered, you told me *you* rejected him all those times. I remembered him kissing you, at those parties. Fuck. I couldn't believe I was fucking this guy. I was so angry. You're leaving the country, and I spent these last few months with *him*?"

I am silent, the sunlight and verdant scent of the woods suddenly tangible, melting in wet trickles down my face, salt in my mouth.

"I'm sorry. For what he did to you." Michael's hand, shocking against mine. Our hands, interlocked over the squirming earth. I wipe my face with the other hand, squinting against the blazing descent of noon. I can't speak. But I look in Michael's eyes, dark as a tree's hollow, whites gone. I nod, assure him I'm fine. My long hair cascading tickles down my neck. My body feels transparent, solid only where I am touching Michael's hand. I feel ethereal, feminine in a way both euphoric and discomfiting. Michael whispers in a language I don't know, that sounds like it is pulled from the ground underneath us, the cackle and hiss of branches and leaves, the drone of insects crawling around us. I see Michael close his eyes. I close mine.

Our hands still touch, in the world behind closed lids, which looks like a bedroom, the curtains half-drawn to the same late afternoon we're in. My eyes snap open as I see Josie lying on the bed in shorts and T-shirt, watching something on his laptop. But I'm still here in the room. "Fuck," I say, and Josie snaps up from the bed and slams into the wall with a thump. His earphones pop out of his ears, pulling the laptop across the bedcover. "What the fuck," he echoes me.

Michael squeezes my hand. He is right beside me, his eyes full black, whispering what sounds like gibberish. "What," Josie stammers.

The curtains billow soft, the sunlight through them pulsing through the room. I've been here, of course; Josie's off-campus place, which he's thinking of staying in with his housemates now that they're all done with college. Michael steps toward him, letting go of my hand. The light from the window passes through him—he casts no shadow. Nor do I. I watch as Michael approaches Josie. I step back, my breath quickened. He is raven-winged, an angel. Arms made of unseeable void, stretching out of his back. Josie is paralyzed, whether by terror or some magic I cannot know. His mouth is a rictus. His shorts darken with growing wetness. The arms unfurled on Michael's back bristle in animalistic display, a spider rearing up, the many hands spreading their sharp fingers. "Don't, don't do anything," I say. Michael turns, the wings of arms folding, embracing him in darkness. I am looking at him in Ember Woods, the sun on our faces. His eyes are full black. He blinks, and they are gray as they were.

"I couldn't have done much anyway," he says, voice flat. "Just a waking dream. A fantasy. I'd have slashed his throat with talons made of darkness for what he did, what he said about you. But his wounds would have healed the moment he realized it's not real."

"Don't . . . go away again."

"We were here. Not there."

"I know. You know what I mean."

"Tarik. That night, you know I wasn't actually in your bed, right?"

"I know. Listen." I look into his eyes. "You're not Josie."

He nods, not looking at me.

"Now, let's stay here," I tell him.

"Okay." His shoulders slump.

"I don't need you to be my guardian, Michael. Just a friend. Like you've always been."

He smiles, looking wan. "I know."

We emerge from the forest as evening melts time fluid again, a liquid that blooms in iridescent bubbles around the streetlights. We are mute as we rejoin the people treading the calm pavements of Lansdonfield on a late spring evening. We stop at our favorite Greek place on North Dietz. We meet a pregnant woman behind the counter, who chats with us. I wonder briefly if I'm dreaming and still in the woods, if Michael has conjured this woman, so warm and kind, in this empty restaurant. As we eat, I get a little sad that she probably won't end up doing our tattoos with her brand-new gun. I'll probably never see her again. Chewing on falafel that feels like alien matter in my body, I ask Michael, "What'll you do after I leave?"

Michael has a smear of tahini on his chin. He shrugs. "Dunno, man. Maybe look for my parents? They keep disappearing on their long-ass road trips, but I usually know where to find them. If I visit them in my sleep."

"That's . . . very cool." My still-sparking brain seems unable to find words.

The melancholy that fills his eyes is offset by the tahini stain. "Is it? I mean, with the internet, it's kind of redundant. Sometimes I just wish they were ordinary parents trying to figure out email, instead of making me do dream quests to find them."

I remain quiet. Tap my chin. He wipes off the tahini with a scrunched napkin. "Or I might just stay in Lansdonfield. Look for a place, play some gigs, get a job at a bar until I figure things out. I have the house for a couple more weeks."

"Don't forget to harvest all your shrooms."

"Oh, I won't." He looks at me. "What about you? Tell me you'll be back in America for postgrad." We've discussed all of this before, but as time together runs out, we reach for assurances.

"If I get in somewhere. Get a full scholarship. Get a visa."

"I'll save up, visit. Somehow. I'd love to meet your family. See Calcutta. Show off all the Bengali you've taught me." As always, he pronounces it beng-allie instead of beng-all-ee, which makes me smile. He can say "How are you?," "Motherfucker," and "Thank you" in the language.

"If you can't make it soon-ish . . . you do have other ways. Right?" I ask.

"The internet?"

"Yeah, yeah. Facebook and IMs is what I mean."

"Okay. The other thing doesn't always work. What we did today, and in our room back then—you were close by. So was Josie. I didn't have to go far. I've never tried crossing oceans."

"You're underestimating your power."

He actually blushes. "Hopefully. Magic isn't easy to conjure in this"—he waves at the restaurant, the TV in the corner now playing a music video because our favorite new cashier switched the channel—"time and place. My parents and I have its memory. That's the only reason we can do what little we can do."

"I do too, now. I have the memory. Because of you."

"Tarik. You'd be amazed at how easy it is to forget. Wait a few years and this'll all seem made up."

"I'll remember," I tell him. "I'll always remember."

He looks at me and raises his tumbler of water. I raise mine, and the plastic rims meet with a dull click.

Michael and I finally reach our temporary home around eleven. We eat leftovers from warm unfurled foil while watching an episode of *Star Trek: The Next Generation*, the ache of childhoods long gone in throats full of chewed falafel. Michael falls asleep on the couch as Jean-Luc Picard eulogizes a fallen crew member, his voice turned soft by the remote in my hand. I'm struck by how vulnerable Michael looks in his baggy flannel shirt, curled into a fetal position, his feet covered in white socks. I know that his frailty is temporary, a gentle lull, a glimpse of the child that comes out in all of us when we close our eyes and surrender. I'm grateful to be able to see him sleep, to know that he trusts me. This journey, I know, is over. I almost don't wake him up but do so that he can sleep in his bed. Since I leave in a few days for India, we end up not getting matching tattoos.

Michael walks with me to the antiquated halls of the Lansdonfield Railway Station, where I'll take the Amtrak to New York City, and then fly out to India from JFK. As we wait on the platform for the train, Michael looks nauseated. I realize he's trying to keep from crying as he squints against the cool breeze streaming past waiting passengers, ruffling their hair as if to say goodbye. There is no magic here, just the waft of early summer over the tracks, a hint of diesel.

The train rolls into the station, waking a stronger gust that lashes hair straight into damp eyes. Michael and I exchange words that are familiar and ancient, incantations against separation, their power dubious. We will miss each other. We will keep in touch. We will take care. We hug. I tell him he'd better come visit me in India. He promises that he will.

Through the train window, I watch Michael recede into time through the strobing flash of sunlight passing through the platform awnings. In the seat in front of me, the little hand of a child, fingers pink with sun, pushes against the glass. The mantra in my mouth: I will remember. We will meet again,

        upon the heath
           of sleep and dream.

ORPHANAGE OF
THE LAST BREATH

Saad Z. Hossain

"Witch? Witch doctor? Kobiraj? Sorcerer? Djinn caller? Djinn fornica-tor?" Mok ran down the checklist. The old man in front of him vehe-mently denied each charge. It was a literal witch hunt. The new police commissar had conjured up the whole thing on a whim, a casus belli to finally eradicate the Great Korail Slum Habitat, which had plagued this part of posh Dhaka for over a hundred years.

Mok looked into the man's rheumy eyes with disgust and shoved him away. God knew what diseases he carried. This slum was a viral hotbed. Sweat trickled inside his helmet, pissing him off even more. He looked around. The lane was deserted, though he could easily see bod-ies crammed into the fiberglass shells, eyes peeping out of windows. It was going to take all day to process these losers, and the squad was only on the outer ring of the slum, where everything was respectable. *Boring.*

"Let's go deeper!" he called out. "Might as well have some fun."

Mok had a gun on each hip, low slung, on faux-leather bandoliers complete with real bullets. The one on his left was his primary weapon, a long-barreled .45 caliber that could stop an elephant. The gun on his right looked the same, clearly part of a matching set, but was instead filled with very complex interior circuitry that could fry a target with a laser at sixty yards. A single touch of the beam was enough to burn a hole all the way through a human skull. It cauterized the wound, however, which was why the laser was classified as nonlethal. To paraphrase Mok's hero, the ancient MMA legend Mirko Cro Cop*, right arm hospital, left arm cemetery.

Besides these two guns, Mok had a machete strapped to his back, with a monomolecular edge, an assault shotgun, a spring-loaded knife in his right sleeve, two throwing knives in each boot, a flashlight in his utility belt, and six throwing stars embedded in his Kevlar vest in a very pretty snowflake pattern. The real kicker was on the top of his head, a halo of four buzzing marbles, orbiting in a figure eight. Reaper drones, the most sophisticated kinetic war gear, controlled directly by the Echo chip in his brain. Mok was part of the elite Delta Squad, named after the Ganges Delta, where they had honed their amphibious combat skills.

Texas Mok, they called him, part of why he played up the drawl and the bandy-legged gunslinger walk. Delta Squad had deployed in the craziness of the American hinterland for a two-year stint, fighting in the bayou for a corporation that felt it could reclaim parts of the Louisiana swamp. They had in fact never been within a thousand miles of Fortress Texas, but people in Dhaka tended to equate America with the Lone Star state, and he could appreciate the fact that Louisiana Mok didn't quite have the same ring to it.

They had returned from America with an enhanced reputation, insofar that they had returned at all from that madness. In the swamps he had learned very quickly that every human being—man, woman, child, or elder—carried an automatic weapon and would fire at you on sight. Proper draw knee-deep in water, and he had been faster. Mok took his boots and his guns, and thus a legend was born.

Back home, working a cushy corporate job, with a daily rate higher

---

* Mirko Cro Cop was a former Croatian cop who became a legendary MMA heavyweight with a pair of nasty head kicks.

than most white-collar workers, the story grew in the telling, until he was considered the fastest gun in Dhaka North, Tri-State Security's poster child. His English was good, too, so the interviews just kept rolling in. He could have taken a desk job but he liked being sheriff, out on the streets, flanked by his squad, dispensing justice, protecting the weak, spinning his guns in a flashy way, etc. With all the extra tactical crap in his head and a military-grade Echo*, he was pretty close to immortal, fit to bursting with killing potential. They gave you all this stuff, but did they ever let you fully unload? Hell, no.

Korail was a lot of things, but most visibly it was a cancerous sore pushing up against the Tri-State, Dhaka's millionaire mini city within a city. Ironically, it housed all the staff that worked in Tri-State, and also provided all the airborne nanotech required to sustain the pristine millionaire microclimate, but that didn't stop ambitious security commissars from trying to eradicate it every decade or so. The land was just too damn valuable.

The outer ring of Korail housed the respectable poor, the gainfully employed servant class. Roughing up these losers always caused problems. Some chauffeur goes to work with a missing tooth and all of a sudden a Monsanto VP is calling his boss and Texas Mok gets reprimanded. The more interesting parts of Korail were deeper in: the multigender brothels, the gambling dens, the body switchers, the raw drug trade, and in the center, the Korail Mansion, the largest house of pleasure in Dhaka, where everything under the sun was allowed. Mok had seen all of this and more, but not a trace of the witches that this Commissar hunted so fervently. He wondered what drove such a man. Were there no easier problems for him to solve?

Anyway, Mok wasn't in charge of policy, he was just a hound. Witches they wanted, and witches they would get. His Number Two,

---

* Echo: implant put into most citizens after puberty, which allows humans to control their digital environment, communicate with each other, collate information, interact with the Virtuality, the sum of the digital world overlaying the physical one. In some cases, it might enhance physical and mental powers.

Hamzat, was also from Delta Squad. They were the only two survivors to return from the Bayou. Hamzat was quick with guns, too, almost as fast as Mok, with the wiry build of a snake, and more cunning to boot. Their third and last member was giant Blue, one of the force's new boys, heavily augmented with machinery in his bones, his sobriquet earned by the bluish sheen on his skin. He moved deliberately, and hardly spoke.

"Boss," Hamzat said, "Kobiraj Lane. Plenty of witches. Easy."

The Commissar was a foreign-educated dickhead who didn't know that a kobiraj was closer to a doctor than a witch, and in these parts, they dealt in alchemical cures rather than black magic. Mok didn't believe in black magic, but Hamzat did, and he had learned to trust his Number Two's survival instincts. Hamzat knew his way around Korail, seeing as he spent more than half his paycheck there.

Kobiraj Lane was a short, narrow alley of five tall prefab buildings, which housed the entire sum of Korail's medical knowledge. Word had preceded Mok's arrival, and the lout in charge of this patch ambled over with a wad of cash, smoking a hand-rolled cigarette. He had a gold earring, and that fat complacency of a criminal who had already cleared his monthly dues with the police.

Mok hated this kind of man with a passion, considering him to be the antithesis of his own lone-wolf persona.

"Texas Mok," the lout drawled. "We already paid this month's tea money."

Mok backhanded him across the face, splitting that stupid grin. The man went down like a sack of shit.

"You didn't pay *me*, you sonofabitch," Mok said, standing over him. "I'm not on the take."

"Wghat ghte gfuck gmann?" Bloody teeth spilled out of the man's mouth as he struggled to his knees. He eyed Mok's drones buzzing around his head and very conspicuously lowered his voice. "Sorry, Mok. Sir."

"Commissar wants witches." Mok pointed at the buildings. "You have a bunch of Kobiraj in there. I want them tagged and reporting to the station."

"But they aren't witches," Healthy said, puzzled. "They don't do any magic . . . they mostly sell quack remedies."

"Even better," Hamzat said. "No magic, no trouble."

"Number Two is a believer." Mok smirked.

"How many bodies you need?" Healthy asked, resigned.

"About two dozen should do," Mok said. "Even split gender is okay—don't send me a bunch of old men. Commissar wants some actual girl witches, too. Rough them up but no permanent injuries 'cos we ain't paying for any time in the healing tank."

"Actual girl witches . . ." The healthcare lout, hitherto sulking through his broken mouth, suddenly managed a sly grin. "We have one, you know. A real one."

"What?"

"A real witch. Exactly what your Commissar ordered."

"Get the fuck out."

"You keep going deep. Near the center."

"To the big brothel?" Hamzat asked. He was an avid customer.

"Past the Mansion. Right after crossing it, you have to take three right turns and three left turns. It's important. Exactly that order."

"What the fuck you talking about?"

"There's a house there."

"Oh ya? Is it made of gingerbread and ice cream?"

"What? No. It's made of bones and blood. She's the black death. Fucking Bibima. Took half the orphanage. Now they send her one a month just to keep her relaxed."

"I never heard of Bibima." Mok frowned.

"She's one of them legendary ones, ain't she? Goddess of cholera or some shit. She takes kids, man. She takes their eyes, their faces."

"Faces?"

"You see a faceless kid," Heathy said quietly. "You don't ever forget it."

"Nothing like that has ever been reported," Mok said.

"What, you think we call cops around here to help us solve crimes?

Think a grandma gets stuck up a tree and we're dialing 999? Get the fuck out, man. Only reason security comes in here is to take tax."

"That is not *me*."

"Yeah, sure, sure. Texas Mok, fastest gun in Dhaka." The lout was openly sneering now. "When you get tired of kicking old men in the balls, try your luck with an actual monster."

Hamzat was tugging at his sleeve with vehement negative head movements, but Mok shrugged him off. His face burned with the peculiar messianic fervor that sometimes overtook him.

"We will kill this witch," he said. "And return the orphans."

They knew their way to the Korail Mansion. It was the one certain landmark in a place of ethereal geography. Tri-Sec got in free, barring tips, not that it helped. The place had a way of carving you out hollow. Plenty of cops spent their entire wages there, regardless of discounts. It was a spick-and-span mansion at the heart of the neighborhood, a huge seven-story Moghul-style palace with creeper-lined exteriors and multiple small balconies artfully lit to entice the voyeur public. Underneath the foliage, the walls were white marble; there was immense wealth in Korail, for those who knew how to see it.

"Three rights and three lefts," Mok said.

"That should spit us out in front of the mosque," Hamzat said, counting roads. "It's black magic."

The ladies called out their names as they passed the entrance, fluttering scarves from the windows. Mok took the first right turn, and their trailing voices sounded like a dirge. The light filtering down changed, a sepia tint washing over them. His hand moved toward his gun, his fingers like treacle. There was nothing to shoot, just a vaguely melancholic air, and the chatter of unintelligible voices.

Mok took the turns, letting his feet follow in a reverie. His eyes saw the alleys, the cheap buildings, and crowded windows, but his brain felt the grandeur of Moghul palaces, of ordered gardens and tremendous blue-tiled baths. He hoped his men were following. He did not have the energy to look back.

At the last turn, the world righted, and he found himself alone, in front of a black marble-clad building, a mirror of the brothel, children adorning the balconies. Their voices were shrill with laughter and lamentation and the normal outrages of youth.

Hamzat? He turned and saw the rest of his squad stagger in. Blue was waving his gun around as if he saw enemies in the air. Mok calmed them down.

"Magic," Hamzat said, rubbing his eyes.

"Mirror image," Mok said. "We are not in Korail anymore, I think."

"Do you believe now?" Hamzat asked. "It's all real, brother."

The slum was gone. Green lawns stretched around the house, broken up by mango trees, an endless tessellation that faded into the inky horizon. The walk to the front door was short, over grass that felt real enough when Mok pulled it out. There was good brown dirt underneath.

He knocked on the door. A child opened it. She had a cracked face, gaps riven with silver, no eyes and no mouth, just a pair of nostril slits. Mok recoiled in disgust, and then remembered the words of the man who had sent him here. *She takes their faces.*

He forced his hand to be steady, and gently placed it on the girl's shoulder. He felt her tense with fear, head swiveling up at him, nostrils flaring in panic, and he felt a mirrored terror rising in him. He tried to pull her close but she twisted away and ran. He called out, and she turned and hissed so he gave chase, the impulse of a natural bloodhound, hand on his gun, and within seconds he was disoriented in the great checkered hall, black and white marble, the sound of tinkling glasses and the laughter of courtesans hitting him with a peculiar nostalgia, ghosts grasping at the living.

He turned and saw Hamzat and Blue splitting away, darting through different doors, weapons out, chasing enemies only they could see.

"Blue! To me!" Mok shouted after the big man, but his words went unheeded. He could hear tittering across their comms, inane nursery rhymes in a slurry of childish voices. *The kind of voices that come from children with no mouths?*

Mok abandoned his chase and turned instead toward the door Blue had raced into. In the old mansion, it had led to the shisha bar, a place for smoking and contemplation, the slow burn of organic opium. In this ghostly version, there was only smoke and the faint smell of cherry tobacco, and cobwebs that Mok burst through in his haste. He saw the back of Blue's heel disappearing across a second doorway, into a narrow hallway, leading off into pleasure rooms, a hallway that had once been adorned with images from the *Kama Sutra*, but now carried drawings made by blind children, horrible nonsensical shapes, no coloring between the lines, paint put on clashing paint, all of it taped neatly to the walls in endless rows.

Mok called for Blue again, but his comms channel was filled with the prattling of those mouthless voices, now a running commentary on the merits of crayons over watercolor.

He kicked down doors at random, and finally saw the faceless girl, struggling urgently as a giant man held her down, a creature with the head of a squid that was holding a knife to the girl's face, trying to carve back in the eyes she had lost, the nose, the mouth, as if she were a Halloween pumpkin.

Mok roared in rage and sent his drones whistling out, deadly marbles, not caring what he hit, just wanting to empty his arsenal, to *erase* this horrific tableau. Chunks of blood and flesh floated away, as time slowed and the drones hammered through those tentacles, even as the monster flung the girl away.

They faced each other for a split second, and then Squid Head reached for his holster. Texas Mok was faster. His hands twitched and both guns were firing, one bullet for each big baleful squid eye, and the monster keeled over, stone dead. The faceless girl shrieked and took off again, her silver skin splattered with blood. This time Mok did not give chase.

The comm was chittering now with childish applause, as though they were seeing through his eyes. He took off his helmet and set it aside. *Blissful silence.* He stared at the fallen body, the head blown off above the jaw, and tried to piece together what just happened, because with the tentacles gone, this corpse from the jawbone down was looking awfully like Blue, even down to his nonregulation boots. He lifted one sleeve, and stared at one dead blue forearm, the skin hairless like a baby's, unmarked, no kills tattooed on yet, no wins, no rep. Fresh meat from the academy, and headless on the floor of a ghost brothel.

Blue. Did I just shoot his head off? He had a knife to that girl. I saw. I fucking heard her shrieking her mouthless head off. Is she even real? Is this murder? Am I supposed to hide the body? He fucking drew on me. Fuck him. I need to get Hamzat and kill this fucking witch. Fucking Blue. I knew he wasn't right. At least I saved one kid.

The hallway felt more solid now. Perhaps the cobwebs were clearing from his head. His helmet was useless, so he left it. He could hear the faceless girl wheezing at the far end, the little thuds of her scrabbling feet. There was a door there, lit by a flickering light bulb. He entered. It was a narrow room, filled with cots of various shapes. Little beds for toddlers. There were wonky mobiles on top of some of them, blankets and teddy bears. He counted ten. Ten kids then, at least. He saw her curled up on a bunk bed at the far end, hiding under a blanket, shaking with fear, her wheezing breath barely audible. The rest of the room was mercifully empty.

Mok looked down, saw that his boots were splattered with blood and pieces of Blue's skull. He slowed his step and let his heart rate go down.

"I'm not going to hurt you," he said. His gun was in his hand unbidden. He holstered it. "Look. I'm not going to hurt you. I saved you from the monster. How many of you are here? Ten? Twenty? A hundred? I will save all of you from the witch."

"Mother?" came the muffled voice. "You're here to kill Mother?"

"The witch Bibima," Mok said. "She has to die." *Fucking Commissar was right.*

The girl made a strangled sound under the blanket. *Was she crying? Or laughing?*

"Can you take me to her?"

The girl rose unspeaking, the blanket wrapped around her like a shroud. Thankfully he could no longer see her face. She motioned to him and he followed. She led him to the hammam, a giant stone-walled room with a deep hot pool in the middle, tiled in blue mosaic. In the Korail Mansion this place had been the hub of relaxation, full of cleansing steam. This bathhouse was subtly altered, the free space cluttered with bathtubs of various sizes, each one labeled with a name, dozens of them. A variety of rubber ducks, geese, and frogs marched like soldiers against the walls. There were towels stacked everywhere, and bottles of shampoo, and their mingled aroma was fresh and cheerful. He saw a woman standing in the hot pool, wreathed in steam, wearing some kind of diaphanous robe. The faceless girl darted into her outstretched arms.

"Stop!" Mok shouted. "Get your hands up!"

Bibima turned her head. There was something off about the witch, and then Mok saw through the fog that the right side of her face was caved in, half her neck and shoulder withered with inch-thick scar tissue. The right eye was gone, orbital bone crushed. It was as if she had taken a bullet to the head. *Good. That means she can be hurt.*

Something moved in Mok's peripheral vision. A shadow slipped in from the far door and he almost unleashed the reapers. There was something familiar about the snakelike movement. Hamzat! A breath later, targeting lasers bloomed on both the witch and her daughter.

"Mok, that you?" Hamzat's voice was calm and low. "I got 'em both locked. Give the word. We shoot 'em all and let God sort it out."

"Not the kid," Mok said.

"You don't get it, man," Hamzat said. "They're both monsters. There are only monsters here."

"She's a damn orphan."

"She ain't even alive. Ask her. There is nothing human here."

"Your friend is right," Bibima said. Her voice was like the rustle of crow's wings on a corpse. "You have come here to die." The girl squirmed loose and turned her faceless glare on Mok. He heard shrill cries in his ears, even though he had left his command helmet behind, as if invisible children were pointing at him and shouting.

"I'm here to save the orphans, witch," Mok said. "Bring them to me, and I will spare your life." The reapers buzzed around his head. He was certain they could outrun whatever power Bibima had.

"Save them?" Bibima laughed. It was a peculiarly beautiful sound. The faceless girl mimicked her, setting his teeth on edge. "Officer. Ask your friend how he knows there is nothing living here."

"Don't let the witch talk!" Hamzat yelled. "Just fucking reaper her."

"What do you mean?" Mok asked. "What is this hell house?"

"You've been to hell before, Texas Mok," Bibima said. "In the bayou. Half-dead in the water, crabs eating your eyes. Do you remember? Does this look like hell to you?"

"No," Mok said. "It does not."

"This house is a sanctuary. Half-life, for those children brutalized, on the verge of passing. Those with wounds so violent and perverse that death would be no release for them. I bring them here to this orphanage, to live in the infinity of that final breath."

"You lie. Why do you not heal them if you have such power?" Mok said.

Bibima lifted the curtain of her hair and Mok saw again the ruin of her face. "I could not even save myself."

"Shoot her!" Hamzat growled. "She's a goddamn witch!"

"Someone else took the girl's face? Who?" Mok asked.

"One night the man you called Blue and your partner here came out of the Korail Mansion, high and dissatisfied. They ran across my orphans begging outside. Hamzat fell over her twin brother. In a fit of rage, he pistol-whipped the boy until his neck snapped. Kira here tried to run away, shouting for help. Blue found it funny to take her eyes, but why stop there? He carved out her nose and mouth, too. Then? They didn't even run away. They went back to the Mansion and spent another two hours there, regaling everyone with the story."

"Those are fucking lies!" Hamzat shouted. The lasers painted frenzied circles on Bibima's face. "I didn't tell no story! I'm gonna shoot her, I swear!"

But Mok's stance changed slightly. His right foot edged out, his silhouette now sideways . . . to Hamzat.

In the steam, Hamzat noticed the subtle shift.

"I pulled you outta the fucking bayou, Mok," he said, desperate. "We wear a *badge*, man. *Police*. You don't believe the perp. Ever. Ain't that the rule?"

"You know the truth," Bibima said to Mok. Her voice had a witchy caress to it, as if she was enjoying the moment. "After all, you saw Blue. Isn't that why you shot him?"

"YOU SHOT BLUE?" Hamzat's scream was full of incredulous pain. "You killed him? What the fuck, man?"

"Blew his head right off," Bibima said.

"And the other kids?" Mok asked. "Are they also like Kira?"

"Worse," Bibima said. "That's why they are hiding. They are . . . shy. Embarrassed to show their missing limbs, the gaping holes in them. *Embarrassed,* can you imagine? Give it some time, and they will come."

"Blue did all of them?"

"Blue, others like him." Bibima shrugged. "Cops. Men with badges. Your kind always come here for fun."

"Not *my* kind. And *your* face?"

"A bullet to the eye, and then set on fire," Bibima said. "The one who sent you today. Your Commissar. He used to come down here every night, before he got promoted."

"Mok, man, you gotta shake out of it." Hamzat said. "Kill this lying bitch. We gotta torch this place and hide Blue's body. You committed *murder*, man, *you killed a cop.*"

Mok glanced sideways at his Delta brother and saw the lasers swing lazily away from the witch. He knew they were pointed at his head now. *Cop killer.*

"I reckon I'm going to kill a few more," Mok drawled.

"So that's it? Texas Mok?" Hamzat sneered. "You gonna pick a damn witch over me, brother? You gonna side with a bunch of bastard orphans?"

"You're the one pointing a gun at me, *brother.*"

Hamzat didn't bother replying. In a way that hurt Mok more, the desultory nature of his effort to make peace. *I guess he hated me after all, being number two all the time.*

In the microsecond it took for Hamzat to squeeze the trigger, Mok cleared his left-hand gun, lifted it, and fired two rounds into his partner's forehead. Hamzat pitched forward, dead. Kira clapped her hands with genuine glee.

Mok felt something wet run down his face. He touched it, saw the red on his fingers.

"He shot me . . ."

He staggered toward the pool and fell at Bibima's feet; as the vision faded in his blown eyes she seemed perfectly beautiful to him. She held him up in the water. Mok felt no pain, only a dull pressure in his head, and knew he was past recovery. His Echo had cut off his pain receptors, was keeping him alive for a few last moments.

"Hussh, my lovely boy, hush."

"My eyes are gone," Mok sobbed, in rage and darkness. "I can't see."

"You are beyond my healing," Bibima said, cradling him. "I'm so sorry, child."

"I'll die here alone then," Mok said. "Forgotten."

"Three cops dead in Korail?" Bibima smiled her terrible smile. "I don't think you'll be forgotten. They will come to find answers."

"They'll call me a cop killer, a mad traitor," Mok said bitterly. "No one will ever know why I killed these *fucking* pigs."

"My poor boy, do you still think they *care* about right and wrong?"

Mok felt an immense lassitude steal over his body; he knew it was time to let go, but all he knew was rage, the hound's rage for escaped quarry, rage for the sneer on Hamzat's face, rage for Blue carving up an orphan with a knife, rage for all the animals who needed killing and would forever escape him.

"You can die," Bibima said. "Or you can choose to live in this last breath, this very moment, in this house, for as long as you want. It is the only thing I can do for you."

"My eyes are wrecked; my face is gone," Mok said. "I am a monster." *Like you.*

"I will pour silver into your face and you will shine," Bibima said. "You will meet the other children, they will see you are one of them, and they will love you."

"I'm not a fucking orphan, to cower here forever!" Mok snarled, defiant still. It cost him. Fresh blood filled his mouth, poured heedlessly into the water. His fingers reached instinctively for guns they would never hold again.

"If you will not stay for refuge, then stay for vengeance. Be our reaper, then. Give answer to what they do. Your brothers will come to see what kind of beast lives here. The Commissar himself will come one day. You will get your chance to put down a hundred like Blue, to *kill them all.* Are you satisfied?"

Mok felt the anguish drain away. There was something here after all.

"I am satisfied," Mok said as the silver poured into the cracks of his face. "I hope they come soon."

THE UNEXPECTED EXCURSION OF THE MURDER MYSTERY WRITING WITCHES

Garth Nix

Dorothy was writing when the ink suddenly poured from her Macniven and Cameron fountain pen in a torrent, to become one giant blot. She scowled in exasperation but made no move to stop the spread of Diamine Blue/Black across the page of Basildon Bond. Surprisingly, it stopped of its own accord at the edges of the paper, eventually making an intensely dark rectangle, which was slightly reflective, a black mirror with a slight blue sheen. A face formed in the ink, or rather an indistinct outline of a face. Not a reflection of Dorothy's own. The mouth opened, shut, opened again, each time revealing the white paper beneath the ink. Finally, it spoke, very softly.

Dorothy frowned again and leaned in close so she could hear.

"Dorothy! Dorothy! It's Agatha."

"Yes, I'm here," replied Dorothy crossly. "Must you use the ink spell? I do have a telephone, you know. Or you could send me a telegram, or even write a letter."

"No, this is urgent," said the inky face. "Ritual business. Besides, you never know who'll be listening on the telephone, or reading telegrams. Some spotty young constable who'll think we're Germans speaking in code."

"Ritual business? But it's not the thirteenth," protested Dorothy. "And I am very busy—"

"So am I, of course," said the face. "Busier, I expect. But Peter just came in, all a-fluster and jumped up on my desk, knocked manuscript pages everywhere—"

"Peter your terrier?"

"Of course Peter my terrier, who else could it be? He jumped up on my desk, put one paw on the typewriter, and using a single, delicate claw typed 'The Beast of Howlrodon is out.' He's such a clever little dog."

Dorothy, not for the first time, wished Agatha had chosen a different name for her dog, no matter how clever he was. Peter was a very special cognomen to her. Something like "Bob" would be so much more appropriate for the terrier.

"How did Peter know? And . . . er . . . what is the Beast of Howlrodon?"

"I already told you he's clever. Heard it from a rat, I expect, a final confession sort of thing before he killed it. He's such a good ratter."

"How does this . . . what is the Beast of Howlrodon?"

"I think it's a sort of giant rat," said Agatha.

"A giant rat?" asked Dorothy skeptically. Any sort of giant animal would attract immediate attention, and it wouldn't need Agatha's terrier to report its presence.

"I looked it up in Mary Sidney and it is in her second *Booke of Secrets*, but only a reference which says 'Howlrodon's most enormous ratte' and 'Blyn 65:6' which I presume is a reference to the Boleyn secret work and you know I don't have that."

It remained unspoken between them that Anne Boleyn's handwritten notes hidden within her *Book of Hours* were written partly in Latin and partly in English, and a peculiar construction of both at that. Dorothy's command of Latin and her general scholarship were far superior to Agatha's, so ownership of the text in question would not have helped the latter. The original Boleyn *Book of Hours* was, of course, in Hever Castle. The notes written in invisible ink between the printed lines could only be raised under the light of a new moon, using a cantrip originally intended for causing warts. Boleyn's notes remained unknown to the world at large, but had been fortunately discovered and transcribed by Elizabeth Strickland, a notable witch, in 1864, and privately published a few years later for a select audience.

"I suppose I can look it up," said Dorothy reluctantly. She made a note of the reference with a pencil on the blotter, so as not to disturb the ink-filled page before her. "But what does it have to do with us?"

"Well, who else, darling?"

"There's Chesterton and his lot."

"Gilbert would forget what he was about before he even started doing anything. As you well know. Besides, for all their wizard talk, I don't think that circle of his is up to much these days. Magic-wise, that is."

"What about Knox?"

"I'm sure Ronald's a perfectly adequate priest if we need an exorcism, but I doubt it would work on an enormous rat."

"I suppose so," grumbled Dorothy. Exorcism was only effective against the spirits of those who had been baptized Christians in life. Sometimes not even then, if their faith had been weak. "But I'm so close to finishing this book—"

"I'm on the last chapter of mine!" said Agatha, not to be outdone.

"I'm simply too busy," said Dorothy, as forcefully as she could.

The face in the ink pursed her lips, then began to recite.

"I promise I shall well and truly employ all my arts of magic, sorcery, cunning, and particularly feminine intuition against Evil-doers, Malefactors, Revenants, Condescenders, Creatures of—"

"Oh, very well!" snapped Dorothy. "You know I can't refuse if you will invoke the oath. I'll look up the reference. It might take some time. I presume you don't want me to telephone you?"

"Definitely not."

"I'm not using the ink spell. I always get it all over my fingers," said Dorothy. "I'll send a raven. Are you at Winterbrook?"

"No, we're in town this week, but remember it is the Lawn Road flat, not the old house. Must it be a raven, Dorothy? Can you at least make sure it comes to the right window?"

"I always tell them," protested Dorothy. "But you know ravens."

"You should get a brazen head," said the face in the ink. "Everyone else has got one. It doesn't have to be Roman or Greek, you know, something inexpensive from Birmingham—"

"I can perfectly well afford a brazen head of sufficient antiquity," said Dorothy stiffly. "My books are selling *very* well. I simply don't want a bust in my study chattering away whenever any of the others feels inclined to gossip. Speaking of them, who have you called? Do we need the full coven?"

"I don't know. I shouldn't think so. I haven't contacted anyone else as yet. You tell me once you've seen whatever Queen Anne wrote about this beast. I have to go. I have to fill in for someone at the hospital pharmacy tonight for a few hours, but I'll be back by ten. They let me test a new poison on a mouse last week. Generally undetectable, save with a most uncommon test. A gift to murderers! Goodbye!"

The ink retreated back into the fountain pen as quickly as it spread, leaving the page pristine and white. Dorothy glared at it. The two paragraphs that had been there were completely erased and she had already forgotten exactly what she'd written.

"Typical!" she snorted. "Agatha and her poisons!"

But she had to admit she was now curious about this "Beast of

Howlrodon." Screwing the cap on her fountain pen, she set it aside, pushed her chair back, and switched off the desk lamp. The single, war-time austerity globe dangling above shed only a pallid light, but she instinctively looked across to the heavy curtains to make sure she hadn't twitched them apart earlier. Though it was still not quite dark outside, the room was small and she had to edge past the window to get to her desk, so she often did disturb the blackout. The local ARP warden was a petty tyrant, and she didn't want to attract his ire. Not because he frightened her, but because it wasted time.

Most of Dorothy's library was in the house at Witham, where she generally resided these days, but since the German bombing had di-minished two months ago in mid-May, she had been drawn back to Bloomsbury. Inevitably many of her books had come with her, more and more on each visit. It was fortunate she had two flats, as the lower one was rapidly filling up once again with volumes.

However, the most precious and esoteric of her tomes were not vis-ibly shelved in either flat. Dorothy went into the sitting room, which was not much larger than her study, and addressed the Edward Bilbie thirty-hour longcase clock with the swan neck pediment and the bronze tide indicator above the phases of the moon in gilt and silver. The central dial showed the time to be midnight, which was wrong as it was actu-ally only a little before eight, but then the whole clock was silent and stopped.

Dorothy stood in front of it, made the requisite gesture, and intoned:

"How flows the tide at Bristol Quay?
It is full flood, a lifting sea
How shines the moon up in the sky?
It is silver-full, to please my eye."

In answer to her words, the tide indicator moved to the full, and the dial of the lunar phase rotated to indicate a bright full moon. Soft silver light shone from the clock; there was a loud click and the front of the case sprang open, revealing neither a pendulum nor any other clockwork, but a row of small shelves, packed with books of antique binding.

Dorothy took out the transcription of the Boleyn secret work. Though only produced in 1883, Strickland's volume had been exquisitely printed and bound in the fashion of a much older book, the leather for the binding being taken from a seventeenth-century coat and the paper from a secret store kept dry in a salt mine for over two hundred years.

She found the reference quickly enough, but had to return to her desk to consult several references, Boleyn's Latin and sixteenth-century English being idiosyncratic to say the least, and even when translated, the meaning cryptic. It took her almost two hours, but Dorothy was confident she had unraveled Boleyn's complications. She copied out the final version in very, very small handwriting on both sides of a cigarette paper, using a silver ink that would be invisible to anyone who did not possess witchsight.

Over it, she wrote with a thick pencil "PUT TEN BOB ON THE SECOND RUNNER IN THE FOURTH FOR MAC TO WIN." It was very unlikely her raven would be intercepted, but if it was, and a sharp-eyed police officer or busybody noticed the message capsule, it would make them think of illegal betting rather than German spying or something of that sort. A precautionary bit of misdirection, more habit than necessity.

Anne Boleyn had quite a lot to say about the "Beast of Howlrodon." Dorothy's translation read:

Who knows from where the Beast did come, for it is not of flesh and bone, but noxious vapours knit to make a shape not unlike a rat, but of vast size. It is eager for meat and bread, and it slakes its thirst on blood, although it has neither heart nor stomach to spark such appetite so wherefore does the sustenance [unreadable]? Howlrodon perhaps knew. He confined the beast to a cess pit at Eltham, but the miasmic breath of the Beast did lay him low, he could not take new breath, and died. The pit has been sealed with stone and lead, and such charms as I can place, I dare not call on [unreadable] or the others, the King has forbade them the palace. Howlrodon's circle is of Scotland, some will doubtless hold me guilty of his death, no matter the circumstance. Perhaps this was the intent of whomsoever raised the beast, my enemies are legion. Or was it Howlrodon himself who called it, thinking to stage a rescue and ingratiate himself, only to prove inept?

To this, Dorothy added a message of her own:

> Evidently this is a variant of a malignant marsh wisp or the like, not a physically embodied giant rat! I deduce it was trapped in a cesspit at Eltham Palace. I suppose the recent building by the Courtaulds of their new house has disinterred it. A trinity should suffice to deal with it. I will get in touch with Elizabeth (I mean Gordon, as she is down from Scotland for one of her radio plays). I think she's the logical choice to make up our three. It were best done tonight. Meet at midnight, above St. Paul's. Don't forget tarnhelm/cloak of darkness and gas mask.

The last sentence would annoy Agatha, because of course she couldn't possibly forget to wear a tarnhelm or cloak of darkness. The Blitz might be mostly over, but there were still occasional German raids, and firewatchers, anti-aircraft battery spotters, and RAF patrols aplenty who would notice a low-flying witch if she were visible. Similarly, while many Londoners had stopped carrying their gas masks everywhere once the bombing became less intense, Dorothy suspected they would be good protection against the "miasmic breath" of the Beast.

She brought to mind what she knew of Eltham Palace, in southeast London. It had long been a royal residence. Henry VIII and Anne

Boleyn had used it, and the infant princess Elizabeth had been housed there for a time, but later it fell into disuse. It had been saved by a scion of the Courtauld cloth dynasty who was building a new house there, or had built a new house, and restored the surviving medieval hall. She had read about it in *Country Life*. It was likely it had since been taken over by the army, or the navy, or by some other government entity, as was the fate of so many great houses in the current war. But that didn't matter. Cloaked in invisibility, the three witches could swoop down, locate the Beast, and confine it once again. Though more professionally, in a silver bottle or something similar, not in a "pitte of turdes" which she had chosen to translate as "cess pit."

Dorothy lured one of the ravens she usually worked with to come in through the attic window with a very unattractive bacon rind, so gristly it had repulsed human appetite even with the current sparse meat ration. She tied the rolled paper to the bird's leg and sent it to Agatha, with firm instructions to tap on the window of the correct flat and not just try all of them until someone responded. The raven was restive, as it was already dark, but it would do as it was told. Not for the first time, Dorothy wondered if it might not be better to employ owls at night-time, but they were so much less intelligent than corvids that impressing instruction into their tiny minds was painful and annoying.

She considered sending another raven to Elizabeth, but unlike Agatha, was not so distrustful of the telephone if those speaking were careful. She went back downstairs and called Elizabeth at her club in Cavendish Street. After first being connected to what was apparently a Home for Abandoned Cats in Battersea, she eventually got through and was soon talking very circumspectly to her fellow witch and murder mystery author, and was once again confronted with the problem of how to address her as this did not concern her Inverness life as Elizabeth, her playwriting as Gordon, or her detective story writing as Josephine.

"Hello, it's Dorothy."

"Yes, I know."

"Agatha's been in touch. Her Peter has uncovered something interesting I thought you would like to know about. Grist for the mill."

"Peter? Oh, yes. Her Peter."

"It's rather historical, Tudor in fact. Anne Boleyn, that sort of thing, involving a chap called Howlrodon. Sixteenth-century horrors! I was thinking the three of us must get together to take a look."

"Oh? I am rather busy at the moment. This radio play—"

"I'm busy too, my new book is almost done. But Agatha has rather harped on about it, I think we must take a look before it's taken away or something happens."

"Ah. I see. What did you have in mind?"

At this point Dorothy dropped the book she'd been holding, with a very audible thump that must have echoed down the telephone line like a distant bomb blast.

"Oh! I do beg your pardon. I must learn not to build absolute towers of books. This one was as high as St Paul's, I think! I was up till midnight last night making notes and just stacking up books by the side here. Very silly of me."

"I see. Midnight. As high as St. Paul's. How very inconvenient."

"Yes. But it seems . . . seemed . . . necessary at the time."

"I understand. Perhaps you could call again tomorrow morning to arrange lunch? I was thinking of spending the day in bed, but of course . . ."

"Yes. Thank you. I look forward to our meeting."

Two hours later, at twenty minutes to midnight, Dorothy crawled out through the attic window onto the roof, dragging her broom "Dante" after her. Like all witch's brooms of the current era, it was made from a huge, three-inch-diameter yew pole that had a crossbar fixed one-third of the way along, a sidesaddle with its two pommels firmly attached to that, the single stirrup currently laid over it. The front of the broomstick had a bat's skull wired to it, with large peridots emplaced for eyes, shimmering green with flying magic. The brush was an enormous and impractical bundle of twigs of broom, *planta genista*, thirteen bunches sewn together with silver wire. The whole thing was more than nine feet long and unwieldy, but anything smaller was affected by strong winds and harder to fly. Some witches had even larger brooms, and affixed low chairs to the cross beam.

Dorothy herself was wearing her tin helmet, driving goggles, and her tweed riding habit, with bloomers under a long apron skirt, and riding boots. A broad leather belt held a scabbarded athame on her left hip and a holstered wand on her right. Her gas mask box was held by a strap over her left shoulder, and a Stanley Super Vac thermos flask (a present from Nancy Bird) was suspended by a strap across her right shoulder. An exquisitely stitched velvet cloak of invisibility, handed down from her grandmother, cascaded down her back, the spell not yet activated.

The blackout was a gift to urban witches. No one could see Dorothy as she whispered the spell to wake Dante. The broom lifted from the roof, high enough to allow her to mount, getting one thigh around the higher pommel and the other comfortable against the lower. She could fly astride as many of the younger witches did, but had become used to sidesaddle in her youth, and Dante seemed to prefer it.

She fastened the last of the three gilded toggles at her neck and spread the cloak behind her. The air shimmered and she felt the familiar faintly electric buzz of invisibility, her skin prickling. Whatever it touched was now unseen. Another word to Dante made the broom rise gently into the night, gaining height in wide spirals.

"Two hundred feet above the dome of St. Paul's, please, Dante," whispered Dorothy. "There's no need to hurry."

It was only a mile or so to the cathedral. Dante climbed to about five hundred feet and headed directly toward St. Paul's, occasionally veering north or south to avoid the tethers of the barrage balloons, though the balloons themselves were considerably higher overhead. Dorothy looked down at the city, a dark, strange mass save for the faint silvery ribbon of the winding Thames. She was glad she could not see the devastation wreaked by the Blitz, the roofless buildings, the stark, broken walls around piles of rubble. It was almost possible to imagine the city whole again, the darkness due to a temporary loss of electricity.

There was a new moon, only a slim crescent, not the ideal phase for any of the chosen three, who were all middle-aged. They would be most powerful under a First or Third Quarter moon. It did provide some light, not that Dorothy needed it. Her witchsight was very strong, stronger than most other witches, though they all possessed the power to some degree, by definition. You could not be a witch if you didn't have witchsight.

She was surprised to see Agatha and Josephine were already circling around the golden ball and cross atop the cathedral, three hundred and sixty-five feet above the ground. They were invisible to ordinary people, but she could see through the charm. Agatha wore a tarnhelm of her own making, a felt cloche hat she'd evidently made in the early 1920s that was no longer fashionable, though of course no one but other witches could ever see it, and Agatha evidently didn't care. Josephine, on the other hand, wore a Scottish bonnet, which was entirely un-magical, and her cloak of darkness was in fact a very stylish and recent Burberry cape she must have enchanted within the last year.

"Dante, raft up," said Dorothy. The broom quivered under her and descended a little, to move into position adjacent to the other two witches whose brooms were slowly orbiting the dome. Brooms could hover, but they didn't like it. It was better to draw up close and continue flying as slowly as possible.

"Evening all," said Dorothy.

"It definitely does not deserve the preface of 'good,'" said Josephine. She wore a leather motorcycle helmet and gauntlets, yellow-tinted goggles, side-laced jodhpurs, and a very rough man's tweed jacket under her cape. She was riding astride a much slighter, swifter besom than Dorothy's, a traveling broom that was made in three sections that were screwed together, and it had an albatross skull at the front with eyes of amber. Its brush was half the size of Dante's and more streamlined, made of broomcorn fastened with harp strings. It would be a much more difficult broomstick to fly, but then Josephine was a former physical education teacher and had the physical dexterity and strength to manage it.

"Agatha has filled me in so far," continued Josephine, speaking a little louder than normal. There was only a light wind blowing, but it was enough to snatch words away. They also had to take care any fire-watchers on the cathedral roofs didn't hear strange shouts from the sky above. It might cause some sort of religious rapture or worse, initiate an alarm to the anti-aircraft guns emplaced nearby who would doubtless start firing. They always did at the slightest excuse. "I have to say this is a very annoying imposition on my time."

"It wasn't my idea!" said Dorothy, bridling. "I told Agatha we should let the wizards take care of the matter."

"Now, now, we agreed they are not competent to do so," said Agatha easily. Her broom was even larger than Dorothy's. She sat in a chair affixed to the crossbar, a George III mahogany armchair, though it had been updated with a safety belt. Apart from her homemade cloche tarnhelm, she wore her dispensing outfit, a white pinafore with a Red Cross badge high on the left side, over a gray silk dress. "Did you bring a suitable vessel for confining this beast, Dorothy?"

"Of course," said Dorothy, tapping the thermos flask at her side.

"Very good," said Agatha. Dorothy struggled to contain a frown. It was annoying that the coven worked on the basis of seniority by age. Agatha was the oldest, so she was in charge, validating her natural tendency to bossiness. It was infuriating.

"As it happens, I visited Eltham Palace in '38 to dine with Stephen and Virginia," she continued. "They are still in residence, I called to ascertain that earlier, from the pharmacy. Can you believe they still have their dear little lemur? A most delightful pet. And their butler, Haydock, who is an excellent man. The Courtaulds had already retired for the night, so he filled me in."

Dorothy gritted her teeth and stared at the bat skull at the point of her broomstick. Agatha always seemed to have some connection with the rich and famous.

"Consequently, I am familiar with the overall layout. I suspect this cesspit must be near the Great Hall, which had some bomb damage last September, it seems likely a bomb might have weakened the seal and aided in this monster's release. In any case, I suggest we fly over the palace, dowsing for the presence of anything unnatural. Discounting ghosts, of course, the place is supposed to be riddled with them. Once we have located the beast, we perform a three-part binding, force it into Dorothy's thermos, and then she can take it out to sea and drop it in the Devil's Hole."

"The Devil's Hole! In the North Sea? That'll take me three or four stages at least! I'll lose two or three days of writing," protested Dorothy.

"It is your thermos," said Agatha.

"Oh, don't haver," said Josephine. "I'll take it. We can get at least as far as Dundee before the dawn if we put our minds to it, can't we, Johnny?"

Her broom reared up, Josephine leaning back, stirrups forward.

"See!" she said. "Fresh as a daisy. I'll stay with Lucy McManus, her place is just outside Dundee, fly over to the Devil's Hole, drop the thermos and come back the same way. I was only going to stay in bed tomorrow anyway, and I can put off my meeting at the BBC the day after if I need to. Val doesn't know I'm here yet. I'll tell him there's trouble getting down from Inverness."

"Thank you," said Dorothy. She looked over at Josephine's broom and couldn't help but be impressed. It was more than four hundred miles to Dundee, dawn was only four hours away, and they still had the Beast of Howlrodon to deal with.

"How fast can you fly?" asked Agatha, who was clearly thinking similar thoughts.

"Hard to say," said Josephine. "I paced some Spitfires a few months ago, I believe they were topping 350 miles per hour. I can't keep that up, of course, though Johnny could, but we have done Inverness to Edinburgh in an hour, and that's a hundred and sixty miles."

"I am impressed," said Dorothy, and meant it. "But shouldn't we be getting on?"

"We must first agree to my plan," said Agatha. "That is, to dowse for the creature and so on?"

"Yes," agreed Dorothy.

"Seems sensible," replied Josephine.

"Very good," said Agatha. She pointed to the southeast. "Away, witches!"

This call to arms was less dramatic than hoped, for her own broom was sluggish. The others shot ahead and then had to circle way back before taking up a vee formation, as Agatha's broom was so slow to even get up to cruising speed.

They followed the Thames eastward, turning south with it toward the Royal Naval College at Greenwich. There were some barrage balloons being winched down to barges there, which required a little weaving around. They descended to two hundred feet, crossing Greenwich Park, before continuing southeast.

Even with witchsight, it was hard to make out landmarks of any kind, but Agatha apparently knew the way, though she did go lower and circle at one point, to find a very straight section of railway emerging from a tunnel. Locating it, they followed this for a mile to Eltham station, then turned right and very shortly after they were above the dark bulk of Eltham Palace, the moat faintly glittering around it.

Unexpectedly, there were a great many camouflaged tents in the garden grounds, and Dorothy could see sentries at various points, some very near the palace. Most were just standing around, but a couple near the moat were ambling alongside it, she could see the shine of their bayonets, fixed to shouldered rifles. She pointed at them, and the three witches drew their brooms close and circled at two hundred feet, talking as quietly as they could.

"Looks like an infantry battalion," said Josephine. "Fairly permanent sort of encampment. Been there for a while."

"I'm surprised the butler didn't mention this to you," said Dorothy to Agatha.

Agatha sniffed loudly.

"They won't be a problem if we keep our invisibility up. I am confident *my* tarnhelm won't let me down. Let's get on with the dowsing."

The three witches drew their wands, and holding them pointed down, flew in parallel ten yards apart across the palace and the grounds, quartering the whole area. They were all experienced dowsers and could easily sort out the various twitches and vibrations of their hazel stick wands, ignoring water, and ghosts and precious metals. The latter indications of these were very weak, gold watches on the soldiers most likely, not buried treasure.

All three noted a strong perturbance at the northwestern corner of the moat, where it terminated in a square pond. Agatha directed her broom down toward it, the others following, and they landed one after the other on the paved path immediately to the south. Dismounting, they laid their brooms out of sight as much as possible in the shrubbery. There was no one else about, the closest sentries were to the south of the great hall.

The water in the moat was still, except in the square pond at the end. The witches gripped their wands as they looked at it, noting the strange ripples when there was no wind. There was a faint reek of sewage, which was unpleasant, but not overpowering.

They did not need to speak to each other. Donning their gas masks, they drew athames as well as wands, silver blades in the left hand, hazel sticks in the right. Agatha stood at the southern end of the pond, Dorothy at the west, Josephine at the east.

Agatha raised her wand and was just about to begin the incantation when a male voice behind them said, "Halt! Raise your hands!"

The witches turned to see a tall, blue-eyed, red-haired corporal, the stag's head badge of the Gordon Highlanders on his bonnet, holding his

Lee-Enfield rifle at the ready, bayonet fixed. A puzzled, bandy-legged private accompanying him hissed, "Who you talking to, corp? There's no one there."

Josephine was the first of the witches to act. She spoke loudly, with far more of a Scots accent than the others had ever heard her use, strong enough to be heard even through her gas mask.

"Is it a Banffshire man you are? The Sixth battalion?"

The private jumped backward and fell over, hearing this Scottish voice come out of the empty air. But the corporal did not move, keeping his rifle held ready to stab, sword bayonet forward. Agatha, who was closest, slowly raised her hands, but did not let go of wand or athame. Dorothy tilted her wand slowly toward the man, the first word of a spell of affixation rising in her mind.

"Aye," said the corporal warily. "Corporal McIntosh, once of Buckie."

"And I'm guessing you had a granny with eyes as blue as your own, and she with the second sight, just like yourself. Did she not tell you of wise women, best left alone to their work in the night?"

"Aye, I had such a granny," said McIntosh. "But the other was of the Kirk and had no truck with wise women."

"So which do you listen to this night?" asked Josephine. "We are here to deal with something of the *brollachan* kind, naught else. I hail from Inverness myself."

The private, who had fallen over, got up and looked wildly around, and stabbed tentatively at the air above him, as if trying to bayonet a wasp.

"I don't like this, corp," he whispered. "Where is the Scottish woman?"

The corporal hesitated for a moment, then lowered his rifle.

"Nowhere," he said forcefully. "There's no one here. Come on, let's get back."

He grabbed the private by his webbing, hauled him around, and pointed him back toward the great hall. The man stumbled away, and the corporal followed. But he could not resist a look over his shoulder as he marched away, his blue eyes bright in the faint moonlight.

He had hardly gone three paces when the square pond suddenly exploded, a giant gas bubble erupting from the depths to burst with a fetid, gagging stench. He spun around and gawped at a miasmic creature rising up out of the water—a beast the size of a hippopotamus, but composed of dense, swirling gases rather than flesh and bone. Its snout was long like a rat's, but there was little other similarity, and when its mouth yawned open its teeth were no more solid than its body, and a gout of yellowy brown gas belched forth, rolling in a cloud across Agatha toward the soldiers.

"Run!" screamed Josephine. The soldiers had their gas masks with them but they'd never get them out and on in time. The corporal reacted instantly, dragging the private, sprinting away from the poisonous cloud which billowed out behind them.

Agatha could be dimly seen within the cloud, almost ratlike herself with her mask on. She had her wand and athame raised, and she immediately began the three-part round to bind the Beast of Howlrodon in place. Dorothy took it up, too, a verse behind as was correct, and then Josephine came in to sing the third part. Their wands wove patterns in their hands, and the blades of their athames shone bright, bright enough to partially pierce the veils of invisibility, so that anyone looking would have seen three low stars, somehow come to earth.

The Beast raged and bellowed forth more noxious clouds, corkscrewing funnels of putrescent yellow that twisted off into the darkness, tornados of poison. The fleeing corporal and his companion shouted, "Gas! Gas!" as they ran, and there was a clamor of alarm in the camp.

Agatha fell silent, and then Dorothy, and then Josephine. Together they spoke the final words of binding, words that any save witches could not speak nor hear. The spell came into being, and the beast was stopped mid-belch, caught like a fly in amber, stuck in a moment of time.

Dorothy sheathed wand and athame, took out the thermos, unscrewed the cap, and held out the flask. The witches spoke another word, one that would burn the marrow from inside their own bones if they had not been prepared for it by the earlier spell. The Beast was freed but only to enter the flask. First, it fell into itself, becoming smaller and denser, and even less like a giant rat, losing snout and legs and what might have been a tail, to become a column of concentrated marsh gas. This in turn drew tighter and tighter, coiling around itself, the gas ever more compressed, until it was a swaying tendril which rose up thirty feet above Dorothy, the end bending down toward her. Then, with a rush, it dove into the thermos, like tea being vigorously poured in, if the tea was thick as jelly, and yellowy-brown, and had a stench that would stun anyone unmasked.

Agatha and Josephine came close, athames and wands ready if the Beast somehow escaped the compulsion at the last. But it did not. The tail of the column followed the rest into the thermos, and Dorothy screwed in the cap. She set the flask down on the paving stone, and took up wand and athame again, to join the others in sealing the lid so it could not be opened, save by a trinity of witches more powerful than they.

"Right," said Agatha. She took off her gas mask, winking into visibility for a moment before her tarnhelm was back on, and wrinkled her nose. The deathly stench had gone, but there was a faint, lingering smell of sewage and decaying vegetation. "That's that. Will you take it now please, Josephine? We need to be away before there are soldiers crawling all over the place."

Josephine did three slow cartwheels across the lawn, somehow not losing either wand or athame, and sheathed both on her way right-side up, finishing with the removal of her gas mask. She bowed and tucked the mask back in its box. Cartwheels and calisthenics were something she did after rituals, a display of both dexterity and control, or perhaps some sort of release of tension. It had been impressive when Dorothy first met her, a dozen years before, but was even more so now, since Josephine was forty-four or forty-five.

Josephine took the thermos and ran to her broom, calling over her shoulder.

"See you on the thirteenth! And not before, I trust!"

Dorothy waved her gas mask in farewell, having just taken it off.

"Me, too," she said. "Thank you!"

"She always makes me feel old," said Agatha as she and Dorothy made their way more sedately to their own brooms. "I suppose I am. I shall be fifty-one this year."

"That is not old," declared Dorothy. She had turned forty-eight the week before.

They climbed on their brooms, spoke quietly to them, and rose up into the air. Below them, there were soldiers running about everywhere, and lots of shouting, and lights being turned on and hooded and turned off again amid a refrain of "gas, gas, gas!" and "watch that light!" In the distance, they could hear the bells of fire engines approaching the palace.

"Not a bad day's work for three middle-aged ladies," said Agatha.

"Not work *we* should have needed to do," replied Dorothy. "Why are we always the ones having to clean up after wizards?"

"Because they'd only make it worse," replied Agatha.

Dorothy did not agree; she thought that this was just a convenient excuse for wizards to avoid unpleasant work. But there was no point arguing with Agatha about this, particularly since she knew the older witch secretly thought *everyone* was far less competent than herself and if something needed doing, she had to do it herself, or at least be in charge.

"Your ink spell sucked back two pars of my new book, by the way. Totally gone."

"I'm sure you'll rewrite them much better," said Agatha. "Though I am sorry about that. The raven you sent tapped on all my neighbor's windows first, by the way. It caused quite a commotion."

They flew on in companionable irritation for a mile before Dorothy spoke again.

"How's your new book coming along again?"

"Mine?" asked Agatha. "Oh, I finished the last chapter tonight after all. That's both books done, and I've started another."

"*Both* books?"

"Oh, yes. I'll have two books out next year."

Dorothy bent close and whispered crossly to Dante. The broom shivered and suddenly accelerated, climbing up toward the crescent moon and the barrage balloons, leaving Agatha far behind.

SO SPAKE THE MIRRORWITCH

Premee Mohamed

Sometimes it began like this. The two men in their stiff and stinking black; the chessboard of light across Calder Ward's kitchen table. They came in broad daylight, showing no fear, calling her *Neighbor* and *Mistress*, knowing full well she had never married. They would not drink her tea—her good tea! She had wasted it on them.

She arranged her face into a blank slab and asked the usual question: "Then may I offer you water from my well?"

The older one fair lunged for it. "Yes, *please*, if you would be so good—"

The younger one cut him off, smiling like a rabid fox. "Thank you, no. We are not afflicted with fleshly needs."

Really. Ward had heard the dry squeak of his lips moving over his teeth. These were the ones you had to watch out for, the smiling ones, particularly the ones who did not know they were smiling. Witch-hunters did that sometimes. All teeth. As they set fire to her kiln or house, as they attacked her animals, as they rushed her with shackles and chains, they smiled.

But they were not coming at her now; and her companions, unalarmed, browsed and scratched placidly enough outside in the dense shade of oak and chestnut. Cruel of the men to hobble their horses so far from the water trough; from the doorway, Ward could see the rolling eyes, hear the aggrieved gasps, as the black and the bay strained toward the brimming tub. Her own mare watched in sympathy.

All the same, perhaps this time it would not end in flames. Ward poured herself some tea, intending to enjoy it despite the blast-furnace of the day.

"Allow me to perform introductions," said the younger one. His skin was sallow under its overheated flush, his hair oily and black. He was thin but large-boned, and the knobs of his wrists gleamed like tallow under his sleeves. Ward didn't like that. The wiry ones tended to be shocking in their strength. He said, "I am Dr. William Charnock. This is my learned associate, Discretion Greenwood."

"And you have come here," said Ward, "to purchase a mirror?"

"We have come," Charnock said, "to *inquire* about them."

Ward rolled her eyes. She had spotted them in her personal mirror—the big one next to the stove—a full hour before their arrival. The gray-haired one on the black, and this spider on the bay, trotting through her woods, sweating, in pious silence, wiping their foreheads with their sleeves.

Their eyes were on that very mirror now, watching themselves and the table and the pot and the cups and the witch: a small dark-haired woman in somber gray, her dipped head lightly covered with the white coif she'd hastily donned before opening the door. Perfectly respectable. Ward smiled coyly at herself in the glass.

"Make your inquiries then, and go," Ward said. "You are eating away the day, and the melt won't stand long without stirring."

"We will not keep you long, Mistress Ward." Charnock's voice was oily and ingratiating. "Perhaps we should begin by saying we are in the process of composing a text . . ."

Ward waited stonily, not giving him the satisfaction. She had already noticed the thick mass of parchment in the satchel slung around his shoulders, invitingly open, insisting someone ask about it.

Greenwood did the work for her, a little too eager, like an ill-used dog who recognizes his master winding up for a kick. "A text about the work of the Devil," he said, drying his sweating hands on his opposite sleeves. "And thusly about his agreements with mortals, by which method witches are created, and witchcraft itself. And the various devices and tests by which one may detect such things . . ."

"So you *are* witch-hunters," Ward said. "*Such* a noble profession."

Charnock glared at her. His eyes were pale gray, like blue after a long illness. "So it is," he snapped. "And in our travels to gather material for the book, we were informed that the local lord's wife purchased a mirror from you recently."

"She may have." Ward covered a yawn with the back of her hand. "I am the only mirror-maker for, I believe, several counties around. I fail to see how it contributes to your great work."

"A *magic* mirror."

"Do not be preposterous. Such a thing does not exist." Ward finished her tea and stood, sweeping her skirts clear of the chair so they would not even come near Charnock's legs. Greenwood watched her with an expression between terror and hope as she approached the mirror next to the stove; Charnock's face did not move from its faint, unpleasant smile.

The mirror had been her pride and joy once; now she easily produced much larger, not to mention more level, glass sheets, since she had built the storehouse behind the workshop. Still, it remained a handsome piece of work: square edges fitted neatly into the polished oaken frame, tapped into place with pegs—not a speck of iron anywhere—and beautifully reflective from her painstaking application of pulverized tin. Ward stood before it and waved her hands, ensuring their eyes followed the motion now and then to the enormous wooden cross hanging on the wall.

Greenwood scratched the back of his head, producing a noise as loud as a metal rasp. "If—" he began.

"The lady to whom we referred," Charnock said slowly, "has been using this devilish mirror for evil purposes, and is taking leave of her senses. It seems that as a result of consorting with the thing she has exiled her lord's daughter to the woods, where the child is now presumed dead; and the servants say their mistress now spends all her time alone in her chamber, speaking to the glass as if it answers her."

"Terrible," Ward said. "Poor child."

"And *you* have not seen the child hereabouts," Charnock said. "Your property being so near, or indeed within, these same woods. Hmm? You have seen nothing?"

"Dr. Charnock," said Ward. "Mr. Greenwood. If you have come to directly accuse me of witchcraft and blood magic, of the taking of innocent children for dark rituals to appease a so-called demonic master . . ."

". . . Yes?"

"Then you are to remove yourselves from my property."

Outside, the crickets sang gleefully in the sun; the leaves whispered the secret names of gods; the thirsty horses pawed at the earth, sending stones pattering against the fence. There was no real magic that Ward could summon under the eyes of such men; she only shouted, *Get out, get thee gone* in her head till Charnock abruptly stood, perhaps seeing the message written upon her face, and gestured to Greenwood.

"We are clearly mistaken," Charnock said. "Good day, mistress."

"Good day, sirs."

Ward finished her tea and washed up, and took the chairs outside to sit in the sun and burn away the contamination of the two unclean men; and she hummed a hymn from her girlhood as she weeded the garden, a pretty song about the lamb of God; and she splashed herself with a dipper of water from the well's deep bucket, smelling sweetly of willow, because the day was so hot. The glass liked hot days, to be sure, but her opinions about it were less charitable.

Inside her workshop, the melt lay quiescent and biddable in the furnace. Hearing her at the door, one of her furnace dragons, glamoured, like the others, into a shaggy brown hunting hound, looked up sleepily and beat his tail against the stone floor.

"They never stop," Ward said to the dragon, forcing down the tremble in her voice. "Do they, pup? No, they don't! They never stop. They are like you—worrying a bone till it wears down to nothing, and then whining to tell me they cannot find it anymore!"

The dragon tilted his head, left then right, then laid it back down upon his paws. Ward worked for hours in silence, occasionally checking her measurements: hotting the pipe, gathering the gobbet, blowing the glass even and thin, laying it on the marble for rolling flat. Ah, that marble! White and pink as a summer rose, all the way from the Old World—perhaps they had marble here in the new, but she had never found it to buy for any price. She loved the cool touch of it on days like today, before the glass came near it.

Occasionally in her head she pictured the witch-hunters watching her at work, their eyes narrowed in suspicion; but what would they see? A small woman in gray, hard at work with her glass and her ruler and her abacus and her sums, a square mirror taking shape on the stone, a dog dozing in the corner, lit in cozy amber light, like a candle . . . nothing demonic here, nothing infernal, and anyway the power of a witch did not derive from anything so silly as their made-up tale of a horned liar.

If only her persecutors *respected* magic, if only they *knew* . . . well, never mind. She was safe out here, she had built a good life for herself in the shade of these old trees. When she rode into town to buy necessities, people touched their cap to her and smiled; no one touched her cart while she went into the stores. Rather strange that those who had once muttered imprecations under their breath had—she glanced at her chemical cabinets filled with glass phials and clay pots—suddenly stopped. But the world was full of strange things.

The village has rejected them, a voice said in her head, taut with warning. *They sought out sturdy men with mattocks and hoes—and no one came. To the Divvil with them, said the fox and his dog, and now they return apace, weapons at hand.*

Ward's head snapped up. She backed away from her marble slab, flung off her gloves, even began to untie the leather apron—no, what weapons had they? A sword or a mace was one thing, but if they had muskets . . . outside, muffled by the stone walls, a dragon began to bay, followed by the piercing cry of the unicorn she had lightly disguised as a white mare. Both could defend themselves, but the *house*—

God! They never stopped. They would never leave her alone. She had been given a short respite from them, indeed she thought the fashion for hunting witches had died out entirely, but she had been wrong; it had only smoldered underground, like a peat fire in the winter, and burst out again unexpectedly when the snow was gone.

Ward straightened her back, thrust aside the apron, and ran full-tilt for the hidden back door of the house, slipping inside and shutting it in silence. Already she could hear the hoofbeats returning on the stony earth of the path—a fast clip, the exhausted wheeze of beasts pushed too hard today. And almost she hated them more for that than for whatever violence they had come here to inflict on her, for at least in persecuting her they had a reason, however flimsy. But their cruelty to the horses had no grounding at all.

The mirror glowed next to the stove, throwing off a dim, clean white light that highlighted every crumb and speck on the floor. Tsk! When this was over, she must sweep the place out properly. Near the top of the oaken frame, the half-familiar, half-unremembered face— for this was the way of her friends on the other side of the glass—drew close, pale, gentle, monstrous, and said, *What is your bidding?*

Ward stayed next to the back door, catching her breath. Sunset filled the room with gold for a moment, then rose, then suddenly, startlingly, crimson. She said, "I would like to deliver an instructional lecture."

Greenwood came in first, murmuring something to Charnock: The door was unlocked, but the witch sleeping in the bed—should he—yes, no, give me the lantern, no, I'll hold it, you go first. Ward watched, smiling, from the darkest corner of the room. She had cheated a *little*—she felt—

and justifiably, doing no more than draping herself in the thinnest cloak of camouflage, as delicate as a dragonfly's wing.

The older man moved softly and cautiously, holding a cheap lantern whose uneven, bubbled glass barely lit a pace ahead of him. A cudgel dangled in his other hand, startling Ward for just a moment—no, she had not allowed herself to believe them truly honorable men, not from this morning's meeting, but this crude weapon brought her firmly back to reality. Look at it! Horrible. And was that an iron nail in the end? Like something you'd use to bludgeon a pig to death—and you shouldn't bludgeon pigs, it was better to cut their throats, and why was she thinking about this anyway, she was getting distracted, and this wasn't her first . . . but both men, *both*. Wait a little longer only!

Charnock pushed past Greenwood, weasel-like, impatient, holding—what was that? Ah, clever. Ward almost admired him. Iron shackles wrapped in cloth so they wouldn't clank against one another and alert a victim. And it was thick rope inside the sack he carried, rather than chains. They had done this before. They had come into a woman's house before like thieves in the night and crept to her bed . . .

Ward waited, waited. Breathed, and watched the faintly glittering veil puff out from her tensed lips.

Greenwood set the lantern silently on the floor; Charnock pressed close, the scrape of their coarse sleeves the only sound in the room. Then they pounced, flinging back the coverlet and snatching at the skirted and bodiced form beneath—a straw manikin, barely concealing a jaw-trap with teeth of broken glass.

Their screams echoed off the stone walls, setting up an answering cry from the animals outside—the terrified dragons, the goats, the chickens startled awake in their coop. And Ward smoothly pulled away her cape of glamour, and strode toward the two men, who did not even notice her at first. By the time Greenwood looked up, babbling something to Charnock, it was too late.

Her hands were empty. The room was small. She took one long step and shoved them, hard, toward the open maw of the waiting mirror. Its softened surface bowed for a moment—stretched—thinned—and then they were through, and the glass was once more transparent and unbroken.

Gingerly she removed the closed trap, and brushed the scattered fingertips to the floor (yes, definitely must sweep up tomorrow), and then she pushed the straw to one side and went to bed, sleepily watching the lantern make its funny shadow puppets upon the wall till the candle inside guttered out.

*In the morning, she rode into town to buy resin for wood varnish, and re-*turned well-pleased with a large jar that Mr. Fenn had set aside for her; and she cooked salted bacon on the stovetop and fried bread in the fat, and sat at the kitchen table eating it and watching the leaves sway outside in the hot endless wind.

"I have taken for myself the use of your horses," she said to the two men screaming silently behind the glass of her mirror. "You were so afeared of my 'enchantments' that you would not even let them share water with my animals yesterday. For shame."

They stopped, stared at her; Greenwood ceased to pound on the invisible barrier with his bloodied fists. He had lost two of the fingertips Ward had rather squeamishly retrieved this morning, Charnock the others. The trap had not snapped as quickly as she had expected. Next time, if there were a next time, she'd oil the hinges. A lesson learned.

She pointed at the glass; a wave of silvery light washed across the surface and voices, distant but clear, began to emerge.

"Please! Please release us!" Greenwood wailed, then cringed as Charnock slapped ineffectually at him and pushed him aside to press his face to the glass.

Charnock gathered saliva in his mouth and spat derisively to one side. "And to think you denied being a witch!"

"I did not," Ward said.

". . . We have evidence now! Evidence enough to convict you a thousand times over—to have you burned, hanged, and buried in a coffin of iron, as befits one who traffics with the Devil!"

"The Devil." Ward sipped her water. "Have you met him? In there?"

Charnock paused, thrown off-balance. Greenwood watched him keenly, enjoying his panic simmering below the surface; it seemed to take all his strength to keep it in check.

"You are in spell-space," Ward said. "A place where witches go to access power, and return with small amounts for needful things. It is not good, it is not evil, it is not holy, it is not cursed; what harm it may contain at any given time is brought in," she said, meeting Charnock's eyes, "from without. It does not exist within."

"But we have seen—" Greenwood began, and fell silent when Charnock turned and shouted incoherently at him.

"You may have seen fell things created by your minds," Ward said indifferently. "Perhaps if you were capable of purer thoughts . . ."

"We are doing the Lord's work!" Charnock shouted. "Let us out this instant and accept your fate! Can you not understand, with your feeble woman's mind, that our service to all of society is at risk here?"

"It seems not." Ward finished her water and got up to refill her cup. The two men's eyes tracked her as she walked to the lidded pail and sat again at the table. She truly did not have time to dally; someone was coming to purchase a mirror in the afternoon, and she must muck out the chicken coop, having missed it yesterday. Still she drank her water—daintily, savoring it, as the two men all unknowing licked their cracked lips behind the glass.

Shame, shame was what she wanted them to feel. She wanted it to hit them all at once and perhaps fatally, like lightning—leaving on their corpses the elaborate curlicues of bloodied ferns. Instead it sprouted hesitantly and grew crooked, a seed planted in poor soil. Greenwood woke first the following morning and whispered, "Mistress, what might we offer you to secure our release?"

Ward studied Charnock's slumped form behind him. Sleeping? Feigning sleep? She said, "I suppose I might release you if I felt you had learned a useful lesson in there. Are the things in there teaching you well?"

"I . . . yes . . . no, I don't know." Greenwood wrung his hands, kneeling. His lined face had developed new lines, spangling out from mouth and nose; his eyes were reddened. "I . . . I am a pious man. I hope I am a pious man. A God-fearing man . . . and even though I am mortal and therefore a sinner, unclean, steeped in the impurities of the world, I am at all times obedient to the Lord."

"Are you? Or are you obedient merely to that little rat terrier who drags you around with his sharp teeth?"

Greenwood gasped. "We both obey the Lord, mistress."

"And the Lord told you to do this," Ward prompted him, pushing her chair back from the table. "To sniff about the countryside like dogs, looking for a whiff of sulfur—to invent it if you cannot find it. To accuse and persecute the innocent, to hate anyone who possesses knowledge you do not, to hate anyone who loves the land, knows the simples, walks paths you do not recognize; to invade the homes of strangers, clap them in chains, and burn them alive. *He* said that? Him, the Lord? He told you to do all this?"

"I . . . we . . ."

Ward raised her hand and shook back her sleeve, preparing to silence the mirror again; she did not know how much more of his mewling defenses she could take. Surely they would be dead soon enough.

"Wait!" Greenwood moved closer on hands and knees, wincing despite the soft, muddy ground. Behind him, in the swirling mass of silver mist, shapeless forms strode slowly, majestically, shaking all the world with their ponderous bulk. Ripples formed in the air around him as if it were the water of a pond.

"Wait?" said Ward.

"But supposing . . . supposing we were wrong about the Lord's work," Greenwood said cautiously, glancing over his shoulder. "That is to say, about what the Lord meant us to do."

"Go on."

"After all, with our feeble mortal minds . . ."

"We," said Ward. "Are you sure, Greenwood? Do you think it is both of you?"

Greenwood swallowed, his throat clicking like a grasshopper's. "I, me," he whispered. "Supposing *I* knew I was wrong. Had done wrong."

"Oh, my," Ward said. "Well. It would be unjust to punish you both if only one of you had seen the error of his ways. But whatever shall we do about it? I cannot open the glass. It might let you both out. I think it would be better to leave you in there. It is educational." She smiled. "It is penance. You like penance, don't you? The idea of penance."

Panic washed across the man's face, and he even moved his hands a little, as if he were drowning and a thrown rope had bobbed slightly out of reach on the waves. "I . . . I could promise . . . I could swear that once I leave I will do you no harm. I will not lay a finger upon you, mistress, and leave this place."

". . . And?"

"And I could . . . do whatever you felt needful . . . to keep the doctor in here."

Ward smiled. "Good."

But the word had no sooner escaped her lips than Charnock was up, like an arrow, no, like the rat terrier she had just deemed him—flying from sleep toward Greenwood, shouting, cursing. Ward stepped back involuntarily from the mirror, startled, even though the glass lay between her and the fight.

It was a strange thing to watch. It was like the world made small: the bigger and slower man defending himself from the relentless onslaught of the smaller and quicker; the older man giving away unwillingly to the younger; the grunts, cries, imprecations to justify the attack: "Thou shalt not suffer a witch to live!" "Let none be found among you that useth witchcraft!" "Or a *sorcerer*! Or a *charmer*! Or those that counselleth with *spirits*! Or a *soothsayer*!"

Charnock's mouth oozed pink-streaked foam, his eyes milky, his bloodied fingertips rebloodied—for their weapons had remained on this side of the glass, and they must fight unarmed. It was rather a clumsy battle, the first (Ward suspected) that Charnock had fought in his life. They were both covered in the wet, dove-gray mud of the place and looked like living statues.

"These are the works of the flesh, Greenwood!" Charnock backed away to catch his breath, snarling like a dog. "Of the flesh! We shall be mortified here—purified! Think not of conducting some foul transaction with this witch, merely to save your worthless flesh! Recant and pray for forgiveness for speaking it aloud!"

"It is not better to die!" Greenwood blurted, hands out. "I wish to live! I—"

Charnock sprang upon him again, and in the tussle, at the moment of what Ward thought might be a killing blow, even if by accident, Greenwood wrestled the thick wad of parchment from the filthy satchel that lay between them, and held it up to shield his face.

Charnock hesitated, as Greenwood must have known he would; and since Ward had guessed it too, she swiftly drew her thumbnail down the glass and murmured a word of power to the spirit in the mirror.

A moment later Greenwood tumbled out, gasping, and lay unmoving on the floor; and the glass had sealed itself up again with Charnock screaming on the far side. Ward gestured it into silence and turned to the bloodied, dazed Greenwood as he hauled himself up, leaning on the kitchen table, then shakily sat.

Together they stared at Charnock, wild-eyed and wide-mouthed on the far side of the glass. Then Ward turned to Greenwood and said pleasantly, "I will put you back in there swift as a thought if you think to betray me." She paused, watching his mouth work. "With *him.*"

"No, mistress! I shall adhere to my word . . . whatever word you tell me."

"As you said before, then," she said. "Go from this place, speak not of it, and do no harm to myself or any other you suspect to be a witch.

Follow the ways of your Lord and keep to your own business," she added, sensibly.

She fetched him a cup of water from the pail and folded her arms, watching him drink. "Idolatry, I think he'll find, is his sin today," she remarked, pointing her chin at the mirror. "If he had only paused to consider that one may follow any book down very dark paths . . ."

Greenwood nodded, cradling the wooden cup in both sticky, gore-spattered hands. "I . . . well, if it weren't for having talked to that lady, I'm sure he would never have come here at all . . ."

Ward went to the mirror and murmured a few words, coaxing loose a single sliver the size of a pine needle; it rolled into the heart line of her open palm and shimmered faintly there as she returned to the table. "The mirrors speak to one another, Greenwood," she said. "And so while it may seem that the lady's mirror is inducing her to do evil, I have heard it speak, and it is she who leads herself astray. Not the words of the glass."

"But the lord's daughter is certainly missing. If . . ."

"I suspect," Ward said carefully, "that the child will be found again in time, and will have come to no lasting harm. Now. Close your eyes."

Greenwood did, and Ward strode around the table and in one quick movement pressed the splinter of glass into the back of his neck, under the bristly gray hair. He jumped, but wisely resisted slapping the tiny wound or touching her, and opened his eyes again, restoring life to his blank, muddy face.

"Magic is real," Ward said. "Pursue harm where harm is being done; and leave people be where it is not. I hope you will remember that."

"I will," he said, visibly restraining himself from touching his neck. "Thank you very much, Mistress Ward. Thank you. I, I . . ."

"Go outside. Take your horse. Begone." She paused. "Do not be tempted to take one of the other horses, if you love your life."

Greenwood left, and Ward spent several minutes pushing and pulling the heavy mirror out of its corner, till at last it faced the stove. It was another fine, clear day, and sweat rolled down her face as she tugged the thing into place. When she was sure Charnock was looking, she took the damp, wrinkled manuscript that Greenwood had left on the table, and opened the door of the stove.

Charnock's mouth worked silently; he pounded again on his side of the glass, but without conviction. Ward noted a coldness seeping into the man's eyes; where once they had been the color of dirty ice, now they were like new-fallen snow.

She forced the bundle flat enough to read the first page, upon which Charnock had scribed, in uneven capital letters, A TREATISE ON THE DETECTIOUNE AND SALUATION OF WITCHES, SOR-CERERS, SOOTH-SAYERS, AND ALL OTHER UNCLEANE CONSORTS (OF THE DEVVIL). "The very idea of it," she said, and—being a sensible woman—removed the pages of parchment from the back that did not have too much writing on them, because it was terribly expensive.

Then she stuffed what remained into the stove and set it alight.

It burned unevenly and sootily, but it burned nonetheless. A great cloud of black smoke erupted from the chimney, and Ward winced, thinking about the mess floating back down onto her roof. Neverthe-less, Charnock's face provided all the satisfaction she needed to confirm her decision.

When the book was mostly ash, she heaved the mirror back into its accustomed place and draped a bedsheet over it. "Send him on a journey or two in there," she said aloud. "Travel broadens the mind, don't you think? And he does so want to *learn* new things."

I quite agree, said the mirror. *I shall see him off myself, and put him on a route with many wondrous sights.*

"Thank you." Ward dusted off her hands and went to get her good broom from the workshop. Work needed doing, the house needed cleaning, and as ever, the glass called her name.

JUST A NUDGE

Maureen McHugh

I was in a fucking mood when I got off shift. I was an ICU nurse and since my hospital was short on nurses, I had two beds that night. One of those beds was a 91-year-old woman who weighed about 100 pounds and had late-stage multiple myeloma and a bunch of comorbidities. The woman was dying and her family had a full code on her. Nine days in the ICU with a trach and dialysis and every known intervention to keep her alive. The hospitalist and palliative care both talked to the family, but they wouldn't budge. The family wanted to know "why we were starving her" (because she could no longer swallow and if we tried to give her even a pureed diet, she brought it back up and risked aspirating; she was actively dying). When she crashed, I had to do CPR and break the ribs of a woman who should have been on lorazepam and morphine, dying in peace instead of enduring twenty minutes of brutal, bone-splintering attempts to keep her alive. She finally died and part of me wished we could have just told the family that we didn't torture people and they could take their full code and go stuff themselves.

The daughter was convinced we could have saved her and screamed at me.

Consent is important. Medicine has a terrible track record of paternalism and doing awful things to people. But two years into the pandemic and I was burned out and angry and so were my patients and their families and it felt to me as though every bad impulse was just exploding out of everyone.

I got home late (I couldn't remember the last time I didn't end up staying a couple of hours past my shift change).

Kayla was up with the baby, nursing in the kitchen at one in the morning. "Hey Jude," she said. Old joke on Jody, my name.

I kissed her and then the top of the baby's soft head. "Bad shift," I said.

She looked up from Isaac in his yellow onesie. She was so soft, sitting at the kitchen table, all curves and infant and light.

"Elderly woman, no code, should have been allowed to die," I said.

"*Meemaw's a fighter*," she said.

I snorted. Kayla's not a nurse, she's an accountant, but she knows a lot of nurse in-jokes.

"*DC to JC*," I countered. Discharge to Jesus.

I got a beer from the fridge and plopped down.

"You should have given her a nudge," Kayla said.

I laughed. My dad had been a powerful witch, and I had learned a lot after he died, but I didn't do magic anymore. My dad gifted me several things: a genetic disposition to gum disease, his book collection including his grimoire, his entire collection of Raymond Chandler, and probably, the impetus to become a nurse. My dad died when I was fourteen of a serious neurodegenerative disease like ALS except not. My mom thought (and I did, too) that it came from him practicing magic.

A lot of nursing school grads are unprepared for the sheer physicality of nursing. The lifting, the wiping, the turning. The shit, the spit, the piss. We had home aides come in but they were expensive and so by eleven I was helping my mom turn my dad every two hours, learning to see the signs of developing bedsores on back, buttocks, and heels. My dad was aware in the cave of his own skull until the end, aware, as his body grew increasingly unconnected from him, the lines of communication going down like his extremities were distant outposts.

I was relieved when he died. He was, too.

I didn't then think, *I am going to become a nurse!* I didn't want anything to do with it. But I didn't know what else I wanted to do except not die that way. I became obsessed with his books, including the grimoire. When I was four, he had taught me the moves of the chess pieces and the simplest of spells, how to create a little blue light in the palm of my hand. By the time I was sixteen, I was pretty proficient. My dad was powerful, and like the child of a great baseball player, I knew the rhythms of practice and the requirements for doing magic well. Then I woke up one morning with my hand numb and I freaked.

It went away in minutes, pins and needles, a clear sign that I had slept on it wrong, but for me it was a warning, and I stopped practicing.

Kayla knew. She knew I could do it—I'd taught her a little spell to make her palm fill with blue light. We joked about it. But she was very supportive of my decision not to do magic. Honestly, technology does a lot of things better than magic.

"I went out into the garden to get a lemon," Kayla said. "Damn mosquitoes."

"Kayla!" I snapped.

"I needed a lemon!"

"Sorry," I said. "I'm just tired. I guess the county has given up on Henry?"

"I haven't seen them come by in weeks," Kayla said.

Kayla couldn't go out into the backyard for the entire pregnancy, and she loved lemons. Loved acid and sour. Loved our lemon tree. But our next-door neighbor, Henry, was a hoarder, and his entire backyard was filled with crap. There was an old car back there, an ancient AMC Pacer, and piles of shelves, buckets, and barrels and furniture. It doesn't rain much in Los Angeles, but there were so many places where water could linger that mosquitoes bred in swarms. All the cases of the Zika virus in Los Angeles involved people who had traveled somewhere else, but West Nile is endemic, and like a lot of new parents, we were paranoid. Kayla avoided processed meats and alcohol and sushi.

I called the county about the infestation, and the LA coalition on hoarders, but Henry, our crazy neighbor, just didn't answer the door when they knocked. The guy who came out to do the inspection called me and told me he would keep trying, and that he'd let his manager know, but in the end nothing happened. Some mosquitoes can breed in as little as a bottle cap of water.

Henry didn't know we called, but I was sure he suspected. When we first moved in, he thought we were roommates and we didn't tell him we were married. None of his business.

Kayla was showing and we were getting groceries out of the car one day when he bicycled up—he didn't have a car—and saw us. He stopped. "Are you pregnant?" he asked her. He was an awkward guy, hard of hearing. We had always been polite but distant.

Kayla smiled tightly and nodded.

"Are you going to get married?" he asked.

My mind went blank but Kayla, who is braver than I will ever be, just said, "I already am," she said.

Henry, shirtless with tanned crocodile skin, looked at her for a moment and I could see when he figured it out. That Kayla was my wife and I was hers.

"Who's the father?" he asked, frowning.

"There is no father," Kayla said, which is not technically true, but also none of his business. "It's just us."

He didn't like that, and I smiled my best "fuck you" smile.

That's when it started.

*We lived in Southern California, so while we had certainly had some ex-*periences with homophobia, we were lucky to have lots of friends and a life where a great deal of the time, we didn't have actively hateful people doing actively hateful things, if you know what I mean. I put Henry in the homophobic asshole category and didn't spend too much energy on his existence. I saw him riding his bicycle once in a while and had that slight angry surge of adrenaline and then went on.

I came home from work one night, relatively on time for once, on the night before garbage pickup to see him going through our recycling bin on the street.

It irritated me. Sure, we were getting rid of stuff, in this case a big cardboard box from Costco—our fourteen-year-old flat screen had died and after about six months we'd broken down and replaced it. Henry was hauling the cardboard out of the tall blue bin. It was being thrown out. Why should I care if he wanted it? I mean, his place looked like shit because his stuff was spilling out from his house onto his porch, and his backyard was completely full of metal shelving units, piles of something covered by tarps, and bricks (which he brought home two at a time in the basket of his bicycle, I assumed, taken from work sites). I glared at him as I pulled the car in and he glared at me and stomped off with the folded cardboard.

Then I went inside and looked in on Isaac, sleeping on his back in his onesie with the milk bottle labeled *40 oz*. Our baby boy, with his fist curled next to his ear and his sleeping look of stubborn concentration.

I didn't think about it until the next day when I saw the cardboard spread out across his driveway. Our driveways were side by side, and he had a homemade parking pad off of his with a bed of uneven bricks and grass growing up between them. He'd covered the bricks with our cardboard.

I said, "What the fuck?"

Kayla frowned at me. "What?"

I told her about Henry taking the cardboard from our recycling bin. "Now it's lying on his driveway."

Kayla came over to the window with her coffee cup. She sighed. "What's that for?"

I had no idea. It stayed for a couple for weeks and I saw it every time I left or came back home and it annoyed the shit out of me. I don't think of myself as a petty person, but maybe I'm a petty person.

Then my uncle died. Timothy was my dad's brother. He had kept practicing witchcraft as a hobby after my dad died, and he taught high school chemistry. He had pancreatic cancer, caught pretty late. I liked Timothy and his wife, Anne, liked my cousins. We bundled up Isaac and made the awkward plane-trip-with-baby to Columbus, Ohio, where they lived.

Timothy looked a lot like my dad, but they were very different people. My dad was an extrovert (and the irony of his death was not lost on any of us—as his nerves de-myelinated and he lost connection with his extremities and lost control of his abilities, including speaking, he was still there, locked in, looking out at us but entirely unable to charm and confide and entertain). Timothy was self-contained.

The funeral was small. My aunt was exhausted by grief and the long final haul. She held Isaac and he gazed up, baby bottom heavy in her arms, blowing a bubble of saliva. There were flowers from the school, and flowers from some of his students, now grown.

I sat with Corinne, my cousin, in Timothy and Anne's suburban backyard, drinking Miller out of a longneck bottle. Corinne was my favorite cousin. We talked about his last weeks. He'd been diagnosed just after New Year's and now it was April, a glorious nonrainy spring day in Ohio. Everything was coming in green.

"Do you think it had anything to do with alchemy?" Corinne asked.

"I don't know," I said. "I was talking about it to Mom, and she didn't think so." Magic is full of weird rules. There are few coincidences in magic. Like calls to like. Everything you do reflects back on you three times. "What was he doing?"

"A lot of research," Corinne said. "He was trying to figure out chrysopoeia."

Chrysopeia is the purification of elements, historically the transmutation of lead into gold.

Corinne continued, "He liked running alchemical experiments and measuring them scientifically. He liked trying to figure out what physically happened." She shrugged.

"Sounds like an expensive hobby," I said. He had a second garage out back that he'd outfitted as a kind of lab.

"Some people have boats, or horses," she said. "Dad had alchemy."

I laughed. "Speaking as a nurse, I'd say that the cancer was just bad luck. People get cancer."

Corinne was tearing up and asking me about end-stage stuff and I was promising her that the drugs her dad received meant that he didn't suffer, when my grandmother walked into the backyard.

A ripple of reaction—a head turn here, a pause in conversation between Aunt Anne and a friend of hers I didn't know—ran across the yard. My maternal grandmother, Lorraine, was white-haired and erect. She wore giant 1980s-style sunglasses and a broad-brimmed black hat. She was tanned and was wearing black capri pants. Perfect for a funeral garden party, which I supposed was what this was.

Aunt Anne was holding Isaac, talking to Kayla about the blanket she was crocheting for him. ". . . got a lot done in the hospital," she said. "Normally I put off projects in the summer because, you know, I'm sitting there with a half-finished blanket across my lap in August, sweating in the AC—" She looked up and saw my grandmother and stood. "Iris."

Isaac stared at his grandmother. He turned and reached for Kayla, starting to cry. He was at the strangers-are-scary stage, and I thought he was going to be like Kayla, who was more of a numbers person than a people person.

Lorraine, my grandmother, took him in her arms and bounced him a little, and he buried his face in her neck.

"He's shy," Kayla apologized.

"It's the age," my grandmother said. "Aren't you a cutie!" She dug into her Birkin bag and pulled out a green bottle the size of her hand. "I brought you a witch bottle for Isaac," she said.

"Gram," I said. "Thank you." We'd had a baby shower and some of the family had sent gifts—a silver cup from my mother's mother engraved with his name, a subscription to a diaper service from a bunch of the nurses I worked with. But I didn't think Kayla was prepared for a witch bottle. "I know just where to bury it. What does it need?" Witch bottles protect against magical attack. They had red thread, rosemary, needles and pins in them, and something from the person they were protecting.

"Some people use hair," my grandmother said. "I prefer to go old school."

"How about a bit of used diaper," I suggested. "Old school" meant piss but I really didn't want to try to collect baby pee. Isaac was a sprayer if I wasn't careful with the diaper change.

We went inside, where my mother was sitting with some people I didn't know and I had some ham, and fruit salad, and hash-brown casserole. Funeral casserole.

My grandmother meant well. She was entitled as fuck, but like many rich people, carelessly kind. She was the reason that Kayla and I could afford a down payment on a place in Los Angeles and she had never suggested that we owed her in the slightest. My dad and my grandmother had issues, and he had never accepted money from her. He had admired my great-grandfather, who had used magic to establish a web of business and financial connections that had allowed him to build a fortune. My father had tried to do the same thing. My father, who I loved, was not suited for business. He was a 1960s guy with a bushy black handlebar moustache and hair like George Harrison and his study was a seven-year-old's dream of a magician's lair. He had an old pharmacy cabinet with drawers I wasn't allowed to open, books and candles, a taxidermized fox with amber marble eyes set on a high shelf. It both fascinated and terrified me.

He wanted to prove something, so he worked in glamours and spells that created bonds between people. Like love spells, they could have unexpected consequences. He had a financial company, kind of a mini hedge fund, I think, but I don't know, by the time I would have been able to understand, he was already sick.

My mother and I diapered him, turned him, and fed him through an NG tube. Home help came every day and night, and my grandmother paid for it all. It was, like witchcraft, ugly and full of piss and shit and the essential matters of life and death.

When he died, I was fourteen and I didn't cry. I was hard and selfish as only a fourteen-year-old can be.

When we got back to Los Angeles, the cardboard from our flat screen that Henry had pulled from our recycling bin was melting into his driveway. Henry had built his own driveway out of bricks, and weeds grew up between the bricks. He battled them with a flat shovel, scraping across the surface of the bricks. He didn't like chemicals, he said. The noise was obnoxious. Before he realized we were heedless lesbians raising our baby without a father, I suggested he try something else, like maybe a ground cloth under the bricks. It dawned on me that this was my reward. It had rained while we were gone, so the cardboard was now saturated and decayed like a layer of papier-mâché.

It was the first thing we saw when we came out our front door.

I was tired from the funeral. You know how annoying a crying baby can be when you're on an airplane? Imagine five hours of that crying baby on your lap. I was embarrassed and exhausted.

Isaac was asleep, lulled by the car ride. (Why are car rides sleep-inducing and airplanes not? Don't answer that—I don't care.) I got out of the car and just stared. Kayla lifted a sleeping baby out of the back and said, "Just don't," to me. Meaning, *Don't go off right now, I can't deal.*

I fumed but didn't go off.

I had to go to work the next night and had a pretty good shift. I had a patient who had been in a car accident, and she needed an MRI. She had nipple rings, and God help me, a navel ring, metal, and in a first, I had to remove them before they could do the MRI. No metal in an MRI. She was conscious—Kayla said my favorite patients were the sedated ones and she wasn't entirely wrong—but she was embarrassed instead of angry. She had her right arm in a cast that extended down to her fingers and even if she hadn't had chest injuries and a drain tube and yadda yadda yadda she couldn't have removed the rings without help.

"My mom always said wear clean underwear in case you're in an accident," she said. "She never thought of this."

I grinned and pretended I did things like this all the time. I had never actually had to remove a navel ring or nipple rings from a patient. Usually, that would probably have been the job of the emergency department, but here we were. I liked her, and she was mortified but game.

I was looking forward to having a fun story to tell Kayla instead of the usual depressing stuff that rode home from work with me but when I pulled into the driveway, there was Henry, going through our recycling bin.

"Get out of that," I snarled.

He turned around. "You're throwing it out," he said, his voice rising defensively.

"I'm recycling it," I said. "Which is better than seeing it thrown on your driveway to rot."

"It's to stop the weeds from growing, like you said." Now he was accusatory.

"I said get a ground cloth and put it under the bricks."

"I'm sixty-seven years old, I'm not pulling up all those bricks. The cardboard works, and it's being used!"

"It's an eyesore, it's been rained on, and it's garbage. Stay out of my bins!"

"Once they're on the street, it's legal," he said.

"I don't care!" I said.

He stepped toward me, chest out. "You can't do anything about it."

"I can call the city and tell them about your trash."

That silenced him. The city had told him to get stuff off his front yard before and ticketed him. I had no doubt he was terrified of the city doing a haul away.

I stomped inside and felt a tiny little bit of victory.

Maybe Henry was why I remembered my grandmother's witch bottle. I found it, square like an ink bottle, and cloudy green. Magic likes metaphor and, of course, my grandmother had found some antique bottle. The pins in it were old, dark, and tarnished. The red thread was bright as a cardinal.

The witch bottle protected against magic. But there was no magic here, just my crazy neighbor. Isaac didn't need protection from spells, he needed protection from homophobes.

The next week, Kayla was working and I was on kid duty. I was tired from work, I'd only slept about six hours, but it was my turn to watch Isaac since Kayla had borne the brunt of it for all the months she was on maternity leave and I was working sixty-hour weeks. Some nights I'd come home and just sit in the car in the driveway and sob. Some days I couldn't bear to think about going back the next day. But we needed my benefits. So I came in the back, stripped and threw my scrubs in the laundry, and prayed I didn't catch COVID and give it to Kayla or, God forbid, Isaac. It was still scary, even vaccinated and boosted.

Isaac looked up at me, serious as a prophet.

"Baby," I said, "I'm going to change your diaper, okay?"

I laid him down on the changing table and he fussed.

"I'll take care of you," I said. "First I take the old one off."

Kayla stopped in the doorway. "You're using your nurse voice." In nursing we tell even the sedated patients what we're doing, as we do it.

"I don't mind wiping your butt," I told him.

Kayla snorted and went on down the hall. She had started back to work part-time—she worked for a CPA and was doing some spillover tax season stuff.

I snipped a tiny, stinking square off the diaper and stuffed it in the witch bottle with a toothpick. I capped it and took it out back. We had a terracotta chiminea that we always meant to use in the back garden— plans to sit out there with a drink, enjoying a chilly evening. It was LA, and there weren't many chilly evenings and mosquitoes had put us off the garden, so we'd used it maybe twice. I started a little fire with scrap wood and turned the bottle in the flames until it blackened, and then buried it in the corner next to Henry's place. Symbolic, at least. Maybe it would protect against sinister influences.

I picked up the recycling in the kitchen and emptied it into the bin. The smell hit me and for a moment I thought it was diapers, ammonia sharp and eye-watering. But we used a diaper service. The recycling bin was half-full and everything in it was drenched in urine.

Henry's revenge.

I wasn't even angry, I was shocked. I dropped the lid on the bin.

"Kayla," I said.

She frowned. I usually didn't interrupt her when she was working. "What's wrong?" she asked.

"Henry pissed in our recycling."

She didn't understand me for a moment. It was one of those sentences that are full of individual words you can understand but take a moment to make sense together. "What?"

"Henry pissed in our recycling. It stinks."

She frowned. "Why?"

"I think because I told him to leave our recycling alone. I threatened to call the city," I admitted.

"Jody," she sighed.

"I didn't expect him to do it. I just didn't want him rooting around in our trash."

"Why do you bait him?" she asked.

"I don't 'bait' him! I didn't want him to take our trash and strew it around his front yard!"

She breathed out hard through her nose. "You deal with it; I've got to find the cost basis on this stock."

She had been doing the lion's share of taking care of Isaac, taking maternity leave on my benefits, and she was stressed about trying to return to work. At least she got to work remotely. But it wasn't my fault that our neighbor was a crazy asshole! "What's to deal with?"

"Well, it's not recyclable, is it? I mean if pizza boxes aren't recyclable, peed-on stuff *really* isn't."

"Fuck," I said, because she was right. "Like I don't deal with bodily fluids enough at work."

"So, you've got experience and you'll be better at it." She turned back to the computer.

Passive aggression 'r' us.

Isaac made a preliminary noise from his crib, the noise that suggested he could erupt at any moment. I went in to check on him. He held out his arms, an imperative *Pick me up!* He could sit upright on the couch but couldn't sit without support. He was so frustrated by not being able to do it. Kayla was teaching him a few basic words in sign language—he understood some things but didn't have the coordination between lips and tongue to speak. He signed *more,* which he used when he wanted something. *More more more.*

"You want a snack?" I asked.

MORE MORE MORE. He *aah*ed and made excited noises. I didn't know how much he understood and how much was just the sheer joy of interacting. On the other hand, I was pretty sure he understood *snack.*

"You're a little piggy," I told him.

He got a piece of banana to maul on and I got his blanket and put him on the floor in Kayla's office.

We always had latex gloves, so I grabbed a pair to use to empty out the recycling bin and took out the paper crap and threw it in a garbage bag. If I were a good environmentalist, I'd have rinsed off the cans and jars, but I told myself that water was valuable, too—LA was under water restrictions because of the drought. While I was throwing the stuff in the garbage bag, it occurred to me that if I saved some of the paper, even just a little bit, I'd have some of Henry.

I didn't do magic. Besides the kind of simple stuff like the witch bottle and good-luck-charm stuff, but it was hard to ignore that I had some of Henry's most personal essence right here. I didn't have to use it. I didn't want to use it. But it was insurance. I went inside and got a press-and-seal baggy, one of the little snack-sized ones we used when we packed cereal for Isaac. I tore a piece off from a piss-soaked hardware flyer and stuck it in the bag. A decent-sized piece. I hid it in a pill bottle in the bathroom. Kayla didn't need to know. She'd worry. I didn't intend to use it. It just made me feel better knowing that I had something on Henry.

"Look," Kayla said over spaghetti, "I know you're stressed out of your mind."

It felt like it came out of nowhere.

"People like Henry? They're like that because of stuff that happened to them."

"Okay?" I said.

"I was reading some stuff online," she said, and took a bite of salad. "Hoarders are usually triggered by some kind of loss or trauma."

"Don't eat with your mouth full," I said. "You're a bad influence." Isaac wasn't even at the table, but he learned all the things I didn't want him to learn and not enough of the things I did want him to learn. I kind of wanted him to have decent manners.

"Just, you should cut the dude some slack. Just let shit like the cardboard and the recycling slide."

"What is this about?" I asked.

"I know he drives you nuts, but really, I think a lot of it is the pandemic. I mean, I know you're burned out and people are shit and you've used up all your empathy on assholes who won't get vaccinated, but we've got to live next door to the guy."

"I haven't done anything!" I said. "He's the one who pissed in our garbage!"

"You threatened him," Kayla said.

"I did not!"

"You said you would call the city," she said. "He got scared. People who are scared do crazy things. You know that better than I do. So he goes through our recycling. We *are* throwing it out."

"That's not the point!" I said. "The point is that his place is an eyesore. And I want our recycling to be, you know, recycled. Not rot on his driveway."

She put her hands up, a gesture of surrender. "Okay. I just hate to see you like this."

"Like what?" I said.

"Touchy. Angry."

"I'm not," I said. "I'm over it."

"You're letting him live rent-free in your head."

"I'm not!" Henry was mentally ill. But he had pissed in our recycling. Which was nasty and mean. I didn't trust him. It wasn't my fault he was damaged. I was tired of being the punching bag for damaged people.

But I wasn't dwelling on it or anything. It wasn't my fault that every time I left the house that stupid cardboard was right there.

The next time I saw Henry bicycling down the street I thought about his life. As far as we could tell, he had no family. Once he had a visitor, a guy in a Toyota Camry that was piled so high with junk that there was only space in the driver's seat and there was no way that he could see anything in the rearview mirror. The guy slept in the car, parked in the driveway. Probably because there was no space to sleep in Henry's. Or maybe the guy just felt better with his stuff.

All Henry had was his stuff. He played the radio; we could hear it through his screen door. He'd had some sort of plumbing issue at some point, and the side of the house farthest from us had plywood covering whatever they'd torn out.

It was a sad life.

I saw a lot of sad lives. A lot of diabetic alcoholics with end-stage kidney disease and congestive heart failure. They'd be intubated and have a Foley catheter, sedated out of their minds, and when I'd do vitals or turn them or clean them, hang a new bag or whatever, I'd still talk to them, tell them what I was doing, because you never know what people can hear. I talked to people who told me (before they were intubated) that the vaccine killed people. I did it for them and I did it for me. I could have a little compassion for Henry.

I said as much to Kayla and she said, "I'm not saying you have to be the guy's best friend, Jodes. Just avoid him."

Which was easy enough. Even if he did live next door.

What Kayla said stayed with me. Since the pandemic, my job had been hard. I didn't want to become that person who hated their patients—even though there were times I hated my patients and my patients' families. People had threatened me, scared me, spit on me. But I was afraid if I gave in, I'd get bitter, and that would infect not just me, but my relationship with Kayla, my parenting.

And here I was doing it with Henry. I mean, part of it was because he was an asshole, but part of it was because of my own stress.

I came back from the grocery on a beautiful Southern California day. The weather was perfect, high seventies. The sky was a clear California blue. Isaac had just had an appointment with the pediatrician, and he was doing great, hitting milestones. I had the day off.

Henry was in his front yard doing God knew what when I pulled into the driveway. I got my bags out of the car—we had a set of matching Trader Joe's bags I'd gotten to soothe Kayla's orderly soul; a blue insulated bag for cold things and five bags for regular groceries. I grabbed handles.

Henry was watching me.

"Hi," I said. And I stopped. "Look," I said, "I'm sorry I got so upset over the recycling."

He looked suspicious.

"That's all," I said. "I was just . . . It was unexpected."

"You were throwing it out," he said.

"Yeah," I said.

He seemed uncomfortable. Oh well, I'd done what I could.

I hauled the bags into the kitchen and was putting them away when Kayla came stomping in. My first thought was *what did I do?*

"Henry has been stealing electricity from us," she snapped.

I honestly didn't understand her. Henry didn't strike me as an electrical whizz. I put the ice cream in the freezer and followed her into the back. I hadn't been in the back since I buried the witch bottle from my Gram. We didn't go in the back because, of course, mosquitoes. She pointed to an electrical outlet—there was one of those orange, heavy-duty extension cords plugged into it. It had been buried, but Kayla had grabbed it and pulled it up, disrupting the dirt, to where it led to the fence between our yard and Henry's mosquito farm of a backyard.

The guy was using our electricity. Our bills had been high, but we thought it was because of all the laundry and stuff associated with having a baby.

I found him in the front, screwing around with a green ground-cover cloth he had spread over the strip of grass between the sidewalk and the street, putting rocks in the corners to hold it down. Kayla came after me.

"You're using our electrical outlet?" I said. "What the hell!"

"What?" he said.

"That's theft, Henry!"

"Theft? Theft?" His voice rose. "I'll tell you what's theft, that area in the back, that's a common area! My mother used those lemon trees! I used those lemon trees! Then you fenced it off!"

"It's our property!" I said. "It's not a common area! And what the hell does that have to do with syphoning off our electricity?"

"You're rich," he said. "What do you care?"

"We're not rich!" Kayla said. "We work hard! And it's stealing! You're stealing from us!"

"You think you own everything!" Henry said. "You think you can tell me what to do! You tell me I can't have the things you're throwing away!"

"Call the cops," I told Kayla.

"If you call the cops, I'll call Child Protective Services! I'll tell them about your baby! About how he doesn't have a father!"

"Don't you threaten me," I said. I felt cold. I had been trying to be compassionate, to be understanding.

"You can't raise a boy without a father! He needs a role model!"

He was red-faced and furious. Ranting. He had clearly been thinking about this for a long time.

I let him rant, let him spew vile things, let him say things to us. I was shocked, partly. I knew he didn't like us, but I hadn't expected this. I hadn't expected him to threaten us, to threaten Isaac. Inside the house, Isaac must have been woken by the commotion, because I heard him wail.

I looked back at Kayla and she got it, went in to get Isaac.

I looked back at Henry, red-faced and screaming. Across the street, one of the neighbors, Sherry, was standing in her doorway, frowning.

I thought, *You do not want to threaten me, old man.*

Abruptly, I turned around and walked back to my door. Henry followed me. "Watch yourself," I said.

I thought he was going to lunge at me. I've had patients get violent, either because they were mentally ill or delirious, or just bad people. Something seemed to register with him that I wasn't going to back down.

Kayla stood in the doorway with Isaac crying on her hip, her cell phone in her hand, videoing. "If you don't get off our property, I'm going to call the police," she said.

Henry backed a couple of steps, and then went back inside his place, slamming the door.

I convinced Kayla not to call the police yet. I went to Lowe's and got locking covers for our external outlets and water spigots. We got a doorbell camera. Kayla wanted a security system. I promised we would get one.

It was nine days to the full moon.

I worked the first day of the full moon and got home at a little after 2:00 a.m. The moon was high and bright. Kayla was asleep. Isaac was sleeping through the night, most nights. Nursing a baby took a lot of energy, and between baby and work, Kayla slept hard these days.

I used my father's recipe for witch ointment. It was a classic version. Henbane and wolfsbane. The active ingredients are scopolamine, atropine, and hyoscyamine, which are poisonous and make you hallucinate. People thought that witches didn't fly, that the ointment just made them trip, but the tripping isn't the point, or rather, the discipline to control the magic while tripping was the point. The only thing I did differently was to use coconut oil instead of beef tallow as my base.

While Kayla and Isaac slept, I went into the backyard and under the moon, I stripped and oiled my body with the ointment, including my vaginal lips. Scopolamine is absorbed transdermally. It was chilly, even in summer. Los Angeles is almost a desert, and the temperatures fall at night. But the bricks in our backyard were warm under my bare feet. Me being me, I thought about how I needed to lose weight. My mouth got dry and I felt flushed and sweaty. Dizzy. I hated witch ointment.

It took a while. The moon got strange, and I forgot where I was. I realized it was working me, instead of me working it. I had to ride this, to rise with it. I was out of practice. But I could do this. I knew how it worked.

Except I couldn't. I couldn't get on top of it. I used to have flying dreams, and sometimes in the dream I would land and then discover I'd lost the knack of getting into the air. At some point I sat down, bare haunches against warm brick.

Then I, I don't know how to say it, I found it. I mounted the very air, rising easily. Below me, I could see my body, slumping to the side, cheek against ground, but I wasn't worried, I wouldn't be long.

I felt disconnected, bodiless. I had the strange sense of being able to control myself without being able to feel anything. Far away, I was maybe scared, or excited, or some sort of strong feeling but without the tension in my muscles, without belly and heart, I couldn't tell what it meant and it made thinking difficult.

But Henry. What if he called CPS and we got someone who didn't like lesbians, who thought we shouldn't have Isaac? What if they tried to take my boy from me? No one else would talk to him when they diapered him. No one else would know that he would eat pureed spinach even though he made a face. That was why I was doing this. Because Henry was an old guy, and Isaac was just starting out, and Henry didn't deserve to mess him up.

I glided through the night air to Henry's front door and then through it. I had never been in Henry's house. There were piles and piles of German newspapers and magazines. I got the sense that Henry's mother was German, although I didn't know if that was witch-sense or just being high as fuck. There were paths snaking through the piles, and giant plastic storage tubs. It smelled of male body odor and mildew. There were metal shelves. Dirty tools like chisels and stirrers with dried mortar on them, stolen, I assumed, from job sites. Plastic bags. So many plastic bags.

And in the center of the maze, curled up on a nest of stinking blankets on the quarter of a bed not piled with crap, Henry slept, mouth open and snoring quietly.

"Henry," I said. "You fucked with the wrong person."

He stirred.

"Wake up," I commanded, above him like an avenging angel, "Wake up up up up."

He sat up and saw me and his eyes grew wide but before he could do anything, I darted in and touched his forehead. "You are paralyzed," I said.

His mouth moved a little.

"I am a witch, Henry. As was my father, and his mother, and her father before her. You threatened my child."

I could see his terror beating in a vein in his forehead. I shouldn't have been able to see, but the tiny space was infused with witch-light.

"I have done no real magic since I was a teenager, Henry. Had no intention of ever doing it again, but you will not threaten me and mine."

I could see him struggling against the paralysis. I hesitated. I wished I knew what I was feeling. I had come here to do this, but maybe I would regret it. I hated witch ointment. Stay focused. That was the trick when you use the ointment. Remember what you planned.

I reached out with my finger to the center of his chest and his eyes rolled wall-eyed like a frightened dog.

"It's just a nudge," I said. Because I always talk to my patients. "It won't even hurt." I wasn't entirely sure that was true, but I didn't want it to.

The skin of his chest was leathery with curling white hairs. My astral finger rested against his sternum, and I felt the wild muscle of his heart, squeezing and squeezing and squeezing, red and striated. There was already damage there, a net of arteries narrowing, stiffening, clogging. Not that he wouldn't probably live for years.

"Stop," I said.

And it did, the ceaseless work of pumping done. Henry sighed and fell back then, eyes open, staring at me, and I stayed with him while he died.

It hadn't taken much. Just a nudge. And at that moment, I didn't even hate myself.

HER RAVENOUS WATERS

Andrea Stewart

My cormorant returned from the river not with food, but with news. "Meihe is angry." He blinked and shook his beak, beads of water hitting my cheeks. The boat rocked gently, the lantern hanging from the end casting a fiery light over the river's surface. A flash of bright scales shone before disappearing into the darkness.

I sighed, wrapping my shawl tighter around my shoulders. "Meihe is always angry."

I removed the rope from his throat and he ruffled his feathers, turning to preening. "This time is different. She will ask for more." And that was all the bird would say.

The water beneath us was deceptively calm; I wondered, if I peered into that blackness, could I catch a glimpse of Meihe at the bottom, holding court in her scaled robes, her sycophants gaping like fish at her fury, giving way before it with little nods and bows? Even now, on the cool surface, I could feel the pull of that heat.

There was no place for me in her court, not after I'd recovered. I wasn't noble born. And there was no place for me back in the town I'd come from. When I'd still been weak from death, I'd lain at Meihe's feet like a treasured pet, sunlight filtering down from the surface as she ran her hands through my hair. "I saved you," she'd said to me time and time again, her voice filled with both lazy wonderment and possessiveness. In the early mornings, I thought I could feel her fingers against my scalp, the nails scraping lightly against my skin.

Most times these days I awoke alone, but sometimes I awoke with Meihe cradling my head in her lap as she whispered into my ear. "There is wickedness in them, Jian. They don't care for one another; they don't honor the old ways. They should be punished. Help me."

"Yes," I would answer, my voice still burred with sleep.

And then she would pull the magic from me, tugging it free as though she were merely uprooting carrots, leaving me empty and spent.

It was better, I supposed, than remembering the feel of *his* knuckles hard against my skull as he'd plunged my face beneath the cold river's surface and held it there.

My husband had made me a ghost. Meihe had breathed her magic into me and had made me a witch.

I flexed my fingers before picking up the oars and rowing back to shore. I couldn't fault Meihe for her anger, not when I had my own. It was in my nature to be angry—it was how my magic worked and how I made a living. Amulets, talismans, poultices, and tinctures, all sold and traded to the immortals of Meihe's court. Each powered by a tendril of rage, nurtured and grown from my heart. Meihe's requests were different, pulling those tendrils up by the roots, twining them with her own magic, using them for her purposes.

But together we made the world right again, altering the path of Snake River, swelling it with our magic until the people who deserved it drowned.

Ungrateful. Petty. Demanding. Selfish.

"She is scheming," my cormorant said as the oars dipped into the water. He'd once been a member of Meihe's court, but she'd cursed him to this form. She hadn't given me permission to take him with me when I'd left, though she hadn't stopped me, either. We were both odd, rejected things—did we not belong together?

"Let her scheme." I opened the basket for him, and he hopped inside.

"Someday, she will ask you for too much," he said as I closed the lid. His voice devolved into a gasping, croaking sound—which happened every time he grew close to saying something Meihe had forbidden him from saying.

He needn't have wasted his breath. There was nothing she could ask of me that would be too much, not after she'd saved me. I owed her everything.

A young woman was waiting for me when I returned home. A supplicant, by the looks of her. But not an immortal.

A townsperson.

Slender and long-limbed, an egret in the roughspun clothes of the lower class, she trembled when our gazes met. I knew what she saw—I was not as I'd once appeared. My skin was paler now, my hair darker than the heavens on a moonless night, my eyes white and bright as stars.

She bowed, and then bowed again. "Witch, I need your help."

Bold of her to come here, to my home, to my doorstep. To wait. To request help. If only someone had helped me before Meihe had. If only someone had seen the bruises and not turned their gaze away, had offered me a place to go. Bitterness twined like vines around my heart. The people I'd lived among were not redeemable. "I'm not in the business of helping mortals."

But she held out the basket on her arm, filled with white radishes and two paper-wrapped packages that smelled of freshly butchered meat. A humble offering. Still, I found myself sniffing the air. It had been ages since I'd had any meat besides the delicate, white-fleshed fish that lived in the river. Not since I'd been mortal.

"Please," she said again, bowing, averting her gaze. Something about her obeisance *was* gratifying.

I relented, beckoning her inside. "Fine. Tell me what you seek."

My hut at the river's edge was much more modest than the house my husband's family owned, and even more so than Meihe's palace at the bottom of Snake River. But I'd found it abandoned when I'd made my way from Meihe's kingdom, the roof in disrepair but the hearth still intact. It was mine alone and there was space to breathe.

Herbs hung drying from the ceiling, the ashes of my fire still warm and sparking when I stirred them. I let my cormorant out of his basket, put a fresh log into the fireplace, and lit it, listening as the woman explained.

"I need a protection amulet, please—whatever you can spare."

I shuffled through my supplies, plucking out a piece of peachwood and threading a cord through the hole in the middle. This would do. Meihe had taught me how to use my newfound gift once I'd grown used to my new shape. She'd shown me how to focus my breathing, how to let my anger rise like the tides, molding it, giving it purpose.

The woman was still speaking, words falling from her mouth like so many loose stones. Her family had offered her as a concubine to a wealthy man with two sons, an agreement that would erase her family's debts. She would do her duty, only . . .

"Only what?" I wasn't sure why I stopped, white, misty tendrils of magic pausing halfway between me and the amulet.

"Only he has a fearful temper. His current wife is still living, but some say he killed his previous one. They say he drowned her in the river."

All the magic pulled back into my core. And *then* I remembered his knuckles hard against my skull, the scrape of river stones against my cheek as I thrashed, as I did my best to *live*.

"What—what is his name?" My throat was tight with the memory of water rushing into my lungs.

The air in my hut suddenly grew cold, thick with the scent of incense. The shutters of a window burst open, a flash of bright-green scales half-obscured by the mist that poured in like fog over a waterfall.

The woman fled out the door, leaving her basket of food.

"Wait!"

It was too late. She was gone.

Meihe stood in her place, robe glittering by firelight. My cormorant let out a soft grunt before tucking his head behind one wing. Meihe gave him a suspicious look but then turned her face to me.

I forgot what it was like to receive the full attention of the river goddess. It was as though I stood too close to a fire, but one from which I couldn't tear myself away. A thin line formed between her brows. "It's been far too long, Jian." At first glance she didn't seem angry. But I could see the emotions simmering beneath the surface of her eyes, a riptide that threatened to pull me in if I stepped too deep.

"A few months, perhaps," I said lightly. Meihe was always indolent during the summer, the lazy swath of her river flowing gently as a breeze guiding loose blossoms from tree to ground. Fall, winter, and spring were when she swelled with fury, every perceived sliver of slight growing into daggers in her sides.

"Too long," she repeated.

I sighed. "Meihe, why are you here?" It had been several years since she'd saved me, and though I'd come to expect her calls, she'd interrupted my business, not even having the decency to knock. I couldn't be angry with her, but I could be annoyed.

"Ah, so rude. I saved your life, you know."

"Yes," I said, my voice soft. "I can't forget it."

She closed the distance between us, reaching out to tuck a strand of hair behind my ear, her fingers cold enough to make me shiver.

"Help me turn the river. Help me drown the nearby town."

I stood frozen, her hand still at my shoulder, caught in the enormity of the task. When I helped her, we swelled the banks, drowning unsuspecting villagers. We'd never turned the course of the river that far. I'd heard it had happened before—stories told by elders to frighten children. But never in my lifetime.

The tugging as she pulled the magic from me was almost painful;

how much more would she need to push the river that far? She didn't come to me with a basket of food, or coins, or jewelry. She was Meihe. She asked and she expected to receive.

I drew back, though her fingers still held the strand of my hair, tugging once before letting go. "Meihe, what has offended you this time?"

She'd never vented her anger on me, but her temper was infamous among the gods. I was different, she'd told me so many times. I was special. Even those remembered words warmed my chest. A *goddess* thought *I* was special.

A wonder I'd been able to drag myself away from her without begging to be allowed to stay.

Meihe threw up a hand. "It's been almost a year and they've not given me any sacrifices. They do not honor me. They forget who I am. To them, the river is just water. It is just a thing they dip their fingers into and pull treasures out of. Everything they get is because of *me*."

I was disoriented, still reeling from the townswoman's visit, my thoughts split between Meihe and my former life. *He drowned his prior wife.* "Is he still alive?" At first, I thought I'd spoken the words only in my mind, but Meihe blinked her black eyes.

"What?"

The words were out, so I cleared my throat and spoke again. "My husband. Is he still alive?"

She waved a dismissive hand. "Jian, that's not why I'm here. And how am I supposed to know?"

Because she had been *there*. She had been there when he'd thrust my head beneath the water. She'd come slithering up through the darkness of the riverbed and had laid her immortal lips against my cold, dead ones and breathed the life back into me. "That woman you frightened away. She said the man who is taking her as concubine drowned his prior wife. He's wealthy now. He has two sons."

Meihe rolled her eyes as though bored. "I came to ask for your assistance, not to reminisce about times long past."

Reminisce. As though these memories were ones I wanted to have.

In those moments after, when she'd gently parted the wet hair from my eyes, when she'd fed me soup and seaweed, a sympathetic ear to my woes—I'd assumed that Meihe had killed him. She was a river goddess. She'd killed many. And was he not deserving of death after what he'd done to me? This is what we did together—scouring the earth of the ones who needed to be purged.

She seized my hand. I felt her magic hot against my skin, contrasting against the coldness of her palm, wriggling into me and meeting the writhing tendrils in my own chest. "Jian, you *owe* me."

Why was I even fighting this? Perhaps I wouldn't have, had that woman not been waiting for me when I'd returned home. But the townswoman's visit had left me with the slick feeling of oil running down my throat. "You let him live, didn't you?"

She let go, abruptly. "Fine. Yes, he's still alive as far as I know. What? You think I should have killed him?"

Yes. The tendrils of my magic licked out, roaring like a fire. He'd taken everything from me—the life I'd hoped for, the children I'd wanted to bear, the dreams of a quiet home. And now he was wealthy. He had two sons. Another wife and soon, it seemed, a concubine as well.

I lived—if it could be called that—in solitude by the river, trading magic trinkets for scraps the immortals saw fit to give me. I could never have the life I'd wanted, could never again be one of them. I existed in the space between Meihe's kingdom and the mortal one—never fully a part of either.

It was his fault and he'd paid no price for it.

"You don't have the power to do this on your own, but together—if we drown the town, we can kill him, too," Meihe said.

I thought of the water rushing into *his* lungs, the fear he'd feel as it closed in over his head, the despair as his home washed away. If I could, I'd hold his head beneath the water myself, digging my nails into the skin behind his ears. The magic came easily to me in that moment, each tendril of it waiting to be shaped to my desires. "I'll do it. Tell me when."

My cormorant attempted to speak to me again the next morning. "She is angry," he said. "You are angry." When he opened his beak again, all that came out was a croaking gasp. I held his beak in my palm, stroking the soft feathers of his throat. Often, he didn't try to speak to me at all. Why now?

His amber eyes regarded me, bright as marigolds. I couldn't discern what emotions lay beneath them. "I'll have to leave you here," I told him. "She won't want you back in her court."

He blinked, resting the weight of his head in my hand. He tried again. "Jian, I already know what Meihe wants and what she doesn't want. What do *you* want?"

"Justice. Fairness. Retribution." I turned and continued to pack a meager bag. This shouldn't take long. Meihe had bade me meet her in her court that evening. Outside, rain pattered against the stones in my garden; the river that had been calm just last night now rose to a roar.

He let out a soft grunt. "If you speak of fairness, you should know you've not met your end of the bargain."

For a moment, I thought he meant whatever unspoken tie lay between me and Meihe. But then my gaze found the peachwood protection amulet I'd begun to work on. I'd used the radishes in a stew and had fried the pork in its own fat, the scent of it making my mouth water, each bite a long-forgotten delight. But I'd not given the woman her amulet in return—she'd fled too quickly.

She'd not returned. After tonight, after the river began to rise, she might not be able to. It wasn't my fault Meihe had appeared, nor was it my fault that the woman had been frightened off. This was a distraction from my task, nothing more. I remembered Meihe's cool fingers against my forehead as she'd woken me from death, as she'd told me she'd made me anew. And then the warning. "But there is a price: You cannot ever return to your town or your people. I forbid it."

I'd laughed back then; why would I wish to return? I had no one there who cared for me, whom I cared enough for in return.

But now I found myself picking up the amulet, recalling the fear in the woman's dark eyes. The edges dug into my palm and then I was thinking of my husband, sending the wriggling tendrils of magic into the wood, shaping them, feeling them settle into the grooves and cracks. Fine. I could spare a moment, at least. I picked up the basket the woman had abandoned in my hut and went to the door.

My cormorant let out a croaking sound, cleared his throat, and tried again. "Jian, you should know—you are not the first witch Meihe has made." And then he fell to gasping, as though I'd tied the fishing rope too tightly around his neck.

I went back to soothe him, running a hand over his wings. "What do you mean, I am not the first? Then where are the others?" But he only blinked and would not speak another word.

I left.

I drew my hat low over my eyes at the threshold, knowing that most people wouldn't give me a second glance in this storm. The dirt path from my hut joined with a gravel road, stones crunching beneath my feet. I sent tendrils of magic into the basket, feeling a slight tug as it led me down the road toward the woman's home.

Houses with tile roofs appeared through sheets of rain, shutters closed against the weather. I took in a sharp breath, and for a moment, it was as though I'd never left. I was cloistered inside my husband's home beneath the watchful eye of his mother, the scent of my own sweat thick in the air as she berated me again for not giving her a grandson. I was in the street, locked out of my home by my husband, people passing, their gazes sliding past me as though ashamed for my tears. I was speaking in confidence to another woman, telling her I thought often about divorce, feeling her pitying eyes on me as she said that no one would have me after that.

The anger surged, wild as the river, tendrils of magic writhing within me. A few people passed me, eyes low, shoulders hunched against the rain. None of them deserved to live. They'd let this happen to me. They were letting it happen again.

I hesitated before stepping onto the main street. Meihe had forbidden me from returning. I owed her my life, but did I owe her my strict obedience? My gratitude to Meihe warred with the bargain I'd made with the supplicant.

Ah, but it was only a short trip; I didn't intend to stay. A few quick steps and I was within the town boundaries and nothing untoward had happened. Meihe didn't have to know where I'd been.

The woman's home lay at the edge of town—flat and wide as the frogs that lived on the banks of Snake River. I knocked.

An older man answered the door.

"Your daughter," I said, careful to keep my gaze averted, "is she here?"

I felt his eyes on me, lingering on my pale skin, my midnight-sky hair. "She no longer lives here," he said.

I itched to look at his face, to know this man who'd sold his daughter as though she were a sack of rice. He'd had to have heard the rumors of my drowning. Had he willfully turned away each time he heard them? Had he listened to his daughter beg not to be sent to my husband?

I met his gaze. He paled, and I felt the satisfaction swell in me—knowing that he was afraid. If I could have slain him with a glance, I would have. "She lives with him now, doesn't she?"

"Witch," he whispered.

Witch, wife, a woman drowned and brought back to life. I didn't need his confirmation to know I was right. I swept away, back down the path, the basket still tight beneath my arm.

I shouldn't have continued on. I should have returned home. But I'd come this far, and I'd made a bargain; I should see this through. I found my feet carrying me down a familiar path, to a house I'd once known as my home. Water soaked in through my shoes, though it did not leave my feet cold. Meihe's magic—now mine.

The house was larger than I remembered, a new wing added, the paint a shade brighter than the rest of the building. Other things had changed. The shutters were newly refinished, the front garden well tended, the gutters cleared.

From inside, I could hear the voices of children, faint above the drumming rain.

I clenched my fingers into fists, heedless of my nails digging into the flesh of my palms. He had *everything*. Meihe should have killed him. She should have dragged him into the water after me, her fingers curled around the back of his neck as he struggled to break free.

But she'd been focused on me, on saving my life.

The gate unlatched beneath my fingers, the feel of the metal and the *click* of the latch both triggering memories I'd forgotten. The apprehension I'd had when I'd first arrived, the touch of my husband's hand on my back, the smile he'd given me when I'd looked up at him, hesitating. There had been kind moments—which made the unkind ones all the more jarring. I'd tried so many different things to please him, to calm his temper.

Nothing worked.

The rain drummed against the rooftop. Water trickled from the gutters. The peaceful scene clashed with the violent memories in my mind. For so long I thought I'd left them behind me, but I could hear the sharpness in his voice as he shouted at me, the crack of ceramic as he broke a dish, that feeling of shrinking—in and in on myself, wishing I could disappear between the wooden floorboards.

My throat went tight, and suddenly I thought of my cormorant, the croaking he'd made when he couldn't say anything more. There was something he wanted to tell me, to warn me about. Yes, Meihe and I were both angry—and though I wasn't sure if Meihe's anger was justified, I knew mine was.

I used the back entrance, the one for servants, and the one I'd used more than once to hide from my husband. The door shut quietly behind me; the brim of my hat dripped rainwater onto the floor, the scent of damp wood filled the air. The hallway closed in around me and for a brief moment I panicked, wanting nothing more than to flee.

He could not harm me. He could not do any worse to me than he already had. Soon, he would be dead.

I slipped farther into the house, searching for the concubine. Everywhere inside were signs of prosperity. Paintings, vases, embroidered silk cushions. I didn't feel like a witch as I wandered the hallways. I felt like a ghost, coming back to the place I'd once lived to find it inexplicably changed.

From behind a door on my left I heard voices. Children shrieking, a woman's stern voice rising above. He'd married again. He had the sons he'd wanted. My hand felt drawn to the doorknob like a magnet to iron. This wasn't my life; I didn't want it, not with him. Yet curiosity pricked at me, urging me forward.

Fingers curled around my wrist. Startled, I turned.

The concubine stood at my side, her gaze downcast. "Don't," she said. "He is inside."

Another voice joined the others—deep and rumbling. Even now, when he could do nothing to me, I could feel my legs tremble, my heartbeat quickening. I wanted to be angry.

But I was afraid.

I drew back from the door as though I'd been burned. I swallowed and then pushed the basket toward her. "Here. The amulet you requested." Unsettled, I turned to go.

"Wait," she whispered.

I sighed inwardly, but turned nonetheless. My husband's concubine held the amulet in her hand, the dim light from a nearby window cutting a crescent across her cheekbone. "Will it stop him from drowning me?"

The way he drowned me? "It will do its best to protect you," I said. "Perhaps not in the ways you wish, but as long as you wear it, your chances of harm are lower than without it." It might not stop him from beating her, or locking her out of their home, or threatening her with worse. She'd be in an even more vulnerable position than I'd been in—a concubine, not even a wife.

Bah. It wasn't my business.

But she reached for me again. "Not that way. He sent a servant to the market. She'll be back any moment. There's another way out. This way."

I followed her past the kitchen, past the formal dining area, our footfalls silent and stealthy—two mice creeping through a place where they didn't quite belong. But when we reached the door that led to the street, I stopped. There, next to the door, was a small shrine.

It wasn't the sticks of incense that caught my gaze, or even the fact that there was a shrine in my husband's household, as he'd never been devout. It was the likeness painted above it: a woman cloaked in green scales, black eyes staring out at the viewer, the swollen banks of Snake River behind her. Meihe.

"Why is this here?" I spoke more sharply than I intended, and saw the concubine flinch. "Did he build it? Did his wife request it?"

She bowed her head. "Forgive me, witch, but I'm new to the household. I don't know. All I know is that the servants refresh the incense every day."

I left the house with more questions than I'd entered with. Only a quick trip, a short diversion. I'd kept my bargain and I should have felt satisfaction from that. Yet now I found myself stalking through the rain toward the edge of town—feeling like I was fleeing, though not sure from what.

I was not the first witch Meihe had made. She said the townsfolk had forgotten her. There was a river goddess shrine in my husband's house. These three thoughts chased me all the way to my hut.

The storm did its best to follow me inside, though I shut the door against it. My cormorant watched me silently as I stripped off my hat, my cloak, as I went to the hearth and stirred the ashes of the fire. I couldn't *think*.

This morning I'd intended to go to Meihe's court, to let her pull the magic from me, to divert the river and to drown the town. Now I wasn't sure what I should do.

I went to my cormorant. "Who were you before she changed you? Why did she do it?"

He blinked his amber eyes and didn't answer—though I knew he couldn't. She'd have forbidden him that.

"How many other witches has she made? Are any of them still alive? Does she visit them, too?" Again, he didn't answer. I lifted his beak, felt his throat move as he swallowed. "What *can* you tell me?"

For a moment I thought he would say nothing again, but then he spoke. "You deserve your anger." I waited, but there was nothing more.

I dropped his beak, pacing the confines of my hut. She could not keep me at court. I could not return to town. I thought I owed Meihe everything, but she had forbidden me the two places that might have come to feel like home. I'd never questioned her reasons before, but the shrine had thrown off all my convictions. Clearly, the town had *not* forgotten her, not completely.

She'd lied to me.

I went to the cupboard and pulled the other cloak from it—the one that allowed me access to Meihe's kingdom. It was plain enough, but three green scales were sewn into the lining. Without knowing exactly why, I bade my cormorant hop into his basket. She might not want to see him again, but at the moment, I wasn't sure how much I still cared. There was the matter of what *I* wanted.

Justice. Fairness. Retribution.

Answers.

Outside, the river was already swollen with the recent rain. I wrapped my cloak around myself, grabbed my cormorant's basket, and stepped into the water. We drifted to the bottom like a coin dropped from the surface. Mud swirled as I set my feet on the riverbed, finding the stone path between the weeds. The rushing currents brushed past my cheeks, tangling my hair. But Meihe's cloak made it feel like nothing more than a warm breeze.

It was a short walk to Meihe's palace. It sprang from the riverbed, aquatic plants cultivated around the walls in neat rows. The tiled rooftops were blue, the color muted by the cloudy skies far above.

The guards at the gates let me pass with only a glance, though one of them stared a little longer at the cormorant basket. Meihe was expecting me, and they didn't dare cause a delay. Neither of them broke away to escort me. I knew my way through these hallways, through the opulent rooms filled with carved coral and pearls.

Meihe waited for me in the courtyard, her back to me, gaze fixed on the surface above.

I set my cormorant's basket down and let him out, the rustle of the basket's reeds catching Meihe's attention. She turned and saw the bird sitting atop his basket. Again, her eyes narrowed in suspicion but she said nothing. Instead, she stepped toward me, her hands outstretched, her green-scaled robe laid out behind her.

"Help me."

Even now, my mind swirling with questions, I found it difficult to resist. The rage in her dark eyes called to mine, demanding an answer. In that moment I wanted nothing more than her touch, the reassurance that I was indeed special and different, that I could somehow help her at the same time I helped myself. My cormorant was right—I did deserve my anger. What had I done to justify the pain I'd endured? Nothing. All I had to do was to tell Meihe yes, and she would pull the magic from me, the river would swerve, and the town would drown. My husband, who should have died the day he'd killed me, would finally face the punishment he'd long escaped. I had *suffered*; was I not owed this one thing?

My magic surged, and I felt Meihe reaching, grasping, tugging at the tendrils embedded in my heart as she waited for my consent. The answer clung to the edge of my lips.

"You made a bargain." My cormorant's voice, cutting through the fog.

Yes, I'd made a bargain, but I'd completed it—what did he mean by telling me this now? I thought of the concubine in my husband's household, her eyes wide with anxiety as she asked me if the amulet would stop him from drowning her. I thought of the river running into town, the scant protection the amulet would provide. I didn't owe her any more than she'd asked for—did I?

My husband had drowned me and I might drown her, and a shrine to Meihe was in my husband's home.

And he'd prospered.

There was something here I was missing—so mired I'd been in Meihe's scheming that I'd not been able to see the web she'd spun around me. I was no cormorant, but with her magic surging through me it was difficult to speak.

I chose my words carefully.

"What was the last sacrifice the townsfolk made to you?"

The look on her face gave me my answers. It wasn't some hapless chicken or goat or cow that had been drowned in the river for her.

It was *me*. I was not the first witch Meihe had made—so there had been others. Others who'd had their heads thrust beneath Snake River's waters, others who had sucked not air but river into their lungs, others who had been claimed by Meihe, their magic and their wrath cultivated to serve her purposes, harvested whenever she felt the need. She hadn't killed my husband for murdering me. She'd rewarded him.

The words my cormorant had spoken came back to me: "You deserve your anger."

Yes. *Yes*, I did.

But Meihe did not.

I pulled away from her, slowly, deliberately, feeling my magic slip from her grasp even as she tried to hold on to it. "Wait," she said, and I felt the power shift between us. "I need this. Jian, please. I saved you."

She'd done that, it was true. But she'd also used me, weaving my anger into her own machinations. I didn't have to live apart from the townsfolk. I didn't have to make trinkets for Meihe's immortal court. I didn't have to help her do to others what had been done to me—all so she could have the sacrifices she so desperately wanted.

"My life is my own. My anger is my own."

And then, without a backward glance, I picked up my cormorant and left.

The town did not drown, and neither did my husband. But then, neither did the concubine. I found my feet taking me back into town the day after my confrontation with Meihe, leading me to the house I no longer envied.

He deserved a worse fate, but then, I could not control everything. But I could help others escape the fate I had.

I strode into the house without knocking, using my magic to unlock the door, to cast aside my husband when he sought to confront me. I'd not forgotten my anger. I found the concubine in the kitchen, scrubbing the countertops.

"Do you wish to stay here?" I asked her. "Or do you wish to come with me?"

She barely hesitated.

In the end, it was she who unraveled Meihe's spell on my cormorant—pointing out that it was not unlike the rope I tied around his neck to prevent him from swallowing large fish. Only this spell prevented him from speaking large secrets. I found the tendril of Meihe's magic tight around his throat, snipping it free with a quick lashing of mine. He did not, alas, change back to his immortal form, though he assured me he was content as he was. He told me of the other witches Meihe had called upon over the years, the ones who were still alive and the ones she'd harvested into nothingness.

They lived scattered along the riverbanks—so many drowned women, so many sacrifices to Meihe. It would take time to visit them all, but I was no longer a mortal; I had time. And how many more women lived with husbands like mine, wishing and hoping someone would see them? How many more could I offer a place to go?

Three days after I'd freed my cormorant, I sent him into the water to fish. I had supplies to gather before I set off down the river. He returned with two fish in his beak, and I retrieved them before untying the rope.

"She knows what you're planning," he told me, his voice smooth and unfettered. "Meihe is angry."

"Good." I picked up the oars and slipped them into the calm waters of the river, my lantern swaying gently at the prow.

"So am I."

DÉJÀ VUE

Tochi Onyebuchi

The lie turns from hiss to howl in the air above the girl's head, around the husband and husband latched like bolted locks onto each other, in the mouth of the witch who looks first at them, then at the ceiling of the mud dwelling, glancing in between, the girl thinks, at the girl to make sure she, too, is playing her part. It is the lie that raises grains of sand into the air and pinches them there so that they hang suspended in the bars of moonlight coming through the slats of corrugated iron roof. The lie that races through the hair of their arms and legs like tickles.

Whenever the witch performed the rite, the girl wanted to hide her face in shame. The girl sees in the faces of the two husbands the same admixture of hope and fear and wonder that she's seen in the eyes of so many others, too many others.

Later, she knows, one of the husbands will take her to the side like others had before him and words will stampede out of his mouth, crash with bone-shuddering earnestness and sincerity, as he will try to thank her for what the witch did. He will say that the hiss that turned to howling had then turned into the voice of their little boy who had died in infancy and who they were convinced haunted the corners of their shack. The girl will be tempted to spit back at them that they could not possibly know the tenor and timbre of their baby boy's voice, because the child had died before it could speak with any intelligence. But she will remember what the witch did to her the last time she threatened to puncture this bubble of belief. She will remember the burn on her wrists and the way the witch's withering stare had overripened her heart to turn it into a shrunken thing. And she will bite her tongue so literally that the taste of copper will fill her mouth. So, for now, she simply watches the two husbands look into the air at the center of the shack's living room. This is where they will say they saw the child's ghost, hovering spectral, angelic, over that one spot on the ground where he had gasped his last baby breaths.

The girl waits for the two husbands to look at each other and see their own hope and fear and wonder mirrored back at them, confirming the vision. And that moment does happen, but one husband breaks the other's gaze and looks at the space where the child is purported to be hovering before the other husband, and this second husband spends a precious moment looking at the first, and the girl sees in it if not a rift then a friction, an instant where the one is, for an infinitesimal moment, unintelligible to the other, the spirit, the soul, blocked off from view.

After, the girl, hands in her pockets, stands outside. The clients are told that this is for reasons of privacy, but the girl knows that it is so she can perform surveillance. Note the passing shadow of a drone or feel in the ground the telltale rumble of a Titan. See if any patrols are performing their "random" neighborhood sweeps, hunt the air for cordite or any scent describing the presence of government munitions.

There's some talking in the shack behind her, people sniffing away sobs, money changing hands, then the wooden back door scraping against the ground of the back alley. The witch palms the girl's head; then, when they're far enough away, she reaches into her sack to pull out a small plastic bag of broken twigs for the girl to chew on.

It doesn't take long for the girl's teeth to work away the coating to reveal the candy inside. It's the same with the stones she lays out in her summoning circle or the leaves she burns in the fire from her lighter—

mentholated things from harmless plants dotting the forest and parts of the scrubland.

Though night turns to morning over their heads, they walk through perpetual shadow. It's this way in all of the slums where you're expected to know where the waste runoff is by heart and which alleys house stray dogs and which ones prodigious orphans working away at junk tech that could one day reverse the burning of the world. Shadows charge the breathable air with electric danger and possibility, shadows through which the only way to walk is with an aura of invincibility. The witch told the girl that the way they would survive is by moving through these places as though they had every right to, though the witch wouldn't tell the girl why this meant they only ever seemed to enter and exit settlements as though they were hiding from someone. Or why, for part of the ceremony, the girl was always obligated to stand watch.

But she knows to keep quiet as they make their way to the settlement's outskirts and feel the day burning suddenly on their backs, hurrying across red landscape to where their Beast is waiting.

The girl is almost up and in her seat before the witch has a chance to pull off the cloaking blanket. The witch looks as though she has something to say, but shakes her head instead, smiling, and balls up the signal shield and stuffs it into the trunk attached to the back of the vehicle. She puts her sack in but only after grabbing a few more snacks and stuffing them into the girl's pockets. Then she seals the trunk, hops on behind the girl, and revs the groaning, grumbling machine to life.

Morning turns to day as they raise an arrow cloud of dust into the desert.

They'd found a cave tucked under a craggy blood-colored outcropping. Free from wandering eyes, the witch pulls strings of moisture out of the air and weaves a curtain of water over the entrance to the enclosure, so that every time one of them has to pass through, they are refreshed with enough water to carry in their skin and their hair for many miles.

From here, the witch sends the girl back to the town they passed along the way, a bustling, half-built thing with no too-tall buildings but a mashing-together of market and home. Optimism still hums in the air. The place, the girl feels, has just edged into that space where thievery and violence begin to sprout. A place becomes big enough, promises enough invisibility, and knives are suddenly sharpened to cut the bottoms out of purses or to sneak in between rib bones. Back alleys gain their threatening cast. Mobs are quicker to form. The girl finds the air infecting her as well.

On the way here, thought of the supplies she would purchase buoyed her. The peppers and legumes and meat, the machine parts for their Beast, face wraps to better keep the moisture in throughout their journey. But the taste of evil in the air is bitter on her tongue and her thoughts turn to how the coin was earned.

The witch lies to people. She preys on their despair. She commercializes their loss, claims to see the ghosts hiding in walls or descending, upside down, from ceilings, claims to hear the phantom wailings and the beseechings whispered on the wind and the commands that the flesh-and-blood left behind toss themselves off of cliffs or drown themselves in rivers so that their spirit can catch up to the ghost's. There are no such things. But for coin and credit, the witch makes sand rise and wind whip and fire sprout from the earth and tells the grieving that this is the work of the lost and loved ones. And the fools truly believe that a night-blue, moonbeam-white apparition hovers over the fire circle and is smiling at them or that in the rain that spills through the holes in their roof, they can see the face of their dearly departed. Risking capture and torture, imprisonment and violent death, all for coin.

Then the girl feels regret. She doesn't know what the witch's life was like before she came into it, doesn't know if she was always a witch or became a witch to feed this orphan, to give this orphan shelter and a chance to see the world outside her hovel. If the witch is risking capture and torture, imprisonment and violent death, maybe she's doing it for her.

A shoulder crashes past hers, then an arm, then another. Before she realizes it, the girl is swept up in a tide of people and shouting. "They got one!" "Hurry, she's in the center!" "We have to get a good spot or else we're gonna miss it!" And suddenly the girl's feet are underneath her again.

For too many moments, as she weaves through the rush, as her body remembers what it was like to be a waif and a pickpocket and a survivor in a city too big for her, she fears she has manifested powers of her own. That she has wished harm into being. Imagining a murder that is now being brought to pass.

She squeezes to the front of the crowd, and it is the same as when they left their last town, a bracing traversal from shadow to light, from night to day, from crowd to space. Like passing through a wall.

On a raised wooden dais, a woman is strapped to a stake, her arms bound behind her, while police stand at attention at each corner, facing outward. A magistrate circles the woman and the pile of kindling on which her bare feet are perched. Her knees are slightly bent. The girl realizes that the discomfort is intentional. They want her to suffer through this. This is not someone the girl knows, and she finds relief in that fact.

"You have the power to manipulate the elements. The rocks that make mountains, the clouds that bring rain. You could darken the sun and lessen its heat. You could revitalize our rivers. You could light our homes in the winter. And yet you do none of these things. You could help so many, but instead, you traffic in blasphemy. Why?"

The girl does not know if the question is rhetorical. The magistrate waits several beats, and the girl wonders if the magistrate is in sincere search of an answer.

"Why?"

The crowd has become silent.

"You waste what you have been blessed with to bring people into a realm that is forbidden to them. You put them in touch with what they should not touch. You corrupt them. We have seen their effects." At this, he turns to the crowd. "The spirit-touched go mad. They take whatever it is that coats them upon engaging with this witchcraft into our world. They rust our metal. They lose their minds. How many of us have lost a loved one to the madness this witch—all of these witches—infect us with?"

The crowd roars to lift him higher, to straighten his spine and raise his chin. To put more muscle on his bones.

To the witch, "You are hereby being charged with the crimes of practicing anti-Riemannian geometry, threatening the integrity of the theory of relativity; conspiracy to engage others in relational quantum mechanics; and necromancy. For which the sentence is death by rapid oxidation."

At the naming of her sentence, the crowd roars like something less than human, something more than human.

A bit of the fever has touched the magistrate's expression as well. His gleaming eyes match the sun-glint off the metal shards that spring from the front of his diadem.

It strikes the girl then that the truly terrifying thing at work is belief. The magistrate, the crowd, they all believe what the witch's clients—the witches' clients—believed. That these priestesses were truly reaching past the known world with its harvests and its seasons and its metal into another and pulling back what they'd found. Pulling back what they'd been asked to pull back. The girl would look in the air over a firepit and observe swirling air. Everyone else would look in the air over that firepit and see a glowing heresy.

Another police officer, this one helmeted, ascends the stairs of the dais with a metal gauntlet around his right forearm. And with a flick of his wrist, a ball of fire comes to life at the end of its nozzle. He neither dares nor spares a glance for the witch before he sprays flames into the kindling. A brief, perfunctory jet, but it is enough to begin the hissing, howling blaze. The girl wonders briefly if the witch herself is stirring the winds to further fan the flames, to speed along her own obliteration.

The girl sees it in the magistrate as well; his posture, body inched slightly forward, expecting something. Daring her. Save yourself, his hunched shoulders tell the witch. If thou be a witch, save thyself.

But the witch does not. All she does is scream until she isn't able to any longer.

The girl returns with supplies. The water curtain slaps her out of her stupor.

"I saw a graveyard on my way from the town," the girl says, setting her sacks full of items down.

The witch upends them one by one, and the bags' contents hang in the air—the machine parts, the peppers, the grinding tools, the jian dui. The girl wants to be angry at the witch's casual disregard for the law, that even now when she doesn't have to, she's working her power, but her mouth waters too quickly at the sight of the jian dui she'd snuck in with the purchases, and the witch looks at her with an eyebrow raised in question. The girl frowns back that, no, she did not steal the jian dui, she paid with their money. So the jian dui floats into the girl's hands while the witch gathers ingredients for the evening's broth.

"It's on the border of the wasteland, but it is far enough from the town that people must journey to get there."

"Good," says the witch. "When the moon is high, you'll go out and scout for potential clients and report back to me. Remember not to talk to them on your own. They cannot know your face, because then when the strange thing happens, they will think you had something to do with it."

The girl munches in silence.

"Did you walk through the graveyard already?"

The girl nods.

"And?"

She swallows a bite. "There was disease or famine six or eight years ago. Many of the deaths inscribed on the tombstones have the same year. Many children."

"Babies?"

"I did not see any that had their own markers."

"Anything else?"

The girl thinks harder but nothing of note comes to mind.

"If there are many men dead," the witch says to herself, "then that must mean there was war recently. Violent death is not good for business. Many eager to move on past it. Different with natural death. Different with drowning. Different with starving. Starving is good."

The jian dui turns sour in the girl's mouth when she hears this.

"When you go out, look for those mourning lovers or partners or babies. Not brothers or sisters. It is easier to hate a brother or sister than it is your child. And passion for your lover runs hotter. If you hate your lover intensely, you can love them just as fiercely."

The girl had seen these things at work during the summonings. Clients in the throes of heated passion, of that whiplashing between loathing and ardor. She realizes now that what she felt watching those emotions play out over the faces of those clients was jealousy. She would only know with her head what they knew with their hearts. She would never feel those things in her bones. Her marrow would never be so enriched with that humanness. And she looks at the witch, letting the broth boil as she gathers her tools, then leaves to work on the Beast, and she wants to ask if the witch has any of this knowledge in her bones, if she'd had to learn it through living or if, like the girl, she had to be told how the human heart worked.

The broth boils.

Darkness turns the cracked gravestones into faces. Foreheads creased in frown or lips twisted into smirks or simply a blank, unreadable stare into the middle distance. It is difficult to tell what's buried just by judging the headstone. Sometimes the big ones house a couple and sometimes they house a single youth and sometimes the tinier ones, barely noticeable, the type to be tripped over, house what looks like an entire family.

The girl hides in a ragged forest, torn and be-holed tree leaves covering her, and watches the place she'd scouted in silence. She had tried to memorize its layout, remember what dates corresponded with what plots, but the execution earlier in the day scrambles her memories. Every time she closes her eyes, she sees the irises of that witch—brown and flecked with shards of morning in a face with skin the color of hardening, red clay.

She is so busy trying to shake away the haunt that she almost misses the robed woman walking—gliding—through the fog that hovers above the ground, that shrouds her ankles. Sprigs of grass and bundles of flowers rise in her wake, and logic has the girl thinking that this is simply what happens when someone steps on them then raises their foot, but to the girl, it looks like every step this woman takes leaves life blooming behind her.

She holds part of her maroon robe in her hands as she walks, and the whole thing gives her an aspect of queenliness. Then she stops at a gravestone and comes down to one knee and brushes a hand against it, as though to wipe away dirt and grime. She lets her hand rest, then bows her head, and the girl wonders if this is what prayer looks like.

Usually, there is some crying—sometimes it is loud and sometimes it is soft and choked—and maybe the person falls to the earth and beats it with their fists and laments. Usually, if the person has come this close to the gravestone—if they haven't rooted themselves at the graveyard's periphery, too terrified or paralyzed by grief to draw any closer—they do something that can be heard by others, an announcement of their sorrow. Or they talk to the gravestone as though the person beneath their feet can hear them, entire soliloquies sometimes, and sometimes they even laugh when they think they hear the deceased tell a joke. But this woman simply remains there with her hand against the stone.

Not a good candidate, the girl thinks to herself. Her grief is not loud enough, not unreasoning enough.

Soon the communion is finished, and the woman rises and turns to walk away.

When she is far enough, the girl, curious, steps out from the forest cover and sneaks to the stone the woman touched and sees the name and the dates and her eyes grow wide because the deceased was only a child and maybe the girl was mistaken. Maybe the woman was a mother. Maybe she was mourning her child.

"Stop." No gravel or profundity to the woman's voice. It's more plea than command. But it freezes the girl where she crouches. "Are you a grave robber?"

If the girl ran, the woman could not chase her, would not. And the girl has not yet turned around so the woman cannot claim to have seen her face. It would be so easy. The girl would not even have to tell the witch of the mistake she made.

The girl stands, slowly, and turns around.

She doesn't know what she's wearing on her face that makes the woman kneel before her and touch her cheek, but at that touch—flesh against flesh—her bottom lip trembles. "Oh, child," the woman says, then brings the girl into her chest, so tightly as to absorb her. And the girl realizes just how cold it has been outside, because the woman is warm, so warm, and she cannot stop shivering.

It's too much.

The girl breaks away and turns to run but crashes into the headstone and falls back. The dam is broken. She can't stop crying.

A blanket covers her, and the woman draws the girl up and smooths her hair and picks twigs and pebbles and blades of grass from it. Sympathy makes her eyes glow as though those eyes were moons off which light reflected. And she looks at the girl then around at the graveyard to see whom the girl had come to mourn. "My child. Who have you lost?"

And the girl can't bring herself to lie; neither can she bring herself to say "no one."

"Did you find any clients?" the witch asks when the girl returns.

The girl shakes her head and walks past the witch, past the bowl of broth the witch has surely been keeping warm with her magic, past the light and into the shadows, and lowers herself to the ground, curling

344

into an apostrophe, trying with all of her might, succeeding finally, in telling the witch no.

The witch does not ask from where the girl got the new blanket.

The witch is angry with the girl, the girl knows.

There is tension in the witch's arms around the girl's body as they ride their Beast from their last encampment and through empty savannah. Maybe the witch thinks the girl is still too unskilled at spotting potential clients, or maybe she suspects the girl of harboring a secret that has somehow managed to interrupt their livelihood. Maybe, the witch wonders, the girl saw something that frightened her and was willing to forego what comforts could be bought with their earnings, choosing, rather, to leave. The girl feels all of the witch's questioning in the way her chest and stomach press against the girl's back.

The Beast purrs beneath them but barks on occasion, more frequently than before, and the witch slows it. Wind picks up, air chills, and as they ride, storm clouds gather above them, thunder rumbling in them in accompaniment to the Beast's noises.

But the witch does not speed their bike any faster. The girl wants to turn and ask the witch if she's okay, if she notices the tempest beginning around them, but she can't move because the witch is holding her fast. Then the girl wonders if she herself is in danger, if this is somehow punishment for what happened in the graveyard. The girl wonders if the witch is powerful enough to have seen that far and that deeply into that night. Or, the girl wonders, something in her own body gave it away, that she had seen a potential client and that she had made the mistake of letting that client see her and then she had run away from what could have given them their next week's food. Maybe a new coat for autumn.

The clouds grow and bunch against each other. Light drains from the world around the girl and the witch, poking through in sharp beams where the cumulonimbi haven't yet met. And it is like they are passing slowly—a parade of two—through a darkened building with stained-glass windows along its ceiling refracting the sun's light.

Fire gilds the underbellies of the clouds. Whips of lava unfurl and strike the ground, fiery lightning that cracks then booms. Wisps of cloud hang to the molten fingers, and yet the Beast refuses to go any faster.

The girl struggles against the witch, tries to break free, tries to leap off the Beast and run along ground that has likely by now grown too soft to offer footholds, ground that would swallow her up in mounds of shifting sand. But logic flees the girl and she starts trying to swing her elbows. She cracks the witch in the nose, but no sound comes out of her. No change in posture, but a further tightening. The wind whistles in the girl's ear, then she realizes, suddenly, that it's the witch, saying "Shhhhhhhhh" so quietly it shouldn't be possible for the girl to hear. "Shhhhhhhh, stay still."

And the girl does.

She loosens to the point of limpness and lets the witch's body hold her like an extension of the Beast itself.

The tongues of lava flick from the clouds to lick the earth at random. From afar, then, increasingly, near. Until one of them snaps the ground immediately to their right. It's close enough for the girl to see the sand sprout like a daffodil into the air and freeze instantly into crystal. The girl can't believe what she's seeing. She wants to stop the Beast and stare at the formation, stare at her face in it, but the Beast is moving, slowly, through the rest of it. And again and again, the lava snaps the earth around them to glass, and a path walled off on both sides by pellucid, crystal daffodils taller than her twice reveals itself in the ground.

Questions whorl like saliva on the girl's tongue. Questions and accusations and wonderings, and she desperately wants to know what part of this is the witch's doing, if it is only the crystals or if it is the whole entire storm, and the girl is reminded again of the witch she saw burned at the stake. How powerful she must have been to be so feared.

If thou be a witch, save thyself.

The girl knows there is a lesson here, that the storm they are riding through is telling her a thing more articulate than any combination of words the witch herself could utter. But this thing around her is still too loud, too immediate, for her to understand. All that fire, so much of it uncontrolled, and yet . . . all controlled by someone, by something. Is that it? That every act of destruction has an author? That the witch is powerful enough to protect them both and she needn't fear harm? No, there must be something greater, and the girl feels herself on the precipice of epiphany, but they pass out from beneath the storm clouds to arrive at a cliff's edge. Below them, a stream and real, living animals coursing through and around it. And she is too struck with wonder at the sight of these to notice that the witch has leaned back in her seat, has let her go.

The witch says nothing. It takes the girl a moment to realize what is happening.

She is being released.

The girl turns and peers into the witch's face and looks for chastisement, for anger or annoyance. But there is only a quiet sorrow, a silent determination, and a soft gratefulness.

"She would have been your age had she survived," the witch says. Then, out of the folds of her wrap, the witch pulls a perfectly preserved crystal daffodil. Her fingers, normally so sure, shake as she fits it behind the girl's ear, the girl too stunned to flinch or fidget. And the witch leans back again, smiling, and this time there are tears in her eyes. "If I keep telling myself that you are her or that you have her in you, I am lying. And that is not my trade."

Easily, the witch lifts the girl off the Beast and sets her down.

"Down there is food easily found and clean water. And if you follow the river, you will find people to receive you and give you shelter and make you your own woman." She revs the Beast. "Do not try to follow me." Then she is gone. There is no storm to swallow her up, but she vanishes wholly and completely nonetheless.

It has all happened too quickly for the girl to process, for her body to do anything other than what the witch commanded, so her steps take her down the cliff and along the river, and it is only when she is greeted by a shepherdess and her wife that she is reminded of the lucent flower in her hair.

Sometimes, while repairing a well, she will catch a glimpse of something in the water and then she will lean over and stare more intently until she realizes that she is searching for that face, and longing for the witch will fill her heart so fully, so utterly, that she will want to call for her. And, again, while shining metal for the village's telescope, she will see it, a reflection of someone's arm bent at the elbow the same way the witch's would be when she was stirring broth. And when the woman sleeps, she will dream of that afternoon passing through that storm and how the wisps of cloud that clung to the tongues of descending lava looked first like arms then like stretched-thin torsos and that when those tongues touched the earth, so too did those wisps of cloud that now looked so much like faces she'd seen before. The longing will be so great she will find herself wishing she had never loved at all.

One morning, entering the barn to bring her horse out for riding, she will spend several moments inside, calming the beast, and she will stop at the door on her way out, realizing that she has been passing through bars of light that fall through spaces between the roof's wooden slats.

And she will wonder if it's the longing that sticks its fingers into the space-time continuum to rip it apart or if the tearing is what opens the way to that which is longed for. If longing isn't her wanting to see the witch again but the witch trying to make her way back to her. And the woman will wish the witch were here to help her finish the algebraic proof she had begun, just the other day, to sketch with her finger into the dirt in the middle of her summoning circle.

BOTANICA: A SONG IN FOUR MOVEMENTS

Sheree Renée Thomas

after Ntozake Shange, Linda Hogan, Sonia Sanchez,
Ai, Paul Laurence Dunbar

SISTREN: A CALLING

She woke, 93 million miles from herself
and silence did not hold her tongue.
Shoulders rising from darkened waters
her voice rang out on the skin of air
She began with lovers, two
on the swept floor of earth.

She was what passed between them.
She was what breathed inside them.

She was the sweet gourd too heavy for the vine
and full of her own wet seed.

Grandmama Gawd kept the red trick bag
the bloodstained cloth that held her navelstring
so she would not forget the other women
she lived inside before Time was ruint
so she would not forget the other lives
that lived inside the river before
its waters were ruint.

Daughter of none, the first sister walked
the muddy river's banks and listened
each soul whispering her name.

Her name was the beginning of hunger.
Her name was the curiosity they called sin.
Desire was in that jackball bag of ribs and bones
and want, the origins of betrayal
but there was forgiveness, too
the dry seeds of the serpent's rattle
that could shake loose a killing
shekere a healing.

She stood naked and painted herself
haint blue, color of the old ways
a blue hand across a blueblack face
Seven axes in the circle of sun.
Masked, she danced counterclockwise
in the ceremony of wayward daughters
in the ritual of those who must birth themselves
again and again
She danced a river of sighs
the dance to call the spirits up
the ones wrapped in night's black skin

the ones whose palms rise to the stars
the lifelines wrapped all around their wrists.
Her spirit disappeared inside its dance.

She is the wild one that lives
in the palm of the river.
She is the marigold in winter
the black dahlia of a hard-frost spring
She is the wild one, the dandelion that wants
to fly away from herself.
She is the wild one who fights
to be her one, true, authentic self.
She sheds the mask they made
from the skin of the other lives
she lived. Now she wears the face
of the future tomorrows she carves
out of the dreams of her true self.
At night she drowns and wakes
her painted blue skin beneath the water
her blue palms reach for me

I know the taste of her. Her hands reach
through time and find the bare earth of me.
I say her names, earth calling water.
She is my mother. She is my daughter.
She is your mother. She is your daughter.
She is no mother. She is no daughter.
She came from a womb. She has no womb.
She is all of us. She is none of us.
She is, the swept earth calling the river, sister.
She is the one who whispers, sis . . .
She is the one who says, resist.

She is the one who will always persist.
She is the one. She is the flow.

FLOW

A woman lying in water
becomes herself
but where does water grow?

Water grew between lands
that once lay together as one.
That was the first separation
the first betrayal, where the stories
inside each grain of sand
older than we are, came apart
holding their secrets
silent, not even a trace
of the first ones, the first love.
No white jawbone turning over
in the sun, in the great salt
of blood that was Eden, no finger, no lips
to kiss the bone, no splinter
of leg or thigh, a hollow temple.
After exile, legs and arms
no longer trapped her.
After exile, she journeyed far
taking the salt of years
with her.

How does water survive?
How does it strip a world

to its bones, how does it dance
without feet, sing without voice
hold with no hands, and follow
the night, shining moon without
a single eye?

What does water see?
Where does water go?
When it is borne up into
the endless sky, its flow never ceasing.

THE FLOW NEVER CEASING

Earth's drum has fallen down
It joins the white clay of the river
where the women bathe before
the rites are wrong
but in our arms
the sun is fire held still
the world breathes through water
dark earth passes like light through us
amber shadows cut through the sky

No man or spirit can mask
the fire that grows between

On nights like this
we promise things
and when dawn comes
we remember just the sound
of dreams.

As lovers we rest on the dark trunks of trees
we plant over and over again.
The trees' eyes have become narrow slits
that mask desire. Lust blossoms
in moss-covered limbs.
We embroider lilies and moonstones
in our sleep, our minds race
for solutions to ancient wars
grief more ancient than any of us.
We know the future is not inevitable.
It will burst from the soil we till now
From the seeds we hold in open palms
From the hope we bury and unbury
over and over again.

How does hope survive?
We wear the mask
that grins and lies
It hides our cheeks
shades our eyes.
How does it strip a faithless world
to its bones, how does it dance
without feet, sing without voice
hold flowers with no hands, and follow
the unknowable night, a shining future
yet to be born, a space for verdant life
not yet seen by a single eye?

What does hope see?
Where does hope go?
When it is borne up with its sisters
into the endless sky, its flow never ceasing.

When it is carried away
by a river of stars, called back into the dark
an ancient new beginning
an ark of generations.

ARK OF GENERATIONS

How comforting the clarion call of space
it carried us like water
like scattered seeds of gourds.
We prayed the whole centuried night it carried us
our tongues spinning in spirals, tripping over
the shells and the saints.
We feared the darkness would rise up
like a great beast
send us flying into oblivion
to drown in the moonlight
the stars our only witness.
We feared the sisters we left below
would forget our names
bury our navelstrings in strange places
no longer thought of.
We feared there would be no trees
left to hold the root of our understanding.
And in our fear, we longed for even
the bloodied trees that held our black
bodies, swaybacked and crooning.
We longed for sleek fires, the familiar face
of burnt out dreams.
But that was just a dark tale
we told ourselves, frightened
in the hollow of sleep.

Great Grandmama Gawd has lit up
the green trails of freedom.
We live in a green house, voices rocked
by weeds, by lilacs.
We have learnt a new way of walking
of talking, which is to say, the old way.
We are the sweet blackfire of dreams.
We sail under a soprano sky.

We wake, 93 million miles from our old selves
and silence does not hold our tongues.
Our shoulders rise from darkened waters of the past.
Our voices ring out a new defying gravity.
As sistren, we know our calling. blues
We began as lovers, generations
on the swept floor of earth.

We are what passed between the old time and the next.
We are what breathes inside all of life. We are our own.
We are the light that never needed an Eden.
We are the light that is its own tree, its own sun.

We are the sweet gourd too heavy for the vine.
And we sing because we are full. We sing
because we are ripe, full of our own wet seed. We sing
because we are Sistren. We sing the songs of earth.

THROUGH THE WOODS, DUE WEST

Angela Slatter

"They say there are only old women left."

Dima, sitting on a stump, dirt and dead pine needles at his feet, hugs his greatcoat tighter around him but it's no use. The cold is unspeakable. He's never felt anything like it, would be ashamed to say so even though he suspects the others feel the same. Pasha, across from him, also on a stump, is hunched so close to the small fire there might be signs of smoldering coming off his boots, but it's hard to tell in this strange dusk. Hard to see much at all. No snow, not yet—how can it be so fucking cold with no snow?—but there's something in the air, not quite fog, almost a veil.

Or maybe he's just tired. Too tired. Scant sleep these past nights as they've traipsed into territory for reasons that seemed obvious at one point. No sleep, really, with the noises around them—if it's not the earsplitting cracks of weaponry trying to destroy people and buildings (admittedly it's a day since that was heard), it's the quiet noises in the depths of the blackness. Light breaths and hard, twigs breaking, the flap of wings. Whispers.

On balance, he thinks the quiet noises are the worst.

"They say all the men died—quickly. But the women . . . even when they were made to leave, when they herded them on buses and took them away for treatment and testing . . ." He sniffs, thinks of his grandmother. ". . . even then the old women came back. Escaped facilities, crawled from windows, under barbed-wire fences. The ones who knew they'd die anywhere else."

"They say, they say, they say." Pasha's angry, but that's his friend's default setting, so Dima doesn't pay him any mind. Pasha, his dark curls hidden beneath a hat with furred earflaps, glares. Dima would kill for that hat. He pulls his own beanie down tighter over his nondescript hair, his undistinguished forehead.

"They weren't old then, of course," Dima continues. "Or not so much. But they had nothing else to lose. No other place to call home. They didn't want to be in the cities, they didn't belong there. They'd grown out of the forest, you see." Dima knows he's starting to babble. Doesn't know why he's telling this tale. Nor does Pasha, apparently. Only they've been waiting for Kolya, and Dima wanted to fill the silence.

"Then where are they? Hey? These old women?" Pasha shakes his rifle, but not at Dima, merely in his direction, the barrel pointing out in the woods so if it were to go off, only a tree would be harmed. He's not that pissed off. Yet. "Huh, Dima? Where?" He makes a noise of disgust. "Fucking bumpkin."

Before matters can go further downhill, Kolya steps from between two trunks, seems to appear by magic, as if pulling himself from the rapidly darkening air. He's grinning; always the peacemaker, even when they were at school together. His bright blond hair catches the firelight, his eyes flash blue. So handsome. "Calm down, Pasha."

"What are you so fucking happy about?"

Kolya holds up his prize: two rabbits. Poor specimens, and wherever his bullets hit there's not much left. Kolya's a city boy, wouldn't know how to tie a snare to save his life. Even if he did, Dima's not sure there's a rabbit alive sufficiently stupid to step into one of Kolya's traps. Mind you, Dima's no country boy either, but he knows enough to know he

knows shit. He's glad he's still got a couple
of ration meals left, and that packet of biscuits.
Surely that will last them to the end of this
trek? Surely tomorrow they'll be out of the
forest. Out of all these fucking pine trees.

They look so straight, so forthright with
their vertical trunks, they grow so neatly, you
think—then step into them and discover the
lie. The trees, Dima's certain, move. Like
a gang of women in a bar, moving in front
of you so you can't follow their friend. Like
a shield wall—by the time you get through, the
one you sought has disappeared. But these trees: You keep walking,
keep pacing farther in because you're sure you can see light somewhere
there, just a little way off. Just a little. A tiny bit more. One more step.

And you're gone.

They'd been lost three days now. Compasses don't work here and
there's no mobile signal; even if there were, their phone batteries are
long dead. Their watches had stopped telling them anything useful,
supplies were dwindling, and Kolya insisted on trying to catch rabbits
each afternoon before the light was spent. Today's the first time he'd
succeeded.

"Well done!" shouts Pasha and it's not clear how much is sarcasm,
how much is glee. "Tell me, Kolya. Did you see any old women out
there? Dima says the woods are thick with them. Runaway old women.
Wild creatures with their scarves and gum boots. Cavorting beneath the
moon."

"I said nothing about cavorting!" Dima protests, but the headscarves
and gum boots aren't too far off the mark. Imagines his grandmother
again, so many brightly colored headscarves, she didn't have to wear the
same one for almost two months. When she died, Dima's aunt sewed
the best of them together to make a shroud. The other sisters called it
a waste, but Aunt Sophia shrugged and said the young women didn't

wear such things anymore. She gave the rest to Grandmother's friends to divide among themselves.

"Hush, Pasha. Build up the fire, let's make a spit for these." He dumped the bodies in front of Dima. "Skin them."

"Me? Why me?"

"I caught them. Pasha is in charge of the cooking. You are the skinner, Dima. It's only fair. A clear distribution of labor."

Later still, only Dima is awake. The other two have rolled themselves into their sleeping bags and are snoring. They ate the rabbits, but Dima did not partake, couldn't bear to eat the creatures he'd dressed for the fire even though the smell was tantalizing. He doesn't mind taking first watch, though; he really won't be able to sleep anyway, is too wired. So, at midnight or thereabouts, when the old woman appears next to him, Dima almost shits his pants.

"Good evening, young man. I hope I did not startle you. May I share your fire?" Her voice is mellifluous, gentle. Calming. He's not surprised she's come to their encampment, dressed as she is in a pair of khaki trousers, long-sleeved shirt, and a sleeveless puffy vest—nothing more. Army issue, he thinks. Perhaps her own, perhaps a husband's repurposed. Stolen. Whatever: Who is going to police such a thing out here?

"Of course, Grandmother," he says, bestowing the title from an ingrained automatic respect. "Would you like my—"

"Keep your coat, boy, I do not feel the cold."

He's grateful and ashamed—it's too chilly, really, for chivalry—then rises, offers his seat. This she accepts. He takes more branches from the pile of kindling collected that afternoon and adds them to the fire, careful not to overwhelm it and snuff the flames. Then he sits across from her, where Pasha had been. The stump is frosty, unwarmed by any backside for some time. Uncomfortable. His own was also uncomfortable but at least he'd been there long enough to make it toasty. He hopes his guest appreciates it. Settled now, he asks, "Are you lost?"

She smiles. The fire splashes orange into her silver hair, makes deeper shadows in the wrinkles on her face as if she's a relief map of life. Not ugly, strangely lovely. "I live here."

Dima's excited. "Your house is nearby? We haven't seen any dwellings in three days! These trees—"

"I live here," she says again. "But what are *you* doing here, young man?"

"We were—we got lost. We were looking for something. But the trees . . ."

She leans toward him, closer to the fire, and sniffs as if she can smell his skin. Her hand reaches out, above the flames, gestures. A shiver travels down his spine, but he obeys. Offers his own hand, feels her fingers on his wrist almost as if she's seeking his pulse. An expression flits over her face, awkward as a bat, and is gone.

"There's part of you that began here," she says, head tilted.

He nods. "My grandmother came from a small village that's close by—*should* be close by."

"One of those removed"—the old woman nods—"who did not return."

"No." Dima feels a little ashamed again, but isn't quite sure why.

"This is no place for you," she says, releasing him.

"But you just said I belonged here, a little." He touches where her fingers were, finds the skin smooth and hard as if frozen or scarred. He must stop himself from looking down because it would be rude, and he senses this is not a woman who'll let that pass.

She's shaking her head. "No. A little of you *began* here. That's not the same."

His bottom lip trembles and he stops it. Tells himself he's a dolt. Why take this as rejection? From an old woman he doesn't know? Pasha's right: He's an idiot.

He clears his throat to ask what's hovered at his lips since she appeared. Hadn't wanted her to think him a coward (deep down Dima knows he is one) but the night is so very dark and he's so very cold, and she's beginning to seem so very strange. He notices, now, that she's not wearing any shoes, and her feet look . . .

"Do you know the direction out?" he blurts. "Can we come to your cottage and use the phone? Call someone to collect us? We'll be no trouble." The idea of a proper roof over his head is intoxicating.

"I have no phone. But I will offer you the route home, for the memory of your grandmother." He follows the sweep of her hand as she gestures off to her right.

A path.

A clear, bright, white path.

A path made of stars, he thinks, lining the forest floor like a silver carpet. Is he dreaming? He can see all the hundreds of miles they've trod to get lost—he can see the way through, the way home to the apartment where his mother and sister wait. Dima smiles with relief. Whether he's dreaming or not, the feeling of hope inside him is warming.

"Thank you, Grandmother!"

"You simply step on the path and you will find yourself home, wherever that happens to be. But there's a condition." One of her fingers rises, a warning; it's a stumpy digit, crooked and arthritic. He wonders how she copes with the cold in her bones out here.

"Condition? Anything, Grandmother." There's always a price. Besides, he's dreaming. Isn't he? He pinches himself. It hurts. He's awake. He doesn't care; he will take any magic as long as it gets him out of this fucking forest.

"You must go alone."

Dima stares at her, glances at the still bodies of the others—they've known each other since they were five; they bicker but they are his brothers-in-arms. He has obligations. "But . . . Pasha and Kolya."

"You walk alone, Dima, or not at all."

He thinks perhaps he can persuade her, if he talks to her long enough, is charming enough, he can wear her down. "I can't go without my friends, Grandmother."

"Then you will not go at all," she says—he likes to think a little sadly—and she is gone.

Dima is less afraid. The forest is filled with strangeness, but she did not hurt him. Not the worst thing he has imagined for himself. And tomorrow the sun will rise. They will find their way.

It's only after he's woken Pasha for his watch, when he himself is snug in his sleeping bag and drifting off, that Dima remembers he did not tell the old woman his name.

In the morning, Kolya is missing.

At first, they don't worry—the fire is out, and they assume he's off to find more kindling. But as the dawn burns through the clouds above, as time wears on, as their stomachs begin to growl at a delayed breakfast, Dima feels uneasy. He and Pasha, sitting on their stumps, keep looking around, over their shoulders, through the trees, seeing nothing more than other trees. When Dima suggests they eat something, Pasha yells that they will wait for Kolya, he will be back soon.

But Kolya does not appear, and Dima's belly gets the better of him. He opens the biscuits and eats two before offering one to Pasha—Dima's no fool, he doesn't hold out the whole packet, knowing his friend's temper might well make him dash them all in the dirt. He takes a single biscuit and pinches it delicately between the tips of his fingers, holds it up as one might a treat to a skittish animal.

Pasha accepts the biscuit after a moment's consideration, crunches down on it as if it's personally offended him. Dima hands over more; they eat until the wrapper's empty even though they know they should be careful with their food. Eventually, without discussing it, they both rise and shoulder their packs. Pasha takes his small axe and cuts an arrow in the trunk of one the pine trees: *This way.* A message for Kolya in case he returns, more rabbit corpses in hand. Every ten trees, Pasha makes the same sign. He does it for hours—Dima is impressed; he doesn't think he'd have the stamina, the belief, for that.

They walk and walk and walk. Sometimes Dima wonders if they'll simply go in circles, come back to their own campsite, the last place they saw Kolya. Where he met the old woman. He does not tell Pasha about her, although part of him thinks he should. But he's still raw from his friend's mockery. He imagines the vitriol. *You're an idiot, Dima. Fucking bumpkin. Dreaming about old women. A path of stars, what the fuck is wrong with you?*

A few hours later, they find Kolya.

It takes a few moments to figure out it's him, however. There's a pack on the ground not so far away, his rifle, his uniform, his greatcoat with the tear in the elbow where he caught it on a fence they climbed through three, no, four, days ago now.

The body hangs upside down from a tree in a clearing, skinless as a rabbit on a rotisserie, swaying a little in the breeze. There's no drip-drip-drip of blood, for that's all poured out—dried up in a black sticky puddle in the dirt. There's a buzzing, though. It's winter. It's so fucking cold. How can there be flies?

The young men rush to their friend, reaching, but there's something about the corpse and its state, something about the lack of skin, the flies dancing on the meat of him, something about seeing every striation of muscle and tendon, and the eyes staring-staring-staring. The teeth without lips, so naked and so white. They don't touch him, no. They can't. They really can't.

Up closer they realize there's still a strip of hair on his head, a Mohawk stiff with red, in place of the golden locks of which he was so proud. They stare. They stare for a long time. Dima doesn't know how long but he only knows that his brain hasn't been working for a while—doesn't kick-start again until Pasha moves. Steps away. Turns his back and walks onward as if their journey hadn't been interrupted.

"We're leaving him?" Dima asks and his voice is high. But he says "we." We are. Not *you.*

Pasha swings about but instead of the expected ire, he's calm, almost glacial. "Do you want to cut him down? Wrap him? Bury him? Do you want to *touch* him?"

Dima thinks about how Kolya will feel beneath Dima's hands, without his skin, like those rabbits Dima *peeled*. Thinks about how, nearer, Kolya will smell even worse. All those flies. Thinks about how he will never get the stink from his nostrils or the memory of that most awful intimacy—that most naked of touches—from his mind.

Dima follows Pasha, doesn't look back.

Eventually Pasha stops.

The sun is setting. They've found a stream and gratefully refilled their canteens. There's a small campsite, too, although how long since it's been used is anyone's guess—spiders have built webs in the remains of the twigs and ashes. A day. A month. A year. More.

Dima gathers wood, starts a fire with the lighter his grandmother gave him when he first enlisted. Before she died. He shakes it, listens; not much left in the reservoir. He thinks Pasha has a lighter, too, but Kolya had matches. Waterproof matches, two boxes, in his pack. But they didn't search his belongings, didn't think to take something to aid in their own survival. Too late now. Too far to go back. He doesn't mention it to Pasha.

There are no stumps here, so they sit cross-legged on the ground, in the pine needles. They pool their rations: three meals, two full canteens, no biscuits. They have to find their way out of here very soon. How much farther can it be? The place they were headed, the base they're meant to blow up. *Two hours through the woods,* their commander had said, *due west.* Two hours, three days ago. Four? Turned around by fucking trees.

Pasha goes to sleep almost as soon as the day turns to dark, which it does with the swiftness of a light switch flicked. He mutters for Dima to wake him for his watch, but Dima's unsure how he's meant to count the hours. They are, he thinks, still crossing that two-hour corridor between *then* and *now*. Between the road where the truck dropped them off and the power station they were meant to destroy. Even if they find it, he muses, it won't matter. Once again, the explosives are still in Kolya's pack—he was the responsible one.

Dima almost speaks, almost wakes Pasha to tell him about the old woman. But before he can weigh up the wisdom of the decision, she's there once again, across the fire from him. She in her khaki outfit, standing straight and tall like the trees, her hair loose silver.

"Good evening, Dima."

"Good evening, Grandmother."

"May I sit with you again?"

"Will it make a difference if I say no?"

She snorts. "None whatsoever, but I will think you impolite."

"Me? I'm beneath notice. Nondescript."

"Sometimes, Dima, that's not a bad thing. To be able to pass beneath notice. To walk in the shadows. You might walk there forever."

"Do you? Grandmother? Walk in the shadows?"

She smiles as if disappointed in him. Yet she gestures once again, just like the first night, last night. "And if I offer you this path again? A way home—what would you say? I should not do so, but there is something likeable about you, Dima."

He looks at the path of stars, at the shiny points that dazzle his tired eyes. At its end—so near and yet so far!—he thinks he can see shadows moving against the windows, against the blinds. His mother, his sister, waiting for him to return. The warmth of the apartment that's shabby but comfortable. It will smell like soup and fresh bread. His sister will be studying, his mother, too. The cats will be by the hearth, purring like small engines. Dima stares longingly, then looks at Pasha.

"But Pasha?" he says, and the old woman's shaking her head even before he's finishing speaking.

"On your own or not at all."

"Why did you do that to Kolya?" he asks with a hitch in his voice, for he's got no doubt it was her.

A pitying look, as if he should know. The old woman leans forward; the light from the flames makes of her a monstrosity, all shadow and furrows. But her expression isn't unkind. Isn't cruel. Just a little sad, a little resigned, as if she expected this, somehow. "Dima? Dima, my boy, you're going to die. Out here. It's so cold. So quiet and lonely." She points at Pasha cocooned tight in his sleeping bag, oblivious. "Do you think he would hesitate one moment? Do you think he wouldn't leave you behind?"

And Dima wants to cry. He thinks of Pasha fighting off Dima's bullies when they were small and Dima was the smallest of them all. Yet he knows, too, that Pasha would leave him in a heartbeat if the old woman gave him this chance, but because Dima's a coward he also knows he cannot do the same. If he runs now, he runs forever. He says, "I can't."

And the old woman is gone.

Dima thinks he must tell Pasha everything, no matter how angry he gets, no matter how much he mocks. Pasha must be warned for his own sake, so he can be alert.

But Dima can't wake Pasha, not even when he yells and shouts and pushes the sleeping man. In the end he gives up. He swallows his fear, curls around it and his rifle, and tries to stay awake.

When dawn burns away the last of the dark and Dima wakes, it is to find that Pasha is missing.

Dima cries until snot runs from his nose and he can barely breathe for sobbing. Finally, though there's nothing left, and he knows he can't sit here by the merry little stream all day, can't spend another night among the trees, he crawls over to Pasha's pack—unlike Kolya's it's been left behind although he can't say why—and ransacks it. He finds four extra ration packs his friend hadn't admitted to. He claims them and Pasha's lighter, the small axe, and Pasha's canteen, which he refills along with his own. He gathers his belongings, takes his bearings for all the good it does.

His first steps are stumbles into the stream, then across it, becoming surer and sturdier as he struggles up the bank. It feels as if he gains confidence from the certainty of his own footfalls, how his boots eat the earth. This way. Surely, yes, this way.

Dima continues for some time, in this fashion.

Until he begins to wonder if he'll find Pasha somewhere in the woods, hanging from a branch like Kolya, turned into a meal for the insects and the crawling things of the day and night. Any foxes that might leap high enough to strip away some meat. He stops in his tracks, looks around, tries to establish where he is.

He has no idea.

Wait! There's a sound! Water.

Dima runs toward it, his heart bursting with hope. There's meant to be a stream where they should have come out, just across from the infrastructure they were meant to destroy.

He steps into the camp he departed this morning. There's Pasha's pack just as he left it, open, the contents disgorged. The cold ashes of the fire kicked over because the last thing he needed was to burn this forest down, or perhaps that's exactly what he needs to do? But no, he won't. Can't.

Dima gathers more firewood, more and more and more until there's a large pile of it, enough to last one final night, he thinks. He looks up. The sun's falling. He breathes life into the tinder; when it's crackling merrily, he sits in the dirt and waits for the old woman. At some point he sleeps and wakes only when she calls him gently by his name.

And this time he does what he's avoided doing the past two nights: he looks properly at her feet. Without embarrassment—with fear, but not embarrassment. Shoeless, fur-covered, sharp-clawed, ridiculously long, rabbity from toe to hock. His mind had shied away the first and second times he saw it, from the memory blanked during the days. But there they are, now, undeniably giant rabbit's feet. Nothing else about her is leporine. No ears, whiskers, or fluffy cotton tail. Just an old woman looking at him quizzically as if she's not sure why he's still alive.

"Will you share my fire, Grandmother?" he asks, voice a little raw from sleep as he sits up.

"Thank you, Dima." She sits, elegantly, her legs folding beneath her, the scimitar curve of the toes dangerous in the firelight. "Have you worked it out yet?"

"Pasha is gone."

"Yes."

"Will I find him?"

She shakes her head and as she does her face shimmers: from old to middle-aged to young, so young. A girl, perhaps ten with silver eyes and silver hair, who opens her mouth—a tooth is missing, waiting for her adult ones to grow in—and says, "No. You won't live long enough."

Dima blinks.

The middle-aged woman repeats, "Have you worked it out yet? Why?"

Dima blinks again, remembers back to that night. Thinks of the scrawny rabbits on the makeshift spit. He blinks yet again. Sees two bodies, impossibly large, not rabbits. Humans. Women. Old women. The smell of their cooking, the drip and sizzle of their fat, their gray hair shriveling in the heat, not catching fire but almost melting. Yes, melting.

"Your sisters?" he asks, swallows.

The old woman, his old woman, is back. "My friends."

"Will you show me the path again, Grandmother?" Dima's voice is so soft, yet it's rich with hope. "I didn't eat them."

But she's shaking her head, as he knew she would. "No, Dima. You had your chance—you had two chances, that's one more than I should have given you. It's too late now, my boy. My poor stupid boy. There are consequences for our actions—you must realize this."

He nods. "I'm sorry, Grandmother, for what it's worth."

"I know."

"Will you stay with me, Grandmother? Until it's time."

"Yes, Dima, I will remain."

And they talk. They talk the whole length of the night. He tells her about his mother and sister and grandmother because he thinks it's important that—at the end—he speaks of them. That their names are on his lips. She tells him the secrets of the forest—the magic, the spirits, the creatures that have watched his progress all these days and nights. When he asks if there was ever any chance for them, him and Pasha and Kolya, if they'd not committed murder in her woods, and she says, *Perhaps*. Perhaps she'd have forgiven them when it was merely *trespass*, but she hadn't had to worry about that, had she? *No*, he says. They talk more and she tells him what she is, who she is, what she will be. She promises that she will tell his mother that he is gone, and he's grateful, for he doesn't like the idea of his family not knowing. He thinks about this witch with her faces and her feet taking the path of stars to his home, delivering a death note to his mother.

He thinks he is at peace with his demise. He thinks, right up until the sun begins to spear through the trees, that he will be calm. He's wrong. Even before it's light enough to see, he's off like a shot, haring through the trunks, hurdling the stream and fallen branches. She doesn't call after him. He hears no pursuit. But he knows she's there.

She's always going to be there.

When his breath runs out, when his hope—that ridiculous little flame—finally snuffs, then he slows. Dima jogs until he comes to a hole in the earth. A ditch, really, but it's just his size. He looks behind, tries to find the trail he's come from but there's no sign he was ever there. No sign he was ever in this forest he should never have stepped into anyway. There's only the glow, back there. A brilliant orange tinted with licks of red, turning the saplings, the old timber into silhouettes, then making them disappear as it gets closer and closer.

He knows he can't outrun it—her. He didn't want to come here, yet he did. And that little bit of blood from his grandmother, that red thread so slender that connects him to her and to this place? It's too thin to keep him safe. Not enough. It won't protect him. She tried to tell him, that old lady, in the cold hours, when she seemed, no, *was*. She was so kind, but he didn't heed the kindness, and tried to tell him it was time to leave. Now, he'll never get away.

He's going to be here for a long time.

He'll become part of the land.

Things will grow from him.

He'll feed them, like the children he'll never have.

There's a comfort in that, he thinks; just a little.

He lies in the grave and watches the last morning stars, waits for the sky to fall.

NAMELESS HERE FOR EVERMORE

Fonda Lee

"On this home by Horror haunted—tell me truly, I implore—
Is there—*is* there balm in Gilead?—tell me—tell me, I implore!"

—"The Raven," Edgar Allan Poe

Dear Heavenly Father, I pray to You in my hour of need and ask that You deliver me from torment. I've reached out to You so often during my terrible grief and been comforted, yet even though nothing is beyond Your power, I fear I can never escape the horrors of my own mind. I've always known that wickedness walks Your earth. I see the false prophets of Hollywood, the ongoing attacks on Christian traditions and values, the rising levels of sin and crime in this country—but not until tonight have I come face-to-face with evil in my own house.

Around midnight, and unable to sleep, I was rereading Isaiah 57 at the kitchen table when I heard a noise against the window over the sink. It was so faint, I might've imagined it. Then it came again, a *tap-tap*-tapping. When we'd first moved into the house, in the summer before Lena began middle school, a woodpecker took up residence in the backyard cedar tree. At random times, I'd hear it hammering at the bit of rotten siding under the eaves, so even though it was the dead of night in December, that's the first thing I thought of: a bird pecking at the sill. When I set down the Bible and pulled back the purple curtains, however, all I saw was my own haggard reflection, backlit by the hanging lamp with half its light bulbs burned out.

I grimaced at the sight of myself. The summer tan I'd worked so hard for was long faded, the fine lines of impending middle age had deepened like thin canyons around my eyes and mouth, and my hair was an uncombed, colorless mess with the dark roots showing.

I looked awful. But since I'd lost Lena, I barely cared anymore.

Letting the drapes fall back into place, I sank into the armchair in front of the television and fumbled between the cushions for the remote. The sudden sound of the doorbell nearly made me leap out of my skin. My heart thudding, I sat frozen in my seat, staring at the front door. Who would ring the bell at such an hour? All the expected visitors had already come and gone. The neighbors had brought flowers and a casserole and earnest requests to please let them know if I needed anything, but we weren't friends. I was quite sure they were atheists. I wasn't about to open the door for a stranger, but the lights were on and my car was in the driveway, so it was obvious I was home. Should I go to my bedroom and lock the door? Phone the police?

The bell rang again. A voice on the other side called out, "Hello? Is anyone home?"

It was the voice of a young woman. Her silhouette appeared in front of the sidelight window as she peered into the house, one hand held above her eyes to block out the glare of the streetlights. She had long, dark hair and a familiar, slim adolescent height. For a second, my heart spasmed with an impossible hope so great and painful that I couldn't breathe. My Lena, returning home one last time as a radiant angel to comfort me with the truth that she was in a better place now, that we would one day be reunited in Your kingdom.

I knew it wasn't true; the girl standing outside shuffling her feet in the cold couldn't be Lena, but I pushed aside the throw blanket and went to the door. "Who is it?"

"Mrs. Allen? I'm sorry to show up so late like this. I should've called ahead but I didn't have your number." A long pause. "Can I come in and talk to you? I was Lena's friend at school."

I unbolted the door and opened it. The girl standing on the porch was older than my daughter, probably a senior, maybe even a college student. I tried to recall if I'd seen her among the handful of Lena's classmates who'd been at the funeral. I didn't recognize her, but that whole day had been a blur; it was possible she'd been there and I hadn't noticed. She was dressed entirely in black: a puffy black winter jacket, black tights, black boots that matched her ink-black hair. She wore too much eye makeup. Lena had never hung out with Goth kids, but this girl looked like the type that might skateboard and listen to satanic music. She was also hunched and shivering, and the red two-door car parked on the street behind her wasn't the sort of vehicle her parents ought to let her drive on a night when the roads might be icy.

I held the door open and let her inside. "You look positively frozen," I said. "Would you like something warm to drink? I could heat up some hot chocolate."

"Yes, please, Mrs. Allen." She blew into her cupped hands and sank into the second chair at the kitchen table. Lena's chair.

"'Mrs. Allen' makes me sound old," I chided her. "You can call me Edi. That's what young people do these days, don't they? You even call teachers by their first names?" I sniffed the carton of milk in the fridge to make sure it was still good before pouring it into a saucepan and starting it warming on the stove. "I'm afraid I didn't catch your name, though."

"Right, sorry," she said. "I'm Raven."

Of course she'd have a New Age name like that. I wondered if she'd gotten it from tree-hugging hippie parents, or if she'd picked it for herself in order to seem cool and special. "You said you knew Lena at school?" I prodded.

"We were in a club together." Raven had been watching me intently as I stirred in the hot chocolate mix, but now she lowered her gaze and picked at the chipped black polish of her bitten nails. "I was her big sister—the older student who's supposed to welcome her and make sure she was doing okay. I . . . didn't do a very good job this time."

An uncomfortable silence fell between us. I was beginning to regret answering the door. If this girl had come to my house to unload her guilt at not having been a better friend to my daughter, I didn't want to hear it. People are cruel hypocrites. A lot of spoiled, rich kids wouldn't give the time of day to someone shy and a bit different. But now that Lena was gone, they acted as if they knew her. At the funeral, they told me how much she would be missed, when all it'll take is a couple days for them to forget all about her and go back to their regular lives.

I brought the hot chocolate over to the table and sat down across from Raven, pushing one of the steaming mugs toward her. She accepted it, wrapping long fingers around the warm ceramic. "So which club were the two of you in together?" I asked.

Raven sipped the hot chocolate. She glanced at the Bible lying on the corner of the kitchen table before returning her gaze to me. "It wasn't a student club," she said. "I brought her into the Greenville Coven. It's the local chapter of a . . . much bigger sorority." She set down the mug and gave me a questioning look. "Did Lena tell you about it?"

I sat back slowly, crossing my arms. "No," I answered. "That certainly doesn't sound like something Lena would be involved in." Sororities were all about parties, drinking, and boys, and we had strict rules about those things. They encouraged vulgar, loose behavior, and were not anything a fifteen-year-old Christian girl ought to be exposed to, much less participating in. And why would Raven and her friends call their club a *coven*?

A terrible thought occurred to me then, one that made me feel sick to my stomach. Had my daughter been recruited into some sort of occult group? I'd heard of teenagers dabbling in that sort of sinfulness. Father Geoffrey had warned in several of his sermons that parents needed to be vigilant against the hidden conduits to witchcraft that resided right under our noses in popular television shows and books. Could there be an occult association *right here* in our town, actively targeting impressionable teenage minds? Lena would've known better than to ever get involved in something like that. She would *never . . .* would she?

"You must be thinking of someone else," I explained to Raven. "My daughter and I were very close and told each other everything. She never mentioned you or your club."

When the girl didn't reply, I breathed a sigh of vindicated relief. I readied myself to forgive her mistake, accept her apology, and show her to the door with prayers for a safe drive home, but then she said, quietly, "Lena didn't tell us about you or her home life, either. I guess she kept the different parts of herself secret. She tried to deal with her struggles alone."

What a miserable thing to say to a grieving mother! It was all I could do at that moment not to throw the girl out of my house. "Lena wasn't struggling," I retorted. "She was always happy and loved and supported. What happened was God's will. A tragic accident that's hard for me to accept only because I'm an imperfect enough person to question Jesus for bringing her home to heaven." Tears pricked my eyes but I blinked them away furiously. I wasn't about to cry in front of a complete stranger, a rude teenage one at that.

I knew what Raven was thinking. What other people in her school and even in church had been whispering. I hadn't been home when Raven slipped and fell in the bathtub. I'll never forgive myself for that. But the coroner said there were no drugs in her blood; she had definitely drowned. That didn't stop rumormongers from speculating, from suggesting the unthinkable.

"Edi." Raven's voice sounded different all of a sudden. She didn't seem quite the hesitant teenager she'd first appeared to be. She was sitting up straighter and her unflinching gaze made a wave of unease overtake me. "What do you remember about that day?"

I didn't know why she asked, or why I answered, if not for some dark compulsion. "I went to Bible study as usual, and Lena stayed home because she wasn't feeling well. When I got back, she wasn't in her room. I walked into the bathroom, and . . . that's when I found her."

Recalling that horrible moment made the sorrow surge afresh. With her eyes closed and the halo of her hair floating gently around her beatific face, Lena had looked as though she were peaceful and sleeping. The water in the tub hadn't even spilled over the rim.

Oh Lord, I know Your will is mysterious and good, but why, oh *why* would You take from me my only child, my reason for being? How am I supposed to go on without her?

Raven's voice lowered compassionately, but there was a growing insistence to it that unnerved me even further. "The ladies in your Bible study group said you arrived that morning upset and flustered, like you'd been crying."

I swallowed my grief and frowned. "They did?" I recalled being in an awful mood that morning and arriving at church late. But now I couldn't remember why. What did it matter? Also, how did this girl—no, not a girl, looking more closely at her face, she was definitely in her twenties, how could I have thought otherwise at first?—anyway, how did she know the other women in my Bible study group?

I gasped as another layer of suspicion dropped like a brick on top of the first. Could a satanic organization have infiltrated even Father Geoffrey's congregation?

"You told your friends at church you were late because you'd gotten into an argument with Lena." Raven leaned over the table and pressed on before I could get my bearings. "Do you remember why? Do you remember the last conversation you had with your daughter?"

"I . . . what? No, no, that doesn't sound right. I don't remember that." Yes, Lena was fifteen and prone to temptation as all teenagers were, but she was a good girl with a good head on her shoulders. We rarely argued, and when we did, we apologized quickly and prayed together for greater patience with each other. If we'd had a fight that morning, I would remember.

Yet . . . I couldn't recall what we *had* talked about before I left. Why couldn't I?

I stood from the table. "I'm not answering any more of your questions," I declared. My voice and hands were trembling. "And I think it's time you leave my house."

Raven nodded and rose from the table, but instead of going to the door, she murmured something unintelligible under her breath as she stepped up to me and, before I could pull away, she touched her index finger to the center of my forehead.

A memory came back to me as suddenly as one of those instances when you're searching for your keys and the knowledge of where you last placed them springs to mind in an abrupt flash.

"I can't make you go to church, but at least I can go myself. I pray every day for the Devil to leave you, Lena, but you have to want him to. You have to close your heart and soul to him. You have to ask for God's help and accept it. I can't do it for you." I'm in angry tears as I grab my purse and wrench open the door.

"Mom." Lena's voice makes me turn. There she stands, splotchy-faced, tears running down her cheeks. "I'm done. I'm just . . . done. You won't remember this, but . . . Goodbye, Mom."

I jerked away and collided with the kitchen counter. "What did you do to me?" I demanded in a whisper of horror. "You . . . you put a vision into my mind."

Raven shook her dark head. "All I did was remove the memory blocker."

An icy wave of fear spilled down my spine. Shaking like a leaf, I crossed myself and clutched the crucifix pendant around my neck. "Lord, protect me from the Devil and his servants," I breathed.

"I'm not the Devil," said the young woman, or demon. She regarded me and bit her bottom lip unhappily. "Like I already said, I was Lena's friend."

"My daughter would *never*—"

Another memory surfaced, unbidden. *I'm home from work early. As I get to the top of the stairs, I see Lena's door is ajar, and I can hear her talking to* someone unseen. *She'd better not have invited a boy home from school without permission!* But when I peek inside, she's alone. She's standing by the window, staring intently at a houseplant she's holding. She's speaking to the plant—no, *commanding* it. The plant grows and sprouts new leaves, becomes full and green and mature, then browns and withers and dies, going through its entire life in the span of a few seconds.

I let out a scream. Lena whirls around and drops the pot. It doesn't fall to the ground but hangs suspended in midair.

I sagged hard against the counter, clutching my head. "What are you doing to me?" Raven took a step forward and I cried out, seizing the Bible from the table and holding it up alongside the crucifix. "Get away from me! Don't come another step closer!"

The woman stopped, but she didn't appear affected by the holy objects. She sighed, her shoulders slumping with understanding. "It seems Lena suppressed many of your memories of her, so you'd remember her the way you wanted to, as a good and ordinary Christian girl. But she wasn't skilled enough to weave a complex spell that would seal away each memory individually. Now that I've undone the primary block, they're all releasing."

I whimpered as another vision filled my mind. *Lena and I sitting together on the sofa watching a movie. I'm holding the bowl of popcorn and she's leaning her head on my shoulder and eating from the bowl, the way she always does. We laugh at a funny part of the movie. Lena chokes on a piece of popcorn and starts coughing. I sit up in alarm and pound her back, but her face turns red. The television screen turns to static. I look up in alarm as the lights start flickering wildly in time with her hacking. She dislodges the bit of stuck food and takes a big breath of relief. The television picture returns and the lights stop blinking.*

I'm on my feet, staring at her. "Get thee behind me, Satan . . ."

I pressed the heels of my hands to my eyes. "Lies, all lies," I moaned. "If Lena was . . . if she was possessed, other people would've noticed. People at her school and at church."

Lena and I shouting at each other in the living room. "What's happening to *you is unnatural, Lena! It can only come from Satan, and we need professional help from the church to deal with it. Father Geoffrey—"*

"It's not evil, Mom! There are other people like me. I met an older girl at school named Raven. She told me—"

"Your daughter was a witch." Each of Raven's oddly gentle words skewered me. "Teenagers can have a hard time controlling their magic when it first begins to manifest. The coven has to find them quickly, to cover up accidents and teach them control. That's why simple glamours, amnesia, and deep sleep are some of the first spells witches learn."

The memories kept coming, no matter how hard I tried to shut them out.

I pull back Lena's sleeve and gasp at the cuts on her arm. I'd remembered that as a tattoo. *Father Geoffrey comes to the house to prepare Lena for the exorcism, but she puts us to sleep over dinner and escapes the house.* Oh, how embarrassed I'd been to find we'd overindulged in wine and Father Geoffrey had fallen asleep on my sofa. Thank goodness Lena had been out at a sleepover. *"It's not your fault, Lena. The evil's in your blood. It comes from that awful, awful man who . . ."* No! No, no, *no.* I'd buried all that. I would never have spoken of those dark things to my daughter!

"Lena didn't slip in the shower." Raven spoke quietly and with terrible conviction. Her mascara-rimmed eyes were black pits of sorrow and despair. Windows into my own purgatory. "She filled the tub and got in. She knew how to cast a sleep spell deep enough that she wouldn't wake from it."

With a guttural scream, I seized the carving knife from the butcher block on the counter and lunged at the witch. She was the reason I'd lost my daughter. She'd filled Lena's malleable young mind with unnatural ideas, turning her away from God and toward darkness and sin. If it weren't for her, my child would still be alive. I wouldn't be alone.

She didn't move as I charged her. I glimpsed in her face a grim lack of surprise. Malice and regret were frozen on her youthful features as I plunged the knife down toward her chest.

A burst of white light, like the pop of a camera flash. I stumbled forward, blinded, and collided with the back of the kitchen chair, swinging the knife into empty space. The witch had vanished into thin air. A black bird flapped over my head, off the edge of the refrigerator and into the living room. It landed with a loud caw on the head of the statue of the Virgin Mary and baby Jesus in the nativity scene that Lena and I had put up by the fireplace two weeks ago, in anticipation of Christmas.

I chased that evil visitor, shrieking, throughout the house, but each time I lunged, it flapped away and landed out of reach. At last, exhausted, I fell to my knees on the carpet, heaving and sobbing. The raven perched atop the bookcase like a gargoyle, and the little remaining light from the lamp threw its monstrous shadow against the wall.

"Lena was perfect," I wept, raising my hands in helpless supplication toward the ceiling, crying out my truth. "She's an angel in heaven with Jesus, not a witch burning in hell."

The raven sat and watched me with coal-black eyes—sad, judgmental, and cruel. It sits there still. I can see the sun beginning to come up outside, but inside this cursed house, it will forever be as dark as the doubt in my soul. Lord, I pray, deliver me!

MASK OF THE NAUTILUS

Sheree Renée Thomas

She awoke in a ruined kingdom, the cold wind blowing through her hair.

"You have not seen me in a long while," Kenyatta heard the voice say, "but I have seen you. Your grief called to me. Come. We are painting in tongues," the masked one said. "Come and see."

Kenyatta rose from her bed, the tearstains of nightmares dampening her pillows and her cheeks. The voice was an invitation, a whispered command, soothing and ominous all at once. Kenyatta knew who it belonged to before she looked outside. A crowd had gathered, their voices raised with wonder; hope, confusion, and anticipation drifting in the wind.

They craned their necks to see the one the elders spoke of, Grandmama Gawd the Great Mask Maker and her ramshackle house, with its painted haint-blue shutters and starry eaves covered in ancient wooden masks. No one alive had seen Grandmama Gawd's face, for she wore a grand mask carved from the world's first tree. Alive with her magic, filled with the spirit of ancestors, the house trembled and shook. Its pennant flags waved and swayed in the wind. The house bowed, standing on its massive chicken legs and feet, decorated with colorful ribbons and bands.

Outside, the children stood watching, in a long circle of sun.

Brightly colored feathers filtered the morning light, floated through the air, rainbow confetti.

Grandmama Gawd's chicken-foot house leaped and danced, to the children's delight. The great masks rattled on their hooks from haint-blue shutters and painted-star eaves.

The masks rang out, sang out, calling the children and their parents by name.

"Waterfall, horseshoe, salamander. This one's for you, Daria Alexander!"

A horse-shaped mask carved from ebon wood galloped across a sunbeam. It shook its dark-stained raffia mane, then floated down to gently rest upon the young one's smiling face. Together they galloped off, leaving the child's worries in a cloud behind them.

"River, treeborn, looky-loo. Laurence Olivier Jones! This mask is for you!"

Gold and bronze, a heart-shaped mask with two curved horns spun on sunlight. Its iridescent, metallic hue reflected the child's hidden treasures. The child clapped her hands and stomped her feet, double-time, then twice more. Painted with light and clarity, the mask's narrow eyes expanded when the child reached up and plucked it from the widening space, the liminal, in-between place. The girl's arc-shaped mouth opened to reveal green vistas and lush, open fields. Relieved, her arms and shoulders relaxed as she entered a deepening space where her young spirit ran fearless and free.

In this land, the masks were louder, more insistent. They shouted and hummed, muttered and moaned. The stories they told, the visions they sang, were more vibrant and boastful than the ones the children had known. Here, a traditional mask, emblem of the masquerade, was not enough to hide the depths that dwelled within. Their grief climbed inside them. Here, lives were plucked, unarmed souls stolen before their time by hands that swore to serve, to protect. The plaintive signs they carried weighed heavily as they had marched and gathered in the streets. The people had grown weary holding their tongues, turning their cheeks. They had raised their voices, sang the songs of hope, but their music was unheard, their pain unseen by Justice.

Blind to all but them.

Before the Great Mask Maker came, Kenyatta's heart had turned away from itself. The bell in her altar only rang in her sleep. Her waking self and sleeping self no longer shared the same blood or chambers. Her spirit walked along the emptied rooms. Where she once felt connected, there was now a great void. The land and all its roots had rejected her. The known world no longer made sense. She longed for the peace she only felt when she was out at sea, so she waited in the twisting line and the heat, her thoughts a tumbling wave inside her.

Swirling in the sounds of newborn suns, in the blueblack knowing that grew inside them, the crowd shouted and yelped, as each mask descended from the wooden shack. With the masks, each soul released its inner burdens. Whether near or far, a bustling city or a tiny town carved from the backbone of land, the Mask Maker's wares were sought out, coveted. Their stories carried memories and maps that led the people through the forgotten forests of themselves.

Without the masks, they feared they would lose whole mountains and rivers.

Without the masks, the strange countries that occupied their minds might disappear. Without the masks, they might recede to the land of myth and forgotten memory.

So one by one, the people came. Some chose their own masks, and for others, the masks chose them.

One child stood in the line, eyes downcast. Unlike the others, he did not watch the masks fill the sky like giant kites. Instead, he dug his heels into the earth, pressing down as if he wished the rich soil would swallow him up. A great shadow overhead blocked the sun. When he looked up, surprised, he found a beautiful plank mask outstretched above him. He stood quite still as the crowd whispered all around. The bright red mask hovered. Its great falcon wings unfurled. The mask rested atop the child's head. Gently, so very gentle. His eyes rolled back, the great wings spread, and the child floated away. The black bottoms of his shoes were the only things visible, as the winged mask carried him off into the clouds. A hush covered the crowd as they watched in wonder, wordlessly.

Like the others, Kenyatta stood in the long, sweltering line that spiraled outside the Mask Maker's mysterious chicken-foot house. She waited, carrying the words she dared not speak, the tears she could not shed in daylight, the crescent moons of her nails digging into her palm flesh. She waited because she too had stretches of land that lay fallow inside her, broken earth that would hold no roots, no gardens, heartbeats and breath she wanted to forget.

At first, Kenyatta could not make up her mind. The first mask Kenyatta wore had a scar, raised above the left eye, spreading and older than the mask they called Reap. Kenyatta had scars of her own. She had walked the path of them so long she could no longer feel her legs. She turned to the crowd; they shook their heads, *no*. The mask would not do, so she chose another.

This one called to her, soft and welcoming, windblown, the sound of the sea. The spirit of the mask whispered Kenyatta's true name, the one she called herself deep in the arms of sleep. It was the self she longed to be. Fragile yet strong, pink and pearly, the nautilus mask offered an open door into a world she could fully enter.

When Kenyatta put on her mask, it felt like hope, warm and wet, slick against her skin. Its scent sharper than the hottest day of anger and despair. They had painted BLACK LIVES MATTER bright against the burnt-black asphalt top, but not a single bone or skull buried beneath that earth could breathe.

For some the mask was not just a small hope, painted into existence. For others it was a broken dream, carved and beaten down into submission. A promise remembered. A betrayal revealed.

When she wore the mask, it felt like a memory repeated bluely. Like the song of her soul, buried in the sea. When Kenyatta wore the mask, she could play a whole tune on one note, a whole song on one string. Her spirit was a diddly-bow, made of coral and starfish. It vibrated with the sheer wonder of living. Inside the mask, she drifted in and out of the past, out of the spaces of the different choices she could have made, the different lives she could have lived. Her shoulders rose, free of their burden of self-doubt and regret. But also, the mask created alternate spaces for her to see a path to a future, one she could believe.

Masked now, the crowd rose all around her. Their spirits joined her in the netherworld. Bodies languid and heavy, the humid air pinned their unruly thoughts down. Here they made a life for themselves inside the dark, winding roads that filled the city's head.

They peer from bodies that have gone weeks without touch. "Help us," their eyes say, something near pain in the strain of their smiles. Lids heavy with desperation, some seek escape, others seek peace.

*A dance that's walked, a song that's spoke.** They wore the masks, too proud to bend, too poor to break. Some wore a mask, but did not believe in its dance nor its destiny. They would craft their own fate, turn down the roads of their own choosing.

Their pain was a spiral of grief, a well of anger and sorrow deep as any ocean.

Grandmama Gawd the Great Mask Maker came to teach them how to claim that water, to take the pain they *were never meant to survive*† and mask it, and with intention, face the darkening world and make it something new.

The crowd moved with slow, sinuous grace. Bare soles packed on the flat earth, they shifted their weight from one ankle to the other, then knees, thighs, hips, torso, and shoulders. Everything come unloosed. Their feet never lifted from the ground, and yet they moved and swayed in waves as if in water.

The Mask Maker's chicken-footed wagon was spirit theater. Its

---

* "When I Think About Myself" by Maya Angelou
† "A Litany of Survival" by Audre Lorde

bright feathers floated like pieces of stained glass sailing through the air. The revelers devoured drumbeats and songs galore. The music drove them from their bodies, the masks contained the new visage of spirits and feelings not yet seen.

The masks contained tongues, a visceral, inner language that spoke of matters too painful, too nuanced, too dangerous to be said aloud.

Was it a piece of fallen tree, roots forgotten? Was it a wooden tongue, voice disembodied?

Was it their own buried anger come back to haunt them, slew-footed specter digging up the ancient past?

They transformed into their own shadows and tracks, crisscrossed, crossroading the blacktop streets and the fields.

When the mask entered her skin, Kenyatta cried out, a wail. A cosmic sound that could be music, water and darkness covering the stars.

In the green blaze of morning turned night, she looked and looked, peering through the slits. The mask had so many eyes. She now wore so many faces, other lives that were now her own.

Could she see a way forward? Could she walk through the dark woods of the forest that is herself? Could she cross the big water she carried inside, the ocean of tears that her spirit cried? Who would cross over to meet her if the distance proved too great?

Like her neighbors, the strangers and the friends, Kenyatta was too tired of dying, too tired of death. The rebirths cost more each day. She was tired of their grief papering the earth red, the only wars unfought were the wars inside themselves.

Kenyatta peers through the mask, its external shell a great shining spiral, a mother-of-pearl trumpet piercing the night sky. Inside she is soft-bodied, born anew. Her spirit is a house of many rooms, a labyrinth of closed chambers that hold her most interior selves. Kenyatta now sees the world through her half prism of pearl. Sees grace where before there was only judgment. And friends in need of refuge, repair, rest. She sees. Beneath the mask there are no strangers. Each life is connected to another.

They are tired of lighting candles, throwing out their hope for justice with the silent stumps of melted wax. They are tired of the markers and the marches, the posters and signs, the slogans and the wailing songs, the makeshift memorials propped up against the cracked concrete walls, the faded, wilted flowers littering the curbs of the streets with thoughts and prayers.

Elijah and Quawan. Breonna and Sandra. Trayvon and Tamir. Amadou Diallo and Philando. Marielle, Eric, Emmett.

The names go on, a litany of pain, a litany of survival. Justice denied is a spirit that haunts itself, its phantom limbs spiraling in the darkness, floating forever out of reach.

But in her mask, Kenyatta has found refuge. She and the mask are now one. Inside she hears the spirit of the sea. She wears white, whirling in the healing waters. Her spirit leaps and dives, over the sea's edge. Seven waves for seven selves.

The nautilus mask curves and spirals out from half her face. A living fossil, fragile but strong, ancient but brand-new, the mask has so many eyes now. The families scatter in the darkness. The birds in the trees count their tears and sighs. They avoid the eyes but watch each other. Their faces are a mirror, a rutted field, revelation. They urge fresh seeds to grow inside themselves. They watch the broken parts grow whole. Black love, a spark of fire in the night. They reach for each other, refuse to be erased.

NIGHT RIDING

Usman T. Malik

My dear girl, believe it or not, you lucked out with me.

Few doctors will take on pain management patients. Many refuse without even looking at the file. The moaners and groaners, road traffic accidents, paralyzed spines, arthritic necks, depressed hypersensitive fibromyalgia types, narc seekers, autoimmune this and gluten-intolerant that—they eat up hours of your life without ever changing one iota of their lifestyles or habits. You listen and nod, give them advice and prescriptions, and they just hunch in those clinic chairs, staring at you.

It makes you feel stupid, makes you feel the weight of those years of training useless before these rocks petrified in their depression and lethargy, who spit in the face of every pill you throw at them. Tricyclics, benzos, anti-inflammatories, antidepressants, opioids. They dry-swallow them then turn around begging for more, pale faces and sleep-hollowed eyes hovering over you.

And when one of them overdoses, guess who's the one that gets blamed?

Easier to not accept such patients—that's the approach many docs use. Well, I say to myself, someone has to take them. Where will they go otherwise? Someone has to refill those pain scripts, release those trigger points, inject those joints.

More fool me, because now I'm stuck with a whole clinic full of them.

But that is why you're here, aren't you? To learn from the famous Dr. Yussef at his Pain Clinic and Sleep Lab. The best treatment to help these long-haulers that others have turned away.

I take pride in my work. I choose my patients carefully and devise personal plans for them. Medical work is detective work, you see. You get into the deep, dark grit of things. You part the evasions and misdirections, you reach for the clues and pull them out, stringing them together, until the correct diagnosis hangs glittering before you, like a pearl necklace.

Do I get stumped sometimes? Of course! Haven't you been listening, my pretty? What year are you again? Final year, that's right. You do look awfully young, you know.

Yes, doctors are often left without answers, as I'm sure you'll discover as you advance along in your medical training.

An example of a case that stumped me? Hmm. Well, several. Bound to be when you've been in practice as long as I have. There was a man with cervical myelopathy who was always in severe neuropathic pain. Couldn't do much for him no matter how many spinal stimulators and pain patches we gave him. Another with complex regional pain syndrome who couldn't sleep at all due to burning pain in his left hand and arm. Phantom limb pain, bone-on-bone joints, sleep disorders. The list goes on.

Speaking of sleep disorders—the oddest was this girl. Pashmina was her name, if memory serves me right. Her brother was a dry-fruit vendor from Peshawar who brought her in to see me at Shalamar Hospital's outpatient department ten years ago or so, and, well, it was such a strange case it's stuck in my head all these years . . .

That interests you? You'd like to hear more?

She was seventeen, I think. A lovely Pashtun girl with the fairest skin, bluest eyes, although illness had cast its shadow on her face. Family had been living in Lahore for some time and she spoke some Urdu but Pashto was her mother tongue, which posed some difficulty in history taking. Her distress needed no translation, though.

"I hurt, doctor sahib," she says to me, twisting the hem of her chador between her fingers. "Top to bottom. I'm stiff and I hurt all the time."

On examination, my resident and I discovered she couldn't localize the source of her pain. Not her hand, her back, or her head. She had tender points all over, and if you touched her anywhere, she flinched and cried.

Pain is a strange thing. A beautiful thing, really. Pain is the discomfiting awareness of a body part you hardly knew existed. Often it doesn't originate in the flesh and even when it does, it is *defined* in the central nervous system. Pain climbs up the ladder of the spine into the brain, where it's processed, neatly packaged, and delivered to your conscious mind. So many checkposts before it is felt by *you*.

Is it any wonder that so many things extrinsic to us trigger and amplify pain?

All our pills are useless if the patient's aches are originating from, say, grief at the loss of a loved one. The hurt in their heart seeps into their bones, spills over into their skin, as I put it to patients. Think of the single mother putting in six days of work every week who comes home to a child always sick with bugs he's picked up at school or daycare? No money, no love, no hope—day after day, year after year. The constant fatigue, the fear, the loneliness. Of course she's going to hurt from neck to toe.

Or the woman with the serial cheater husband. The widow with six daughters and no prospects. The retired army major who "disappeared" activists in Baluchistan and now has nightmares about lifeless bodies digging their own graves. The boy whose stepfather knocks on his bedroom door every night . . .

You see, I suspected Pashmina's pain had its origin in her mind.

"How's your sleep?" I ask.

She doesn't look at me. "What do you mean, doctor sahib?"

"Do you sleep well? How many hours in a stretch? Do you wake up feeling refreshed?"

"I sleep okay," she says.

The girl's brother cocks his head to the left. "Come, Pashminay Gul. You must speak honestly. Never hide things from doctor sahib. We must tell him."

"Tell us what?" I ask.

Her gaze low, Pashmina speaks softly, "I . . . I don't sleep well sometimes."

"Doctor sahib," cries her brother, rising to his feet. "She is up all night. She doesn't sleep a wink. She hasn't for months now." He paces around the room, fists clenched, until the words explode from his lips: "My sister's haunted by the khapasa," after which he sinks into the chair and puts his face in his hands.

My chief resident Sameer and I look at each other. "By the what?" Sameer says.

The girl's face is white. Her clasped hands tremble in her lap.

We lean in and the girl starts talking.

When she was sixteen, Pashmina went to her village in Peshawar to attend a cousin's wedding. There, bedecked in flowers and dazzling reds, she danced for hours until her skin shone and her cheeks glowed. Laughing, friends and cousins told her to sit down lest the bridegroom lose his heart to her instead of his promised.

Later, they went to the bazaar where they feasted on naan and chapli kebab and soda water until they were fit to burst. Her cousins went to the market lavatory, but Pashmina, who abhorred public bathrooms, snuck into a grove of trees, and, behind an old peepul tree, she lifted her skirts, squatted, and let go. The relief made her smile, until she looked up and saw a tall, gangly figure hanging from the branches, its upside-down face mirroring hers.

Later Pashmina would tell her best friend that the creature in the tree held a lock of her hair between its teeth—but how could that be, she said between sobs, when the creature had no mouth?

The next day she left for Lahore, where she sought refuge in the bustling crowds and roaring traffic. Lahore, with its high-rises and shiny cars and girls in elegant, sleeveless dresses made it easier to believe the tree specter was just in her mind. She had imagined the whole thing. Pashmina smiled and hummed, as she ironed the plain white shalwar kameez she and her little sister wore to school before settling in for the night.

She dreamed she was on a winged dark horse, leaping from roof to roof in her village. The animal snorted and swooped, then soared into the night sky, carrying Pashmina deep into the void. *Slow down*, she tried to tell the horse, *take me down*, but the animal shot up and up until the air thinned and her breaths turned long and shallow and the moon was shrouded by the plume of the horse's wake.

Pashmina woke gasping, certain she was dying. A crushing weight pressed on her chest and windpipe. She opened her mouth, her tongue quivered, and her jaw moved soundlessly.

In the dark, the outline of a woman crouched on her chest.

Pashmina tried to scream, tried to buck and sit up, but her limbs were like marble. Her heart thundered in her ears and sweat poured into her wide-open eyes.

"Khap, khap," came the sound from darkness where a mouth should be but wasn't, as twiglike hands dug deeper into the girl's throat—and were gone.

Pashmina wheezed and fell out of her charpoy onto the stone floor of her two-room house. Her scream, when it came, woke her sister, who began to cry, and her brother, who rushed in. All Pashmina could do was point at the narrow skylight near the roof, where a crow sat staring at them at this ungodly hour. It cawed once and took flight.

Her brother heard about her nightly visitor. In the days that followed, she would tell him the story many times, as if the telling would extract the terror of it from her heart. Gul Daraz dismissed it as a nightmare, was even angry when she refused to sleep in that room unless he bricked up the skylight. A few weeks later, choking sounds drew him to her room where he found her curled in the charpoy, foaming at the mouth, her teeth grinding. It took a good amount of shaking and a bowl of cold water splashed in her face before life returned to her eyes, and Pashmina shrieked, "I rode her. This time I—" before collapsing in a bundle of gasps and tears.

Gul Daraz was still hugging her when someone hammered on their door.

"Gul Daraz, where's your sister?"

Qasim, their neighbor, face swollen and eyes red with sleep, asking about his sister. "Sleeping," replied Gul Daraz. "Where else, you big fool?"

But Qasim was not to be put off. He waited while Gul Daraz went and brought Pashmina out in a burkah, the girl still wiping her eyes.

"A hundred thousand curses be upon you, here she is," Gul Daraz said.

"Then who was in Sara's room?" Qasim said.

Qasim's ten-year-old daughter Sara had woken a while ago to find a figure sitting on her chest, its sharp fingernails an inch from the child's face. Sara wet herself before screaming for her father. By the time Qasim turned on the light, the room was empty except for Sara, knees pulled up to her chest, weeping into her hands.

"I'm sure she pulled a terrible prank on my child," Qasim said, glaring at Pashmina. "Maybe she climbed back into her room through a window."

There was no window in Pashmina's room. Just the crevice of the skylight.

Gul Daraz cursed and told Qasim off, but his heart hammered with foreboding. In the next few months, teenagers and children around the mohallah reported waking up with squeezing chest pain and breathlessness to find a shadow riding them, its tongue lolling between stretched lips. Try as they did, no parent could catch the intruder, yet uniformly the youths identified it as fifteen-year-old Pashmina.

There was no escape. Word spread through the neighborhood that the girl was possessed by the khapasa. Can you imagine? they whispered with nervous excitement. Pashmina is visited by the *khapasa*.

"The hag visits her at night," said a boy, kicking his football on the playground, "and sits on her chest. She can't move or breathe. It wants to steal her breath because it has no mouth and nose of its own."

"It tries to choke the girl." The second boy head-butted the ball and chased it. "But she can't, for she has no thumbs and can't finish her hold around Pashmina's throat."

"So it steals her body instead," said the seamstress's daughter, wide-eyed, and winced when the needle slipped and stabbed her thumb, raising a red drop. "Uses it to consort with jinns and demons."

"I heard she's a churail now, too. That they ride in the night together," whispered fifteen-year-old polio-struck Parveen. "That's why I recite the Throne verses every night, for what would I do if she came to *my* bed?"

So the gossip went and so Pashmina suffered her fate twice. Mullahs and amils were called. Shrines and mosques were visited, hakims and homeopaths solicited, but not one could help. The nocturnal visitations continued.

Terror kept Pashmina from sleeping most nights. Her mind was a mess and now her body began to give way. She lost weight, her hair thinned, and her cheekbones protruded. Every night she prayed for delivery and every morning she groaned from pain and whatever nightmares had been visited upon her the prior evening.

"Khap. That's the sound it makes," Pashmina tells us, as she finishes her story, her dull gaze upon the table. "Like a knock on the door. Khap, khap."

A rather terrible story, wouldn't you agree, my dear girl?

Even though I'd personally never seen such a case, Sameer and I—

you've met Dr. Sameer Shehryar? Associate professor at Mayo? Back then he was my chief resident—we had the same thought: sleep paralysis. A well-known condition often accompanied by hypnopompic hallucinations. Sameer was particularly excited, for this would make a great publication for him if he played it right.

Immediately we suggested an overnight sleep study. A polysomnogram and Multiple Sleep Latency Tests. The girl shall be brought to my partner's private sleep lab, I told Gul Daraz. We will monitor her sleep patterns to rule out disorders like narcolepsy and sleep apnea, and perhaps capture one of her episodes. Should one study fail, we'll attempt others. It will be a bit expensive, of course, but we'll see if we can tap into the provincial Dar-al-Maal funds and get it subsidized. One of the perks of being a public servant is access to public funding, Sameer reminded the girl's brother with a smile.

Hope flashed in Gul Daraz's eyes. And that will help my sister? Not just her pains but the haunting as well?

Well, there's no haunting. I laughed. Recurrent isolated sleep paralysis is a powerful, terrifying parasomnia. Once we rule out other problems, we can start a personalized treatment regimen.

So it was that later that week the girl found herself hooked up with electrodes in a comfortable bed at Mansoor Sleep Clinic in DHA. Even ten years ago it was a good setup and now, as you might see if we go upstairs to the Sleep Lab, my dear, you will find it absolutely state-of-the-art. My group has bought it, you see. A tour? Certainly. You can even try out one of the beds if you wish, ha!

Back to our girl. So, the first night Pashmina is up till 4:00 a.m., tossing and turning in bed. No unusual blips on the monitor, but she does stir a lot in her sleep. The next night we get more of the same, except she's up till even later, 5:00 a.m. or so. Such terrible sleep hygiene, we tell her brother the next day. She really has been messed up by her ordeal.

The third night, though: it's around 10:00 p.m. and she's wide awake. I'm in the tiny bunk bed in the on-call room—Sameer and I'd decided to take turns overseeing this extraordinary study, we told Gul Daraz—and the sleep tech is yawning in the control room, occasionally glancing at the camera pointed at Pashmina.

Soon the clock strikes midnight and the girl's finally asleep on her stomach, head angled to one side, lulled perhaps by the whirr and beep of machines in the dark. Who knows how long she has been sleep-deprived. I watch her on the call room monitor. By now I'm nodding off as well—when from the direction of the girl's room comes a sound.

I sit upright. Except for the distant beep of machines, it's quiet. No, I become aware of a droning, a *flowing*, as if I've woken up underground beneath a waterfall, punctuated by . . . moans?

My gaze is drawn to the monitor. It's an old thing, not fancy like the flat screens these days, and it flickers, snowstorms bursting onto the screen. I see the outline of the girl, sheets and blanket piled over her, one arm trailing off the bed's edge. Her room is unlit and for some reason the scene reminds me of a student painting I once saw at NCA of a beautiful, buxom girl reclining in bed, hand outstretched, a reproduction of some Renaissance painting.

Flicker. Except is the mound of fabric atop the girl's abdomen moving? And is that a head with a cloud of dark hair rising from the bedclothes, hovering over Pashmina—that turns to the camera and therefore me?

I fumble out of bed and run barefoot to the control room.

The machines are pinging when I burst through the door. The sleep tech must've been sleeping in his chair right before whatever happened; a string of saliva hangs from his collar when he looks at me, brows raised. "All well, doctor sahib?"

I glance at the monitor showing the girl's room. "Thought I heard something. She okay?"

"Jee. She had an apneic episode. Numbers went nuts for a couple minutes. Heart rate jumped up to 160. O_2 down to the 80s, and then"—he shrugs, reaching over to switch the sensor alarms off—"things normalized. Routine stuff, maybe a bit longer than usual."

The silence is loud. I concentrate and can't hear the strange rushing sound of water, the echo, almost like a whale song I once heard on *National Geographic*, that woke me up. I bend to look at the tracings, then study the girl again. She is sleeping soundly.

No monsters.

Except I heard something. And the sleep tech didn't.

I lean over and turn up the microphone in the girl's room. "Leave us."

He looks at me. "Sure, janab?"

"Yes."

I send the tech home, then I call Sameer. He comes right over.

Together, we examine the tracings. Sure enough, there are at least three apneic episodes when the girl wasn't breathing. She will need a follow-up MSLT to rule out narcolepsy and other hypersomnias, but this seems to be pretty much it: she has garden-variety sleep apnea.

But . . .

I tell Sameer what I thought I saw.

He grins. "Sir-jee, sounds like you had a nightmare yourself." When I don't smile, he says, "Well, we're both here. We can monitor her overnight. Why don't we take shifts, keep an eye on her?"

And, my dear, that's what we did.

For the rest of the night, we took turns watching the girl. Besides a couple more apneic episodes (when she briefly woke gasping for air), the girl's tracings and sleep remained extraordinarily ordinary.

There were no sleep paralysis episodes in the three nights the girl had spent with us. Just good old obstructive sleep apnea.

She finished her tests; we followed the polysomnograms with an MSLT, then fitted her with a CPAP mask. She was asked to follow up with ENT to rule out mechanical obstruction in her airways and sent home. And that was the end of that.

But that brief vision—likely a hypnopompic hallucination; I was, after all, half asleep—well, I'll have you know, it still discomfits me.

Far as the girl goes, we never heard from Pashmina and her brother again.

We had cured her.

So, there you have it, my dear girl. An unusual, somewhat disturbing story, but in the end nothing otherworldly about it.

And with a happy ending to boot.

The doctor pauses. He's in his early fifties, very tall and thin, shoulders hunched under his tailored suit and Polo tie that vanishes under his spotless white coat so seamlessly as if it were a part of it. When he talks, he waves his long brown arachnoid fingers about his salt-and-pepper head. A spider in a white coat, one might think.

"A fascinating study, no?" he says with a flourish and a grin. "Then again, that's what we've done for the last many years. Some of the most interesting pain and sleep cases—"

"Yes, fascinating, sir." The med student looks at him with interest, then at the clock on the wall: 6:45 p.m. They're having tea and biscuits in the doctor's office on the ground floor of the Yussef Pain and Sleep Disorders Clinic. Patient visits ceased around 4:00 p.m.

The med student is in her twenties, tall, brown-eyed, very pretty, with glowing skin and long black hair that falls in layers to soften her oval face. She balances her stethoscope around her neck and says brightly, "Dr. Yussef, I'd love to see the sleep lab, if that's okay. Are there any procedures planned tonight?"

"Always. But the sleep patients don't get here till about eight. Sure, let me take you upstairs."

They go up in the elevator to the third floor. He shows her the control room, where two sleep techs sit monitoring a bank of screens, then walks her through the patient bedrooms, pointing out the soft quilts and ornate headboards ("We spared no expense, as you can see").

His eyes glitter as he opens the door to the on-call room.

"And here we are. A few times a month I take calls here myself for VVIP patients. Politicians, bureaucrats, military generals. Like to make sure they're taken care of well. Isn't this grand?" he says. "Of course, the junior doctors have their own on-call room farther down the hall."

The med student looks at the broad balconied window with a view of the park, then at the mahogany bed, lava lamps, rich brocaded curtains, and the painting of Paris in the rain hanging above the bed. "This is lovely." She runs her hand along the headboard, tracing the winged horses carved into its wood, then takes off her white coat and sinks into the bed, sighing at its softness. "Heavenly."

Dr. Yussef picks up a remote from the bedside table, presses a button, walks to the mini-fridge in the corner, and returns with a bottle of wine. The med student watches with lidded eyes as he pours red wine into a cabernet glass to the soft music of "Strangers in the Night."

"Do you drink?" he asks without looking up and swirls the wine.

"Sometimes. With friends." She smiles. "Don't tell my family, though. They're pretty orthodox."

"Wouldn't dream of it." He pours another drink. "You're full of surprises."

"And you're such a good host."

They clink glasses, sit on the bed, and sip. She giggles at one of his jokes and he grins, letting his fingers brush then linger on her thigh. Her eyes shine. He leans in and begins kissing her.

She kicks off her heels and climbs onto his lap. Their lips still locked, his hands run through her hair then wrap around her throat and briefly squeeze before releasing. She moans and thrusts her tongue into his mouth. He attempts to lift her but she pushes his head to the pillow, rising and grinding against him, eyes closed. He sighs and her palms come down hard on his chest, pressing as she rides him, surprisingly, erotically heavy, both of them still clothed.

"Oh, I've missed this," she says and bucks. The movement makes him gasp. "Easy now," he says, laughing. But her right hand has found his groin, her left hand his mouth, fingers slipping between tongue and teeth, his eyes closing with pleasure. He sucks her fingers one by one: pointer, middle, ring, pinkie, then—he tries to feel her thumb with his tongue and opens his eyes.

She is unbuttoning his shirt, her right thumb hooked in the button-hole, and looks down at him. "How odd, my dear." He laughs again. "For a moment I thought—"

But she's shushing him, her mouth lowering, licking, going places, her dark shining eyes a dream he might have dreamed as a young man. His skin tingles, his flesh feels malleable, he is more alert, more alive than he has been in years, he thinks. He thrusts his thumb into her mouth, groaning as she sucks, then she gently bites down on it.

He gazes at her beautiful face above his groin and smiles—then his smile and her mouth and *his* thumb are gone.

As the girl's thumbless hands scuttle their way up his chest to his lips, the good doctor screams.

The girl begins to speak with her nostrils.

My dear doctor.

You lie with such eloquence. Such wonderful conviction.

Your lies have made you powerful; brought you here, to the beginning.

In the beginning, my mother was. I could not understand because I was not. She rode the night and her children's bodies. She found the ones who shone brightest—as she and her sisters had found others for thousands of years—and they rode with her: to clouds, villages, towers, minarets and mosques, though they knew not why. She was theirs and they hers, until their bodies finished changing, upon which the world would change for them, become like putty in the palms of their hands, as it had for others like them—after which she would leave.

Her will was ancient, her compact affirmed, but they remem-bered not.

Sister, sister, they would call her only after she left them.

But you took them both. In the middle of her change.

You impaled my two-mothers, you raped them. You and the other who had no business being there. Night after night you and the other came and rode my two-mothers, even as you lied to their brother, who knew not; as you have lied to so many brothers who knew not what happened to their sisters and daughters in your sleep clinic.

You took their screams and molded them and my two-mothers froze, shocked, petrified inside the change. You took their silence for triumph, for cure, and sent them away after you were done, you and that other.

Shush, you don't have to explain. No time for explanations tonight.

Pashmina's brother took my two-mothers back to his house, but they didn't stay in Lahore. They went back to the village, where, like a thawing winter rose, slowly my two-mothers came to life.

And as they did, so did I.

I was a speck in the belly of my two-mothers when you came inside them. I was born from your seed and Pashmina's virgin blood. I grew like a pregnant cloud and as I became aware of my two-mothers' womb world, I realized who I was, *why* I was. Months went by and I grew and grew, but try as I might, I couldn't escape my prison. You had imprisoned them and me inside.

As well, for I was outgrowing my two-mothers and they knew it. A new compact was contrived and reached. And thus, through love and bitterness and understanding of my two-mothers, I was freed.

Yet I wasn't *free*.

You see, my dear doctor sahib, you were responsible for this. Your unholiest act had shackled my feet. I could walk, but I could not *fly*. The bond between you and my two-mothers was a leash that held me to the ground, so the sky and darkness, the wings and night steed—my birthright—were denied to me.

Not for long, though. Because there is another way.

And that is why I am here, dear father. To carve out my freedom.

To claim my birthright.

The good doctor is gibbering.

"What is all this, a trick? Where is my thumb!" he cries, twisting under her weight, staring at the place where the girl's mouth should have been but isn't, then at his thumbless right hand twisted around the yellow bedsheet that doesn't have a drop of blood on it. The nub of flesh where his thumb used to be is smooth and shiny. "This isn't possible. Your story is crazy. Oh, why does it hurt so bad? I never raped that girl. I only—"

But the girl, no, the woman, isn't interested in explanations.

She takes off her shirt and turns around.

The doctor's protests die suddenly, and then he screams.

Two faces, so close to the surface they may as well be trapped under an iced lake, stare out at him from below the skin of the woman's back.

One is terribly familiar, the face of a young Pashtun girl.

The other is the stuff of his worst nightmares. A face he once saw in the camera of a darkened sleep lab.

Two pairs of lidless eyes blink rapidly at him before narrowing in absolute hate.

The woman turns back to him, lowers her head close to his. A pulsing blood vessel–laced membrane, like a bat wing, covers her face from what would've been the philtrum to her chin, and, ridiculously, even in the midst of his plight, or because of it, the good doctor can't help but trace out the membrane vasculature—the facial vessels squirming up, branching into the horizontal creep of the labial artery and vein, and the vertical thrust of the angular arteries.

They pulse when she speaks with her nostrils. "Father, Father, my two-mothers and I do still need to fly."

She waves a hand and Dr. Yussef's back arches suddenly. The skin of his forehead ripples.

"God, what is this?" he manages to whisper. "This can't be real, this—"

But the woman is rolling off him. She raises a hand and his mouth snaps shut. His teeth grind. There is a cracking sound as his jawbone splits and softens; his forehead protrudes, then elongates with the bridge of his nose and his jaw, sending chips of bone and bone dust scurrying in the air. His soft brown eyes recede to each side, his lips pouting and stretching into an impossible moue, blood spraying from his nostrils and lips, turning his face into a grotesque mask.

And all the while the doctor moans through clenched, rapidly enlarging teeth, blood filling his mouth.

Even as his neck lengthens and his occiput broadens; his chest expands and bursts out his white coat, the stringy Polo tie flapping uselessly on it.

He writhes and falls off the bed onto the floor. His arms swivel forward from their sockets, the bones cracking, tendons and muscles tearing and popping, sinking deeper inside the chest until his armpits are all but gone and his elbows have turned into knees. His torso expands and curves, his hips and lumbar spine broadening, the vertebrae thinning and rearranging themselves on his skeletal tree as they narrow and dip caudally, raising a mound of flesh above his anus into the semblance of a fleshy blood-soaked organ, reminiscent of a naked mole rat perhaps, before settling into a well-formed mammalian tail.

A rustling in his withers—impossible to call them anything else. The woman smiles (the membrane stretches wide) as from the place where once scapula poked through the flesh of the doctor's back a pair of black wings erupt and flap, shedding chunks of gristle and fat all over the expensive brocaded quilt puddled at the foot of the bed and beneath his hooves.

The doctor tries to screech but whinnies instead.

"Here there be winged horses," the woman says and claps her hands in delight. She reaches forward to caress her father's mane; it is rich and wet with red.

"Pain," she tells him as she swings a leg over his back, one thumbless hand strongly gripping his mane. "You told my two-mothers and me that pain is a beautiful thing. Father, I promise you will be in its blessed company for a long, long time."

He rears on his back legs, then stomps the floor.

"Khap." Her lips brush his long, pointed ear. "Khap, khap. The evening is still young and we have to pay an old friend a long-overdue visit."

She is still whispering lovingly in his ear as the good doctor crashes drunkenly through the bedroom window and wings off into the night.

WITCHFIRES

E. Lily Yu

The business breakthrough came with the perfection of the portable crematorium, seven feet by four feet of brushed gray steel, lined on the inside with gas jets, and easily towed behind Ron's white pickup truck. In the ten years prior to this development, Ron Morgan had had to content himself with the occasional cremation of one or another of his followers, hardly a growth business; now he could cover hundreds of miles in a day, if he needed to, the truck rattling with strapped-down propane tanks, to reach the next body.

He rarely drove more than twelve.

His fifteen followers accompanied him in a tour bus draped with polyester flags and equipped with Wi-Fi. When not taking a shift at the wheel, they tapped away at their laptops, identifying the next community they would stop in, as well as individuals in the community who might be congenial to their cause. By technological sleight of hand, through multiple accounts and automation, the fifteen of them appeared to be a much more persuasive several hundred online. They also ran a very healthy donation portal. Ron was quick to acknowledge their hard work with warm words and handshakes.

The truck and bus turned off the freeway into Pinoak, California, in the late afternoon. The light was sweet and golden, and Ron's followers dispersed among the restaurants downtown to enjoy pulled pork tacos and seared salmon nigiri, Cuban sandwiches and pink-boxed donuts. Ron waved off their enthusiastic invitations and instead checked the crematorium's various valves and dials, making sure the dust and jolts of highway travel had not interfered with their function. One could never be too careful.

At 7:30, the sixteen of them flashed tickets and filed into the Pinoak Arts Center, where the Pinoak community orchestra's evening program, printed on two sheets of folded and stapled pink paper, featured Shostakovich's Symphony No. 4. Ron was pleased to see how elegantly his folks had dressed, from emeralds in earlobes to gleaming tiepins. They had come far in the ten years it took to find them.

Listening to the music with his eyes shut, Ron would not have believed he was hearing an orchestra of hobbyists in a second-rate town. The musicians demonstrated an excellent grasp of both technique and color, and a high, fine sense of drama and tension. More than once, his breath caught. His muscles tensed. After the celesta's soft minor thirds had died away, the auditorium vibrated with enthusiastic applause.

Sighing, shaking off the broken enchantment, Ron walked down the worn carpeted aisle to the stage to congratulate the conductor.

"Miss . . . Seong, was it?" he said, glancing at the effusive biography on the program—Juilliard this, Northeastern that, a fineness that was entirely out of place in Pinoak. The program did not mention that she was single and had no family in town, though these were, to Ron, salient and suggestive characteristics. "An astonishing evening. One to remember."

"Thank you," the conductor said, tucking her baton under her arm. There was a thin sheen of sweat on her brow and a sense of exultation in her movements.

"It's a pity," Ron said, tapping the program. "Such a pity."

The conductor said, "I know, but they were out of yellow. And you can't read black text on green."

"I didn't mean the program."

"Then what did you mean?"

"You could have worked hard and developed your obvious natural talent. You could have succeeded honestly. Instead, you relied on witchery for this success."

She stared at him, her face wavering between incredulous laughter and unease, then turned away.

"I've spent twenty years hunting women like you," Ron said. "Witches have tells. Wands—the one under your arm, for example—cats, mysterious abilities . . ."

"You're a nut," she said over her shoulder. "If you don't leave, I'll call security."

Community arts centers did not hire security. The Pinoak Arts Center most certainly did not.

"Tell me, Jessamine," Ron said to the blond concertmaster. "Have you noticed anything odd about Miss Seong when she conducts?"

"Oh, yes," Jessamine breathed, her face pink with glee.

The conductor froze.

"She's always muttering to herself. Making passes with her wand. She smells like rotting cabbage. And if you don't agree with her, she gets *aggressive*."

If the next conductor wasn't Jessamine herself, or someone selected by Jessamine and kept under her French-manicured thumb, Ron would eat his own vest.

"What about you, Andre?" Ron asked the clarinet, who was dividing and cleaning his instrument with exaggerated care. By now, most of the community orchestra had packed up and left, enveloped in flowers and the embrace of relatives. Three-quarters of the chairs on the stage were empty. Thanks to the fifteen people murmuring to each other behind him, Ron knew the names of all the musicians who remained.

Their names and their grievances.

"She's not very nice," Andre said, grinning at the conductor. "Kind of uptight. Can't take a joke."

"Bit of a cocktease," the first trumpet said.

"She chooses strange music," Jessamine added. "The Shostakovich made me uncomfortable."

"Sounds like a witch," Ron said, and the musicians began to nod, yes, that was sensible, that was it. Everyone knew what to call women who didn't laugh and didn't say yes, and what right did some foreign woman with fancy degrees have to come in and command them, anyhow?

When her own musicians seized her and dragged her out into the parking lot, into the fine California evening, the stars pricked prettily in bears and dragons overhead, the shocked conductor made no sound. It wasn't until Ron's folks closed the steel cover and latched it that she began to move, to beat her fists and feet against the lid. But Ron had, with commendable foresight, connected the propane tanks and hoses before the concert, so it took no more than two seconds to light the crematorium's jets.

Then there were only clean blue flames.

It takes three hours at over a thousand degrees Fahrenheit to reduce the greatest genius to so many blackened bones. Tracy Millford had been with Ron through the most witchfires, and so he trusted her to sort the jewelry and metals—hip implants, gold fillings—from ash and bone, once everything had cooled.

After Tracy had sifted the ashes and pronounced them clean, Ron gathered up two handfuls of grit and crumbled them into the air over his followers' bowed heads.

"You are virtuous and worthy," he said. "We've done a good work here. Our thirtieth witch is now ash and smoke."

The slivers of bone fell to the pavement at his feet, but the wind lifted the finer particles and brushed some of it into the hair of those present and spread the rest with a loose hand over the sleeping town of

Pinoak, which would wake, soon enough, to find itself safer and more secure, lighter by one witch, warmer by one fire.

The handful of orchestra members went home, their primitive hungers satiated. Ron's people bedded down on the bus, ashes still caught on their eyelashes, smiling sleepily at each other. They were part of something larger than themselves, something that blazed bright enough to inspire action, powerful enough to immolate human beings. There on the purple-flagged bus, typing siren songs to anyone who might listen, they had found at last the meaning of their narrow mouselike lives.

Ron himself checked into a hotel, washed the dust from his hands, and slept soundly on four-hundred-thread-count sheets.

The silver pickup with its smooth gray trailer cut a meandering path through California into Nevada.

Ron's thirty-fifth and thirty-sixth witches were a local journalist and a county commissioner. The county commissioner stood and watched, white-faced and openmouthed, as the thirty-fifth witch burned at the center of a circle of Ron's people, in a wooded and hidden lot not far from the municipal complex. Unlike the journalist, who favored sweatshirts and jeans with pockets deep enough for notebooks and tape recorders, and who went yelling into the portable crematorium, the commissioner had blond hair ironed flat and wore nude lipstick, a pencil skirt, and black patent leather pumps with three-inch heels. She said very little.

"You're not like her at all, are you?" Ron said.

The county commissioner shook her head dumbly. The propane flames hissed.

"Frankly, you're not like any other witch I've met. You respect societal niceties. You're aware of the importance of appearances. You have, in short, a great deal of potential," Ron said. "It would be a waste to send that up in smoke."

She was nodding now. Her necklace of brass plaques shook.

"Perhaps you could demonstrate a change in loyalties." Ron consulted the temperature gauge: The interior was still two hundred degrees below optimal. "Show that you regret your past ways and have reformed. You'd need to apologize publicly . . ."

Her nodding intensified.

"And to show you mean business, you'll introduce an ordinance prohibiting witches. No, an ordinance providing for the hygienic and appropriate disposal of those identified as witches. If you *have* a witch, let her be disposed of *properly*. You do have the authority to issue ordinances, don't you?"

A fraction of a second's hesitation before the nodding resumed. Ron sighed.

"Even if you can only draft them and bring them before the board of commissioners for a vote, that's useful. You'll find a way to influence them, I'm sure."

He glanced at the crematorium. It had reached its peak temperature.

"Though I've been wrong before. I *thought* I'd found a sympathetic journalist."

The county commissioner flinched. Ron beckoned over one of his faithful.

"Daniel, Ms. Guzman. You'll help her draft her ordinance, won't you?"

"Pleased to meet you," Daniel said with his most disarming smile, as if he had not been one of the six purposefully nondescript people who had surrounded the county commissioner as she walked out of her office. He stuck out his hand.

Ron observed the long moment in which the county commissioner resembled nothing so much as a wild horse run to lathered exhaustion, eyes rolling at the noose, before she bit her tongue and shook Daniel's offered hand.

"I'm so glad we could reach an understanding," Ron said. "A word to the wise, by the way—and I'm speaking from experience here. You'll find that your colleagues in the police department across the way won't believe you, can't be bothered to investigate if they do in any way believe you, will tell you simply to quit the internet if that's where people

started **threat**ening you, and will prove suspiciously deaf to your en-
treaties. Above all—and please understand that I am trying to be kind
here, and spare you wasted effort and crushing disappointment—you
must not underestimate how many strangers can be persuaded to hate
you, and how many friends will say nothing while you burn. It is so much
easier to mobilize outrage against a single woman than, well, anything
or anyone else."

"Please," the county commissioner said, finally provoked into
speech. "It may be a local office, but I *am* a politician."

"And a witch," Ron said.

"By your definition."

"By my definition. Which is the only one that matters."

He bowed to her. Daniel, taking the hint, produced legal pad and
fountain pen.

The ordinance that County Commissioner Linda Guzman proposed became
the model for similar ordinances in fifteen counties across Nevada and
neighboring states, which led to far more business than Ron Morgan
could manage on his own. He purchased more buses, built more portable crematoria, split his followers into teams, and recruited hundreds
more.

As a token of thanks, he sent Linda Guzman a handsome reliquary
of repoussé silver set with garnets and windows of rock crystal, con-
taining a handful of fragments from the thirty-fifth witch, along with
gently worded instructions to display it upon her desk.

"What the fuck is a witch?" the eighty-third witch asked as she was tossed
into the crematorium, hands zip-tied behind her, while her whole
school watched. Led by one of her rejected suitors, they had voted her
Most Likely to Be a Witch. One of the recently issued local ordinances
specified the consequences.

Ron's helpers shouted over each other.

"A worker of iniquity!"

"A bleeding horror!"

"Malice incarnate!"

"A sulfurous breath of hell!"

Prodded, her classmates and teachers volunteered their own versions.

"Someone disloyal, without school spirit."

"A whore!" the spurned boy howled.

"A prude."

"A slut."

The girl looked more bewildered than terrified. Ron bent over her and whispered, "Anyone I say is a witch, is a witch."

She stared at him. "That's it? That's all it—"

The lid closed on her words.

Tracy touched Ron's shoulder while the student burned. "They're getting younger," she said, her forehead creased. "I thought most witches were older women. I had no problem with purifying the world of unrepentant evil, but that girl—she was only seventeen."

"Witches are pernicious," Ron said. "They know how innocent our children are. How precious and pure. Of course they'd corrupt them. We just have to move faster."

"Of course, of course," Tracy said, the lines on her forehead unchanging, and Ron looked at her sharply and thought, *Her then*, and *It happens*, and *When?*

By the time Tracy herself was a heap of black cinders, two hoop earrings, and a few rings and fillings, hardly worth forty dollars in total, the Kennewis pawnbroker said, frowning as he slid two twenties under the bulletproof barrier, all of Ron's thirty-eight new permanent crematoria were open and doing brisk business. The fees his various facilities charged their municipalities more than covered fuel and payroll, given that only his ten most valuable followers received any wages. The primary motivation for participating in his movement, Ron often said, was the satisfaction of serving a righteous cause; he would not cheapen their motives with something so debased as cash. Righteousness, moreover, cost less than propane.

It burned for longer, too. As soon as the last witch cooled and was sifted, before the smell of burnt hair had dissipated, each community immediately found the next one. Had Ron's various crematoria been open pyres, one would be able to fly coast to coast by the light of the witchfires constantly burning.

If Ron had retained any illusions about inherent human decency, the behavior of the friends, colleagues, and neighbors of the accused would have stripped them away. They were silent. They averted their gazes. One or two picked up the chanted insults. It was inconvenient, even dangerous, to be known as a witch's associate. Any minute, the pointing fingers might swing toward *them*.

A few, professing idealism, though their trembling suggested self-preservation, pledged themselves to Ron's group and in return received various online logins and a brief lecture on the qualities of a witch.

"Few powerful friends," Daniel recited, ticking off the points on his fingers. "Not well known and liked in their community. Significant differences of demographics or lifestyle or politics from the local majority. Little family support in the area. Precarious employment. Warts, moles, or birthmarks. A predilection for cats and toads. Accusations of outrageous behavior by past romantic partners. Gossip and nebulous mutterings from colleagues. Unusual talents or extraordinary accomplishments. Often of mature or advanced age, though we're sadly seeing very young ones these days. Above all, some tremendous, suspicious *difference*."

"Given enough time and experience," Ron said, "you'll know it when you see it."

Sooner or later, they learned.

After a town had been emptied of its witches, there was a dead echo to it. One could walk and walk and not find a single breath of colorful life captured in a bottle or on a canvas or on the brick side of a building, and not hear a single burst of delighted laughter, and only encounter the gray squirm of rats vanishing into pipes and the thin film of ash clinging to storefront windows and the skin of those remaining. The wind stank of charred meat and carried, more faintly, the thin metallic tang of suspicion. The few visitors that stepped off plane or train or out of a car felt a shadow pass over them, and they tugged down hat brims and shrugged up the collars of their coats, keeping their eyes on the pavement so as not to attract attention.

North Coll, in Pennsylvania, had become that kind of town. One of Ron Morgan's more successful fixed operations, the North Coll witch crematorium had produced, in the three years since it opened, enough bone shards and teeth to send any archaeologist into paroxysms of joy. The dusty glass jars that lined the facility's walls evoked, in Ron, a deep and quiet pleasure.

He had come to North Coll because his employees had requested help. There was a rumor of one last witch in North Coll, a witch who kept to herself and did not flaunt her opinions or publish her business and was thus difficult to winkle out and burn.

"But I know she is one," Victor Holbrook told him. Victor had signed up to work shifts at the crematorium after watching one of his cousins go up in smoke, but he had not met Ron before, and was quivering with his sudden proximity to power. "I'm sure of it. I just can't prove it—"

"Do you have her address?"

"I know the neighborhood she lives in."

"But not her address."

"We're not sure which person it is, which house—"

"Everybody," Ron said, "has a friend, or acquaintance, or neighbor, who will sell her out. Who has been dying to throw her on a pyre. Everybody. Most have at least two."

"I'm sure you're right," Victor said. "But we may have burned all of them."

"Really." Ron scratched his ear, which had grown dry and scaly in recent days. "Huh. I can't fault enthusiasm, even if it wasn't very forward-thinking of you. Show me the neighborhood."

The neighborhood Victor brought him to, like many neighborhoods in North Coll, consisted of rows of dandelion lawns of varying tidiness, boxy white shotgun houses, and peeled-paint porches. No one sat on the porches these days. Some of the houses had the sightless haunted air of a home left vacant.

It didn't take long. Ron walked up and down three blocks before he spotted it: a house much like the others, but with papered-over windows, a flourishing garden with sunflowers as tall as men, and a yard full of milkweed horns, dock, sorrel, and huckleberries.

"Have them bring the portable here," he told Victor. "1485 Balsam Lane."

Victor pressed his cell phone to his ear. Ron went up the steps and rapped on the door.

The woman who answered was not the witch; he could tell that immediately. She wore a blue cotton shirt and a thin gold wedding band, and had a face creased with laughter. She adjusted her cat's-eye glasses to see him better. "Hello," she said. "Who are you?"

"Who's that, Mira?" a woman called out from farther in the house.

"Ron Morgan," he told her. "I was actually hoping to meet your . . . roommate?"

"Wife," Mira said, cooling considerably.

"Can I come in?" he said.

"Who is it?" they heard again, and then the witch tromped across the kitchen to the door. Her brown curls were streaked with white, her shirt was streaked with paint, her feet were bare, and her green eyes saw through Ron, pierced clear through him, as though she'd thrown a knife.

He tried to smile. "My name—"

"I told you not to open the door to strangers," she said to Mira.

"But he's dressed nice, and he was polite—"

Ron wedged his steel-toed boot in the door before either of them could bang it shut. He heard the pickup truck roll up and park at the curb.

"Ron," he said again, offering his hand to the witch. "And you—"

"Get out," she said.

"Unfortunately," Ron said, "that's not going to happen."

He wrapped his hands around the witch's wrists, tight as a python.

"Let go of her!" Mira said.

He had pulled the witch halfway down the steps before she saw the portable crematorium and dug in her heels. Around them, curtains twitched in the windows of the houses that were still occupied, though none of the neighbors stepped outside.

Ron batted aside the broom handle that Mira jabbed at him, and then his followers were swarming up the steps, tearing the broom out of Mira's grasp and overwhelming the witch.

". . . false prophets," the witch gasped as they carried her down the steps and across the front yard. "Inwardly they are ravening wolves . . ."

Ron's smile stretched until all his teeth showed. "The Bible?" he said. "Look around you—how many people here, do you think, worship a God besides themselves?"

"Take your hands off my wife!" Mira said, flinging herself forward. She wrapped her arms around the witch, and they both collided with the side of the crematorium. That *was* a problem, because the portable was only large enough to hold one body at a time.

It was, however, solvable.

Ron twisted a knob. Though the lid was open, the jets spouted blue and yellow, a minor defect he had never fixed because he had always held that accidents were not tragedies but the revelation of submerged guilt in whoever had been burned. The witch's hair caught fire; her arm was in the path of the jets. She screamed and jerked away.

Weeping, Mira pushed her wife to the ground and smothered the flames with her clothes and body.

"Leave her alone," Mira said. "She hasn't done anything!"

"And because of us," Victor said brightly, "she won't."

"It's for the good of the world," Ron said.

"You're dogs, all of you," the witch said, spitting the words out in a froth of fear and pain. "Serpents. Vermin. Vipers. Beasts."

A forest of hands reached for her, to drag her out of her wife's arms and into the crematorium. The witch bared her teeth at them. Then her eyes went wide.

For the faces of Ron and his followers were lengthening, lips loosening and slavering, eyes losing their whites. They hunched over, hands groping for the earth. Scales formed out of skin. Fingers fused into hooves.

"You're goats, crows, cockroaches. Leeches, lizards, rats." She was counting them now, naming what she saw. "You're wolves. You're mosquitoes. You're lice."

"Wolves," Mira muttered, casting about for her broom. "Great."

"You're centipedes, vultures, weasels, bears."

One or two of the canids snarled at the women, but the rest, shrinking or growing, curling into themselves, becoming crooked and furred and clawed, lost interest in the pair. They began snapping and pecking and tearing at each other, the large ones crunching up the small. The rattlesnake that Ron Morgan had become hissed and struck and sank its curved fangs into the leg of the bear that once had been Victor, which promptly trod on the snake's tail and crushed its rattle.

Mira helped her wife to her feet. They retreated into the house and bolted the door behind them.

"I did read that the black bears around here were thinning out," the witch said, glancing out, her face pale with pain.

"I'll call an ambulance," Mira said, and did, and thought a minute. "Also Animal Control."

Then she filled a plastic bag with ice and wrapped it in a towel for her wife's blistered arm.

They waited in the kitchen for the ambulance.

"So you *are* a witch?" Mira said.

"No."

"Because it seems like you could have mentioned it a little sooner."

"I'm not a witch," the witch said through her teeth. "I don't know why they changed."

"The way I see it," Mira said, "some folks choose to become beasts. Choice by choice, day by day. They chase greed, cruelty, and fear, and call it justice, kindness, righteousness. When you twist words to breaking, you lose human language. Harm enough people, you lose humanity itself. When they heard you name them for what they were, they could see it, too." She shrugged. "Though maybe they had some help with that."

Her wife thought about this. Sirens wailed in the distance, closer every minute. "So you're saying *you*—"

Then red lights flashed in the street, and Mira had to swing her broom and shout at the bear so the EMTs could leave the ambulance, and it was quite some time before her wife recollected the question.

THE ACADEMY OF ORACULAR MAGIC

Miyuki Jane Pinckard

In the final year of the Great Famine, on the night of the autumn equinox when the world shuts the door to summer, my mother came home to find the most beautiful woman she'd ever seen at her threshold.

"And so," she would tell me, "that's how I came to entertain a fox for supper."

It was her favorite story.

"But how did you know she was a fox?" I asked her. I was four, I think, but I already knew that only the truly wise could see through the cunning animal's disguise. My mother was the shaman of the village, and the wisest person I knew.

"I saw her snowy white tail," she said. "Who's telling this story? Finish your dinner."

The fox was the messenger of a great spirit, Yonadari. She said to my mother: "Tomorrow, the drought will end and the rains will come. Rice will be planted again in spring. And you will have a daughter born on Midsummer Day, as beautiful as the moon, who will become the most powerful sorceress in the Dragon Isles.

"And then," my mother sighed, "you arrived."

I was born on the right day, that much is true: on the longest day of the year, at twilight, that liminal time when the window between waking and dreaming is open, when the moon shares the sky with the sun. I was by all accounts a pretty baby, with a thick black patch of hair and wide, curious eyes. Ironically (from my mother's perspective) I also had a penis. All the same I was her heir, her pearl, and she named me Shinju.

From the time I could walk my mother included me in the shaman's trade. I assisted her through exorcisms, festival rituals, prayers for good fortune, illnesses. She would perform the rite and then ask me, "Did you see? Do you understand?"

I suspect she was watching me for signs: Would I be her daughter, her heir? Or simply her child?

I was a quick student, I can say without arrogance; I learned the chants and the movements perfectly. But no spirits answered when I called. No ghosts responded to my exorcisms. There was no hint of my mother's power in me, and after year after year of nothing, I started to believe I'd failed her, and that the fox's words had been a mistake.

But I did not let that thought deter me.

One warm evening, a month before my thirteenth birthday, I walked to the shrine at the top of the hill. The great river Ura flowed in a waterfall down the mountain, and if I followed it downstream, I'd arrive at Heikyo, the Tranquil City, the source of everything that mattered. All the best scholars, the best musicians were there. The best mages, too.

The next morning, I told my mother that I wanted to attend the Academy of Oracular Magic. It was then and is still the most prestigious institution of its kind. For twenty generations the ministers of the Imperial Bureau of Divination have been selected exclusively from the graduates of the Academy.

"If I'm to be the best," I said, "I must measure myself against the best."

My mother made a face as if she were spitting. "The city-bred mages know nothing. They practice their foreign magic, their divinations with painted sticks and books and astrology charts. You can't learn magic from books. Real magic flows through the body itself, a gift from the gods!" She flung her arms out wide. "Listen. Real magic rides on the wind, in the air. It stirs the leaves in the trees and pushes grass from the dirt beneath. Real magic speaks, and we listen; and we shape it by the telling."

"I can't do what you do," I said.

She chewed her mugwort leaf in silence, watching me.

"Mother, I have only ambition to offer you, only the promise of the fox's prophecy. Can I become the greatest sorceress in the Dragon Isles while trapped in a dusty village on the ridge of a bleak mountain?"

She said, "Only highborn Keishi clans are allowed to send their children to the school."

"Let me tell you a story," I said with a smile. "One day I will disguise myself, like a fox, and walk into the Academy and become the best student they ever had."

On Midsummer Day, at noon, I walked up to the gates of the Academy of Oracular Magic in the Tranquil City. The guardian dragon statue that wound its body over the roof glared at me as I passed under it. The dragon is a creature of opposing elements: yin and yang, water and fire. Its ferocious eye interrogated me.

"You there, in the stolen robes," it said. "You think you belong here?"

I hoped it could not see how I trembled behind my veil, snatched off a noble's baggage cart. "You should show me more respect," I said. "You're talking to the girl who'll become the most powerful sorceress in the Dragon Isles."

The dragon only laughed.

I doubt the Grand Master believed I was a Keishi daughter fallen on hard times, but she let me in anyway. As a student escorted me to the dormitory, I overheard the Grand Master speaking with her steward in the corridor: "She's a country bumpkin. Her accent! And did you see those eyebrows!"

"Like monstrous caterpillars," said the steward. "I'll consult the genealogy tables at the Imperial Registry."

"Don't bother. I'd bet my right eye you won't find a trace of her family there. All the same, she traveled quite a long way to be here. That says something."

Desperation?

Or ambition.

The Grand Master was scandalized when she discovered I could not read Shiran, the language of scholars. She assigned me as a tutor a girl called Harui.

I did not seek to make any friends at the Academy, because the other students intimidated me, and I was angry at myself for feeling so. But Harui seemed inclined to mix her mockery with appreciation, even affection. She was a true-born Keishi—graceful, elegant, quick-witted. I found out later she was of a family, the Furuda clan, that had been ruling the Dragon Isles in all but name for two centuries. Her ancestors were illustrious and proud and there were stories whispered of their ruthlessness in pursuit of power.

She was a harsh teacher. She laughed at my mistakes and chided me that children of five wrote with a neater hand than I. But she also made me feel like the only person in the world when we were together, and I found that over the course of her tutelage I longed for her respect, even admiration. When she finally smiled faintly at my copy of the famous poem by Bai-Li, and pronounced it not bad, I was transported by pride and relief.

Afterward the servants came to collect our practice sheets to be used as fire starters. I pretended to drop my ink brush so I could slip my hand over one of her papers and slide it into my sleeve. In private I marveled at her beautiful hand. Her calligraphy was a painting, expressive and poignant. I folded the paper and kept it next to my chest, tucked into the folds of my robe.

A month or so after I'd arrived, we had a lesson about ghosts.

Lingering ghosts were a common problem in the village where I'd grown up, because of the famine. I'd assisted my mother at many exorcisms. Ghosts are restless when they've died without peace.

The instructor asked, "What is the technique for banishing a ghost back beyond the Bridge of Dreams?"

I did not know enough to hide my knowledge, so I said, "You must listen to its story. Understand what it needs and try to help if you can."

There was silence in the room, so I went on: "It's dangerous, of course. Your own spirit must be strong enough to stand up to the ghost, in case it tries to possess you. A strong shaman can send a ghost back over the Bridge of Dreams to the spirit realm, where it belongs, by telling it a powerful story."

The instructor's mouth opened and closed and her eyebrows went up and down. Faint laughter chimed from somewhere in the room.

"Never, never speak to ghosts," said the instructor, when she could talk. "It is forbidden. Dangerous. Apostasy." (At the time, I didn't know this word.)

"We are not witches," she scolded. "We are not country shamans, burning herbs and shaking sticks. We are training to be the greatest cultivators of magic in the Dragon Isles, and we use rationally derived techniques that have been tested by our predecessors for a thousand years." She took a deep breath. "Such arts as you describe are forbidden."

I could tell my cheeks were flaming, bright as poppies.

"The proper technique," she continued, calmly slipping back into her lecture, "is to write the protection mantra on a piece of pure white paper as a talisman. Hold the paper in front of you and focus on it. Chant the mantra until the ghost disappears. Then use the water divination technique to ensure that the ghost has departed this realm."

I learned not to answer questions in class after that and I was ashamed I hadn't known better.

Harui came up to me after the lesson, her eyes laughing, but not in a way that made me feel diminished. "You really put that teacher in her place," she said. "No one here can do *real* magic, not like the kind you're talking about. Did you know there's a ghost here in the Academy? Or that's the rumor, anyway. Have you seen it?"

"No," I lied. In fact, I had noticed it, but it was a bitter spirit, too powerful for me, and I knew to leave it alone. It was an ancient ghost that seemed to linger around the pond in the south courtyard. I avoided it, assuming it wasn't a danger to anyone. I was wrong about that, as it turned out. But in that moment, all my attention was on Harui.

Her eyes were bright with curiosity. "Where did you learn about ghosts, Shinju? Where's your clan from?"

"The mountains," I replied vaguely. "I've got to get ready for supper."

Harui fell into step beside me as we walked back to the student quarters. Behind us I heard someone say in a loud whisper, "Should *he* really be in the *girls'* dormitory?" followed by scattered snickers.

Harui turned, her head lifted, her lips curved in a proud smile. "Kazemi, I thought I recognized your nasally voice. Didn't I hear the Grand Master say you're failing your classes? Probably because you're spending so much time thinking about someone else's business instead of minding your own. Come on, Shinju."

Harui threaded her arm through mine and we strolled on. Her hair smelled like peonies.

In my first year at the Academy, I learned to miss my home village, where I was simply Shinju, accepted as my mother's daughter. Children in the village dressed alike, played together, were praised and scolded together, regardless of whether we were boys or girls or neither. The Academy had layers of expectations I didn't understand: how to walk, talk, dress, smile, drink tea—so many details were endlessly scrutinized.

My mother's way remained closed to me, so I explored other avenues of accessing power. The Academy taught that power was born of ritual, in writing and speech, in the chanting of mantras, in the sacred incense used in the meditation chamber, in the rune-covered stones and star charts used for divination. I read everything I could. I methodically explored the vast library, starting at the southwest corner and working my way across the shelves.

I became known as "the ghost of the library" because I hardly ever left it. Sometimes Harui came in with her friends, and I could feel her gazing at me, curiously. I no longer needed her help but I missed our practice sessions and I wondered if she did, too.

One evening, in the second winter following my arrival, Harui did not come to supper. I overheard that she was ill, and rested in seclusion in the infirmary.

The steward wouldn't let me in, no matter how much I pleaded. "We fear contagion," she said. "Not even her family is allowed."

That night, I escaped the dormitory and went to one of the small courtyards in the Academy complex. I stood by the small pond there, underneath the plum trees slumbering in the cold.

I took out Harui's poetry practice sheet and kissed it. On the back, I wrote a prayer of protection and healing. Then I folded up the paper while chanting the mantra quietly under my breath and released it into the pond.

"Yonadari, listen to me," I said. "You sent your fox-messenger to my mother for a reason. I am that reason. Hear me, and answer. I am your anointed. I need your help."

There was no answer.

I waited in the shadows outside the infirmary until the acolyte on duty shuffled off toward the privy, and then I slipped inside.

Harui lay in her bed behind a screen, in a room filled with the scent of sacred incense. Her breath came in rattling gasps, like a fish flopping on the riverbank, and her skin was gray. This was no illness. I recognized the signs: She was possessed.

There was no time to fetch a shaman or a medium. In a panic, I did what my mother always did: addressed the ghost directly.

"I'm here," I said. "I'm listening. I call you with respect to tell me your story."

There was no answer, and Harui's condition was unchanged. I put one hand on her heaving chest and one on her damp forehead and closed my eyes. I said, "Yonadari, help me reach this ghost. Ghost, I'm listening. Tell me what anchors you to the world of the living where you do not belong."

There was nothing. Tears flowed down my chin. Harui could be lost forever, her bright eyes dulled, her mischievous laughter silenced, her fearlessness snuffed out.

Real magic flows from the body itself, my mother always said. I took a deep breath. I raised my voice and unleashed my anger and fear into the room: "Ghost, why have you invaded the soul of this innocent girl?"

Innocent?

The voice was so full of venom that I almost fell backward.

There is nothing innocent in this daughter of the Furuda clan. She deserves to suffer as I have suffered.

"Don't be afraid," my mother had always said. "Ghosts may be vengeful or angry but most of all, they long to be at peace and leave the human world."

I tried to remember that as I wrestled my fear under control.

"Ghost, tell me what has been done to you. I'll listen to your suffering."

Furuda killed my son, as surely as if she'd slit his throat.

"No. Harui did not do that."

Her mother did. It's only right I take the daughter's life in payment for my son's.

"Ghost, I doubt even her mother is responsible, for I believe you've been dead for generations. You are an ancient spirit. Still, I'm sorry for what happened to your son."

The ghost did not reply, but Harui convulsed under my hands.

"Stop," I said. "Stop, ghost. This descendant of your enemy means you no harm. Vengeance is not justice, and taking her life will give you no peace."

She must die, the ghost said. *I demand it. I have waited for this chance, to take from the Furuda clan what they took from me.*

"Ghost, listen to me. The longer you stay here, trapped on the human plane, the more you'll forget who you were and who your son was and how much you love your son. So let this go, and mourn, and be at peace."

You know nothing. You are a child. Harui's body jerked so hard I thought her limbs would crack.

In desperation, I did the only thing I could think of—something that my mother would have said was foolhardy, something that was certainly forbidden at the Academy.

"Take me," I said. "I offer myself as a vessel for you, that you may experience life once again, in recompense for the life you lost."

Just then, someone entered the room behind me: "What's happening here? What are you doing?"

I ignored it. "Hurry, ghost. I am ready to accept you." I arranged myself in the pose for meditation and closed my eyes. "I invite you in."

A voice that sounded far away shrieked. Footsteps rang in the corridor. I focused on myself, on keeping my soul open to the ghost. I had no idea if this would work, or if the ghost would even take my offer.

Suddenly it felt as though my entire body had been dropped into cold water, except I wasn't wet. The ghost's soul crawled into my body, into my chest and belly. I shook with the shock of it. The ghost was made powerful by her rage and grief. She had been brooding for years, decades, probably, waiting for her chance.

She opened my mouth and spoke in her own voice: Wake up. Wake up, girl.

Harui opened her eyes. I was aware of the presence sharing my mind and my eyes, staring down at her. My heart, normally full of affection for her, crackled as if it had been set on fire.

The borrowed voice said, "The Furuda clan owes me a blood debt."

"Who are you?" said Harui. Her voice was a faint rasp.

"I am Kitagao, mother of the boy killed through treachery in the service of your clan."

By now the Grand Master and the Master of Healers and the steward were at the door. The steward tried to reach for me but the ghost inside shot out her hand and struck. A flash of light knocked the steward back against the wall. The Grand Master pulled out a scroll and a brush and began to write. Her mouth moved as if she were chanting but I heard nothing, nothing but furious rushing in my ears like a waterfall.

The ghost inside me reached out and grabbed Harui's shoulders. I fought back, gentling the touch. Harui trembled, but she was, after all, a Furuda. She tilted her head up to look at me and I knew she was not looking at me, but at the presence inside me.

Harui said, "Your name is unfamiliar to me. If your son was killed unjustly, on behalf of my mother and my mother's mother and all my ancestors, I apologize to you and pledge recompense. We will light incense for you and say prayers, every year, as long as my clan lives."

The fury stoked hotter inside me and I fought it down.

"You don't even know what happened. That's how much my son meant to you."

My hands reached for Harui's throat. I couldn't stop them.

People around me were shouting. Harui looked at me calmly. She said, "Shinju. I believe in you."

I snatched my hands back and held them tight against my body.

I struggled to find my own voice. "Kitagao, you have your answer. The Furuda will remember, and pay their respects. You will leave now and go across the Bridge to the land of the dead."

Kitagao was growing tired, but so was I. If she didn't leave soon, I wasn't sure if I would have the strength to expel her.

"I see this Furuda child through your eyes," she said at last. "You love her."

Harui's eyes flicked at mine.

432

"Let me tell you a story," I said. "You will pass now over the Bridge of Dreams. You will go with peace in your heart."

"And if I refuse?"

"I am Yonadari's anointed, and I will destroy you."

The ghost flared inside me again, pressing against my bones as if testing my strength. Sweat dripped from my forehead but I held still.

The ghost sighed. "I will leave, then. Say your prayers for me, children."

I began to chant the mantra for protection and peace. In a whisper, Harui's voice joined mine. My words grew stronger and stronger with each repetition until finally, I felt in command of my entire body again. Whole.

I opened my eyes. Harui watched me intently. Behind her stood the Grand Master and the steward, their faces rigid.

The Grand Master said, "You have violated our most important code. The punishment for this is expulsion."

I bowed to the head of the school. "I understand."

Harui said, "I object! She saved my life."

"Shush, Harui. This is not a matter for children to decide." The Grand Master frowned at me. "You were so ambitious, Shinju. So eager. You threw away all your hard work in one night."

Harui kept her eyes on me as the steward and the Master of Healers fussed over her. I smiled at her, promising with my eyes what I didn't want to say in front of everyone else. Her answering smile, and her nod, assured me she understood.

"I'll leave right away," I said.

By the time I'd gathered my few possessions, dawn streaked the sky. I passed under the dragon's glare. As the sun's light hit its crown, I thought I saw a white fox perched there, laughing, her tail waving in the breeze.

The dragon said, "You came here to become the most powerful sorceress in the Dragon Isles. And now you leave in disgrace."

I laughed. "Disgrace, is that what you think?"

"What else do you call it?"

"I'll tell you when I return," I said. "I'll tell you when the Empress calls upon me to serve her, me, a mountain-bred girl of no wealth and no name. I'll tell you when Furuda—no, Harui—the woman I love, is the Chancellor and invites me to her villa for tea and moon-viewing before we retire to her chamber. I'll tell you when I bring real magic out of the mountains into the Academy, into the halls of power, straight to the heart of the Empire."

The dragon grinned. "You have learned the truth of oracular magic, Shinju. You have learned to shape your own destiny with words of prophecy. Until we meet again."

I walked upriver toward the mountain, toward home and my mother. She would want to hear what had happened.

THE COST OF DOING BUSINESS

Emily Y. Teng

Annie sliced her finger off working the pendulum blades, which was really no one's fault but her own. She wasn't paying attention, and next thing you know, there was a scream and blood all over the factory floor. Went straight through her ring finger, right where a wedding ring would go.

It's bad enough that she needs professional attention, but when I tell her I'm taking her to get it seen to, she balks. She tries to insist she's fine, holding the dripping stump of her finger. I wrap the severed digit in a hankie and near drag her to the factory witch.

The factory witch's office is a tiny closet off the break room crammed with pots and potions and bottles and bundles of dried frogs and old bones hanging from the ceiling. A carved idol head leers at us from the back wall. Barely any room for the workbench where she mixes up all her brews and keeps an efficiency-sized cauldron bubbling on a Bunsen burner. A real witch's hovel. There's a sign hanging on the door that changes what it says each time you look. Usually it's something cute and rhyming about kittens or small dogs, but right now reads: EYE OF NEWT, WING OF BAT, DON'T STICK YOUR HAND IN WHEN THE BLADES ARE STILL MOVING, YOU MORON.

Oh, yeah, she knows we're coming.

When Annie opens the door, a bat swoops down from out of nowhere straight for her face. She shrieks. The bat swerves a bare inch from her nose and circles the lone light bulb overhead, chattering with laughter.

"Vlad," the witch admonishes. "How many times have I told you not to do that?" But she sounds more amused than angry.

The witch has Annie sit on a stool in the tiny bit of clear floor space she's got while I hover outside the open door. She tsks, examining the finger. "Nice clean cut. Well, it would be, wouldn't it? Anyways, it'll attach back just fine."

She washes the cut out with stinking liquid number one and swishes the finger around in stinking liquid number two. She uses thick black thread on a sliver of a needle to sew it back in place. Then she smears the whole thing with the final, smelliest concoction of all, and covers it all with gauze. She's brisk and efficient. She's also muttering the whole time as she works, but just loud enough that I can tell it's not a spell, just her cussing a blue streak under her breath.

"Need a note for worker's comp?" She fills out an incident sheet, consulting a thick, color-coded binder that hangs from a hook on the wall. Standard recompense for dismemberment of a digit (straight blade, second knuckle) is three work shifts. Annie signs, pricking her thumb to dab some blood on the signature line. The witch tears off the flimsy and hands it over, adding, "Next time you cut a finger off, see if you can do a thumb. I've always got good use for a fresh thumb or two."

She's joking, I'm fairly sure, but that doesn't stop Annie going pale and sprinting for the break room door.

The witch winks at me, and shuts her door in my face.

The boss is in today.

The boss doesn't come to the factory often, once in a blood moon, and whenever he does it means there's hellfire and reorgs coming down the line. Rumors swirl of a satellite campus being opened—the demand for the boss's repertoire of industrial torture has never been higher. The witch is up there with him in his plush office digs, and from the way little jags of lightning splash periodically against the glass, she's not happy about it.

When they finally emerge, there are thunderclouds in her face, and her hair frizzing up beneath her regulation hard hat. The boss clears his throat. He's got a booming voice made for proclaiming apocalypses. Hardly needs to project at all.

"It has come to my attention that the number of workplace-related incidents has reached unacceptable levels. So many worker's compensation reports have been filed that questions are being asked. Is it negligence or is it malice?" He laughs, inviting us to share the absurdity of the speculation. The witch glares murder at the back of his head.

"A government inspector will be investigating these incidents. Any incident over the last six months that required more than a half day's equivalent of recompense"—the word curdles on his tongue—"will be subject to review. I expect everyone's full cooperation." No one misses the pointed look he sends the witch's way. The witch least of all, if the way she brushes a lock of hair out of her face using her middle finger is any indication.

"Let's keep up the good work, girls."

He bows to us like we're queens of hell, then snaps his fingers and is gone in a sulfurous puff of smoke.

The witch spends the rest of the day stomping around the factory floor, making an ostentatious show of burning bundles of sage and dried wort, to cleanse the place, she says in answer to no one's question. The smell of burnt herbs mixes with the boss's lingering sulfur aura, which refuses to dissipate like it should.

"Government inspector," she mutters loudly enough for everyone to hear. "What does he know? Old man's got a pitchfork up his ass so high he could roast himself on a barbecue. See him down here poking his nose in the cogs?"

By the time the end of shift rolls around, all her temper's settled into a cold, clinging, wonderfully foul aura. Annie's supposed to go get the stitches pulled today, but no amount of threats are enough to make her knock on the witch's door. We wind up in the break room with its first aid kit between us. I snip the threads with tiny scissors, then use tweezers to pluck them out one segment at a time.

"Is it really that bad?" Annie says in a low voice.

"Must be, right? If the bureaucrats are sending someone in."

"But, there hasn't been anything except—" She wiggles her finger right as I'm cutting, and I nearly slice right through it a second time. I hiss and yank on her hand to make her hold still. "Right?"

"Right. Right, but . . ."

The *but* hangs between us. Annie lowers her voice. "We could ask *her*, right? She would know. She's the one who files all the incident reports."

"Who's we? I'm not going to do it. Are you?"

"Like hell," she shoots back, and her mouth twitches into a grin.

I pull out the last of the stitches. The witch did a good job; the only sign Annie's finger was ever sliced off is a ring of pale tissue, so neat and smooth it looks like it was done on purpose. Annie wiggles it experimentally as I return the first aid kit to the drawer below the coffee urn. Which is, as usual, completely empty.

The government inspector is a round little imp with the impressively waxed goatee of someone who thinks he's more important than he actually is. He wears a starched houndstooth suit, tinted glasses, and a small name tag that invites us to call him Asmodeus.

"You will address me as 'government inspector,'" he says.

The witch stands in front of him, arms crossed, glowering like nobody's business. If it were me, I'd be running for the nearest bomb shelter right about now.

"Irina," he greets her. "How's the pact?" And when she snarls, he smiles a daggered smile. His teeth are fine little needles the color of jaundice.

He sets up shop in a disused secretary's office, where he heaps files and folders in big, meaningful piles on the desktop so that everyone can see them clear through the window. Every now and then he summons one of us in for an interview—with no time recompense, of course. The office is on the other side of the factory floor. To get to it, you have to pass the break room, which means passing the witch's office, whose door is now open twenty-four/seven so she can stare at everyone who goes by, while he folds his hands over the top of the desk and smiles. He has a list of our names and works down it in alphabetical order.

Which means Annie is one of the first workers called.

I'm working the turbines that day, so I miss it when he calls her name, but I see it when she exits his office. Brown file folder tucked under one arm and eyes jerking back and forth like they'll wither if they settle. She catches sight of me and mouths *bathroom*. Maybe says it, though with the distance I wouldn't be able to hear it, even without my earmuffs on.

I nod.

We end up crowded into the third stall from the left. The flush mechanism is broken, so no one ever uses it. Perfect place to have a talk, even if it gets cramped with two people in there.

Annie's hand trembles as she lights a cigarette. She's sitting on the tank with her feet on the closed lid while I lean against the door, and it takes her halfway through her smoke before she finally lets out a billowy breath. "Do you remember when I burned my eyes out with the arc welder?"

"What? When—"

"Or when my foot got caught in the mangler?"

"I don't—"

"How about when I broke my right hand with a mallet? Or lost my ears to the pendulums? Or dislocated my shoulder trying to realign the oil vats?"

"Annie, I have no clue what you're talking about. The only thing that's ever happened is you cutting off your finger a few days ago."

She drops the remains of her cigarette in the toilet bowl, then holds out the file folder to me. "Take a look at these."

The incident reports rustle like dry leaves. There are so many of them, and so varied, that all I can think at first is that they're fakes. A whole leg lopped off almost to the hip isn't something that's likely to slip your mind anytime soon. Except that the witch's handwriting is on each and every one, alright, and Annie's blood on the signature line. The injuries go back months, all the way to when Annie started working.

"There's got to be some mistake."

Annie works a second cigarette from the carton. "The government inspector had these all. He had them organized nice and neat in a brown folder with my name on it. He started off asking me about them, but then he was asking about the witch—what was she like? Did I ever see her on the factory floor between shifts? How often did she leave her office, and at what hours?"

"What did you tell him?"

"That I have no fucking clue, of course. But why would he be asking about the witch? And why don't I remember the injuries?" The lighter trembles as she fires up her third cigarette in as many minutes. Workplace regulations forbid any sort of nonindustrial flames on the factory floor, but the bathrooms have always existed in something of a blind spot. "You saw how many boxes he had? All his files and folders?"

"Yeah?"

"How many of those do you think are yours?"

I don't answer.

She finishes her cigarette and climbs down from the tank. As we head back to work, her hand drops down to her right hip—the side she'd lost her leg on, according to the incident reports—and hovers on it like she's massaging a phantom pain.

440

As part of his investigation, twice a week the government inspector emerges from his office to tour the factory floor. In deference to safety protocols, he trades in his glasses for a pair of safety goggles. He wanders around, taking notice of working conditions and workplace hazards and the safety signs taped up on the sides of the cutting machines. He stands up on tiptoe to peer over our shoulders, watching how we operate the pendulum blades and making notes on his clipboard.

The witch never makes an appearance during these inspections. Instead, she shuts her door, the only time it's closed nowadays, and it stays that way until the government inspector has retreated back into his own office. I think she's avoiding him, but Annie points out it could as well be the other way around: that it's the government inspector who's waiting until the witch is out of sight, out of mind, before he emerges to make his rounds. The sign on her door displays nothing now but excerpts from Emily Dickinson about buzzing flies. I find myself missing her kitten couplets whenever I go to the break room to make a new pot of coffee.

And then I hear the government inspector's voice, sliding like an oily film across the hiss of bubbling tar: "Serena Cho."

It takes a relative eternity to reach his office. The door stands open, invitingly. On the desk in front of him is a single plain brown folder, at least half an inch thick with papers. At the sight of it, something in me runs cold.

"Close the door," he says. "Sit."

The only other chair is a cracked plastic one taken from the break room. He waits until I'm seated before opening the folder. He makes a show of looking it over. From this angle, the words are an illegible skein of slants. "Serena Cho, indentured worker at Luciferous Works?"

I nod.

"Length of term?"

"Thirty years."

"And how much time do you have left to go?"

"Nineteen years, seven months, eight days, twelve hours, and thirty-one minutes. Would be twenty-six minutes if I wasn't here talking to you."

He ignores this. "What was your contract for?"

"Does it matter?"

He raises an eyebrow and makes a note in the file. He takes his time forming the letters. Demon talons evolved for teasing guts out of living abdomens and carving runes into flesh, not clutching writing utensils.

After an age he sets his pen down and leans forward so he can peer over the tops of his glasses at me. He's sitting taller than I am, probably with a couple books stacked under him, but knowing that doesn't make it any less effective. Out of the corner of my eye I can see his tail, curled around a desk leg. "I have here copies of incident reports filed for injuries that you've sustained since you began working here. I'd like you to have a look through them and see if anything stands out to you. Take all the time you need," he adds with a flicker of malice, sliding the folder across to me.

Some of the reports are so old that the ink has faded, and the words blur together in my sight. I page through the whole mass, then drop it all back on the desk. "Okay. And?"

"Did you not read them?"

"I don't need to."

"Then you remember all of these incidents? All those injuries taking place?"

"Maybe."

"You're being very blasé about this whole thing."

"We handle big knives and heavy implements on a daily basis. Accidents are bound to happen."

"Accidents such as"—he extracts a sheet at random—"your right foot getting trapped in a mechanism whose fail-safe failed to engage properly, that resulted in your foot being pulverized?"

"It's the boss's factory. You have any issues of equipment malfunctions, take them up with him."

The sheet flutters down into the folder again. "Tell me about Irina."

"Who?" Then I remember: That's the witch's name. "What about her?"

"Humor me." He smiles, utterly humorless.

"She's the factory witch, that's all. She wards the place against industrial sabotage and treats us whenever we get hurt."

"And she's on friendly terms with the workers?"

"She's not on friendly terms with anyone."

"What about the boss? He's the one she made a pact with."

"If that's what you consider a basis for friendship, I feel sorry for you."

"How often does she tour the factory floor?"

"Once, twice a week maybe."

"And what does she do then?"

"Her job, I assume. Why don't you ask her yourself?"

He stares at me hard. I fix my gaze on his lower jaw. A little glob of wax clings to the underside of his chin, half-melted in the room's heat. "Is there a reason you're being so . . ." He hunts for the word. ". . . recalcitrant?"

"I sold my soul and now I'm working in a torture factory. Forgive me if I'm not inclined to be as cooperative as you'd like."

The glob of wax quivers. He sits back in his chair, folding his clawed fingers together with an air of finality. "Thank you for your time. You may go now."

My hand is on the doorknob when he says, "Oh, I nearly forgot." He holds up the folder. "Take this with you. It's yours, after all."

I stop by the locker room to put my folder in there, then go to the break room. I don't really need coffee, but I do need to let my mind settle. The pot is, predictably, empty. I've just tossed out the old grounds when I hear a low hiss. "Psst!"

The witch. She's peering out through her door, gesturing at me. I glance through the break room window. The government inspector's door is closed; likely he's interrogating someone else. I set the coffeepot down. "Can I help you?"

"What did Ass talk to you about?"

"Ass?"

"Asmodeus. The *government inspector*." She sneers the title.

"I don't know if I should tell you," I say truthfully.

Vlad chitters from somewhere in her office. The witch stares at me hard. The fluorescent overheads catch in her eyes and make the pact-runes of her irises glow infernal. It takes everything I have not to squirm. "He was asking questions about me, wasn't he?"

"No."

"You're a shit liar, you know that, right? Ass. What a grease stain of an entity. I should've known he'd end up a bureaucrat." Her eyes narrow. "What's wrong with your foot?"

I follow her gaze to my right foot. I realize I've been favoring it. I make myself stand normally, and a bolt of pain shoots through my ankle so that I have to bite my lip to keep from yelping. "Nothing."

It doesn't sound convincing, even to me, and from the look on her face she doesn't buy it one whit. Suddenly I want coffee even less than before. I leave the pot—empty—on the counter. Carefully limping, I hobble back out to the factory floor.

The next time the government inspector is out on inspection, the witch is there, too. They run into each other by the cauldrons.

"Ass."

"Irina." His moustache quivers. "What are you doing here?"

She holds up a bucket. Cockerel blood slops over the lip. A hot, coppery tang rises and mixes nauseatingly with the smell of boiling tar. "Refreshing the safety wards on all the equipment. Part of my job duties, you know."

"How fascinating. Might I trouble you to let me watch? I've rarely had the opportunity to observe witchcraft in person. It would be such an education."

"By all means," she says sweetly.

For the rest of the day, he trails her as she hauls the bucket here and there, leaving sticky little puddles on the floor, and paints runes and hex wards over every piece of machinery, right down to the nuts and bolts. In some cases, she has to squeeze herself into vents or fly herself up to reach a hex ward panel, and the government inspector has to scramble to reach it and copy the design down on his notepad before it's sucked in greedily by the metal. By the end of the day the bucket is empty, the notepad is three-quarters full of cramped black notes, and the government inspector is wilting. And they're only a third of the way through.

The witch climbs down from her last target. "There we go. Done for the day. I'll pick up again bright and early tomorrow morning."

"Tomorrow?" he echoes weakly.

"Of course. Can't neglect my duties."

The government inspector visibly sags. His eyes dart toward his office like he wants nothing more than to crawl into his seat and collapse, maybe for a month. But the witch is radiating studious diligence like the reek of myrrh, and so at last he manages, "Then I will see you tomorrow morning," before staggering away, drooping and wobbly.

The witch watches him go with a look of savage satisfaction. She whistles all the way back to her office, empty bucket swinging.

Dark circles ring the government inspector's eyes the next morning like he got punched good and hard. The witch greets him with a welcome so cheery I wouldn't be surprised if birds started trilling. They vanish into the sea of pendulum blades and are out of sight for the rest of the morning.

I'm sorting flails and lashes when a shriek of rending metal tears through the air, louder than even the wind howling through the turbines. And right after it, a scream.

And then silence.

I'm not the only one who leaves her station to see what happened.

There's a crowd milling around by the time I reach the boiling vats, those giant, bubbling cauldrons of blood and tar for those in the seventh circle. A huge rip splits down near the entire length of one of the vats, the metal buckled and crinkled, like it was crumpled by a giant hand. Hot tar dribbles from the edges and spreads across the floor in a boiling lake.

A body is slumped right by the torn vat. Whoever it was, she must've been standing right by it when it broke. She never had a chance. She's so covered in tar that she's little more than a lump, all except for a single, miraculously untouched hand, draped bonelessly on top of the tar like a used rag. A line of pale, new skin circles the finger right where a wedding ring would go.

"Move, for fuck's sake. Move!" The witch. She shoves through the crowd and catches sight of Annie's body. She freezes.

But only for a moment. Then she plunges right in, wading through the tar like she doesn't feel it. She reaches Annie's body and hauls it up. Her face is white, pinched, and angry. Vlad flutters over her head, cheeping in agitation.

"What a pity." The government inspector has followed her. He stands at the edge of the tar. His voice is utterly devoid of pity. "A tragedy, this loss of life, I'm sure."

The witch glares. "What," she snarls, "do you *want*, Ass?"

The government inspector looks up and down at the broken vat. "Such an . . . unforeseen equipment failure, I'm sure. Such a shame. You warded this vat yesterday, did you not? Yes, I recall, you did. I was right there with you. I watched you do it, in fact. Too bad your hexes weren't able to do a thing. Too bad there seemed to be such a glaring weakness to them."

More figures arrive. The official response team, wearing heavy boots and thick gloves. They produce shovels and buckets. A couple of them take Annie's body from the witch, who gives it up without protest.

Production shuts down for the rest of the day. Normally there'd be bitching at the loss of work time, but on this occasion there's not so much as a peep. The more conscientious of us take the time to make sure all equipment is properly secured for the day before clocking off. The break room crowds, then overcrowds, with workers waiting for transport back to the factory dorms. The witch has retreated to her office and shut the door, the sign a mute slate.

I go clear out Annie's locker, taking her cigarettes and mascara. I fill my pockets and am about to shut the door when I notice the brown file folder shoved into the back. Her incident reports.

I almost throw it out right then and there, but something makes me open my own locker and slide it in all the way to the back, right next to my own. Then I head back to the break room. I put the mascara and cigarettes on the counter for anyone who wants them, saving only one pack for myself.

When we arrive the next morning, there's a notice tacked up on the locker room bulletin board informing us that the witch is being removed from her post, effective immediately. No other explanation, not that any's needed. "Serves her right," someone mutters, loud enough to be heard as we all prepare for the shift. A general mutter of agreement rises up. The witch made herself no friends in this place.

But all I can think of is the look on the witch's face when she saw Annie's body. The way she plunged in, hands digging into the boiling tar to pull Annie out. As I reach into my locker to hang up my jacket, my hand brushes against her file folder, cold slivers through my hand like I dipped it into the ice of the ninth circle. I yank it back and ball my fingers up into a fist, fighting back tears against the painful chill.

A bell chimes the five-minute warning. Lockers bang shut, and the room begins to empty. Hastily, I yank on my work vest and rake my hair back into a regulation ponytail.

Industry doesn't stop for anything. Or anyone.

Work is lighter than normal today. The boilers are still being repaired, meaning shift assignments are shuffled around to find an opening for everyone. No one wants to lose out on their scheduled time, and so the overseers have to scramble to find a spot for everyone. But that's their problem, not ours.

The day crawls by. Time expands, each second ballooning out to unbearable lengths until the bell finally clamors the three notes that signal the end of shift. I strip my gloves off and hurry to the bathroom before anyone else has so much as looked up and stretched. There, I shut myself in the third stall, climb on top of the tank, and rest my feet on the seat.

There's rarely a post-shift bathroom rush, but you always get some people who can't hold out for the ten-minute ride back to the dorms. I light up one of Annie's cigarettes and smoke it as the bathroom fills with murmurs of conversations and flushing toilets. I'm halfway done by the time the last person leaves and the doors slam shut with a final sound. I grind out the cigarette, pocket the half-finished stub for later, and exit the bathroom.

The factory is quiet. Machines looming out of the darkness like great shouldered beasts. I thread my way through them to the break room and to the closed door of the witch's office. I put my hand on the knob and am about to turn it when I realize the light is on, shining through the crack. I back up a step. Too late.

The door slams open. "If you've come to fucking *gloat*, you miserable bastard—" Then she sees who it is. "Oh. You. What do you want?"

There are a thousand things I could say. But when I open my mouth, what I blurt out is, "What are you doing here?"

She leans against the door frame, arms crossed over her chest. "Seriously? Do you have to be such a dick about it?"

"If you're here for more sabotage . . ."

She shoves the door open wider. I glimpse half-empty shelves and bare rafters, cardboard boxes stacked by the door crammed full of all her books and bottles and colored candles. "I'm packing, you nitwit."

"Oh," I say.

"Oh," she echoes mockingly. She pushes off the door frame and whirls back into her office. I follow after her, even though she didn't ask me in.

I don't know what I was expecting to find, coming here—proof, perhaps, of her guilt. Malevolence baked into the very stones, the witch's malice steeping her surroundings in a pervasive aura of evil. But all that's here is the feel of an emptied room and a plug-in air freshener trickling out a lemony scent too sunny to be anything but artificial. This room was never a witch's hovel after all, just the skin of one plastered over cinder block. Vlad, huddled on a nest of dried herbs poking out of the top of one of the boxes, sneezes.

The witch starts pulling bottles off the shelves. Her fingers, I notice, are swathed in bandages. Thick ones, so much so that she can barely bend them. "I'd offer you something to drink," she says, "but I already packed away my teapot."

"I'm not touching anything you give me."

"And here I thought you'd never learn. Well, then, tell me why you're here when anyone with a scrap of sense would be avoiding me like the plague."

"I want—" I stop, uncertain.

"Just spit it out already. I haven't got all day."

She glares at me, but her expression looks worn. Tired, even, which is not something I would have ever guessed she was capable of. I'd even pity her if I didn't think she'd curse my eyeballs to jelly for it. "Why were you hexing us?"

"I never hexed a single one of you."

"But—"

"Someone comes in to see me, and three days later their foot gets lopped off? If that was how it went, you wouldn't need Ass to come around poking his oily fingers everywhere. No, it was the coffee. My own special little brew to . . . encourage accidents. That swill you guys drink is so close to battery acid anyways I could've dumped a whole gallon of lye into it and no one would've tasted anything different. It's even got a special drop of something mixed in so you don't remember afterward. Which, you're welcome, by the way."

Vlad chitters scoldingly. The witch sighs. "Oh, what does it matter if I tell her? It's not like he can sack me. Again."

"Do you hate us that much?"

She looks surprised. "Hate? Why would I hate you?"

"Why else do that?"

"To make a point." She looks at me, and something of that familiar acid twists her expression. "Oh, come on. Don't tell me it never crossed your mind, either."

"I literally have no clue what you're talking about."

"Your contracts." She drags out the syllables like I'm an idiot. "Oh, for—okay, look. Everyone who signs a deal with the boss does it for a standard contract, thirty years' time, grievous injury clauses, you know the drill. But it didn't used to be that way. Used to be, when you made a deal with the devil, how well you came out of it depended on you. It was a duel, you see, who could figure out the most loopholes and twists of language and come out over the other. Cleverness *mattered*. But now everything's by the book. It's all standardized. It's all *bureaucracy*. And the big man goes on sitting in his office acting all smug at wringing every last drop out of you, but tell me you don't think it's fucking idiotic. Sure they're milking the contracts for all they're worth now and very efficiently, but all they're doing is following rules. There's no art in it anymore. The devil is a fucking bore. God, hell is *boring* now."

There's a ringing noise in my ears. "So you killed Annie to—what, protest a policy change?"

"I didn't kill her."

"Don't you fucking *dare*."

"You don't get to be a witch by being nice, but that doesn't mean you have to be a total sociopath. Hurt her, yes. But kill? You really think I could do that? No, don't answer that. Answer this instead. Who's the one person who'd be able to override my wards? The one person in this whole factory with more power and authority than me? Maybe some-one who suspects what I've been up to and wants to rig an incident in full view of a pedantic, vindictive little government inspector he called in so he has an ironclad excuse to boot me out on my ass without having to fork over any severance pay?"

"You're lying." The words leave my mouth without thinking. "It's in the contract. He can't break his own contract like that."

"He's the devil. He can do whatever he wants. And if you don't think that, then you deserve everything that landed you here in the first place. In any case, not my problem anymore. Whatever happens next, that's up to you." She finishes taping up the last box, hoists it in her arms, and jerks her head at me. "Move. You're in my way."

After the witch leaves, I remain there, rooted to the spot. I think about Annie. I think about injury, and fault, and obligations. I think about what we owe and what we're owed in turn. I think about con-tracts and the cost of doing business.

Then I leave the husk of what was once the witch's office and walk out onto the factory floor.

The place looks no different without her hex wards, but then again, it wouldn't. That was the whole point of the factory witch: invisible, constant protection of the factory's assets, including the workers who kept the industry of hell grinding away eternally for a boss who only ever cared about us in terms of the hours he could sieve from our lives. And I know that however much we were just instruments in the witch's personal crusade, what she felt toward us was still a thousand times more than what the boss ever felt.

My feet carry me to the nearest machine: a slicer, a beast of blades and biting steel capable of flensing a soul more delicately and thoroughly than a whole battalion of devils could ever manage. Ten years, five months, and two days working it, and I've come to know it as close as a lover.

I reach into its guts. There are three safety latches in there among the blades that get flipped whenever the machine needs to be dismantled for cleanings. Proper procedure is to do a check first thing every morning to make sure the latches are secured before the machine is turned on for the day, but no one ever does that, because who needs to?

I flip the latches. The blades give a little shudder, as if anticipating the next time the machine is turned on and they, no longer secured, will come flying off, right into the assembled crowd of workers just starting the day's shift. There will be screams. There will be blood. Possibly dismemberment, or at least some very serious nods toward it. The witch's hex wards would have prevented someone from reaching in so casually and doing what I just did, but that was then.

The boss is going to have hell to pay for recompense.

My half-finished cigarette from earlier catches flame in a way it never would have been able to before. I take a long drag and spit the smoke out between my lips as I leave the factory and start the long walk home.

JOHN HOLLOWBACK AND THE WITCH

Amal El-Mohtar

The witch had no name that he knew. John Hollowback found her house at the far end of a fallow field, browning with the fall: a small cottage of wattle and daub, with a thatched roof and a smoking chimney, nestled up against a forest of birch, poplar, and pine. He could see a well nearby, a tidy garden, and a store of seasoned wood stacked against the eastern wall.

It was a pretty place. He thought perhaps he was mistaken; it did not look like the home of a witch. Still, he walked to the door and knocked three times.

The woman who answered was most certainly a witch.

Her hair was dark, greasy, wisped in gray and falling messily out of a loose topknot; her skin was sun-browned and crinkled around her eyes, which were a strange, flashing blue. She did not look very old, but was hideous enough to be recognizable as one who practiced magic.

"What do you want?" Her voice was low, but clear.

"I want a whole back, instead of a hole in my back," he said, firmly.

She squinted at him, and gestured for him to turn around, poking at him curiously while he did.

Though he walked without a stoop or limp, John had a hollow in his back. Where spine and sinew were meant to make a bold line from neck to tailbone, they vanished instead into an oval cavity the size of a serving plate, lined with pale, soft skin.

"I used to be called John Turner," he said, bitterly. "Now folk call me Hollowback, like an old tree. Owls could nest in me."

She placed her hands against his shoulder blades, knocking against them like a door. She rapped her knuckles down his back until they met wood and the sound rang out hollow indeed. He winced.

"I made myself a board to cover the hole. I daren't be alone with women—"

"You're alone with me," she observed.

"You know what I mean. I have seen doctors, and they can do nothing. Can you?"

She pulled her hands back, folded her arms, and considered him.

"Perhaps," she said. "Come in."

She led him toward the hearth and sat him down; he turned his back to her, lifted his shirt, and unfastened the leather bracers holding a thin sheet of wood against his hollow like a lid. He shivered as she felt around its edges, hissed when her fingers brushed the tender flesh within.

"I see," she murmured. "I see. You're missing a pound of flesh. Who did you cross?"

His shoulders slumped beneath her hands. "No one. I have no debts, and some money put by. A year ago I was to propose to my love; a year and a day ago I woke with a hollow in my back, and this frightened her away, and she never spoke to me again."

"Mm." She withdrew her hands. "A pity—it is difficult to restore that which has been taken by another."

"Then you cannot help me?"

"I did not say that." She tapped a thoughtful rhythm against his back. "But it will take some time. You will have to stay here for the duration. What have you brought with you?"

He lifted the flap of his bag and pulled out a leather-bound book.

"I thought you might value this, and take it as payment" he said, offering it to her. She raised a thick eyebrow, picked it up and thumbed through it.

"It's blank," she said, looking at him curiously.

"It's magic," he said, "I think. Anything I try to write in it vanishes. I have no use for it, but I thought, perhaps, someone with your craft—"

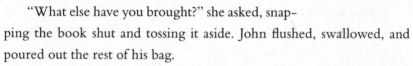

"What else have you brought?" she asked, snapping the book shut and tossing it aside. John flushed, swallowed, and poured out the rest of his bag.

He had packed sensibly: a change of clothing, some food, some money, along with his tools. But from among his belongings the witch singled out an apple, a comb, and a bit of string. John blinked; he had not packed them.

"These," she said, "will be of some use. Tomorrow we'll begin tending to your back. You are a woodworker, I see?"

John nodded.

"I will take my payment in trade, then. Go to sleep."

The witch sat in her garden, puffing on her pipe, while John slept. He didn't remember her; that much was clear. What he *did* remember remained to be seen.

She clicked her tongue in the language of bats until one swooped merrily around her head; she whispered with it a while, then watched as the bat wheeled away into the velvet dark.

John woke to the witch shaking him gruffly by the shoulder.

"We begin today," she said. "You'll do chores while it's light; at night, we will work together on your back. Is this fair by you?"

"Yes," he said, straightening, "yes, of course."

"Good. You must understand that once we begin this process, it will be difficult to stop. It is as though you are carrying a knife stuck in your back; if I pull it out, a dangerous gushing will result, and if you do not let me complete my work, it will go badly for you. I say this because it will be painful, and I will not hurt you without your consent. Do you understand?"

John felt suddenly unsure. "It will hurt?"

"Most likely. Great changes often do."

"Only, I don't remember it hurting when it happened."

The witch only stared at him, waiting.

John chewed his lip, then nodded. "And I only need to do chores? You don't want the book, or . . . a promise, of . . ." He swallowed what might be an insulting assumption. ". . . some future thing?"

The witch looked more pitying than contemptuous. She reached up to clap him on the shoulder.

"John Hollowback," she said, "you have absolutely nothing I could possibly want."

On that first day, John swept the witch's floors, scoured her pots, drew water from her well, and scouted a space outdoors to set up a spring-pole lathe. She'd said she expected trade, but nothing else; he wanted to be prepared. By the time the witch called him in, he had most of it done, and had worked up an honest sweat; she'd set out a robust dinner for the two of them, bread and cheese and a thick vegetable stew. They ate in silence—not quite companionable, but not awkward, either.

Once they'd finished, John cleared the table and washed up; the witch, meanwhile, set the apple on the table, and waited for him to join her.

"Take off your shirt," she said, "and your board, and lie down on your belly."

He did as he was told, if reluctantly; it was not easy to show his naked back. He found he was less ashamed about it with the witch, though; perhaps because she wore her own ugliness so brazenly, he didn't so much mind his own. Wherever he came face-to-face with people, they found him handsome: He was, after all, tall, with straight teeth and a small nose, high cheekbones and honeyed hair. But when he turned his back, he knew people shuddered at the shape of him, whispered about the odd way his shirt hung off his shoulders, a strange sag at his belt.

He propped his chin up on his folded arms and gazed into the dimming embers of the fire while the witch moved around behind him.

"I'm going to make a scrying bowl of your hollow," she said, "by painting it black, and filling it with water. While I do this, I want you to tell me the story of this apple."

She held it out to him. He frowned.

"It's just an apple. I must've packed it for a snack and forgotten about it."

"It spoke to me," she said, simply, "from among your things. You seem to be missing more than flesh, John Hollowback—there are memories you carry outside your body, and I don't think you'll be whole again until you've recalled them." She sat down next to him on a low stool, swirling a paint brush through a pungent stone jar, and began applying its contents to his back.

He hissed—it was cold—then wrinkled his nose, annoyed. "That's nonsense. I'll grant I don't remember my hollowing, but I've a decent memory in general, and—"

"Eat it."

He blinked. "What?"

"Eat the apple. Take a bite."

He was rather full from dinner, but he shrugged his shoulders, parted his lips, lifted it to his mouth—and stopped, suddenly wracked with nausea. He gasped, sick-drool pooling around his tongue, and turned away from it, panting—but could not drop it, though he felt it growing warm in his hand, echoing something thumping hard in his chest.

"You can't eat it," said the witch, her voice rougher than he would have liked, "any more than you can eat your arm. But you can tell me the story of it." She laid another long, thick line down the bowl of his back while he caught his breath.

John turned the apple over in his hands. It was, he thought, a lovely specimen, red and round, its stem flying a single leaf like a flag; it looked just picked, carried the scent of the orchard with it, the fizzy smell of ferment rising up from fruit crushed underfoot. Nothing in his bag had broken or bruised its surface; he owned as that was odd. But a story? The story of the apple was that it was a mystery, though the more he looked at it, the more he cupped it in his hands, the more he felt an unaccountable tenderness welling up in him.

He flinched as the witch poured a pitcher of cool water into his back, exhaled as she stirred her finger through it.

"I see," she murmured, "a great many trees, and among them a wagon, brightly colored. There are women picking apples, but the wagon . . ."

"Oh!" said John, suddenly. "Of course, yes—that was when I first met her. Lydia, my—" He grimaced. "She was working, bringing in the fruit, and she was singing . . ."

The witch said nothing, but slowed her stirring. John found himself tugging at the thread of memory—perhaps this was what she meant by telling the story? The apple reminded him of something, and he shared it? He groped his way to a better beginning.

"I was traveling with a troupe of players—not a player myself, of course, but I'd make their sets, mend the boards they trod, and they gave me a share of the take. William and Janet, they were married, and Brigid, she wasn't their daughter but may as well have been. We traveled in a caravan that was both advertisement and stage—or, well, they all did, being a family. I usually followed after them on a mule, stopping in towns to ply my own trade and sleep in a bed before catching them up at the next stop; more comfortable for everyone that way, the wagon was only so big.

"Well, we were setting up in this orchard with the farmer's permission, and this girl was up a ladder. She was fine enough to look at, but

her voice was something else. She was singing, leading the other workers in a song, call and response, and it was like hearing a lark among
crows. I stopped setting up, stopped everything just to listen to her. And
when the song was done, I strode up to her and said as how I'd loved
her singing, and her voice was a gift, and why was she picking fruit
when she could be traveling the country and sharing out the gold of her
music? And she blushed and smiled and plucked an apple from a branch
near her cheek and held it out to me, and said that was very kind, but she
was only a country lass. But we got to talking, and I brought the players
out to meet her, and she watched our show. And that did it. She was off
with us the next morning."

The water in his back felt warm now, not unpleasantly.

"Give me the apple, John," said the witch, quietly; she coaxed it
from his hand—he found it hard to release—and then rolled it around
the edge of his hollow. A ringing rose in his ears, a pain, a sharp slic-
ing of grief—and then water sloshed over the edge of his hollow and he
cried out, spun quickly to face her, scuttling back and away on his palms
and making a mess of the floor.

The witch looked at him coolly.

"There. That's one." She looked from him to the puddle on the
floor, and stood up slowly. "Enough for now, I think. Mop that up.
Don't bother putting your board on tomorrow—it won't fit. Best give
your back a little room to breathe."

She walked out to the garden, leaving John gasping, reaching
around to touch the familiar contours of his hollow, and finding, instead, an inch more solid back than he'd had before.

The next morning, John woke late; the witch had let him sleep in. He was
glad of it: He felt sore and stiff throughout his body, as if he'd spent a
long night drinking. He stretched, and scratched, and reached cautiously toward his hollow. His shoulders slumped in relief when he
found his new flesh still in place. He looked around for a mirror, and
saw one hanging on the wall; steeling himself against the possibility that

it might do him some mischief, he approached it and tried to catch a glimpse of his back in it.

The hollow was certainly smaller—but a thin black ring marked its previous circumference. He frowned. Perhaps it would fade in time.

He could hear the witch puttering out in the garden, and dragged himself to the bread and cheese she'd left on the table, next to the leather-bound book she'd refused from him as payment. Or had she accepted it? She was an odd one; she spoke plainly, but John felt there was much she didn't say.

As he munched his breakfast, he decided there was no harm in opening the book.

Then he choked.

The first few pages had writing on them. Not just any writing; the story he'd told the witch last night.

Well, he thought, that made sense; who better than a witch to write in a magic book? Perhaps that had always been its purpose—to be a witch's grimoire, inscribed with spells.

Funny that she'd write his own story in it. Odd, too, to see his story laid out by another, in writing. It seemed, at a glance, much longer than his own telling.

He skimmed over the memory of apples, and felt, again, the pang of losing Lydia, the sting of betrayal, the anger and shame of it. There had been so much promise at first, and then, at the end, no hint of anything amiss until she was gone.

"Good, you're awake," said the witch, standing in the doorway, tugging off her gardening gloves. John startled, slammed the book shut, and turned to her, equal parts furtive, guilty, and defiant.

She did not seem to notice. "The day's getting away from us. Do you need me to make you a list, or can you get on all right just looking around at what needs doing?"

She made him a list, in the end, and once he'd chopped wood and hauled water to her satisfaction, he turned back to finishing his lathe.

He thought he might make the witch a bowl, as a small joke, since she'd made one of him. He found a likely birch log, split it in half, and began chipping out a rough shape. He'd just gotten as far as fitting it onto the lathe when the witch came out to see him, and he noticed the hour gone late and golden around him.

The witch looked at the lathe with frank curiosity. "I see you've not been idle."

John's hollow back straightened somewhat. He took pride in his work.

She stepped around to his side. "Would you show me? Or is it a trade secret?"

John demonstrated the mechanism: how the treadle tugged the pole down and spun the wood to be shaped in one direction, then the other as it released. "You only cut on the downstroke," he said, "slowly, carefully. Then it springs back up—it's called reciprocating action—and you push down again, until it takes the shape you want."

"Fascinating," she said, quietly. "Very clever. Does the wood ever break, or crack?"

"Not if it's sufficiently green, seen to by a steady hand."

"I see," she said. "And is this light enough to work by?"

"No," he admitted. "I should leave off for tonight."

"Wise. And so shall I—I don't think you're entirely recovered from yesterday. Come and have something to eat."

That evening, their meal together was more genial; the witch asked about his back, whether he felt any pain after their ritual.

"No," he said, "but there's a black ring—"

She shrugged. "Sutures leave scars. It's all part of the process. I can't undo what happened to you; I can only help mend it."

She asked, then, about his memories of traveling on the road.

It had been a bright and venturesome time; they'd performed in villages and taverns, but also led the occasional masque or revelry in a grand country hall. Their summers they spent on the road; in winter they sought the shelter of familiar fields, farmers and sometimes gentry glad of the entertainment during long, cold nights.

It was while holed up together that they came to know each other best, he and Lydia. Her arrival had expanded the group's repertoire: Where before they'd performed scraps of entertaining miscellanies, told stories, made use of John's modest skills in puppetry, now they had a full complement of players, though it meant Brigid usually took on trouser roles to play a young lover opposite Lydia's ingenue, or else a puckish troublemaker needling William and Janet's grumpier elder roles.

But Lydia was indisputably the star.

"Did you never perform with them?" asked the witch, pouring them both a fragrant tea after they'd eaten.

"I did before, if they needed someone to be a prop, or a mark, or to move a puppet. I'm no actor, I know that—hard not to when you travel with those who have the gift. But once they had Lydia, it was better to keep to making and mending. She cast a long shadow."

"Were you jealous?" she asked, with a frankness that felt like a slap.

"No," he said, staring at her. She held his gaze. Eventually he looked away. "No. But Brigid was."

The witch chuckled, and John frowned. But she stood and asked him to tidy up after their meal, putting an end to the matter, then walked out into the garden. He was asleep before she returned.

The next morning John woke early, but not earlier than the witch, and found a bowl of porridge laid out for him as well as some late plums. The leather-bound book was there, too.

He watched it while he ate. He looked out toward the garden, where the witch likely was.

He pulled the book toward him, opened it, and read.

Lydia picked apples and sang as she worked; she loved hearing her voice strong and high, feeling her call pull in a chorus of responses, as if she cast a net to catch her fellows' breath. But when she stopped, she felt eyes on her, and turned to see a tall, spindly young man staring.

"That's a terrible ladder," he said. "It's dangerous, you could fall. Let me fix it."

Lydia laughed, for the ladder had borne her weight without wobbling all season, but she hopped down and let him have his way. As he shook his head and set about tightening the rungs, he said, "You have the most beautiful voice I've ever heard. And I've heard plenty. I'm John. What's your name?"

"Lydia," she said, smiling. "Thank you, that's kind."

"No, it's just true."

She asked if he was with the caravan of players, and he said he was. Her eyes shone, and she said she was looking forward to the show, that she loved the music and stories; he paused in his work and said he could take her to meet the players, if she wanted.

She did want, very much.

She met William, Janet, and Brigid in short order; John introduced her as the voice of the orchard, and she rolled her eyes, but said she did love to sing. Brigid's eyes caught hers, and she asked about her favorite songs, and they fell to talking like they'd known each other for years but had not seen each other for more, familiar and starved for each other, while William and Janet exchanged fond looks and John sat silent and looked at everyone apart from himself.

John tasted copper before realizing he'd bitten through his lip. He shut the book, then opened it, fingers trembling. Then he shut it again.

How dare the witch? He'd come to her with his hollow, his history, and she had made of it—whatever this was, a fanciful embroidery, some kind of cruel taunt.

Had he even said he fixed the ladder? He recalled, now, that he'd tightened the rungs, but it hadn't seemed worth mentioning. Was that really the first thing he'd said to Lydia?

He shoved his porridge aside and stormed out to the lathe.

The work soon soothed him. His world narrowed in focus to angles and pressure and speed, the beauty of wood smoothed and shaped, every rough part sheared off into a tangle of delicate blond curls. By the time the witch came out to find him, the finished bowl gleamed.

"Here," said John, stiffly. "Trade."

The witch raised her eyebrows at him, and took the proffered bowl, turning it in her hands. "It's lovely. Well done."

John flushed, but looked away. The witch eyed him, then said, lightly, "I know just what to do with it. Come with me."

He followed her into her garden, where she wandered, stooped, cut lettuces and herbs with a short sharp knife. Whatever she cut, she placed in the bowl, until it was heaped with brilliant, tender greenery.

"Walk with me, John," she said. "We'll not be long."

"Where are we going?"

"To visit a neighbor. Now, what's the matter?"

He scowled. "Nothing."

"It's the wrong season for lemons," she said, "but you look like you've been feasting on little else. And you didn't clean up after breakfast; that porridge'll be crusted to its bowl like a barnacle."

He rolled his eyes. "Pardon me for having made you a better one."

The witch stopped walking, and looked up at him. Her eyes flashed—literally, magically—and he looked away, fuming.

"John Hollowback," she said, calmly, "you'll keep a civil tongue in your head when you speak to me, or else you'll keep a home in your back for owls. Is that understood?"

He chewed his lip. "Yes."

"We made a bargain, and I have asked very little of you. Tell me what's wrong or keep your own council, but do not think to insult me or my crockery with your backhanded foolishness while accepting my hospitality. Shame on you."

She walked on, and reluctantly, he followed.

Eventually they came to a cottage, and were warmly received by the couple inside: a woman, heavily pregnant, and her husband beaming solicitously alongside her.

"I brought these for the cravings," said the witch, pressing the bowl into the woman's hands. "Make a salad of them, they'll be good for you." She looked to John, and smiled. "John here made the bowl."

John stood awkwardly by while the couple gushed their thanks; they pressed a small loaf and a jar of bramble jam on them, which the witch handed John to carry. Mercifully she declined their offer of dinner. They began their walk back in silence.

"I made that bowl for you," said John, who wanted to be angry, but was mostly tired. The witch shrugged.

"And I traded it for bread and jam. I did say I'd take my payment in trade." She looked at him, levelly. "And that I wanted nothing from you. I always mean what I say, John."

"I thought," said John, who wanted to be vicious, but wasn't up to the task, "that witches hated giving up their greens. That they punished people for taking from their gardens. We did a whole show about it once."

She chuckled. "And why not? Everyone wants to see a witch punish someone for stealing from her. A witch is a kind of justice in the world. It makes for a fine story. No one wants to admit the truth, for all it stares them plainly in the face."

"What's that?"

"Steal from a woman long enough, and a witch is what she'll become."

They'd reached the cottage. John drew a deep breath.

"I'm sorry," he said, grudgingly. "For being rude. But I saw what you'd written in the book, and I didn't like it."

He didn't like, either, the pitying way the witch looked at him now.

"John," she said, "I've not written anything in that book."

She laid him down shirtless in front of the hearth again, painted another layer of black into his hollow. She handed him the comb, poured water into the bowl of him, and propped the leather-bound book open to a fresh page where he could see it.

"I believe I understand," she said, "what has happened to you, and the way it came about. But it's a little like trying to rebuild a tree from a pile of wood shavings. There is so much you don't remember, and it's necessary that you do. So, tell me the story of the comb."

She began stirring the water in his back again.

John looked at the comb: It was very elegant, long-handled, and decorated with flowering vines carved out of the wood. He recognized his own work.

"I made this for her," he said. "I made her lots of things, but I could say they were for the troupe, if I were building scenery that would show her particularly well, or making improvements to the wagon. But I made her this as a gift, from me to only her, and she let me comb her hair with it, and I knew then that she loved me, to let me stand so close to her."

The water in his back heated up much more quickly this time, and less comfortably. He shifted on his belly and looked from the comb in his hands to the open book in front of him.

It was filling with writing. He squinted to read it.

John prided himself on introducing people to each other. He was *no great performer, but he liked to say that he was the trusses that held up the stage, that he carried them all on his back. Sometimes he would ride ahead of the wagon and make connections through his woodworking, connections which he then leveraged into performance opportunities, and sometimes he would hang back after the show to glean gossip and carry that back to the group. He had an uncanny knack for placing himself between people, and resented the existence of any closeness that did not widen to admit him.*

He resented Janet and William's direction; he resented Brigid and Lydia's friendship; he resented Lydia's passion for performing, and the audience's passion for her. And the more he resented them, the more he plied them with gifts, words and wood and wooing coated in the venom of his need.

John hissed. The water in his back steamed. "It's not true," he gasped, "it's not true."

466

"Tell me what is, then," said the witch quietly, stirring all the while.

"I loved them." His lip trembled. "I loved them all."

But he looked back to the book, and read,

For William and Janet, he made a pair of beautifully turned bowls, *and while they ate together he spoke grave rumors of unfriendly villages ahead, dislike of outsiders, a dwindling of prospects leading to a hard winter.*

"Some say it's unnatural for women to play men onstage," he said, his eyes soft and sad, "and mutter dark things to each other. Honestly, I fear for Brigid, but I'm sure these words will pass like weather. It's probably nothing."

And William and Janet paled, and reached for each other's hands.

For Brigid, he made hand-carved dice, and played games till they were deep in their cups, and spoke of Lydia's talent, her brilliance.

"But I worry," he said, "that she'll only ever be thought of as one half of a pair—that she'll be stamped like a coin into one role until she's spent."

And Brigid frowned, and John looked contrite, and said, "It's not that I think you're smothering her," and paused, "but I do think she feels smothered."

And Brigid looked stricken, and the next morning went with a pounding head to have a word with William and Janet, and was soon visiting nearby family for a spell while Lydia's heart shook to see her go.

For Lydia, he made a hand-carved comb, beautifully wrought with flowers and vines, and offered to dress her hair before she mounted the stage, as Brigid used to do.

"You know," he said, combing her long, bright hair, "when you stand onstage you shine."

She smiled softly. "Thank you, John."

"But sometimes," he said, "You shine so bright that it hurts to look at you. You're like a small sun, and lesser stars can't be seen when you're out."

Lydia's throat hurt. "Does it bother you?"

"No, no, of course not." He paused. "But I think it bothers Brigid."

And Brigid put distance between them, and Lydia dimmed herself, until soon they couldn't see each other at all.

And so John made room for himself.

John hardly felt the witch take the comb from him, stunned by the words and the gulf they opened in his chest. But when she began running it along the outside of his hollow, he screamed: It burned, as if the comb's teeth seared grooves around his bowl-back's rim. The water that spilled over the edges of him scalded; he panted, then drew his knees in close to his chest and wept while the witch watched.

"That's two," she said, low and gruff, and left him.

The next morning, John awoke to voices in the garden. The witch, and one other beside. He tried to rise—and groaned, his body a patchwork of pains and aches, then groaned more deeply as he remembered the source of it all.

The visitor sounded agitated, but he couldn't make out the words. The witch's voice came clear.

"I'm sorry, but I'm busy now. Come back tonight, and we'll speak more of it then."

She came in a moment later, looked at him, then busied herself in brewing a pot of mint tea while he found his way to a seat.

He stared into nothing while she poured him a cup.

"What must you think of me," he whispered, "to hear me say what I do, and then read what's written in that book?"

The witch shrugged. She poured herself some tea and sat down. "What do you think of yourself?"

"I hate it," he said. "I don't recognize the man in those pages. It isn't how I remember it."

"But you didn't remember any of it, at first" she said, lifting her cup, sniffing it. "All you remembered was losing your lover."

John kept silent. He blew gently on his tea.

"I don't want to wait until tonight" he said, finally. "I'd like to get it over with. Can we do this by daylight?"

The witch sipped her tea as she looked at him. It struck him, suddenly, that she wasn't ugly at all—he couldn't remember how he'd thought that.

"We can. But it will hurt you terribly."

He looked into his cup, and nodded. "I know."

Laid out on his belly again while the witch painted his back, he twirled the string this way and that between his thumbs and forefingers.

"I used this," he said, his voice a shallow croak, "to measure her finger for a ring. I wanted to make her a wooden one—I was going to ask her to marry me. But then everything went wrong."

"How? What happened?"

John's throat worked, but he couldn't remember. He shook his head. "She was gone when I woke. They all were."

The witch stirred the waters in his back, smaller and smaller circles, he felt, as his flesh had filled in, though he could take no joy in it, and said, "I see a great hall done up with harvest revelry—sheafs of wheat, garlands of asters, great rounds of braided bread."

"Yes," said John, "the troupe's last performance. William and Janet had decided—they'd"—he drew a deep breath—"they'd lost their taste for travel, and the take wasn't what it used to be. There was no better time to ask Lydia to marry me; I'd look after her, and we could be our own troupe together, if she wanted. I could set up shop in a town, she could sing in a proper theater—I would've built her one from the ground up, I knew enough of the right people. I had something to offer her, and she had nothing to lose—"

"Because you'd taken everything from her?"

John gritted his teeth. "I never *took* anything from anyone. I had nothing, I came from nothing, I built everything I had for myself. I never forced anyone to do anything they didn't want to. I only ever tried to help."

He glared up at the book, daring it to contradict him. For a moment, nothing appeared.

Then black ink bloomed from the blank pages and sank John's heart to his stomach.

The night of the final performance, Brigid brought her mother to see *the show, and to meet John and Lydia, of whom she'd heard much spoken. John was genial and spoke expansively, praised everyone but himself; Lydia smiled, demure, said little.*

Brigid's mother looked at them together: how John's arm wrapped too tightly around Lydia whenever anyone else was around, how she wilted near him, how, if ever his gaze went elsewhere, if he were called away, she seemed to relax, to straighten, to smile more easily and speak more freely.

She looked, too, at her own daughter: how she floated away from the friend she would not cease praising in her visits, but orbited her like a moth near a lantern.

She saw that some sick magic was at work.

"Lydia," she said, "would you lend me this fine fellow of yours? John, I noticed some odd carvings under the seats here. I wondered if you could tell me about them."

And John, flattered, turned his back on Brigid and Lydia, whose eyes found each other, and whose hands soon followed, and who, haltingly and in a daze, remembered how to speak.

Tears brimmed in John's eyes and he knuckled them away as he turned his face from the book. "You can't hold me responsible for them drifting apart!"

The witch stirred his waters placidly. "Who are you talking to, John?"

"Look, if they'd really loved each other, nothing I said or did could have changed that. I only wanted them to love me too, as I loved them!"

"How did you love them, then?"

"They were everything to me," he said, fiercely. "They were my life, all of them together, and I was just—a tool. A handyman. I wanted to be everything to at least one person."

"Reciprocating action," she said. "Isn't that what you called it? Your work with the lathe. You'd pull her to you, and cut away what you didn't like, and then if she bounced away she was less, until you caught her again, and cut and carved until she fit in the palm of your hand."

"*I* discovered her! *I* made her a star!"

"What happened with the string, John?"

"I don't know! The performance went well. Lydia was more dazzling than she'd been in ages, she was pressed on all sides afterward by admirers, and I couldn't find her for hours. But we were all going to sleep together in the hall that night, after the show, so I just waited. I waited a long time into the night, and when she finally came in, it was her and Brigid together, and I couldn't—I didn't want to interrupt, so I pretended to be asleep until they were. And then I got up, and—"

He gasped as the water in his back began to boil. The witch pulled her finger back a second before it burned, shook the heat out. "Go on, John."

"I crept closer . . . I tried to tie the string around her finger without her waking, but . . . she did, and—"

"What are you doing?" she hissed, snatching her hand from his, *looking at the string in horror. "What's this?"*

"Nothing, nothing, go back to sleep."

"Is this a spell?" She tugged at the string on her finger, in a panic, in a rage, as Brigid stirred beside her. "Is this how you—what are you doing to me?"

"Lydia, please," he said, finding his way to one knee, looking at her, his eyes large and beseeching as a dog's, "I wanted to ask you to marry—"

The string around her finger glowed like metal in a forge, then snapped and sizzled away to nothing. Lydia herself began to glow, as if stars melted into her veins, and rose up from her blankets, rose further still, until she floated above him, her hair high and wild as the lightning, and the air around her crackled with power.

"Liar," she hissed, and the word burned bright as her hair, "Liar! You've tried to cut me and bind me like wheat all this time!" And she spoke back at him every truth she'd untwisted from his words, every piece of her he'd taken while

seeming to give her gifts, every day he'd ruined with his sad jealous eyes reproaching her for hurting him with her happiness.

And as John watched a witch being born, he felt a great gouging at his back, as if a giant hand in one single stroke had sheared spine and flesh and blood and skin from him, and out from the coring of his body tumbled an apple, a comb, a piece of string, and a book, and he fell down among them in a swoon.

When he woke up, it was midday, and the hall was empty. He picked up the objects around him without seeing them, put them in a bag, and carried them with him for a year and a day.

He screamed his throat raw as the witch rolled the string into his hollow. The water turned to vapor; the thick paint on his back smoked and peeled. Bones jutted beneath his blackened skin like mountain peaks, twisted like serpents coiling, cracked and rumbled like a thundering sky—but settled, finally, solid and sound as good joinery. He panted and sobbed while the witch rubbed circles along his newly filled back; whole now, but for a small gap an inch wide and a few inches tall, surrounded by three black rings.

"Good, John," she whispered. "Well done."

John slept the day through. As the hour grew long and blue the witch sat in her garden with her pipe, waiting for her visitor.

"I can't believe," came a voice bitter and hot, "that you would help him. After everything he did to us."

"Sit, Lydia," she said, gesturing to another stool. "How was your journey? How's Brigid?"

Lydia narrowed her eyes. "She told me not to murder you. How could you?"

The witch shrugged. "He came to my door and asked for help."

"And that's it, then? He's whole now, and anyone who looks at him will see just another smiling charming man and not know to shun him? It wasn't for you to fix him!"

The witch raised an eyebrow. "Did you want the task?"

"Of course not."

"Or Brigid, or who, then? Be honest, now."

Lydia's eyes flashed, literally, magically. "I didn't want him fixed at all. He doesn't deserve it."

"Ah, there we come to it. And that's why I did it." The witch held her gaze. "For you to carry less of it. For him to carry more of it."

Lydia's face twisted in disgust, and she shook her head. But she sat down, and stared out into the darkness.

"I'll never forget what you said that night," she said, her voice full of burrs. "*A witch is a kind of justice in the world. And here you are, undoing it.*"

The witch tapped the ash from her pipe.

"When you came into your power," she said, "what he'd done to you came back to him fourfold. But that was the end of your story with him. You began a new one; so too should he, with the remembrance of all he did written into his body."

"Why tell me, though? You must have known I'd hate it."

"I wasn't asking permission. But I thought you should know." She pinched herbs from a pouch and packed them into her pipe. "I wasn't going to let him become a secret I kept from you."

Lydia breathed deeply, and exhaled slowly. "I won't see him, or speak to him. Not ever again."

"Nor should you."

"You don't want me to?"

"No. I'd put seven seas between you first." She tilted her head toward the cottage door, listening. "In fact, you'd best be away; I hear him stirring. Give my love to Brigid."

Lydia looked toward the cottage door. Then she hugged the witch to her, kissed her cheek, and said, "I will."

She left. The witch went back inside.

John was awake and waiting for her, still pale and shaken from the pain, but calm. She crouched down next to him, took his temperature with her wrist against his brow.

473

"You're Brigid's mother," he said, quietly. "I didn't remember you."

"Hard to remember a witch," she said, amiably, "at the best of times."

"You knew who I was from the beginning."

"I did."

"And you helped me?"

She shrugged. "You asked for help. I'm not sure you're happier now than when you came, though, are you?"

He chuckled bleakly. "No."

"Then perhaps all I did was enjoy seeing you punished."

"May I stay?" His eyes were wide and soft. "I'll keep helping. I could make you chairs and spoons . . ."

"Absolutely not." The witch's gaze was sharp, and he flinched from it. "You're good at your craft, John. But people aren't blocks of wood for you to turn to your liking, and you've not quite learned that yet, in your bones." She stood, and walked over to the leather-bound book that lay closed now. "Have you tried writing in it since coming here? It might keep your words now, if you choose them carefully."

She found him ink and a quill. He sat with it awhile, reading through every word, feeling his memories shift and spike and settle like the objects in his back.

He tried writing, "Lydia," and it wouldn't stay. He tried writing, "I wish," and it wouldn't stay, the ink swallowed by the page like a pebble by a pond.

He wrote, "I'm sorry," and the words stared back at him like eyes, and stayed.

He closed the book.

"I'm ready," he said, and handed it to the witch. She took it, turned him around, and angled the book carefully at what remained of his hollow.

It slid into place like an ending.

ABOUT THE AUTHORS

Linda D. Addison is the award-winning author of five collections of prose and poetry, including *The Place of Broken Things* (written with Alessandro Manzetti) and *How to Recognize a Demon Has Become Your Friend*. She is the recipient of the HWA Lifetime Achievement Award and the SFPA Grand Master, and her work appears in *Black Panther: Tales of Wakanda*; *Black Fire—This Time*; *HWA Other Terrors*; *Predator: Eyes of the Demon*; and *HyBriD*. Online at: LindaAddisonWriter.com.

C. L. Clark is a British Fantasy and Locus Award–winning editor and the author of Nebula finalist *The Unbroken*, the first book in the Magic of the Lost trilogy, and sequel, *The Faithless*. She graduated from Indiana University's creative writing MFA program and was a 2012 Lambda Literary Fellow. She's been a personal trainer, an English teacher, and an editor, and is some combination thereof as she travels the world. When she's not writing or working, she's learning languages, doing P90-something, or reading about war and (post-)colonial history. Her work has appeared in Tor.com, *Beneath Ceaseless Skies*, and *The Best American Science Fiction and Fantasy*. Online at: clclarkwrites.com.

P. Djèlí Clark is the author of the Nebula Award–winning and World Fantasy Award–nominated novel *A Master of Djinn*, and is the award-winning and Hugo, Nebula, and Sturgeon-nominated author of the novellas *Ring Shout, The Black God's Drums*, and *The Haunting of Tram Car 015*. His short stories have appeared in Tor.com, *Heroic Fantasy Quarterly, Beneath Ceaseless Skies, Griots*, and *Hidden Youth*. Online at: pdjeliclark.com.

Indrapramit Das is a writer and editor from Kolkata, India. He is a Lambda Literary Award winner for his debut novel *The Devourers*, and a Shirley Jackson Award winner for his short fiction, which has appeared in a variety of anthologies and publications including Tor.com, *Slate, Clarkesworld*, and *Strange Horizons*. He is an Octavia E. Butler Scholar and a grateful member of the Clarion West class of 2012. He has lived in India, the United States, and Canada, where he received his MFA from the University of British Columbia. His most recent book is the novella *The Last Dragoners of Bowbazar*. Online at: indradas.com.

Amal El-Mohtar writes fiction, poetry, and criticism. She won the Hugo, Nebula, and Locus Awards for her 2016 short story "Seasons of Glass and Iron" and again for her 2019 novella *This Is How You Lose the Time War*, written with Max Gladstone, which also won the BSFA and Aurora Awards and has been translated into over ten languages. Her reviews and articles have appeared in the *New York Times* and on NPR Books. She lives in Ottawa, Canada. Online at: amalelmohtar.com.

Andrea Hairston's novels include *Mindscape*, shortlisted for the Philip K. Dick and Otherwise Awards and winner of the Carl Brandon Parallax Award; *Redwood and Wildfire*, winner of the Otherwise and Carl Brandon Awards; *Will Do Magic for Small Change*, a *New York Times* Editor's pick and finalist for the Mythopoeic, Lambda, and Otherwise Awards; and *Master of Poisons*, listed on *Kirkus Review*'s Best Science Fiction and Fantasy of 2020. Her play, *Thunderbird at the Next World Theatre*, appears in *Geek Theater*. Her short fiction has appeared in *Lightspeed, New Suns: Original Speculative Fiction by People of Color* and *Trouble the Waters: Tales from the Deep Blue*. Her next novel, *Archangels of Funk*, is out in 2023. In her spare time, Andrea is the Louise Wolff Kahn 1931 Professor of Theatre and Professor of Africana Studies at Smith College and the artistic director of Chrysalis Theatre. Online at: andreahairston.com.

Millie Ho is a writer and artist based in Canada. Her short stories and poems have appeared in *Lightspeed*, *Nightmare*, *Uncanny*, *Strange Horizons*, and elsewhere. Her work was a finalist for the Ignyte and Rhysling awards. Online at: millieho.net.

Saad Z. Hossain is a Bangladeshi author writing in English. He lives in Dhaka. His war satire, *Escape from Baghdad!*, was published in 2015 and included in the *Financial Times* best books of 2015. It was translated into French, as *Bagdad la Grande Evasion*, which was a finalist for the Grand Prix de L'imaginaire 2018. His second novel, *Djinn City*, was released in 2017 and also translated into French. His novella *The Gurkha and the Lord of Tuesday* was published in 2019 and was a finalist for the Locus and Ignyte Awards for 2020. His third novel, *Cyber Mage*, was published by Unnamed Press in America and ULAB Press in Bangladesh. His latest novella, *Kundo Wakes Up*, was published by Tor.com.

Kathleen Jennings is an Australian writer and illustrator. Her Australian Gothic debut, *Flyaway* (2020), received a British Fantasy Award (the Sydney J. Bounds Award) and was shortlisted for the World Fantasy Award, the Crawford Award, an Australian Shadows Award, and the *Courier-Mail* People's Choice Book of the Year Award. Her short fiction and comics have received several Ditmar Awards and been shortlisted for the Aurealis Awards and the Eugie Foster Memorial Award. Her debut poetry collection/written travel sketchbook is *Travelogues: Vignettes from Trains in Motion*, and she also maintains the Gothic Twitter bot *Girls Running From Houses* (@girlfleeshouse). She is currently undertaking a creative writing PhD and posts about illustration and writing regularly. Online at: tanaudel.wordpress.com.

Alaya Dawn Johnson is a Nebula Award–winning short story writer and the author of eight novels for adults and young adults. Her latest book is YA science fiction novel *The Library of Broken Worlds*. Her adult novel, *Trouble the Saints*, won the 2021 World Fantasy Award for best novel. Her debut short story collection, *Reconstruction*, was an Ignyte Award and Hurston/Wright Legacy Award finalist. Her debut YA novel, *The Summer Prince*, was longlisted for the National Book Award for Young People's Literature, and the follow-up, *Love Is the Drug*, won the Andre Norton Nebula Award. Her short stories have appeared in many magazines and anthologies, most notably the title story in *The Memory Librarian*, in collaboration with Janelle Monáe. She lives in Oaxaca, Mexico. Online at: alayadawnjohnson.com.

Cassandra Khaw is an award-winning game writer and former scriptwriter at Ubisoft Montreal. Khaw's work can be found in places like *The Magazine of Fantasy & Science Fiction*, *Lightspeed*, and Tor.com. Khaw's first novella, *Hammers on Bone*, was a British Fantasy Award and Locus Award finalist, and their latest novella, *Nothing But Blackened Teeth*, was a *USA Today* bestseller, Bram Stoker Award nominee, and World Fantasy Award nominee.

Fonda Lee is the author of the epic fantasy trilogy Green Bone Saga, consisting of *Jade City, Jade War*, and *Jade Legacy*. Her most recent book is a novella, *Untethered Sky*. She is also the author of the acclaimed young adult science fiction novels *Zeroboxer*, *Exo*, and *Cross Fire*. Her short stories have been published in *MIT Technology Review, Uncanny Magazine*, and several anthologies. Fonda is a winner of the World Fantasy Award and the Locus Award, a four-time winner of the Aurora Award, and a finalist for the Hugo Award and Nebula Award. The Green Bone Saga has been translated into multiple languages and named to *Time's* Top 100 Fantasy Books of All Time. Fonda is a former corporate strategist and black belt martial artist residing in the Pacific Northwest. Online at: fondalee.com.

Darcie Little Badger is a Lipan Apache writer with a PhD in ocean-ography. Her critically acclaimed debut novel *Elatsoe* was featured in *Time* as one of the Top 100 Fantasy Books of All Time. *Elatsoe* also won the Locus Award for Best First Novel and is a Nebula, Ignyte, and Lodestar finalist. Her second fantasy novel, *A Snake Falls to Earth*, received a Nebula Award, an Ignyte Award, and a Newbery Honor and is on the 2021 National Book Awards longlist. Darcie is married to a veterinarian named Taran. Online at: darcielittlebadger.wordpress.com.

Ken Liu is an American author of speculative fiction. A winner of the Nebula, Hugo, and World Fantasy Awards, he wrote the Dande-lion Dynasty, a silkpunk epic fantasy series (starting with *The Grace of Kings*), as well as short story collections *The Paper Menagerie and Other Stories* and *The Hidden Girl and Other Stories*. He also penned the *Star Wars* novel *The Legends of Luke Skywalker*. Prior to becoming a full-time writer, Liu worked as a software engineer, corporate lawyer, and litigation consultant. Liu frequently speaks at conferences and universi-ties on a variety of topics, including futurism, cryptocurrency, history of technology, bookmaking, narrative futures, and the mathematics of origami. Online at: kenliu.name.

Usman T. Malik's fiction has been published in *Al-Jazeera*, *Wired*, and Center for Science and Imagination (Arizona State University), and in *New Voices of Fantasy* and several "year's best" anthologies, including *The Best American Science Fiction and Fantasy of the Year*. He has been nomi-nated for the World Fantasy, Locus, and Eugie Foster Awards, and has won the Bram Stoker and the British Fantasy Awards. Usman's debut collec-tion, *Midnight Doorways: Fables from Pakistan*, won the 2022 Crawford Award from the International Association for the Fantastic in Arts (IAFA), was on *Washington Post*'s 2021 list of best new science fiction and fantasy collections, and was shortlisted for the World Fantasy Award. Online at: usmanmalik.org.

Maureen McHugh has published four novels (including the Tiptree winner *China Mountain Zhang*) and two collections of short stories. She has also written for Alternate Reality Games, including *I Love Bees* for Halo and *Year Zero* for Nine Inch Nails. She recently moved back to Austin, Texas.

Premee Mohamed is a Nebula award–winning Indo-Caribbean scientist and speculative fiction author based in Edmonton, Alberta, Canada. She is an assistant editor at the short fiction audio venue Escape Pod and the author of the Beneath the Rising series of novels as well as several novellas, including *These Lifeless Things*, *And What Can We Offer You Tonight*, *The Annual Migration of Clouds*, and *The Butcher of the Forest*. Her short fiction has appeared in many venues. Online: premeemohamed.com.

New York Times bestselling novelist **Garth Nix** has been a full-time writer since 2001, but has also worked as a literary agent, marketing consultant, book editor, book publicist, book sales representative, bookseller, and as a part-time soldier in the Australian Army Reserve. He has written numerous books, including the Old Kingdom series beginning with *Sabriel*; the Keys to the Kingdom series; *Frogkisser!*; and *Terciel and Eleanor*. His most recent novel is *The Sinister Booksellers of Bath*. He also writes short fiction, with over sixty stories published in anthologies and magazines. More than six million copies of his books have been sold around the world and his work has been translated into forty-two languages. Online at: garthnix.com.

Tobi Ogundiran is the author of *Jackal, Jackal: Tales of the Dark and Fantastic*. He is a two-time Nommo Award nominee and also a British Science Fiction Association, Shirley Jackson, and Ignyte Award nominee. His work has appeared in *Beneath Ceaseless Skies*, *The Magazine of Fantasy and Science Fiction*, *PodCastle*, and *Africa Risen: A New Era of Speculative Fiction*, as well as in *The Year's Best Fantasy* and *The Year's Best African*

Speculative Fiction. A trained physician, he's taken a break from medicine and is currently pursuing an MFA in creative writing at the University of Mississippi. Online at: tobiogundiran.com.

Tochi Onyebuchi is the author of *Goliath.* His previous fiction includes *Riot Baby*, a finalist for the Hugo, Nebula, Locus, and NAACP Image Awards and winner of the New England Book Award for Fiction, the Ignyte Award for Best Novella, and the World Fantasy Award; the Beasts Made of Night series; and the War Girls series. His short fiction has appeared in *The Best American Science Fiction and Fantasy*, *The Year's Best Science Fiction*, and elsewhere. His nonfiction includes the book *(S)kinfolk* and has appeared in the *New York Times*, NPR, and the *Harvard Journal of African American Public Policy*, among other places. Online at: tochionyebuchi.com.

Miyuki Jane Pinckard writes fiction about magic and space travel, and nonfiction about games, technology, and culture. Her work has been published in *Strange Horizons, Uncanny Magazine, 1up.com, Electronic Gaming Monthly, Salon Magazine*, and other venues. A graduate of the Clarion Writers Workshop, she's a member of the SFWA Diversity, Equity, and Inclusion Committee and a board member of Dream Foundry, and serves on the programming committee on the Board of Directors of the World Fantasy Convention. She was born in Tokyo and currently lives in Venice, California, where she's teaching herself piano (badly). Online at: miyukijane.com.

Kelly Robson grew up in the foothills of the Canadian Rocky Mountains. Her novelette "A Human Stain" won the 2018 Nebula Award, novella *Waters of Versailles* won the 2016 Aurora Award, and novella *Gods, Monsters and the Lucky Peach* was shortlisted for the Hugo, Nebula, World Fantasy, Theodore Sturgeon, and Locus Awards. Her most recent books are the collection *Alias Space and Other Stories* and novella *High Times in* *the Low Parliament.* Kelly and her wife, SF writer A. M. Dellamonica, now live in downtown Toronto. Online at: kellyrobson.com.

Angela Slatter is the author of five novels, including *All the Murmuring Bones* and *The Path of Thorns*, and eleven short story collections, including *The Bitterwood Bible* and *The Tallow-Wife and Other Tales*. Her work has won a World Fantasy Award, a British Fantasy Award, a Ditmar, two Australian Shadows Awards, and seven Aurealis Awards; her work has been translated into multiple languages. She has an MA and a PhD in creative writing, teaches creative writing, and occasionally mentors new authors. She's collaborated with Mike Mignola on a new series from Dark Horse Comics, *Castle Full of Blackbirds*, set in the Hellboy Universe. Online at angelaslatter.com.

Andrea Stewart is the daughter of immigrants and was raised in a number of places across the United States. Her parents always emphasized science and education, so she spent her childhood immersed in *Star Trek* and odd-smelling library books. When her (admittedly ambitious) dreams of becoming a dragon slayer didn't pan out, she instead turned to writing books. Her debut epic fantasy trilogy, The Drowning Empire, is out with Orbit Books. She now lives in sunny California, and in addition to writing, can be found herding cats, looking at birds, and falling down research rabbit holes. Online at: andreagstewart.com.

Emily Y. Teng graduated from Texas A&M University, where she studied psychology and creative writing. She currently lives in Seattle, Washington, where she works as a narrative designer in the gaming industry. In her free time, she paints embarrassingly bad portraits and practices anime theme songs on the piano.

Sheree Renée Thomas, a 2022 Hugo Award and Ember Award nominee, is an award-winning author, editor, and poet whose work is inspired by music, natural science, and mythology. Her short fiction is collected in *Nine Bar Blues: Stories from an Ancient Future*, winner of the 2021 Darrell Award and a nominee for the Ignyte, Locus, and World Fantasy Awards. Her fiction and poetry also appears in *Sleeping Under the Tree of Life* and *Shotgun Lullabies*. She is the author of *Marvel's Black Panther: Panther's Rage*, a contributor to *Black Panther: Tales of Wakanda*, and a collaborator with Janelle Monáe on the story "Timebox Altar(ed)" in the *New York Times* bestselling collection *The Memory Librarian: And Other Stories of Dirty Computer*. Her poetry is included in *The Future of Black: Afrofuturism, Black Comics, and Superhero Poetry*. A 2022 winner of the Dal Coger Memorial Hall of Fame Award, she is a co-editor of *Africa Risen: A New Era of Speculative Fiction* and *Trouble the Waters: Tales of the Deep Blue*. She is the editor of *The Magazine of Fantasy & Science Fiction*, founded in 1949, and associate editor of *Obsidian*, founded in 1975, and also edited the two-time World Fantasy Award–winning groundbreaking anthologies, *Dark Matter: A Century of Speculative Fiction from the African Diaspora* and *Dark Matter: Reading the Bones*, which introduced W. E. B. Du Bois's science fiction. A former New Yorker, she lives in her hometown, Memphis, Tennessee, near a mighty river and a pyramid. Online at: shereereneethomas.com.

Tade Thompson is the author of six novels, including the critically acclaimed *Rosewater*, the first in his award-winning Wormwood Trilogy; *Making Wolf*; and, most recently, *Far From the Heaven* and *Jackdaw*, as well as the Molly Southbourne series of novellas and several short stories. He has won the Arthur C. Clarke Award, the Nommo Award, the Kitschies Golden Tentacle award, the Utopiales Award, and the Julia Verlange award, and been shortlisted for the Hugo Award, the Philip K. Dick Award, the British Science Fiction Association Award, and the Shirley Jackson Prize, among others. Many of his titles are currently in development for film and TV adaptation. Born in London to Yoruba parents, he lives and works on the south coast of England, where he battles an addiction to books.

E. Lily Yu is the author of the novel *On Fragile Waves* and the story collection *Jewel Box*, both from Erewhon, as well as the librettist of the short opera *Stars Between*. More than thirty-five of her stories have appeared in venues from *McSweeney's* to Tor.com, as well as thirteen best-of-the-year anthologies, and several have been finalists for the Hugo, Nebula, Locus, Sturgeon, and World Fantasy Awards. Online at: elilyyu.com.

ABOUT JONATHAN STRAHAN

Jonathan Strahan is a Hugo and World Fantasy Award–winning editor, anthologist, and podcaster. He has edited more than one hundred books and is reviews editor for *Locus*, a consulting editor for Tor.com, and cohost and producer of the Hugo Award–winning *The Coode Street Podcast*.